Bounceback

Rachael Derrick & John Derrick

A W.H.A.M. Novel

For Ken Sauer, alligator wrestler, and Ken Cooper, wanderer in the 4th dimension: superheroes indeed, like all great teachers - JD

For Blue - RD

Cover art and design by Cory Thomas - www.seethomas.com

W.H.A.M. logo by Jaydot Sloane

Table of Contents

Tuesday Dec. 22, 2023

Psychologists generally concur that the psyche of the supervillain does not form in a vacuum, but stems from a childhood full of emotional neglect and/or outright abuse, poorly developed social skills, and above all, an environment that fosters both a sense of entitlement and an acceptance of aggression as a method of conflict resolution.

Dying for a Laugh: Thematic Felony and the Modern Fool
Caroline Henderson, 2023

"At least a third of these people wear only black and are pierced in places that would have horrified my grandmother," mutters Jamie, studying the line of fans snaking its way through the bookstore. "This is normal. It's a healthy fan base for you."

"Why are there so many kids here?" I murmur back. Some of them are unattended and under 12.

"Also normal. Most of them will grow up just fine. You ready, Caroline?"

"Absolutely."

"Be excited, smile big, just don't let all this go to your head," Jamie says as we take our seats behind the table. "Your book's only been out for a week. They're not actually here for you."

Given the volatile nature of the people I write about, a book tour assistant like Jamie is a gift from god. Or from my publisher, if you want to get boringly literal about it. Unfortunately, she's also a bit of a buzz-kill.

I know these people aren't here for me. It's only a couple of shopping days before Christmas, yet close to 200 people wait in line to shake my hand and watch me scribble my name on the title page of *Dying for a Laugh*. They're here because I interview supervillains for a living, and bad guys are sexy. Always have been, always will be.

One by one they step up. Under a pithy quote or the reader's own carefully dictated personal message, I scrawl my autograph. Over the course of the first half hour, "Caroline Henderson" becomes "Carlne Hendsn," then "Carl Hen_!"

I listen to people whose siblings died in pterodactyl attacks, neighbors who'd thought the flashes of green and purple lights from Dr. Atrocious' basement simply meant he was running an unlicensed disco, and a mother who fears her daughter's growing love of

4

ventriloquism is the first step on a dark road toward novelty larceny. I squeeze hands and murmur vague reassurances.

I answer countless breathless questions. At least a dozen folks want to know if Deathripper is a boxers or briefs man. Which is just weird, since D-Ripper's first and possibly worst crime was the revival of the underwear on the outside of the pants fad, a style no one had pulled off in public since the early 1990s. Apparently his under-undies are an ongoing topic of online debate.

Personally, I never really got into the whole bad-is-sexy thing. I didn't spend my teen years dreaming of super-powered criminals in tight leather pants. Corny as it sounds, I just wanted to be a journalist like my mom, a columnist for the *Cleveland Plain Dealer*.

In college, I interned for a local news blog, and got assigned to cover supercrime. I quickly learned that an interview with a pro hero is a serious pain in the butt to schedule, and a miracle if it lasts longer than five minutes. A villain, on the other hand, always has time to talk about himself. Most supervillains fail because they cannot resist dangling their brilliant plan on a line before their foes, fishing for compliments. Somehow they're always surprised when they hook a gorilla-strength knuckle sandwich instead.

While my college friends went on dates or played four-hour board games, I spent most of my free nights and weekends at the Cuyahoga County ExtraMax prison, recording interviews with extraordinary miscreants. By the time I'd graduated, I'd turned this into a blog of my own: Thematic Felony. The blog really took off after one of my better attempts at amateur psycho-analysis got retweeted by a couple of well-loved superheroes, and soon took up more time than my day job reporting for a small-town newspaper. I worked up a book pitch about the inner lives of supervillains, and two years later I've got someone scheduling tour dates.

Jamie is putting the line of fans on hold so I can duck down to take a swig of water when a familiar voice says, "Caroline Henderson. Can you *believe* I just waited twenty minutes in line to stand here and look at your silly face?"

I look up into the teasing smirk of Sarah Gordon, my best friend since the first grade.

"What are you doing here? I thought you were out with Geoff tonight."

"I am," Sarah says. "I'm letting him shop the kitchen store. He can splurge on whatever toys he wants as long as he buys me a fondue pot."

"Good deal."

"Isn't it, though?" Sarah sighs, already blissing out at the thought. "Anyway, here." She hands me a copy of the book.

"I already signed your copy," I remind her. "I circled your name in the acknowledgments and everything."

"I know," Sarah says. "But I had to come out and show my support. At least I thought I did!"

I grin, nodding at the still lengthening autograph line. "Isn't it unreal?"

Sarah was with me for my big panic attack two months ago, after I heard how the ratings had crashed on MTV's *Who Wants to Be a Hostage?* I'd convinced myself the supervillain craze was over. But since then, Xarax had come back from the dead, Golem Grim had fallen off the heroism wagon (again), and Leather & Mace had unveiled her line of Amazonically Proportioned Dolls for Young Men.

"They're not really here for Caroline," Jaime says again. Sarah sticks her tongue out, which is excellent, because it probably wouldn't be professional for me to do it myself.

I sign Sarah's book: *To My Stalwart SareBear. Where would I be without you?*

"Up the proverbial creek without a thingy, probably," Sarah informs me after reading. "This is totally worth the $34.95 cover price."

"Yeah, yeah," I say, catching the sarcastic undertones. "I'll buy you lunch. What else do I have to spend my royalties on?"

"Love you!" Sarah says, and skips away into the mall.

I return my attention to my adoring public, and sign another dozen books before my fingers start to sting. I'm setting down my pen to shake them out when a tall man steps up to my table. He throws back his trench coat to reveal an elaborate 19th century naval uniform: deep blue wool over a white vest, with gold epaulets and shiny gold buttons. His right hand clutches a wide bell-shaped black hat, no doubt impressive in Napoleon's day but somewhat ridiculous to the modern eye. The left holds the unholy plastic lovechild of a revolver and a ray gun. He places the hat on his head and levels the blaster at mine.

"I've waited a long time for this," sneers the Vice Admiral. He's a third-string supervillain featured heavily in chapter six of my book. He's never actually served in any nation's navy, but gave himself that name as if he could defeat Captain Freewill, Colonel Hooah, or Private Defiant simply by outranking them. He gives new meaning to the term 'petty officer.' "Not to mention the—" He checks his watch. "—47 minutes it's taken me to get through this line of your drooling sycophants."

"You don't think that would've gotten you cutsies?" I reply, nodding to his gun. Several people waiting in the line laugh.

"No, don't do that!" Jaime hisses in my ear. "Rule #1, if a subject shows up, is *don't antagonize them!*"

"Right, thanks for that!" I hiss back.

"Silence!" roars the Admiral, antagonized. "This is not a show! Anyone who doesn't want to end up as painfully dead as this woman is about to be, shut up, and don't move!"

The entire bookstore freezes like a broken GIF. Only the eyes move, customers watching the staff, staff watching me, idle browsers in nearby aisles trying to determine if they can slip round the end of the nearest bookcase unnoticed.

My gaze flickers to the copies of *Dying for a Laugh* stacked like ramparts on either side of me. The book's in hardcover, 437 pages. It weighs at least three pounds. Could it knock that revolver from his hand? I'm not sure I'm fast enough or that I would actually hit him if I tried. I've never been what anyone would call an athlete. But the Vice Admiral's ray gun is already swinging back my way. My options here are limited.

Just as I reach for a book, the doors opening on the parking lot are flung wide, and another man in a long coat stomps in. This one is stocky, Latino, and wearing a powdered white Colonial wig.

"I don't believe this!" he grouses at a theatrical volume. "I'm running a little late, and this preening imperialist thinks he can pilfer my victim!"

The Admiral snaps his head sideways to glare at the newcomer. His gun remains pointed steadfastly at the tip of my nose. "And just who are you, sir?"

"I, sir!" The man in the wig drops his coat to the floor, revealing a costume to match the hair: a long brown jacket, a lace-cuffed shirt, breeches, hose, and buckled shoes. He too holds a sinister hi-tech firearm, a laser rifle easily three times the size of the Admiral's gun. "I am Tomás Pain! And I am here to deliver this author the well-earned honor of my name!"

Tomás Pain is profiled in chapter ten of my book. He's ultra-conservative and before his arrest went around dressed as a Founding Father, viciously assaulting politicians, pundits, and activists who he accuses of "failing to live the ideals of this Great Nation!" The background check I ran after our interview exposed him as a citizen of Canada, not the U.S.

"Oh, this is good!" Jaime whispers gleefully. "Assuming someone intervenes and we don't die, you can't buy this kind of publicity!"

I whisper back, "Has this kind of thing happened before?"

"Once. And I was only in the hospital for like six weeks. The author was out in three. We'll be fine! Just sit back, and let them distract each other long enough for help to arrive."

Realizing nothing Jaime is going to say right now is actually going to help my nerves, I turn back to the villains. I'd heard Pain managed to swing an early release for good behavior, but I hadn't expected this. Obviously, neither had the parole board.

"Your slanderous book ruined my life. I can't even arrive at a simple book signing-slash-homicide on time anymore!" Pain spits.

"Hey!" I say. "A book isn't slander; it's libel. And my book isn't libel, it's true!"

The Admiral seems more amused than angry at the interruption. He waves in the general direction of the queued fans. "There's a very convenient line, Mr. Pain. I suggest you get in it." Without waiting for a reply, he turns back to me, thumbing a button on the back of his ray-revolver. A low hum begins to build in the barrel.

"George Washington, Thomas Jefferson, John Adams! These men never waited in lines in their lives," proclaims Pain. He stalks towards my table, hugging his rifle into firing position. "And just what, pray, is your grievance 'gainst the lady?"

"If you must know, she described my ship as 'rather small.'" There's more sniggering from the line. The Admiral shouts, "Quiet!"

"That was my editor's addition!" I say. "He said he didn't want readers to feel intimidated." Jaime misses the convincing train by several seconds, but nods emphatically anyway.

"You also called it a boat."

"That was him as well."

"You see? Clearly the lady meant you no offense. Now why don't you just run along, and leave her to me and the Second Amendment?" Tomás Pain says, hoisting his laser rifle.

"I'm not sure that's a very good idea," I say, carefully catching the Vice Admiral's eye. "Why don't you tell us more about your weapon? Mr. Pain's gun may be larger—" The Admiral bares his teeth, and for a split second I'm sure I've overplayed my hand, "but yours looks much more impressive!"

Surprised, confused, and all-too-easily flattered, the Admiral hesitates. "Actually, it's…"

Jaime nods encouragement. Every moment we delay is another chance for one of my fans to upload a video of this little gathering to a website that is almost certainly monitored for villainous activity. The bookstore has a very nice skylight, and any minute now some urban avenger is going to come crashing right down through the glass, her cape draping nicely as she lands on top of that New Releases table.

"...harmless to elites like myself, but causing hideous mutation, terrible pain, and agonizing death to mere mortals like Ms. Henderson," finishes the Admiral.

"'Tis to be admired, I'm sure," says Pain, "in any company but this. For this gun, my gun, can unravel the very weave of temporality! Turn backward the clock of life, from infirmity to cradle to never-was-at-all!" He glares at me, lip curling. "You unwound my life, miss, right to the hidden shame at my root. I'll make you wish you'd never been born, in the torturous seconds before your wish is granted."

"I'm sorry," says the Admiral. "Was any of that in English?" It's the worst thing he could have said. Pain's first victim had lobbied successfully against a National Language bill.

Pain whirls, squeezing off a shot at the Admiral. The Admiral ducks, and the gun's green ray hits a display of *Frankenmonster* teen romance novels. The books are instantly reduced to a puddle of ink, string, and wood pulp.

The very next moment, the Admiral brings his weapon up and fires at me.

There's a crackling pop and a flash of violet. Too late, I shield my face with my arm, feeling my whole body tighten up.

Ten full seconds pass. I open my eyes. My stomach executes maneuvers that would do the Navy Blue Angels proud, but otherwise I am conspicuously unscathed.

"You're okay," Jaime says, reaching out as if to squeeze my shoulder, but hesitating just shy of actually touching me. "Just a harmless flash."

The Vice Admiral curses, slapping the ray gun's butt against his palm.

Tomás Pain raises his own weapon at me, laughing heartily. I notice a small blinking light on the side.

"Is that a low battery warning?" I ask.

"What kind of super villain puts a low battery warning on a time gun?" scoffs Pain.

He pulls the trigger.

Chapter 1: Reawaken

There are those [villains] who suggest that their impulse toward
evil awoke in them suddenly, most often at the onset of
puberty. Few consider their early attempts at crime as a
rebellion against their guardians; they imply their actions
were simply the next logical step in their lives of self-
centeredness. Those who did identify themselves as rebels
spoke of an amorphous being or group known as "the
system," to whom they ascribed a variety of sinister
attributes. Almost half of those interviewed recounted
witnessing a defining episode of violence in their formative
years.

- Dying for a Laugh

I woke up suddenly, with a whole-body spasm that set off a
throbbing headache. Had Jamie and I gone out drinking after the
signing? It didn't seem likely, but for some reason I couldn't
remember the end of the night.

I fumbled for my phone to check the time. Instead of tapping the
cool wood of my bedside table, my knuckles hit the wall, which should
not have been that close. As my eyes cracked open, I realized there
was a pounding noise in the room to match the feeling in my head.

A familiar voice yelled, "Get up, dweeb face! Mom wants us to
go to the grocery after breakfast."

I looked around and saw the childhood home I thought I'd left
behind for good when I went to college. I was tucked into my twin bed
with my fuzzy purple comforter, over there were my bookshelves
filled with an eclectic mix of philosophy texts, comic books, and
trashy romance novels. Plastered across the walls were pages I'd
ripped out of magazines, pictures of Janelle Monae, Little Mix, and
Justin Timberlake.

Oh good grief, I thought. *Not the back-in-high school dream!*

Wrapping myself into a comfortable blanket burrito, I buried my
head under the covers and waited for my brain to stop spinning. The
headache was fading slowly as my dream-brother stood outside my
dream-bedroom and yelled. Clearly I wasn't going to be able to ignore
him, so I slid out of bed and went to open the door.

"Shut up, Hank," I said. In his worn t-shirt and jeans, he was the
very picture of his college freshman self, down to the scruffy stubble
he cultivated in an attempt to look carefree.

"You shut up," he said nonsensically. "Quit being a lazy butt."

"I'll be down in a minute," I said, expecting the dream to shift ahead even as I formed the words. Usually at this point we'd be halfway through the meal already. I turned my head, waiting for the world to rearrange itself around me.

It didn't. I looked back at Hank, who had clearly been expecting resistance. He raised an eyebrow.

"You look like you got hit with the ugly stick. Did you forget to eat while I was away? Or did Mom and Dad miss me so much they gave up cooking?"

"Ha ha," I replied automatically. "So funny I forgot to laugh." We stood there for another few seconds before Hank walked away, muttering something about the unfathomable mind of the little sister. I blinked, wondering why I was dreaming something as banal as standing in the doorway of my childhood bedroom after an unremarkable conversation.

Oh no, I thought. *What if this isn't a dream? What if -*

Shut up, I thought back at myself. *You're 26 years old and signing your awesome book, and the next thing you know you're waking up in your childhood bedroom. What else would it be, Caroline?*

Grabbing my old robe from the back of the door, I headed down the hall to the bathroom. I hit the light, turned automatically to the mirror, and jumped.

That was not me staring back at me. At least, not the me I was expecting.

Yesterday morning my mirror showed a comfortably padded young woman with a wry grin. Today I saw a pale skinny girl, tight-lipped and overprotective of her newly straightened teeth. Her hair was the same dark gold, but sleep-matted and too long. In lieu of pajamas, she sported boxers and a worn Led Zeppelin t-shirt, her bony elbows poking out from the wide sleeves. She lacked definition, like a pencil sketch awaiting ink.

Unfortunately, definition is not the same thing as detail. This younger me had plenty of detail, red and splotchy and all over my face. That's when I realized this wasn't a dream. Because who dreams zits in this kind of excruciating detail? The same stupid zits I'd had when I was 16!

The memory of the double confrontation at the book signing reappeared, fully formed. I'd been shot, twice, by experimental weapons built by certifiable sociopaths. And at least one of them wasn't fully powered.

"Oh, HELL no!" I shouted at the mirror, and spun away, as if by not looking I could force myself back into my proper age and shape. Instead, I received another painful reminder of just what it meant to be 16, as my uncoordinated feet overstepped and I fell into the wall.

"Caroline? You okay?" I heard my mother yell from downstairs.

"I'm fine!" I shouted back, and somehow managed not to follow this up with hysterical laughter as I sank to the fluffy bathroom carpet and put my head between my knees, thinking hard.

It wasn't a dream and probably not some magical illusion, although I couldn't be sure of that. And even if it were an illusion or virtual reality, I was stuck in it until whoever put it in my brain took it out again. I could be reliving my own memories, but in that case I wouldn't have control over my actions. My consciousness could have been implanted into a clone or a robot duplicate, but why? And my brother, my teenage brother was here too? No, only one thing made sense.

Time travel. Somehow, Tomás Pain had literally shot me back in time. Instead of simply de-aging me like he'd threatened, Pain's weapon had pushed me backwards through my own lifetime.

The part about the weapon not performing as advertised didn't actually surprise me. Everything else about the situation was as surprising as crap, but temporal weapons had a bad reputation for doing precisely not what they were fashioned for. This was why fledgling villains ClockWatcher and Mr. Minute had been defeated early in their careers.

The former gained notoriety because his first crime, a bank heist, had actually been successful, until his ClockStopper ray malfunctioned and forced the mastermind and his henchmen to perform the heist again in reverse. After the security guards finished laughing, they'd cuffed the ClockWatcher and taken him in. He could have gotten just a few years for the attempted robbery if he hadn't also used stolen plutonium for his weapon, which put him in a federal penitentiary for 25 to 40.

The unfortunate Mr. Minute was found in his own lab, surrounded by elaborate plans for not-yet-committed crimes, locked in a personal temporal flutter. To him, time was passing normally, but to the outside world, he froze for thirty seconds of every minute. He'd done some time for conspiracy, but as he couldn't actually commit any crimes, he was released and started a fairly lucrative eBay business.

Tomás Pain's normal modus operandi involved antique muskets and fireworks made with illegal amounts of gunpowder, so he probably hadn't made the weapon himself. For a moment I wished I'd gotten a better look. Then I realized I was wishing for a closer acquaintance with a strange energy weapon, and wished for a physicist instead.

The Vice Admiral's weapon didn't seem to have had any effect at all, though I did recall some formulation of the word "mutation," which worried me a bit. When I got back to my own time—which I assumed would be soon, because no way could something this weird be permanent—I would get myself to a Geiger counter, and make sure I wasn't putting my possible future children at risk of having two heads.

The bathroom floor here in my parents' house was significantly tidier than my own, I noticed. So at least here in the past, I'd benefit from my father's insistence on a regular cleaning schedule.

After a quick hot shower, I returned to the bedroom to inspect my closet. The insecurity of my youth meant that I normally wore clothes a size or two larger than I needed, so I dug through my drawers until I found a pair of boot-cut jeans and a blue sweater from junior high. I brushed my hair into a ponytail and grabbed some shoes before running down the stairs to the kitchen, narrowly avoiding another fall as I rounded the corner. Hank was digging into a pile of eggs and toast while Mom read the paper and drank her morning tea. Dad was at the stove, cracking another egg into the pan.

"Morning, Dad."

"Hey Caro. Eggs?" He reached for the butter to grease the pan.

"Yeah, thanks," I said. "Wait, no. Let me make you an omelet."

He looked surprised. I've matured some in the past few years, but even now my idea of breakfast is waffles in the toaster. I'm not sure teenage-me had ever volunteered to chop veggies. Mom peered over her newspaper as I rummaged around in the fridge to find mushrooms, half a green pepper, and a bit of cheddar.

I didn't miss the quick look that passed between my parents. "I'll have some too, please," Mom said.

Hank finished shoveling his food into his mouth just as I was cutting the omelet into three pieces. He looked at his watch. "I'm meeting Chris to go to the mall at 12:30. We need to get back with the groceries before 11:45 or you're putting them all away yourself. Hurry it up!" Hank was extra annoying at fraternity age.

"Mom, since I'm not done eating, can't Hank go by himself?" I asked sweetly.

"What? No! It'll take twice as long!"

Thankfully, Mom was in fluffy egg and cheese heaven, and not above bribery. "Then you'll just have to move faster, dear."

Grumbling, Hank went to get his keys and coat. As soon as he was safely away, I finished my food and jumped up myself. "Going to Sarah's, back soon."

Dad buttered his third piece of toast. "Well played, kiddo."

I could have told my mother about the whole time-travel thing, I suppose. She did work for a major metropolitan newspaper, which spent a lot of its ink on super-crime. But she would have insisted on telling my dad, and it would have become this whole big thing. Assuming either of them even believed me. I mean, they thought I was 16! No one takes 16-year-olds seriously. I was barely taking myself seriously.

So I went to Sarah's instead. Luckily, it wasn't far. When Sarah and I were in the fourth grade her parents made the brilliant decision to buy a house in my neighborhood, so she and I could spend the next decade cutting through five backyards to spend practically all of our waking hours together, before leaving together for Kent State. We shared a room there and then an apartment in Berea until a year ago, when Sarah moved in with Geoff, and the advance on my book finally allowed me to get a swanky downtown apartment of my very own.

Reaching the Gordons' back door, I turned the knob, entering the house unannounced as usual. I ran up the stairs, passing Sarah's dad in his study.

"Good morning, Caroline," he called out.

"Hi, Eugene," I replied, and if I hadn't been in a hurry I might have stopped to see what Sarah's dad looked like ten years younger.

I found Sarah sprawled face-down across her bed reading a book. Her cheeks were too round, her hips narrower than the Sarah I was used to. But that Sarah wasn't here, so this one would have to do.

"Hey," I said before she could look up. "First, you have to tell me what day it is, including the year, and then I'll tell you why."

"Okay. Random much?" she said calmly. Flipping her dark hair over one shoulder, she checked the calendar on the wall. "It's Monday, December 23, 2013. A whole year after the end of the world. Suck it, Mayans."

I'd been knocked back *exactly* ten years.

"All right, skip the part where this is ridiculous and impossible, we'll come back to it later. But I'm from the future," I said, less coherently than I would have liked.

Sarah's left eyebrow went up. "Yeah, we'll definitely come back to that. What do you mean 'the future'?"

"Last night, I was 26 years old in 2023. This morning I woke up here, and I'm 16. I pissed off a supervillain and he shot me with an age-regression ray. It's a job hazard."

Now both Sarah's eyebrows were up. "Wouldn't that just make you 16 in 2023?"

"That would have been a more logical outcome. He wasn't a very good supervillain. He was actually trying to kill me. Plus there was this other bad guy, also wielding a techno-weapon, and maybe the energies kind of overlapped?"

"Lucky for you," Sarah said, and climbed off her bed to give me a hug. "You're not the delusional type, and this is too subtle and pointless to be a prank, and plus I love you and stuff, so I believe you. But y'know, some kind of proof would be good."

I hugged back hard. "I can tell you about the extradimensional invasion of 2015, or who the next President is, or how you're gonna con one of your college professors into letting you turn in your novel-length *Hunger Games* fanfic in lieu of your senior thesis, but I can't actually think of anything specific from the next 24 hours to prove that I know the future, so we're sort of stuck."

"So I'm going to be an English major? Huh. Did not see that one coming."

"No, actually. That's why it's so brilliant. Or it would be, because that's all I'm going to say."

"What? You're the one who just said you wanted to prove you'd traveled through time!"

"Yes, but then I realized what a stupid, possibly dangerous idea that was. Look, you're my best friend—okay, teen version, but still. Can't you just trust me?"

The brat rolled her eyes at me. "All right, how about this: tell me a little about my awesome future boyfriend, and I'll consider us square."

"Well, there is a friend of the boy persuasion, and he is pretty cool. But future-talk is risky! The more a resident of the past knows of what's to come, the more likely she is to either avoid or hasten the events in question without knowing all of the pertinent details, which greatly increases the odds of a paradoxical event." I took a breath, having run out of air, then confessed, "I read that in a novel, but I still think it's good advice."

Sarah did the slow nod thing. "O-kay. I got that, mostly. And, 'cause I've never heard you use the word 'paradoxical,' that's about all the proof I needed."

"Thank you."

"So what now?" she asked, sitting on the edge of her bed. "How long are you gonna be here? I mean, when are you gonna be 16 again? And will you remember being 26? Or will the you that's 26 just be gone? Or, wait—where is my you now? Age-16 you, I mean? Is she in your body in 2023? Did you, like, swap places, or did you just take over her brain?"

"Sarah, please," I said. "I have no clue how long I'll be in this body. Or if this is my body, regressed after all, and your Caroline is stuck someplace else. The bad guy didn't exactly show me the user's manual before he shot me. From what I know of these kinds of things—which isn't a heck of a lot, because they tend to be pretty random—the ray's effects may wear off quite quickly, or they may take a few weeks to fade. I may even wake up tomorrow and find myself in the body of my 7-year-old self."

"That could be fun. Finger painting without shame." Sarah realized this wasn't the most helpful thing to say and went on, "Or you might be here for a while. Like you said, you don't know, so don't worry about it. Just enjoy having your youth back for a while."

I frowned. "What are you talking about? I'm 26!"

"Yeah, do you remember being 16? Anything after college is like, ancient," she said. "So what's it like being grown up? If you won't talk about my future, can't you tell me about yours?"

"I'm a writer," I said. "I write supervillain biographies—"

"That's what you meant by job hazard! Oh man, that would be so cool! And dangerous, obviously. Have you been attacked before this?" Sarah clutched a pillow, watching me like I was the latest episode of her favorite TV show.

I shook my head. "This was my first event, the first stop on my first ever publicity tour. Hell of a way to kick it off, huh?"

"Shyeah, no kidding. Okay, new topic: your boyfriend or girlfriend. What're they like? Do I know them? They're not from our school, are they? Ohmigod, is it someone from our school?"

Her relentless enthusiasm was a little annoying, but I smiled anyway. "Nope. At the moment, I'm in an entirely non-dating phase."

"You are?" I'd announced I was from the future and Sarah had barely blinked. Now she was shocked. "Is everything okay? I thought for sure you'd have your forever-partner locked down before we even graduated from college."

"So did I, but it didn't turn out that way. It also turned out to not be as important to me as I thought it was gonna be."

"Wow. You really did grow up. But you're happy?"

"I am awesome," I assured her, and I meant it. "I'm being paid to do what I love, and I'm good at it. It's brilliant. Y'know, except for this minor thing with the extreme critical response and the time travel. I can't wait to get back there."

"I'll bet," Sarah said. "But I'm sure it'll happen soon."

We talked for several hours more, until my stomach was rumbling loud enough for Sarah to hear and offer to make lunch.

"No, thanks," I said. "I should get home and see what my parents are doing. But this was fun. And hopefully the next time you see me, I'll have no memory it ever happened."

"Huh?"

"Because I'll just be 16 again."

"Oh, right. You want me to remind you?"

"What did I just tell you about paradoxes?"

"Sorry!" she said. "But ten years from now?"

"Absolutely," I said. "See you then, and we'll laugh about this."

But the next time I saw Sarah, I was not laughing.

I spent most of that first afternoon and some of the evening helping my Mom finish decorating the Christmas tree, and by the time I was again a free agent, the Gordons had left to go see Sarah's grandparents in Youngstown. I wasted the rest of the night zoned out in front of the TV watching holiday specials, half expecting my very own Ghost of Christmas Past to appear before me at any minute.

The next morning I woke up, and quickly realized I was still a kid. Then I realized it was 8 a.m. on Christmas Eve, turned over, and went straight back to sleep until noon. If you're going to be a teenager again, do it all the way, I say.

The rest of Christmas Eve and then Christmas itself more or less passed in a blur. It felt half-remembered and half-lived, an odd mix of nostalgia and déjà vu. There was baking, and the eating of baked things, and my father's terrible reindeer jokes. There were the first halves of several of my brother's vulgar fraternity stories, which Mom never let get any further than that; luckily I'd long since found out all the endings, so I no longer had to follow him around unsuccessfully begging for the rest. There were plenty of presents, and thus plenty of opportunities to feign surprise and delight, but the bigger trick was in faking just the right level of anticipation when Dad or Mom or Hank tore open their gifts from me, which I no longer remembered selecting.

All in all it was a strangely ordinary holiday. It was a nice day to relive, but nothing particularly formative, nothing to suddenly shift my perspective about myself.

The following morning, Mom shook me awake at what my actual teenage self would've called the butt crack of dawn, asking if I wanted to brave the after-Christmas sales with her. I remembered the long lines more than the joy of consumerism, so I sweetly said "No thanks," and pretended to go back to sleep. As soon as Mom had gone I got up, got dressed, and walked over to Sarah's.

"All right," I groused as I walked into her bedroom. "This is officially not funny anymore."

"Hello to you too, Caroline," Sarah said. "So I'm guessing it hasn't worn off yet?"

"Nope," I said. "And it's starting to get annoying. Reliving the holidays is one thing, but I am NOT going back to the eleventh grade!"

"Relax," Sarah said. I love her and stuff, but has anyone ever said that word without making the recipient want to punch them? "We've still got like a whole week and a half before that happens. And high school isn't all bad."

"It wasn't. But I'm done with all that now, and college too. I finally have a real life, and some jerk supervillain goes and hits the reset button on me? Screw that."

"All right," Sarah said. "So what can we do? Is there someone we can call, someone who knows about time travel and stuff?"

Of course I'd already thought of that. The problem was that what little evidence of actual time travel existed in the public record was anecdotal and contradictory, flummoxing the best scientific minds of the age. Stephen Hawking's last paper on temporal mechanics had been just four words long: "Hell if I know."

"The only person I can think of is Ruby Goldberg," I said. "I interviewed her for a chapter in my book about time villains. I mean, I will interview her."

Sarah's eyes got huge. "You know Ruby Goldberg? Girl genius slash superhero Ruby Goldberg?"

"A bit. But not yet. She's only 17 herself at this point. She won't start time traveling until college, and the type she used required a rocket ship, a precisely aligned binary star system, and a math prodigy with a prehensile tail."

"Well, still," Sarah said. "She'll have the best shot at figuring out what the heck her future self is thinking."

"True," I said.

Sarah searched "Ruby Goldberg" on her phone and found RubyTech.com, but far from the polished, professional corporate website I'd seen in the future, it looked like a generic school project. It did have a contact form, so Sarah handed me her phone to type in a message. I entered my name and email address, then clicked the drop-down box labeled "Subject." Between "Alternative Energy" and "Genetic Engineering" was "Time Travel." I entered my first name and email address, then the words, "Back from 2023" and hit "Submit" before I could talk myself out of it.

Immediately my phone buzzed from my pocket. It was a bounceback email from mailer-daemon@googlemail.com. I showed it to Sarah.

Address not found
Your message wasn't delivered to ruby@rubytech.com because the address couldn't be found, or is unable to receive mail

"That can't be right. You sent it from her own dropdown form!" Sarah said.

"Wait," I said. "Look."

The smaller print at the bottom of the email read:

The email account that you tried to reach does not exist.
https://support.rubytech.com/?1struleoftimetravel=youdon
ottalkabouttimetravel.70=rtmtp

Reaching over my shoulder, Sarah jabbed the link. It only lead to a "Page Not Found."

"I don't get it," Sarah said.

"It's right there," I said. "'The first rule of time travel equals you do not talk about time travel.' What if I've been part of a classic Ruby Goldberg overcomplicated plot all along?"

"You mean like—no! You're not saying she was in league with the villains?"

"Not like that. I can't see her going evil or anything. But on the other hand, how does a novelty thug like Tomás Pain get his hands on advanced temporal weaponry?"

"You think he stole it from Ruby?" Sarah asked.

"I can't think of anyone else who could even build something like that."

"Well, yeah," Sarah half agreed. "But it's not like it did what it was supposed to anyway."

"So what if she *intended* for Pain to steal the gun, because it was never a gun at all, but a gun-shaped time machine?"

Sarah looked dubious. "Really? Where are you getting all this?"

"As a supercriminal biographer, I'm a professional leaper-to-conclusions. Trust me; I know how to fill in the blanks."

"Yeah, you're great at Mad Libs."

"A supervillain shows up at my book signing and tries to kill me. Well, two of them, but I suppose the Vice Admiral could have been a fluke," I said. "Look, villainous plots always fail for one of two reasons. Sometimes the bad guys are a victim of their own overconfidence, in which case it all blows up in their own faces. But usually villains are defeated because a hero outplays them. The time gun worked, but it didn't kill me. Ergo, a hero wanted me to travel through time."

"Ruby Goldberg is kind of known for making all her toys way more ridiculous than they need to be," Sarah said. "But why send you back here now?"

"I'm not sure yet," I admitted. "But whatever it is, I don't think it's really about me. I don't have any great unresolved high school issues or anything. There's nothing in my own past to fix here. This isn't one of those feel-good reliving-your-life movies. What I do have is a whole lot of knowledge about felonies that haven't been committed yet."

"So it's more of an action-thriller, then?"

"Maybe just a crime drama. Hopefully a simple one. For now, we need more information."

"And if this whole theory turns out to be a load of hooey?" asked Sarah.

"Doesn't matter," I said. "At the very least, it's a framework to help me cope with being a freaking high schooler again without completely losing it. I'll make adjustments as I receive additional data."

"Whoa. You ARE older and wiser."

I couldn't tell if Sarah was kidding or not.

We didn't have long to wait for my next clue. I stayed and ate dinner with Sarah's family that night, and afterward her parents vanished upstairs so she and I could indulge in random sitcoms. Five minutes in, *Brooklyn Nine Nine* was interrupted by a Special News

Bulletin: the TroubleShooters were fighting Sugar Mama downtown in Public Square.

On the screen, a grainy white giant loomed against the Terminal Tower, shaking her massive rock candy fists. As the name implied, Sugar Mama had the ability to transform her body into a sweet granular form which she could move and reshape at will. I'd come to know the woman and her abilities well in the last few months. My publisher was trying to pair me up with a popular TV chef for my next book, *A Taste of Redemption: Confessions, Confections, and Jail-Cooked Meals from Your Favorite Super-Villains.* I still hadn't decided if publishing a true crime book with recipes at the back was going to make my career or kill it dead.

In the foreground, as Sugar Mama's long arms flailed, I glimpsed a couple of tiny figures in bright red and blue, the official colors of the TroubleShooters, Cleveland's teen hero team.

"Oh cool. Superfight!" Sarah said.

"Shush!" I said.

"Speak of the whatever," Sarah said, ignoring me. "There's your Ruby Goldberg right there, with the ginormous raygun. Think maybe we could drive down there and talk to her before they're gone?"

I shook my head. It'd take at least 45 minutes to drive downtown, and the Shooters would almost certainly be gone by then. But I knew this fight, and my mind was turning.

The camera zoomed, closing in on a very short Latina girl with a dark ponytail and a red domino mask, wearing a blue leotard with red leggings and balanced on a pair of ridiculously high spike-heeled boots. She had her right hand held back and above her head, like a waitress carrying a pizza. And six feet above that hand, hovering in midair—

"Is that a Prius?" Sarah said.

It was. An entire car held aloft by the invisible power of that teenage hero's telekinetic brain.

Sugar Mama slammed one of her massive hands to the ground, but the TroubleShooter was too fast for her. She danced easily out of the way, and as the grainy fist rattled the pavement, the hero's arm snapped forward, hurling the Prius right into Sugar Mama's face. Sugar Mama's head snapped back. Her enormous dark eyes blinked, great syrupy tears dropping to the sidewalk below.

A second later, the Saccharine Scoundrel tumbled back against the Tower. She hit the stone and collapsed into a mound of unmoving white crystals, the Prius sticking out at a spoon-like angle.

"Yes!" Sarah cheered and punched the air.

The camera cut away to a reporter in a trench coat, holding a microphone in one hand and clamping a shiny blue hard-hat to his head with the other, grinning ear to ear. "Outstanding! Just a phenomenal knockout there from team leader Lift."

I pressed my hands to my mouth. My stomach had gone cold.

Sarah tilted her head at me. "You do not look impressed. How was that not awesome? I mean, I know it's a rerun for you—"

"This is it," I said, more to myself than to her.

"This is what?"

I didn't answer, too busy watching the TroubleShooters deliver Sugar Mama into a highly specialized police containment van, one sandy white shovelful at a time. Too busy listening to the reporter rhapsodize over Lift as he waved her over for an interview. "This year, Cleveland has had the privilege of watching this young woman really come into her own. She truly is a hero in her prime."

Sixteen should never be anyone's prime, whatever Hollywood says.

"What was going through your mind during that fight?" the reporter asked Lift.

"Really I was just looking for the nicest mid-sized sedan I could find," the hero said. "That's how I always do it, if I'm going to throw a car. I'd rather not have to throw a car, but if I do, then I figure the more expensive it is, the better the chance that the owner will have insurance that covers Acts of Super."

I pointed at the screen. "This was the last footage most people ever saw of Lift in action. Two days from now, on December 28, 2013, she gets killed fighting Grammar Cop."

"Who?"

Lift was on TV, alive and well and half a city away. "This is why I'm here. I know where, and when, and how, and I can be there and make sure that it doesn't happen!"

"You are *so freakin' cool!*" Sarah cheered, jumping forward to tackle-hug me. "Future Ruby Goldberg sent you back to save her friend!"

"I will! I can do it," I said, feeling sure of myself for the first time since I'd seen my own acne-covered face. "And then I can go home."

"All right! We have a plan!"

"No, actually we still need one of those."

Chapter 2: Revise

Psychotherapists have long distinguished between villains whose methods are non-lethal and those who show no compunction in killing. It was not until the 1970s that a third category came under scrutiny: villains who at first used tactics that posed little or no danger to others but eventually graduated to maiming or even killing victims. It was discovered that a large percentage of this third group came to cause harm by accident rather than by design.

Tragically, once a villain has caused the death of a non-combatant, use of deadly force tends to increase in subsequent heists. Criminologist Anna Heffernan (2019) identified this behavior as a response to the cognitive dissonance created by the villain's sense of self-righteousness. "Once [a villain] kills, he has to tell himself that he meant to do it, that it's worth doing to get his point across. Otherwise he's just crazy."

- Dying for a Laugh

With Sarah's help, the plan was planned by the time my Mom texted to ask when I was coming home. Because it was 11:30 by then, and even if it wasn't a school night, she still expected to be kept informed of these things. I loved my parents, but I really had not missed living with them.

I texted back *OMW*, hugged Sarah goodbye and hurried back to my own house. I didn't need to make things any tougher on my actual teenage self than they naturally were, once I'd leapt on back to the future.

The next morning, Mom went to work as usual—journalists don't get much of a holiday—so I challenged my brother to a game of *Halo 4*. I was woefully out of practice and thus got my butt thoroughly kicked. I giggled my way through every onscreen death, which annoyed Hank so much he eventually threw up his hands and left the room, so I still counted it a personal victory. After that I helped Dad make lunch and bake cookies. Lawyers get very nice holidays, so he had a whole week to laze around the house with us and eat meals in front of the TV, which Mom never let us do when she was home.

The kitchen door creaked open right as Dad was pulling the last tray of cookies from the oven; I'd forgotten Sarah's knack for showing up just in time to be offered dessert. She and I each took two cookies, and I planted mine in a bowl of ice cream. Sarah laughed at me, enjoying frozen treats in the middle of winter, but my teen self didn't seem to feel the cold the way I was used to. I bolted for the stairs the instant Dad handed me the spoon, nodding for Sarah to follow me up to my room.

"So I'm thinking we need to throw you a party tonight," Sarah said the instant the door closed behind us.

"A party?"

"Not a trash-somebody's-parents-house-and-maybe-the-cops-come party," Sarah clarified. "A going-back-to-the-future party. It's your last night in the now. We should get the whole gang together and have some fun. Responsibly."

Yep. We were those kids. I liked that about us.

"I dunno," I said. I picked my own brain for the "whole gang" in question; this was my junior year, so we'd mostly have been hanging out with who? Tamika? Nate? I hadn't seen either of them in years. Aside from Sarah, I'd never been very good at staying in touch with people. "It sounds pretty awkward."

"Come on, it'll be great!" Sarah, on the other hand, was extremely social and felt it was her duty to keep me connected with the rest of the world.

"What would we even say we were celebrating?"

"Reasons are for old people. And anyway, couldn't you just tell them like you told me?"

In the time it took me to glare at her for the 'old' crack, I considered that. "No, I don't think so. For the same reason I haven't told my parents."

"Because you're pretty much the same age as them, and that's weird?"

"I am not!" I said, fwapping her on the shoulder. She acted like it hurt, and I rolled my eyes. "I haven't said anything because there's no reason to. It'll be over soon, so there's no reason to go weirding everyone out and making them look at me funny."

"Why'd you let me in on the big secret, then? And like, instantly?"

"Because I knew I could trust you to just go with it, and I had to tell someone."

"So wouldn't it be nice to share this with a few more someones?"

"I'm good, thanks."

Sarah let go of the party idea, and we talked our parents into letting her sleep over instead. We stayed up watching TV until Sarah could no longer keep her eyes open for longer than twenty seconds at a stretch. I wasn't even a little bit tired myself; I was too consumed with anxiety about the day to come. As my bed wasn't big enough for two, we nested in a pile of sleeping bags, blankets, and pillows on my bedroom floor. Sarah commenced snoring the moment I tucked her in.

In the morning Sarah and I ate a hasty breakfast, then dressed in a few more layers than our temperature-controlled destination required, just in case. I found Dad in the laundry room sorting lights and darks.

"Morning Caro, what's up?"

"Dad, I need the truck," I said. "I mean, can I borrow the truck, please?"

"Going out somewhere with Sarah?" Dad said.

"Yep."

"I could just drive you. You know I like spending time with you."

"No. Thanks. Can I just take it?"

Dad sighed. "I get it. The time has come, the Walrus said. I'm just the old man now…"

"It's not that! I just—we don't even want you to know where we're going, because I'm going to, um, shop for Mom's birthday," I lied. "And we both know how bad you are at keeping secrets from her."

"Fair enough," Dad said. I gave him a quick hug and a peck on the cheek, then bounded up the stairs.

"Hey, wait a minute!" I pretended not to hear Dad call after me. "When did you learn to drive a stick?"

On the drive, we went back over everything I knew about Grammar Cop, mostly to make sure we had our timing down. Markus Strunkenwhite to his mother, in his own eyes he was 'the heroic Grammarian,' waging a one-man war to 'restore the tarnished English language to its rightful shining glory.' His weapon of choice was the Punctuator, a gun of his own design that hurled heavy plastic punctuation marks at high speed.

I remembered sitting in an uncomfortable metal chair in a stuffy prison viewing room in 2017, watching Strunkenwhite as he watched the hotel security footage from today. Every few seconds I glanced towards the clock at one corner of the screen, etching the numbers carefully into my notebook in pencil. Later, I would lay the key moments out for the world in my book, in a chapter entitled, 'Beats, Shoots and Leaves.' I even did my own reading for the audiobook. We recorded this segment on the very first day, and I was nervous, so they made me do three takes on the chapter before I got it right. Each minute was burned into my brain.

At 11:25 a.m., the video showed a crowded meeting room in the Simonson Suites Cleveland Hotel, an assortment of colorful characters filling a dozen rows of folding metal chairs. 'Characters' was in fact the technical term, as more than a third of the room's occupants appeared to be AmaZone swordslingers, dark-robed Trikmagi, or techno-armored thundertroopers. This was CrossCon '13, the first official sci-fi convention dedicated to the Star Crossers trilogy. At the front of the room sat Osbourne Taylor, the talented puppeteer and voice actor who brought to life Sensei Gryphon, one of the most beloved—and linguistically eccentric—characters in film history. The actual puppet rested on the stage beside him.

At 11:31, Mr. Taylor opened the floor to questions. Lines formed behind standing microphones at the head of each of the room's side aisles. Strunkenwhite joined the line on the right. On screen he was a tall, broad-shouldered man in a tweed jacket and bowtie. His hair was dark and lank, his nose crooked, his smile unassuming. From 11:32 to 11:45, Strunkenwhite patiently waited his turn.

At 11:46 Strunkenwhite stepped up to the mic, resting a large hand on his lapel in a professorial manner. In a congenial British accent—a complete affectation, as the man was born and raised in Minnesota—he asked if he might have a few words with "Sensei Gryphon." There was a roar of agreement from the crowd, whistling and applause and a few shouted quotes from the film.

Mr. Taylor gamely picked up his puppet and tugged it over his arm. "What question have you, Earthchild?" he asked, in a high-pitched yodel only half an octave above his already puppetish everyday voice. "What wisdom seek you from yon ancient Sensei Gryphon?"

"This is for the Queen's English, you semiliterate buffoon!" cried Grammar Cop, pulling the Punctuator from beneath his jacket. He opened fire. A quotation mark, three periods, and an exclamation point tore through the WELCOME CROSSER'S! banner hanging behind Taylor.

I asked Strunkenwhite what he was feeling right then, as those first shots went wide.

"They didn't," he said. "I'd only just noticed the bloody apostrophe!"

At 11:47, the room erupted. Everyone sensible ran for the double doors at the back. The slightly less sensible did so shouting. A trio of AmaZones carrying the better quality replica laser swords fought against the tide, trying to get between Strunkenwhite and the stage, where Oz Taylor and his puppet stood with mouths agape.

There were two convention staff members in the room, medium sized guys in black t-shirts with the word SECURITY printed in yellow across the back. One pulled the fire alarm, which only served to intensify the chaos. The other started shouting into a walkie-talkie, then gave up and threw it across the room at Grammar Cop, knocking the Punctuator from his hand more or less by sheer luck.

At 11:48, Grammar Cop dove under a chair after his fallen weapon. The three cosplayers leapt on top of him. The second staff member now with a cell phone to his ear, gesticulated wildly. A transcript of that call reveals that instead of dialing 911, the staffer called in to Leviathan's emergency line directly. Grammar Cop elbowed one of the AmaZones in the face and hit another with a chair.

By 11:49, Strunkenwhite had managed to recover the Punctuator, and immediately resumed shooting. Most of the punctuation bounced off the cosplayers' well-padded foam chest plates; even at exclamation-point blank range, the projectiles would leave nasty bruises but do no lasting damage. A lucky comma managed to shatter a laser sword, spattering its owner with tiny shining shards of safety glass. Her face bled from a dozen minute cuts. One of her costumed companions turned away from Grammar Cop to make certain she was all right.

By 11:50 a.m. the room was all but vacant, the remainder of the crowd having squeezed out through the doors at the back. The third AmaZone stumbled after Grammar Cop through a maze of empty folding chairs, half of them kicked over in the mass exodus. The security staffers were still present, but crouched low along the walls, keeping well back from the action. As Grammar Cop took more potshots at the stage, Mr. Taylor finally thought to duck down behind the moderator's stand. Three more exclamations spanged loudly off the hardwood podium.

"Come out and face the consequences of your lexical transgressions!" shouted Grammar Cop.

At 11:51, three members of Cleveland's teen superteam, the TroubleShooters, arrived on scene: Lift, Match, and Ruby Goldberg. They called for Grammar Cop to lay down his weapon and surrender. The speed with which they'd responded suggested they were nearby, perhaps attending the convention in their civilian identities.

The standing cosplayer dropped to one side. Her friends flattened themselves on the ground, clearing the field between Grammar Cop and the heroes.

Grammar Cop spun around, firing in a panic as the TroubleShooters rushed towards him. In the lead, Lift made only a *cursory attempt to deflect the shots with her telekinesis. She waved her hand, like someone swatting at a fly. Three of Grammar Cop's shots flew wide. The third bounced harmlessly off Lift's shoulder.*

"We knew his punctuation marks were made out of plastic," Ruby Goldberg would state in her report. "They couldn't really hurt us."

Just after 11:52, a sharp and ironically misplaced semi-colon hit Lift, slicing her jugular vein. Clutching her throat, she stumbled and fell, crashing down onto the chairs. Her teammates rushed to her side, applied pressure to the wound and called for a paramedic.

By 11:55, Lift was dead and Grammar Cop had fled the scene.

"That was the day Grammar Cop stopped being a joke and became a true supervillain, when Lift became the first casualty of his war on the sloppy vernacular," I said. "He claimed her death was an accident. For what it's worth, I believed him. But afterward, he upgraded his Punctuator ammo to lead instead of plastic. Later he added the toxic ink. His crimes grew bloodier by increments, each one an attempt to justify to himself the one before that, recasting his mistakes into some noble quest in whatever part of his mind he could get to fall for that."

"But we're gonna stop him from killing at all. Right?" Sarah said. She'd never seen what Grammar Cop was capable of. She only knew what we were capable of, and we were teenagers, so that was anything.

"Maybe," I said. "We're absolutely gonna stop him from killing today."

"Hey—if we pull this off, the universe isn't gonna blow up or anything, is it?"

This version of December 2013 was already a little different than the life I remembered. I'd spent more time at Sarah's and less at the grocery store with a cranky brother, for one thing. Now I was contemplating real change. If I could save Lift, a hardworking semi-pro superhero, not only would she get back a life I'd never seen her live, but she would almost certainly go on to save other unsaved lives herself. How far could such changes ripple outwards?

I had no idea. For all the wonders of our world, time travel is still a rare and mysterious thing. All I knew for certain was that a human being was scheduled to die. I refused to just let that happen.

"I mean, the other day, you were the one going on about dangerous paradoxes and stuff," Sarah added.

"Well, sure," I said, as if my stomach wasn't a butterfly net. "But that was before I figured out I'd been sent here on a mission."

We pulled into the hotel parking lot at 9:54. By 10:33 we'd survived an agonizing wait in the registration line, picked up our tickets, and downloaded the complementary app with the convention schedule and a map of the pertinent areas of the hotel onto Sarah's phone.

"Here! Here he is, Oz Taylor, Conference Room 3-B!" Sarah hissed.

"Why are you whispering?"

"Why aren't you?"

"Why bother? We're just two excited fans," I said.

"Oh. Right," Sarah said. I winced as she turned to yell at the next passing stranger, "OZ TAYLOR! Sensei Gryphon in DA HOUSE, everybody, WHOO!"

"Not that excited."

"Old people are no fun."

We hurried through the thoroughly classy 4-star hotel, padding double-time across its patterned carpets, dodging between thundertroopers, demon-hunting cowgirls, and assorted incarnations of the same Time Lord.

Twice I had to grab Sarah's elbow and pull her along. "You can go back and get pictures later."

"You're walking too fast!"

"Deal with it."

By 10:41 we'd arrived at Conference Room 3-B. The doors were just opening, Taylor's fans being allowed into the room for the 11 o'clock panel. Spotting Strunkenwhite near the front of the line, I caught Sarah's shoulder and guided her around the crowd, straight up to the yellow-shirted convention volunteer holding the door.

Given the circumstances, it wasn't difficult to make myself look worried. "I am so glad you're here!"

The volunteer's eyes flicked from Sarah and me to the mostly-orderly line her partner was in the process of waving through the door. "Everything all right, folks?"

"Not really. I mean, maybe not?" I took a breath, then another, so I wouldn't stumble over the lines. I'd practiced this bit in front of the mirror. Smooth and slow. "We were here earlier, waiting, and that guy, the one in the tweed jacket, he had a gun. In his pocket, not a holster. And it didn't look like it was peace-bonded or anything."

At this or any other genre convention, every fifth attendee was armed with some flavor of costume weaponry. Such weapons were for show, kept out in plain sight, and by regulation peace-bonded: tied into their sheaths or holsters with brightly colored plastic ties.

"Are you sure that's what you saw?" the volunteer said, looking over to Strunkenwhite with a frown. "I mean, he doesn't really look the type, does he?"

God, it sucked being 16!

"Excuse you?" Sarah said. "Dude, you need to go grab him instead of just standing there with your face—"

"He really upset my friend," I said right over the top of her. "Obviously. Do you think you could just have someone check this out? Please?" The volunteer rolled her eyes, but she also pulled the walkie-talkie from her belt and made the call. Several minutes passed, and then two more con staffers arrived at the door: the same pair of black t-shirt wearing security guys I remembered from the video footage. By this time, the fans waiting for Oz Taylor's panel had all been seated. The volunteer gave the newcomers a hushed rundown of my accusation. Sarah and I nodded emphatically, and were led into the room so we could point out Strunkenwhite from the back.

The three con staffers then huddled up for a private conversation. One of the security dudes hissed into another walkie-talkie. By this point it was 11:03, and the crowd was starting to get restless. With any luck, the con staff was holding Mr. Taylor back until my accusation could get sorted out. No one approached Strunkenwhite.

"Caro, what are they waiting for?" Sarah murmured.

"Someone with more than a t-shirt," I said.

Just after 11:07, another dude arrived, this one dressed in the uniform of actual hotel security. One beefy hand rested on his belt, the other on the butt of a nightstick. He conferred with the convention staff, then led them down the main aisle, stopping beside Strunkenwhite's row.

"Sir?"

Sarah and I held hands, squeezing so hard it hurt.

Strunkenwhite calmly stood and crossed to the aisle, apologizing for the feet he stepped on along the way. He listened reasonably as the hotel guard spoke, pointed to Strunkenwhite's jacket, and presumably asked to check for the weapon.

Then Strunkenwhite pointed up at the stage and said, loudly enough for everyone in the room to hear, "OH LOOK, A DANGLING PARTICIPLE!"

The hotel guard and all three con volunteers actually fell for it, looking away just long enough for Grammar Cop to bolt for the room's side entrance.

"Oh crappity crap," I said.

The guard charged out after Strunkenwhite. The con security guys started to follow, then looked at each other, spun around and raised their hands instead, exhorting the room to remain calm. Sarah and I ran right past them.

Zombies, aliens, and a tall white-faced dude in a black leather face-thong spilled out of the way as Grammar Cop barreled down the hotel hallway, the guard right behind him and brandishing his nightstick. I raced after, legs pumping, surprised by the extra boost I seemed to be getting out of 16-year-old muscles.

"Hey!" I heard Sarah yell. I glanced back, and found her already twenty feet behind me. I didn't recall being so much faster than her. In fact I was fairly sure I hadn't been. She played softball in the summers; they ran laps.

"Mr. Taylor! I AM NOT A FAN!" I heard Grammar Cop bellow from the cross-hall up ahead, and then a sound I knew too well: PTANG! PTANG!

The Punctuator Mark 1. My stomach lurched and the rest of me almost followed. I nearly tripped over my own toes as I skidded around the turn. There, Oz Taylor cowered against the wall, covering his head with Sensei Gryphon. A large plastic quotation mark jutted from the foam beneath the puppet's glass eye.

"Sorry, buddy!" Taylor said.

"Hmmph, a fine friend you be!" Sensei Gryphon replied.

The puppeteer himself seemed unharmed, but the guard had stopped to check on him. I raced after Grammar Cop, spotting his tweed coattails vanishing down another hallway, away from the crowded convention spaces and down an empty row of guest rooms.

Strunkenwhite had a mean sprint, but even as he came up on the next intersection I was closing on him. He turned, running half-backwards, raising the Punctuator to slow me down.

Before I could even cover my face, a heavily panting Sarah slogged around the corner in front of him and punched him in the jaw.

Grammar Cop's running momentum plus Sarah's punching momentum achieved the magic one-hit knockout amount of force that it takes most supers years to master. He slumped to the carpet.

"Huh!" Sarah gasped. "Cool."

"How the heck did you beat me here?" I said.

"I pulled up the hotel map on my phone, and went around the other way," Sarah said.

"Well, nice job."

I kicked the fallen Punctuator safely away down the hall, then crouched to gingerly poke Grammar Cop. He was definitely unconscious. "I think we did it!"

"But you're still future-you?"

"I guess it's not instantaneous."

We heard raised voices and scuffling feet, probably more hotel security or helpful convention-goers resuming the search. Or maybe more than that.

"I heard that one guy calling for a hero. The TroubleShooters will be here any second," Sarah told me. "Sure you don't want a medal?"

I shook my head. Get in, get out, and let history go quietly on its way so that I could go on mine. That was the plan and I was sticking to it.

"Then go!" Sarah said. "I'll hide in the crowd, make sure they pick him up okay."

"Thanks—love you!" I gave her a fast hug and dashed away, certain I was running back to my future.

I underestimated my own momentum.

As I slammed through the door at the end of the hall, my feet carried me right over the top edge of the stairs. My toe rebounded off the steps like I was wearing Kangoo Jumps and suddenly I was airborne, hurtling at vicious speed towards the concrete stairwell wall. I squeaked and threw my arms around my head, and somehow that slight motion was enough to flip me right over.

As the bottoms of my feet hit the wall, my knees bent, and my legs coiled like springs before pushing off again, seemingly of their own volition.

I somersaulted through space at a speed which should have made me instantly dizzy and nauseated. For the briefest instant I wondered if all this frenzied motion was how time travel felt when I was conscious, since I didn't remember the first journey. Then my left foot caught the railing, spinning me into a sideways midair cartwheel. The next thing I knew, my right palm slapped the wall, which somehow did not break my wrist, but instead bounced me right-side up again.

I landed on my feet.

I took one more experimental bounce, on both feet, and nearly hit my head on the stairwell ceiling.

Slowly I sat down on the steps.

Grammar Cop was in custody, or near enough. Lift was alive. I was still stuck in the past. And now, apparently, I had superpowers.

Chapter 3: Recapture

In contrast to the development of the modern superhero, it seems that superhuman abilities are neither required nor desired by the typical villain. In fact, of those powered villains who have consented to interviews, nearly one third admit that they at times found it difficult to plan heists that made full use of their abilities and would have preferred to hire powered stooges according to the needs of each scheme.

- Dying for a Laugh

"And you're sure you didn't get powers before?" Sarah asked.

We were parked in a corner booth of the McDonald's just down the street from the Simonson Suites, our preplanned rendezvous point in case we got separated.

"I think I'd have remembered that." I fidgeted with my cell phone on the table, peeling the blue post-it off the front and thumbing it back down. The note read, 'CALL SARAH.' By now I'd expected my actual 16-year-old self to be back in my place, possibly with no memory of the last six days. "At least this explains what the Vice Admiral had to do with Ruby Goldberg's plan."

"It does?"

"Think about it. Like Pain, the Admiral shows up at my signing with a piece of experimental weaponry, which I'm now pretty sure also came from Ruby's lab. This toy, he tells me, is supposed to cause some kind of mutation."

"Wasn't that supposed to be a bad thing?"

"He clearly thought so, but I'm thinking either Ruby Goldberg somehow knew I had a latent superpower gene, and built a gun to activate it, or her machine just straight up gave me the enhancement."

"So she deliberately turned you into a superhero?"

"Or a supervillain. I haven't decided yet."

"Oooh, yeah, a life of glamorous crime could be good. Steal me pretty things?"

"Heh." I chewed thoughtfully on my ketchup-drenched fries. "But it makes sense, right? My knowledge of future crimes makes me a pretty effective time agent already, and Ruby Goldberg made sure I'd have the abilities to go with them."

"Yeah, I guess so," Sarah said. "Too bad she hasn't actually told you what you need to do."

"There's probably a good reason for that. Some enemy keeping tabs on Ruby herself, or monitoring the timeline in some way. But I've already managed to save Lift, and that has to be a good thing. Whatever other changes I need to make, I can figure those out too. When we get home I'll make up a spreadsheet with all the upcoming crimes and dates I can remember."

"You're such a dork. Can I come up with your hero name?"

"No."

"You could be the Blonde Dynamo!"

"Yeah, no. Seriously, I doubt I'm going to be here long enough to need a codename."

"But what if you still have your powers when you get home?"

"Then I'll worry about it then. And you'll have had ten years to come up with much better ideas."

That night, while watching an awesomely unremarkable TV news story about the TroubleShooters' capture of Grammar Cop at CrossCon, I wrote out a list of every future crime I could recall. It was an extensive and detailed list. My memory isn't quite photographic but it is pretty good, and I scribbled until my hand hurt. But the earliest incident I could think of wasn't until the end of January.

I groaned.

"What? What's wrong?" Sarah said.

"School starts back next Monday, right? I'm on a collision course with high school!"

"Oh, that."

I slumped back into the couch. Sarah cackled.

"I can't do it," I said. "I can't face pre-calc again. I don't even remember my locker combination. I'm going to destroy my GPA and ruin my chances for college."

Sarah's evil laugh trailed off as she recognized my very real distress. "Oh, come on. It won't be that bad, I promise."

We camped out in Sarah's room with a plate of brownies and planned for battle. Sarah wrote me out a copy of my class schedule. She pulled a copy of the Laketon High floor plan off the school website, and we made sure I could more or less remember where all my classrooms were, and my locker. Then we burrowed into the stuffed animal sanctuary sometimes called Sarah's bed to catch up on the reading I'd been assigned over break.

Sarah had already finished her own reading; she did that within the first four days of vacation every year. Now she took half the stack of my textbooks and began jotting detailed notes onto a yellow legal pad. I cracked open *McGillicuddy's Comprehensive Survey of U.S. History, 1620-1988* and reached for another brownie. My fingers brushed only crumbs.

"I got the last one," Sarah said. "You can have it if you really want. But you did eat the last 12."

I blinked. "Twelve? There were not 13 brownies on that plate!"

"There were 15. It's cool, Mom won't miss 'em. That was the pan I made, the bottoms were all burny. See?" Without looking up from the book in her lap, she held up the last brownie so I could see its black and crispy bottom.

"And I really ate a dozen of them?"

"I've never accused you of having standards," Sarah said. "Also, being teenagers makes us hungry. A super-metabolism probably multiplies that?"

"I accept the premise."

I skimmed the history pages, which were vaguely familiar, and then the physics chapter, which was less so. Then I picked up the one thin paperback sandwiched between all the thick, heavy hardcovers. *The Great Gatsby.*

"Oh, you I don't remember at all," I said aloud to the cover, the great big eyes hovering in blue space over a flapper and a Model-T. "I hated you!"

"That seems kinda contradictory," Sarah said.

"I remember the hate. Hate sticks."

"That's true. Oh, and you have a ten page paper due on the book's symbolism, the day we get back from break."

"Oh crap, I do!" I remembered. "I won't even start it until the night before. I don't finish until twenty minutes before my alarm goes off to get up. It's the night that made me a coffee addict."

"So that much of your future's still on track," Sarah said. "Wanna watch the movie?"

"Not even Baz Luhrmann can save this story."

"Okay, well. I *guess* I could write it for you."

"You'd do that?"

"For fifty bucks."

"Deal," I said. I dug my wallet out of my jeans and handed her two twenties and a ten.

Sarah raised her eyebrows. "Seriously?"

"I already wrote it once," I said. "Therefore this no longer counts as cheating. Besides, at this point you probably write more like me-at-16 than I do."

"Hmm. Yeah."

Twenty minutes passed before I broke the silence again. "Are you missing her at all?"

"Her who?" asked Sarah.

"Sixteen-year-old me. The now-me. The one I replaced."

"She never gave me fifty bucks to write a paper."

Suddenly I frowned. "Wait a minute. Didn't you once pay *me* to write a paper?"

Sarah nodded. "Ten bucks, a fortune in eighth grade. *MacBeth.* You didn't think you were paying for quality, did you?"

I chuckled.

"But seriously?" Sarah said. "You're still you. Mostly, anyway. And the ways you're not, they're kinda fun."

"Yeah?"

"It's like having a new friend, but without all the hassle of breaking her in."

Sarah had a dangerous gleam in her eye when she showed up at my house the next morning. "Y'know how my parents belong to that stupid country club they hardly ever go to, unless my dad's trying to pretend he plays golf around other businessmen?"

"Uh, sure?"

"They've got racquetball courts there."

"Okay," I said, not seeing her point.

"We should totally go there this afternoon to try out your powers!"

While it was true that the best description of how I'd felt on those hotel stairs was indeed, "like a racquetball," I didn't really see the point in this, and I told her so.

Sarah's retort was, "How are you supposed to be a superhero if you don't even know the full extent of what you can do?"

"I'm not a superhero. I'm a writer with a specific and limited mission. I've got foreknowledge and the element of surprise on my side, I'll be fine."

"Limited mission or not, it's not like we really know how 'limited' that's going to turn out to be. You could be fighting bad guys for months for all you know. Or years."

"Don't even joke about that."

"However long you're doing this for, you're a hero," Sarah said. "And as your steward, I have to insist you put in some responsible training hours."

"Sarah, I don't need a steward. If I did it would absolutely be you, but I don't." Steward was a catch-all term for registered hero crew, encompassing everything from the receptionists at Everett Mansion to the mechanics who serviced the Guildmobile to doctors and nurses with the specialized training needed to serve extranormal patients. A few professional heroes were known to employ steward personal assistants, but it was rare, and I'd never heard of a teen hero with a steward all to themselves. The TroubleShooters all shared support staff with Leviathan, the professional superteam also based in Cleveland.

Sarah's jaw tightened. "Let me put it another way. Either I'm your steward and you allow me to help you practice your powers, or I'll stop helping you with your homework. I'll refund you for the paper and everything."

"You'd really hold my homework hostage? That's evil. And I know evil."

"I'll do it, if that's what it takes to keep you from going out and getting yourself stupid killed before you're even old like you're supposed to be!"

It was only then that I noticed the damp shine of Sarah's eyes. She was really and truly frightened here. I gave in, and gave her a hug.

"You're right," I said. "I'm sorry, and you're right."

We dug some elbow and knee pads and Hank's old skateboard helmet out of the garage, hid them all in my backpack under an actual racquet, then Sarah borrowed her mom's car to drive us to the club. When we arrived there was one game in session and five empty courts, but we weren't sure how much they'd be able to hear us, so we waited. We spent an hour talking about school, books that hadn't been written yet, and boys for Sarah, though I still refused to tell her anything about her love life past age 16.

Eventually the other game cleared out, and no new players arrived to take their place. Sarah ascended to the second level, standing guard in the hall overlooking the courts, watching me through the wide glassless window there for coaches and referees. I walked into center court, took a deep breath, and spent the next twenty minutes literally bouncing off the walls.

Whether it was my hands or my feet that tagged the wall, or the floor, or the ceiling, the slightest push-off sent me bounding. The tiniest shift in my weight could spin my whole body around, and by twisting my head or pointing my shoulders I could direct myself where I wanted to go. A slightly more forceful shoulder-tuck flipped me completely, enough to get my feet under me for a better push off the next surface.

I expected to experience dizziness or motion sickness, but did not. Perhaps whatever altered my muscles changed my brain chemistry or my eyes in some way as well, allowing my perceptions to keep up with my movement. After the first few minutes, I actually began to enjoy myself. I could hear Sarah giggling the whole time.

Stopping took a bit of practice, but I soon got the hang of that too. It mostly involved keeping my elbows and/or knees from uncoiling again once my feet or hands had impacted a surface. Apparently my first instinct now was to treat every wooden floor and concrete wall like the giant trampoline in Sarah's backyard.

After an hour I started to feel tired. Just a little, the way you're tired after a brisk walk around the neighborhood. Not the tired one usually feels after sustained physical exertion.

I leapt straight from the floor to Sarah's high window, catching the edge beside her hands, pressing my shoe bottoms to the court wall to steady myself as I hung there opposite my friend.

"Okay. I admit it. This is pretty cool."

Sarah spent most of the drive home suggesting more hero names. I spent most of the drive rejecting them. I still wasn't convinced I needed one. I was here in the past to do a job, not to insert a whole new me into the annals of herodom.

"Foo-Fighter!"

"No band names."

"SuperTeen!"

"Generic much?"

"The Bouncing Bowman! Bowgirl? Bow-woman? No, that's clunky-"

"No, no, and no thanks."

"C'mon, think about it! We'll get you some of those trick arrows, with the boxing gloves and the net-traps and the silly putty and all that. They sell them all off the internet, I've seen them. And you can—"

"Still no, dude."

"All right. What about taking the name of a classic hero who's not active anymore?"

"Isn't that kind of pretentious?" I said. "And besides, the intersection of Public Domain plus Not Totally Ridiculous plus Relevant to My New Powers makes for an intensely narrow Venn diagram."

"That's true. But don't give up yet. I'm going to figure this out."

The next day was more or less evenly divided between working on my homework and playing video games. The day after that was New Year's Eve, a classic night for supercrime. The Alliance of Avarice would attack Wall Street sometime around 4 in the morning, but be handily repelled by Chiaroscuro with no help from me. I was free to party, which given my apparent age meant sleeping over at Sarah's house and enjoying a junk food feast starting at 8:30, since Sarah's parents were well over the whole midnight ball-drop thing and planned to be in bed by 10.

It also meant the surprise arrival of Tamika, Nate, and Liz. I hadn't seen Tamika or Nate since Sarah's last birthday. Liz I hadn't seen at all since graduation, although she had pinged me on Facebook Messenger one night a while back. I had seen her status change to "Single"—her wedding was only 9 months earlier—and didn't know what to say, so I hadn't responded.

I yanked Sarah aside while her dad distracted them with polite coat-taking.

"Why didn't you mention everyone was coming?"

I'd seen Sarah's exact grin on the faces of any number of my supervillain interviewees. "You're going to be seeing them all in school next week anyway. This is me throwing you in at the deep end. Relax, you'll be fine!"

I'm pretty sure all three of them caught me staring like a freak at some point. I could hardly help it. Tamika still had her hair in the short, tight 'locs she cut off in college. Nate was a total beanpole. He was a trombone player, and every bend of his bony elbows evoked the movement of the slide. Liz's hair was Kool-Aid red. She still had her retainer in!

And then there was the endless yammering on about OH SO IMPORTANT things.

"I still can't believe he picked a sophomore over me. A sophomore!" Tamika moaned. The 'he' in question was the high school band director, Mr. G. The previous week, he'd given first chair saxophone in the Symphonic Band to Rory Isbell. Rory was headed for Juilliard, but I could hardly tell Tamika that.

Nate, meanwhile, had just blitzed his way through his third break-up in as many months. In the course of twenty minutes, he managed to corner Sarah, Liz, Tamika, and me separately over the chip bowl or while we were switching Pandora radio stations to ask, "What about you? What do YOU think actually makes girls happy?"

"Good grief, Nate," I said when my turn came. "Could you be any more cliché?"

When Liz started going on about how her boss at The Cafe Crusader "is a total ogre! Not literally, he's not a magical person, but he won't even let me study at the counter..." I fled upstairs. They could all think I was on an extended bathroom break.

Sarah followed me up two minutes later, and found me in her room, listening to Snow Patrol through her tinny old laptop speakers and playing Angry Birds on my phone.

"We can hear the music from downstairs, you know. Everyone knows you're not in the bathroom."

"The stereo down there doesn't drown it out?"

"Do you hear anything from downstairs right now? We totally turned it off to spy on you. Are you going to come back down or what?"

I still hadn't looked up from the phone. "You'll have more fun without me, I promise."

"I can't have fun unless everyone else is too. Those are your friends down there, and the least you could do is act like it."

"They're kind of my friends, and kind of not so much. Even when we were the same age, I'm not sure we were ever the same age."

Sarah huffed. "I'm the same age as them."

"You're different." I set my phone down and turned my chair to face her properly. "I just—"

"You're embarrassed," Sarah said.

"That makes it sound petty. I have a right to—"

"You're embarrassed, and you think it's because I embarrassed you. Because I invited everybody over here without telling you."

"A little," I started to say. Sarah flushed bright red. Crap. This WAS her fault, really, but I hardly wanted to deal with her tantrum on top of everything else. "I embarrassed myself, okay? They probably think I'm a jerk, and it's not even nine o'clock."

"They don't think you're a jerk. They think you're *being* a jerk," Sarah retorted. "Because you are."

I put my face in my hands and breathed in and out a few times, until I could speak quietly and reasonably. "I don't know what I'm supposed to say. It's not like I remember anything about what's going on with anyone." I did not add, *And it's high school crap, so I really don't care.* "Can't you just make some excuse for me?"

"If I really thought that would make anything better, maybe I would. But isn't being weird up here sulking just as weird as being weird not talking down there?"

It took me a moment to follow that sentence. "Maybe," I finally admitted.

"We're teenagers, remember? We think everyone's a weirdo anyway. Does that ever go away?"

"When we get older, you mean? Not exactly. We just realize that the weirdos include ourselves, so it's best to accept it and let everyone get on with it. That's what you and I did, anyway."

"Well, okay then. Weirdo. Look, I'm going back down to the party with our friends. You do what you want," Sarah said.

She got as far as the door before I leapt up to follow.

"Sorry, guys. I'm okay now," I announced to the gang when we got back down there. They looked up from their game of Settlers of Catan—Liz with a smile, Tamika and Nate with narrowed eyes.

"Whatever," Tamika said.

The next twenty minutes or so were agony, but agony I could now see was of my own making. I had to earn my way back to the group. So I told Tamika she was a way better saxophonist than that sophomore punk. I told Liz that her boss was the worst, and Nate to stop thinking of girls as a monolith. By the time Sarah was sure her parents were asleep and the jokes started getting raunchier, I was getting just as many laughs as anyone. More, probably. I had ten extra years of material to work from. My memories of this time were still a jumble; I hardly remembered anything that had mattered to me at the end of 2013, let alone what my friends had been into. But I coasted through on context. I managed not to spoil Tamika for the first *Veronica Mars* movie and feigned enthusiasm for Nate's favorite reality show, *Hero Island.*

I spoke the least to Liz, because every time I looked at her I just wanted to shake her and say, "Don't marry that jerk! Don't even date him! Write his name down right now, look at it every day, and remind yourself!" But even if we'd gotten past the bit where she thought I was obviously delusional, I wasn't sure I had the right. Rescuing Lift, saving a life that had been cut short, that was one thing. Meddling with a person's emotional history was another. Sometimes our worst experiences turn out to be our best teachers. Maybe that's doubly true of bad relationships.

On January 6, my mother shook me awake at 6:45 a.m. while my clock radio blared, "Now you're just somebody that I used to know." I think Mom was a bit surprised by its utter failure to penetrate my stupor, but chalked it up to the SuperMonday effect of the first morning back after vacation. I dragged myself into the shower, cursing the U.S. education system and its complete disregard for natural teenage biorhythms. By 7:45 I was at school. Or possibly in a newly discovered hell dimension that smelled like textbooks and hormones.

No, I realized around 10 a.m. as I commenced my two hour block math class, *this* was the worst of all hell dimensions. English and history I could pretty much coast through, stealing enough details from my classmates' comments to neatly overturn their arguments. But life is too short for me to make sense of pre-calculus once, and a ten-year rewind just made it worse. Mrs. Porter spent the first hour lecturing to the people who already understood anyway, then turned us loose on some practice problems. I spent both hours staring out the window or through the open door into the hall, willing the bell to ring and trying not to fall asleep.

The day got a little better after that, but not by much. Afterwards I went straight to Sarah's and ate an entire carton of ice cream, necessitating a run to the store to replace it. Seeing my agony, Sarah agreed to help, in exchange for a very reasonable percentage of my allowance, and on the condition that I continue to respect her role as my steward.

"That's it?" I said. "That's all you want, and you're willing to help me prep for all my tests and take on practically all of my homework? That doesn't really seem fair to you."

"Hey, you'll still have homework. Just different homework. Here—" Sarah said, handing me her iPad.

"What am I looking at?" I said. She'd set up a YouTube playlist, but it looked nothing like her usual dance-pop marathons or Korrasami fanvid collections.

"The other night I couldn't sleep, just thinking of all the cool stuff you can do now. So I started going through all these clips from gymnastics and martial arts and Parkour and everything. The links are all there. I'll be sending you regular updates, and I've been working on an email with the timestamps for all the best bits."

"You've been putting a lot of thought into this."

"Please," she said, "Have you met me?"

Sarah's steward initiative didn't end at YouTube videos, either. Pretty much any time we didn't spend mired in schoolwork, she was coming up with some new activity to further test my powers. The second Saturday after school started back up, she took me bowling to gauge the extent of my strength and control. I picked up the balls with ease. I could probably have juggled them if no one had been looking, and if I knew how to juggle. Still I threw more gutter balls in the first five frames than I ever had in my life.

"Wow," Sarah said. "You used to be much better at this. And by used to, I mean last month."

"Thanks," I said. "I'm trying not to punch a hole through any walls. Or possibly some poor employee working in the back."

"Oh, you'll be fine!" Sarah scoffed. "Let's talk codenames."

I swung back, and into my next throw. "We already talked codenames. What part of 'no' was less than transparent?"

"Oh come on!" Sarah said. "Didn't you ever dream of *being* a superhero, not just writing about their douchey nemeses? I know you did, I was there."

"Of course," I said. "What kid doesn't? But then I grew up, went through puberty, and did *not* get powers. Getting them this time is kinda cool, sure, but it is *not* worth growing up all over again. Nothing is. Hero is just a phase I'm going through. Hopefully a short one."

"Pfffft," Sarah said.

"Don't you 'pffft,' me, young lady."

Gradually, over the course of the next few hours, I did manage to regain my coordination. And I only shattered one pin.

Early on the following Saturday, Sarah barged into my room with wild hair, dark circles under her eyes, and a brown paper bag. Setting the bag on a chair, she pulled out a sturdy blue tracksuit with purple accents. On the left breast of the jacket was a circular logo patch with a stylized letter 'B,' the curves of the letter a dotted line that seemed to trace the path of a bouncing ball.

"What's this?" I said.

"It's you, Caro. It's your costume. You're Bounceback!"

"Sarah, I told you, I don't think I need—" Sarah gave me a ferocious glare, worse than the time I spilled coffee all over her autographed picture of Michael B. Jordan. I took the tracksuit from her hands, folding it up to get a closer look at the patch.

"I was up all night making that on my mother's embroidery machine," Sarah said.

"I could tell."

"Took me three tries. But this is it! Your very own heroic icon."

"Bounceback." I rolled the new codename around in my mouth. "You're sure it doesn't sound—I dunno, porny?"

"What? No! What is wrong with you?" Sarah snapped.

"Also there's the back-in-time thing. I wasn't really planning on advertising that."

"No one but us will even think of that. I think it's hilarious," Sarah said. "Besides, if you're going to show up and stop a crime before it happens, you're going to have to explain it somehow anyway."

"I'm not giving away the time travel thing," I insisted. "I'll just say I'm 'vaguely psychic' or something."

"Sure. Whatever," Sarah said, clearly not worried about that part.

I looked at her. "You really think this is me?"

Sarah nodded so emphatically I feared for a second her head was going to fall off.

"Then 'Bounceback' it is. You're Bounceback's steward."

"Yay!" Sarah said. "But I can trade up to a cooler hero later, right?"

I gave her a shove. She flopped onto the bed and started snoring more or less instantly. I picked up the paper bag to throw it away, only to find it wasn't empty. There was a new pair of sneakers in my size, really nice ones that would be good for running and jumping, and a balaclava to conceal my face. The mask was open at the top, to let my hair out—or my ponytail, anyway. I had no clue how all those heroines managed to fight with their hair all down and swinging around their face. But otherwise only my eyes and the bridge of my nose were left exposed, and I could always add a pair of goggles if I felt the need. Taken all together, Bounceback's ensemble wasn't something you'd ever see on *Project Up, Up, and Away*, but it would do the job.

There were also a couple of folded pieces of paper printed out from the W.H.A.M. licensing website. Sarah had already registered 'Bounceback' as an amateur superhero, and herself as my steward. Anyone could apply for amateur hero status, and receive a serial number and a printable license from the World Heroes Advisory Mission. Essentially it meant that if you performed a citizen's arrest in costume or assisted a superhero in doing so, you could give a legally admissible statement to the police without directly divulging your identity. W.H.A.M. would have your name, home address, and Social Security number on file and would be able to independently verify. How Sarah had figured out my Social Security number, I hadn't the foggiest. But she was crafty like that.

Cleveland's next major supervillain attack was less than a week away, and Thursday's test on polynomial functions aside, I was ready.

Chapter 4: Reacquaint

Despite overwhelming evidence that mind-controlled civilians or stooges are more often detrimental to the average villain's plots, more than 60% of villains questioned stated that they had attempted to influence one or more people to do their bidding. Of these attempts, fewer than 2% resulted in full or partial mind control; about 10% resulted in brain damage for both villain and stooge. The odds of a controlled stooge assisting in a successful heist are less than one in 5,000.

- Dying for a Laugh

I could feel my brain turning, drip by drip, into frozen yogurt. Not even the good kind, but the evil stuff with fake chemical sugars in it and the word "lite" on the package. The worst part was there wasn't even a bad guy to blame. Not officially, anyway. If the Scholastic Aptitude Test ever applied for Recognized Evil Status, I'd no doubt it would be rubber-stamped like nobody's business.

The test and I were to do battle in the morning. Aside from a short dinner break with Mom and Dad, during which I'd failed to convince them to let me take the test later in the year, I'd been engaged in final cramming operations for the better part of four hours. I was studying alone, since Sarah's mother wasn't making her try for any early college admissions. She got to hold off on her test until fall, when I knew for a fact she'd skip the SAT altogether for the kinder, gentler ACT. Slacker.

Just as I was contemplating a TV break, an alert popped up on my computer. I'd programmed my future crimes spreadsheet into Outlook and set it to send me reminders one day, six hours, and one hour before I needed to go kick someone's butt in righteous fashion.

"Oh thank goodness," I muttered, and grabbed the new Bounceback outfit from my closet.

I passed Mom working in her office. "Taking a break," I said. "Borrowing the car, back in a bit."

It was January 31, and as I drove downtown, a charter bus full of basketball fans from Cleveland State was on its way up to Detroit to watch their CSU Vikings take on the Titans. Or so they thought. One of the students, the same campus rep who arranged the bus as a promotional venture with SharkJuice Energy Drink, had also slipped the driver some extra cash to double back into the city. Worse, he'd spiked the SharkJuice with a mind control agent. The free drinks were being liberally consumed by everyone aboard, so by the time they arrived at their new destination, the students would be convinced they were actual Viking warriors out for a fine night of pillage and plunder.

I thought about calling Sarah as I drove. If I was lucky, this could be my last chance to talk to 16-year-old Sarah before I was zapped back to the future. But she was 16. She thought she was invincible, and she would've insisted I bring her along. I would've refused, and I had a terrible feeling she'd drive her non-powered self downtown anyway and blunder right into trouble. I'd changed the password on my computer for the same reason, so she couldn't get at my list of upcoming crimes.

Nevertheless, I had another "Call Sarah" post-it stuck to the phone in my jacket pocket, for the benefit of my possibly-clueless younger self, just like the day we went after Grammar Cop.

I found a decently-lit 24-hour parking lot a few blocks off the river, and exited the car with my balaclava tucked under my inside-out jacket. Whether I was going home tonight or not, the last thing I needed was some sharp-eyed parking attendant connecting Bounceback's costume to my mom's license plate. A little further up the street I ducked into a shadowy doorway, flipped the jacket and pulled on the mask. I should have been glad for it, as Cleveland was enjoying a particularly bitter winter this year, but I didn't seem to feel the cold the way I used to. Another benefit of an enhanced metabolism, I guessed.

Swinging myself up the nearest fire escape, I climbed to the top of the building. Jumping from one rooftop to the next, I made my way down to edge of the Cuyahoga River.

Yes, that's the river that burned in the '50s and '60s. I swear, one little waterway catches fire a few times and nobody ever lets your city forget it.

Clevelanders knew this area as The Flats. Various stores, bars, clubs, and concert venues ran along the water's edge, many inhabiting old warehouses, relics of livelier days for the city's shipping industry. From my classic superhero vantage point behind the neon sign atop Club Mask, I spotted the bus approaching on the road above the waterside. Through the tall windows I saw two dozen college kids wearing a comical assortment of mismatched costumes, including RenFaire-esque barbarian wear, basketball jerseys, and several football helmets with plastic horns super-glued on top.

The bus turned down the hill. Stowing my binoculars, I raced to intercept. Leaping and running across three more buildings, I landed atop a restaurant just as the Vikings pulled up out front. I figured a perfectly timed drop off the restaurant roof would add to the intimidation factor as I told the brain-drained sports fans in no uncertain terms to stay on the bus and go home. I also figured a three-story drop straight down onto concrete would be no trouble at all for my newly shock-absorbent legs.

I was pretty sure, anyway.

I jumped.

I was right about my legs. At least I think so. It was hard to tell exactly, considering that I managed to land right on a patch of black ice. My sneakers flew out from under me and I cracked my head hard on the sidewalk, causing little dancing lights to bloom before my eyes. Whatever boost my muscles had gained, it didn't seem to have added much fortitude to my cranium. So, now I knew that.

I was only dazed for a minute, the lights fading quickly, but by the time I'd pushed back to my feet, the sports fans had already cleared the bus, and there were screams coming from inside the restaurant. Spitting out a few of my Mom's more creative swear words, I charged in after them.

There were faux Vikings everywhere, belching, chanting, and waving homemade wooden clubs, axes, and impractically large swords lightly covered with foam padding. The weapons, courtesy of the mastermind behind tonight's show, had been stolen from a storage locker belonging to the CSU Live Action Role Playing Society. The mind-controlled sports fans snatched food and drink from the tables in front of the paying patrons. Some of the patrons fought back; there were a couple of games of tug-of-war going on over large pitchers of beer. Several of the servers had been cornered near the bar by five of the invaders, who beat their swords and axes rhythmically on their shields. One waiter had already been knocked to the floor, his arm bent entirely the wrong way.

"No sacking the city tonight, gang! Row home and sleep it off!" I yelled, vaulting a table, but in the two leaps it took me to reach the bar, the hostess got a firm grip on the lead Viking's impressively braided black beard and kneed him between the legs. He curled into a fetal position on the ground, and the other four fled for the fire exits.

Following the hostess' lead, I picked out the biggest Viking in the room. He was happily occupied by the dessert buffet, shoveling chocolate cake into his mouth with his bare hands, and not bothering anybody. I picked out the second biggest Viking, jumped up behind him and hit him carefully in the head.

He bellowed, unfortunately more with rage than pain, and turned, swinging clumsily with his padded war-axe. I wasn't really sure of my new strength yet, or just how hard to swing against a fragile human body, but I dodged and hit him again, a little harder this time. He blinked and lashed out, this time fast enough to connect with the back of my knee. I fell backwards, catching myself on a table's edge just in time to avoid my second head injury in as many minutes. A crowded restaurant, I was quickly learning, is not the ideal place for a fight scene.

I shoved myself upright again, hands up in a guard position before my face. He stared back warily. Or possibly he was waiting to burp.

I could have spent the next twenty minutes experimenting on this dude's thick skull, seeking just the right amount of force to put him to sleep without causing brain damage. Or I could do what I did, which was to yank that axe out of his hands, flip it around, and use it to break his left arm just below the elbow, trusting that the pain would distract him from the fight.

He screamed and fell over. I caught him and eased him to the floor.

I turned, grinning under my mask as I found every Viking in the room staring at me with dropped jaws.

"Anyone who doesn't want the same, get your butt back on the bus!" I shouted.

Every single one of them turned and ran. Unfortunately they headed out every door *not* leading to the bus, in search of easier mayhem. A testament to the strength of their pillage-programming, or just their own foolish stubbornness? I gave chase, slamming through the side doors and back into the sharp night air.

The Vikings fanned out amongst the various waterfront hot spots, waving their weapons over their heads. Night-clubbers ran screaming, half of them probably convinced this was a full-on invasion of actual time-traveling Norse raiders, which happened back in '82. A couple of Nautica security guards were attempting to organize a resistance, smashing up patio chairs for arms, while the Club Mask bouncers waved the last of their waiting line inside and barred the door behind them. More shouting, more atonal singing, more cries of "Dude, what the hell?!" rang through the night.

So did Tchaikovsky's *1812 Overture*.

I hadn't expected that for another ten minutes at least. But in the version of history I knew, there were only three TroubleShooters to answer the call, and they were still in mourning, barely a month after Lift's death at the hands of Grammar Cop. Of course that affected their response time.

I ran three steps, flipped myself through the air, and landed right in front of a Norsewoman wearing a batting helmet with blue construction paper wings glued to the sides.

"Hear that thunder?" I asked as the *1812* cannons boomed. "Thor is really ticked off, and he wants you to go back to the bus!"

Wings ignored my words and swung inexpertly for my hair with her hammer. I caught it one-handed, yanked it away, and slammed it as hard as I could into the pavement, shattering the wooden head to splinters. Wings fell to the ground, bawling like a toddler who'd lost her pacifier.

I ran on. The Tchaikovsky was getting louder, so instead of pouncing on another Viking, I ducked out of sight down the nearest alleyway. It was a nicely narrow space, two brick walls staring each other down with only fifteen feet or so in between. Visions of the *Prince of Persia* video games danced in my head, a recurring component in Sarah's training regime. I ran at one wall, leapt, kicked off the brick one-footed, then twisted in the air to kick the opposite wall and bound higher still. Bouncing myself from side to side vertically up the alleyway, I reached the top and rolled on to the nearest roof.

There I turned and dropped flat, hunkering down behind the roof's edge to watch as a red and blue 1966 Volkswagen minibus barreled down into the Flats from the highway. The *1812 Overture* blasted from the van's powerful subwoofers: the TroubleShooters' public-domain theme song. Back in the 1980s, the Shooters had traveled all over the country in that bus in search of wrongs to right, taking down bad guys, working out their natural teenage aggression in a socially constructive fashion. The team settled down in our fair city in 1992, after they formally came under W.H.A.M. supervision. They remained a team of teenagers, older members graduating out to collegiate training programs, professional adult franchises, or solo careers as new young heroes signed on. The current members had meeting rooms and shared training facilities at Leviathan's HQ, adjacent to the Cleveland Museum of Art, and they were assumed to attend school nearby in their well-protected secret IDs.

For the moment at least, my fight was done. I pulled the binoculars from my jacket again, peering through and adjusting the focus onto the wide front window of a bar four buildings down on the other side. Meanwhile, the ShooterVan squealed to a stop a few hundred yards away. The side door slammed open, and the first hero jumped out of the van, a dark-skinned young woman with close-cropped black hair, a blue domino mask, and a chunky laser blaster in each fist, strafing the Vikings with little yellow bolts of light. Three of the marauders fell to the ground, stunned unconscious.

I was used to seeing Ruby Goldberg flying around in a giant indigo robot that occasionally turned into a spaceship, but in 2014 she was still some time away from perfecting that tech. Here, just seven years earlier, even her blasters looked primitive. They actually trailed wires, hooking into a bulky metal backpack strapped on over her red and blue TS letter jacket. Everything Ruby Goldberg invented started out gigantic and cumbersome; she could only ever figure out how to miniaturize after the fact.

Grinning, Ruby charged the largest conglomeration of Vikings, firing as she went, criss-crossing the laser-bolts before her in a visually stunning if not particularly efficient pattern.

Behind her, a second TroubleShooter dropped from the van, a compact white kid in a red mask and a red hoodie with a bright blue M on the chest. A half dozen Vikings ran at him, letting out a mighty roar. The kid laughed and raced to meet them. The lead Norseman brought a massive foam mace hammering down at the hero's head, but the teen ducked inside the stroke, catching the weapon's handle. His hand glowed suddenly blue, then flared white, as a second mace, identical to the first, appeared in the TroubleShooter's other palm.

He was Match, with the power to duplicate any non-living object he touched. The copies faded after an hour, so they weren't exactly the miracle of modern manufacturing, but they served him well enough in a fight. Backhanding his attacker across the face with his copied mace, Match yanked the original weapon from its owner's slackening grip, then spun on into the press of Vikings, taking them on with double the bludgeoning power. His reasonable competence with a wide range of other people's weapons would soon become legendary.

Leaping third from the van came Manaaki, tall and wide-shouldered, in a blue mask, red and blue rugby jersey and soccer shorts. Manaaki was from New Zealand, of Maori descent, with curly black hair and russet skin. He slammed the van door shut behind him, before turning and pounding across the pavement after the others.

I felt my heart skip a beat.

Three of them. Why were there only three of them tonight? Unless I'd somehow missed her exit. I checked the bar again, making sure my quarry was still there, then quickly scanned the crowd below, looking for the sparkle of her leotard. I spotted each of her teammates in turn engaging the Norse, but no Lift.

There were tons of perfectly reasonable explanations for this. Lift could have been called away on a solo mission tonight, or gone out for field-training with one of her mentors from Leviathan. She could have been out of town with friends, or eaten some bad fast food. Okay, heroes usually power through that last one, I think, but even so.

There was no reason to think she was dead after all. That history had somehow autocorrected my fix. No, I'd have heard. It would have been on the news. My mother would be working on the story.

Unless they were keeping it secret for some reason, maybe as part of an ongoing investigation.

But in that case, Lift's friends would not be smiling and laughing right now as they knocked over tipsy college kids.

Unless they were just putting on a brave face.

No. No! I saved her. *I saved her, dammit!*

That's about as far as I got into my panic before gravity stopped applying to me and I flipped up into the air, head down, ponytail dangling, my feet kicking at the dark sky.

Tilting my neck back, I found myself looking right at Lift. Except for being upside down, she looked just like she had on TV. The same sparkly blue domino mask framing her dark eyes, the same confident smirk. Even without the whole suspension issue, I think my stomach would have flipped anyway. How many times had this face stared back at me from the glossy center pages of my book, underlined by the years she had lived?

Even strung upside down, the blood rushing to my face, I couldn't help but sigh in relief. I'd really done it.

"Hey there!" she said. "You don't *look* like a Viking. So I'm guessing you're either a new hero in town or the evil mastermind behind all this."

"Uh, hero," I said. "Absolutely."

"Thought so. The tracksuit-balaclava combo is way too subtle for most wannabe Viking chieftains." She spun a finger at me. Suddenly I was right-side up again, and my feet dropped back to the roof.

"Thanks," I said, quickly reclaiming the ten percent of my hair that had gone AWOL from my ponytail holder. "How did you know I was here?"

"Manaaki spotted you running out of the fight as we drove up, so I snuck around to check you out."

"Oh geez, that must have looked totally suspicious." *And how much more suspicious are you looking now,* my internal editor asked too late, *by commenting on the fact?* "Sorry! I just didn't want to get in anybody's way."

"You wouldn't have," Lift said, seeming to take me at face value. "We're pretty good at this whole combating the forces of chaos thing."

Just like with Grammar Cop, my plan had been to get in, make sure the guy responsible for tonight's stupid got caught, and go home, hopefully for real. I'd worn Sarah's silly costume and fought Vikings to limit the damage until the licensed semi-professionals could get there. Also, yes, because I had boosted strength and super jumping powers now, and it was awesome. But so was being an adult. An adult with my own apartment and no SATs to take in the morning.

"Any idea what happened here tonight?" Lift asked.

"Um, yeah, actually—" I began, only to be cut off by another piercing scream. Both of us looked down to find a dozen Vikings and twice as many rambunctious bar patrons crashing together in the middle of the road. The full-on street brawl portion of tonight's mayhem had begun, and the rest of Lift's team was right there in the middle of it.

She turned back to me with the carefully friendly face of someone in a hurry but trying not to be obvious about it. "How are you with the talking-while-punching?"

I could hardly say, *No thanks, I'll just stay here, creeping on that bar down there.*

Instead I said, "Haven't really tried it. But I'm sure I'll figure it out."

The next ten minutes involved the TroubleShooters and me punching a lot of drunken would-be Vikings, also punching quite a few drunk civilians who refused to back off and let the heroes do their job, and me trying to yell an explanation for all this over the noise.

"Okay! That's good with the punching!" Lift encouraged. I felt a hand grab me from behind and grabbed a wrist, throwing my assailant into an open Mini Cooper convertible. Who leaves the top down in Cleveland in January? "Really good. But you're kinda mumbling. Is it a Viking plague? Is it spreading?"

Kicking a sword out of a Viking's hand, I pushed my hot and sticky mask up enough to clear my mouth. "No, they're just drunken sports fans! Someone spiked their drinks, they're being mind-controlled!"

"Oh! All right then!" Lift tapped the glowing TS insignia on her watch. "Hey Ruby!"

"Kinda busy, boss!" Ruby Goldberg's voice answered. Lift had put her comm on speaker, presumably for my sake.

"The Vikings are drugged! Get a blood sample and do me a fixer!"

"On it!"

Across the fight, I spotted Ruby making a dash for the van, clearing herself a path with her blasters. Match followed close behind with a giant mace in either hand, battering back the Vikings who tried to give chase.

"Dude, you know this is way easier, right?" Ruby called over her shoulder. Her stunguns picked off another three Norsemen in quick succession. "Just make a copy!"

"Dude!" Match dropped to one knee, hammering Vikings on either side of him in the shins, knocking them flat on their faces. "This is way more fun!"

The pair made it to the van and vanished inside.

Ten seconds later, I heard Ruby Goldberg's voice from Lift's wristcomm again. *"All right. Slight hiccup."*

"What is it?" Lift replied unhappily.

"Remember that whole thing last week with the door-to-door vampires?"

"Yeah?"

"We're fresh out of syringes."

"Okaaaaaaaay," Lift said. "Well, figure it out!"

"No, yeah, I got it," Ruby promised. *"Just gimme a minute!"*

The rest of us fought on. Lift levitated her opponents two at a time, spun them about until they were too dizzy to stand, then set them down in groaning heaps, Vikings to one side, civilians to the other. Manaaki just slammed his way through the pressing crowd, parrying swords and axes effortlessly with his bare arms, his big hands gripping the shoulders of anyone about to be on the receiving end of a drunken blow. Manaaki's power was a personal force field that he could expand around any person or object he touched. Every weapon that hit him or those under his protection splintered and broke, and every punch and kick just bounced off. It was a lot of fun to watch, except for the moment when Manaaki grabbed my own shoulder and a Norse war-hammer broke apart across the end of my nose. I heard the force field hum, felt the hair stick up along my arms, and squeezed my eyes shut as the splinters flew. Manaaki didn't let go until they'd all safely hit the ground. I felt bad when Manaaki moved on and I realized I'd forgotten to thank him.

Gradually we wore the brawlers down, though we were starting to tire as well. At least I was. I wasn't really used to that anymore, not since discovering my new powers.

"Ruby!" Lift called into her comm. "Any time this year?"

"On our way!"

The ShooterVan door slid open again. Match dropped out first, foam maces at the ready, but by then the false-Norse forces were dwindling. Ruby Goldberg popped out right behind him, with a brand-new contraption in her hands. This thing had clearly started life as a crossbow, but now boasted an acetylene torch rigged to one side of the stirrup in front, and a glass tube above the stock where one would expect to find the targeting sight.

Ruby took aim across the parking at the nearest Viking. As she fired, so did the acetylene torch, sterilizing the crossbow bolt on the fly. The Viking yelped as it stabbed deep into his bicep.

"Aww, c'mon, ya big baby!" Ruby said. "You guys should love this! It's a mini harpoon!"

The crossbow bolt was affixed to a long cord trailing back to Ruby's weapon. She thumbed a button above the trigger, and the Norseman whimpered again as the bolt was abruptly yanked free of his arm and back into the glass collection tube.

"Ta-daa! One blood sample acquired, one fixer coming right up," said Ruby. She hopped back up into the van and slammed the door.

The police arrived to help contain the civilians, while the Shooters corralled the last conscious Vikings in an empty corner of the Club Mask parking lot. They'd more or less stopped resisting by this point. I stood back with Manaaki, who bounced a fist warningly against his palm and fought not to ruin the effect with a smirk. I also kept sneaking glances at the bar I'd been watching when Lift found me, in case my suspect made a break for it.

"So, Bounceback," Lift said. We'd introduced ourselves during the fight. "Were you here when the Vikings attacked? We were on patrol when the call came in. We didn't expect anyone to beat us to the scene."

"Not exactly?" I said. "I'm kinda psychic? Just a little bit."

Crap, did that ever sound flimsy out loud.

But Lift grinned. "I get it. It's not just the jumping. You see a terrible future, and you bounce it back. I love it. I love it! So you had a vision of the Vikings before they got here?"

"Nothing that specific. I just had a feeling something was going down here tonight. Once I saw the bus pull in, I got a sense of who and why."

"Like they stunk of booze and brain-tampering?"

"Something like that."

That was all the explanation the Shooters needed. Growing up in an age of atomic ninjas, robot tigers, and talking gorilla astronauts, you learned to go with the flow.

Ruby Goldberg joined us soon after that, with the antidote that she'd cooked up in the van's chemistry lab. We mixed it with coffee, kindly donated by one of the restaurants nearby, in the hopes of taking the edge off the students' inevitable hangovers.

I then stole a horned helmet and beard off one of the Vikings, put them on over my mask, and announced, "Grog! Warriors, drink up!"

It worked like a charm. Within minutes the sports fans were peeling off their beards and armor and blinking in the suddenly harsh light of the street lamps, as their brains resumed normal service. The police took charge of the lot of them. Lift, Manaaki, and myself helped sort and load the unconscious and the wounded into a bus or an ambulance as needed.

"I don't suppose you know what evil genius was behind all this?" Lift asked as we were wrapping up.

"Feels like he's nearby," I said, as if it were just coming to me. I didn't want to show off too much, but it felt pretty cool to have actual heroes asking me for help.

I led the TroubleShooters right to the bar's front window. On the other side sat Aiden Kingsley, Cleveland State's campus SharkJuice rep, a flaxen-haired white boy nursing a scowl and a beer. He hadn't grown the mustache yet, but the foam on his lip mimicked it anyway, completing the face I'd come to loathe in the writing of "Flash Mobster."

The chapter title was Sarah's idea.

I waved. He bolted.

I ran for the bar's front door, while the TroubleShooters split along the side alleys. It was Lift that got Kingsley, flipping him upside down as he ran out the delivery entrance and dropping him right into the dumpster. The heroes all laughed long and hard at that, and I faked laughing with them.

Aidon Kingsley was 22 years old. Tonight's stunt had been his first grand chemical experiment. He went on to invade Des Moines with circus folk, St. Paul with a soccer tournament, and Reno with the Guiness record holder for world's largest knitting circle. People died in Des Moines and in each attack after. When he was finally caught and jailed, Kingsley laughed about his first tango in Cleveland, watching from the safety of a bar window as his Vikings failed to pillage anything of value. He'd sneered at the TroubleShooters, their clumsy victory over his clumsier Vikings, but he never mentioned being captured by them. Because he wasn't, back then. So who could say what would happen to him now?

Maybe the world would get lucky, and he'd be put in with one of those magic cellmates you find in Stephen King novels, who would teach him to be a better person and write in a journal. But if I'd just saved Des Moines and St. Paul and Reno and the future, then why hadn't I been zapped back home yet?

Maybe he'd just grow bitterer, humiliated by those jerks who put him out with the trash. Maybe he'd escape, as he did from Alcatraz in 2018 with the aid of a trio of witches and a post-hypnotic suggestion he'd planted years before. Maybe he'd live it all again just the same, or worse.

"Okay, maybe we should let him out now, and help him clean off the worst of, umm, whatever that is," I said after a minute.

"Dude, are you kidding? He earned every second of this," Match said, making the L gesture at his forehead and yelling into the dumpster, "LO-SER!"

"Besides, the cops will hose him off before they throw him in the van," Ruby Goldberg said. I wondered how the officers would feel about that, or the smell. "So, Denny's?"

"Denny's," Lift agreed. "Bounceback, you're welcome to join us."

I still had a standardized test to face in the morning, but how many times in your life do you get asked to go out with actual superheroes?

Apparently the team ate out in costume, and it didn't make much sense for me to change into civvies, follow the Shooters across town, then try and find someplace discreet to change back into hero-gear. So I got to ride with them in the freaking ShooterVan, the absolute coolest vehicle ever seen on the streets of Cleveland.

It's possible I was fangirling a little. On the inside.

We waited for Ruby to fold her mobile lab up and the rear seats back down, then Manaaki took the driver's seat, Lift rode shotgun, and I slid into the middle seat behind them. Ruby and Match took the back, and immediately started an intense discussion of either a video game they were playing, or an actual fight they'd participated in last week, I wasn't sure which. Lift and I made friendly small-talk for several minutes, mostly about what we were going to eat, before Lift cut herself off, pointing at my balaclava.

"I'm sorry. You've gotta be sweating up a storm in there!"

"I knew someone who did that literally," Match said. "It was his power. Way gross."

Lift ignored him. "You can go ahead and take it off. The windows back here are tinted pretty dark, and we're friendly."

I trusted the Shooters. It wasn't as if any of them were likely to know my face, and Lift was right about the sweat, so I peeled off the mask and set it next to me on the seat.

"Well hello there," Ruby said.

Had she recognized me somehow? Maybe her future self had managed to warn her I was coming. Or maybe she was just being flirty.

I decided to go for a subtle test, something that wouldn't force me to tell my story in front of the whole team, or risk some time-shattering paradox if future Ruby needed Ruby-now to remain oblivious for some reason.

I said to her, "Ruby, you're up on your completely hypothetical weird science stuff, right?"

"Theoretically," she replied, with a seriously cheesy grin.

"My friend's always watching these physics shows, and then she gets stuck on the goofiest questions. Like, if a person were to travel back along their own timeline, into their own younger self, how long would something like that take to wear off?"

"Huh," Ruby said, pursing her lips. "You know, I don't think I've actually heard of a case like that happening in the real world. Not our real world, anyway. But if I do? You'll be the first to know."

And then she winked at me.

I fought to keep my smile normal. Maybe she'd pass me a note later. Spoiler alert: she did not. But it was good to know she was on the case.

In the meantime, I went back to chattering about nothing.

We crossed three suburbs and drove past two Denny's restaurants before arriving at our destination, which looked just the same as all the others.

"This is our place," Lift said. She stopped me as I reached for my ski mask. "You're not gonna want to eat with that on! Here, I've got a spare."

She handed me a classic superhero's domino mask, two linked rings of something that felt like vinyl.

"I know what you're thinking. How can little raccoon rings around the eyes actually keep anyone from recognizing you?" she said. "But there's a trick to it."

The outward surface of the mask was covered in an intricate network of raised lines. I picked them out with my fingertips before I could see them, and they reminded me of the scoring on computer memory chips. Lift explained that they were subliminal triggers, like they use in advertisements. Only instead of making people crave delicious burgers and fries, these worked to block any possible connection in a brain between someone's face and their name.

"It's not that difficult. Turns out people are really crap at facial recognition anyway," Ruby said. "It's why IMDb is so popular."

On the back of the mask was a thin layer of reusable adhesive, which Lift assured me was all natural and kind to the skin. It also contained a genetic bonding agent that made it difficult if not impossible for the mask to be removed by anyone but the wearer. I pressed it on around my eyes.

"Looks great! Your own mother wouldn't recognize you," Lift said. "That's totally a lie, they never fool the moms. Anyone else, though."

We went in. A bored hostess coloring in a kids' menu waved us towards an empty corner with a crayon, where we pulled a couple of tables together, wiped off a few greasy spots the staff had missed with napkins, then passed around a stack of laminated menus. Eventually a waitress came over to get drink orders, introducing herself as Anne. The TroubleShooters were suddenly all grins.

"New waiters are the best," Ruby told me quietly after Anne had gone to get our drinks. "They're not used to serving supers, and their manager told them to treat us just like everyone else, only they can't keep the big stupid smile from twitching at their faces. It's priceless!"

Several minutes later, when Anne came back for orders, Manaaki raised his hand to go first. He held up the menu and pointed at one entrée, then another.

"Which one?" Anne said.

Manaaki raised an eyebrow and pointed to a third item, then another and another.

The waitress blinked. "Oh. All of it. Okay, start over," she said, scribbling furiously on her pad while Manaaki patiently pointed to half a dozen dishes on the menu.

She looked around at the rest of us, her eyes narrowed but that smile still tugging at her mouth. Now that Ruby had pointed it out, Anne's starstruck face was practically the loudest thing in the room. "The quiet guy ordered for all of you, huh? Okay, funny."

Anne started to depart as the TroubleShooters snorted and giggled. Match called after her. "No, miss? That was just for him."

Anne turned back, nodding cautiously now, pulling her pencil and order pad back out of her apron. She turned to Lift. "All right. And for you?"

Tiny Lift pointed a thumb at large Manaaki. "I'll have what he's having."

All five TroubleShooters erupted in great heaving belly-laughs. I laughed too, though I was abruptly aware of some very strange signals my stomach was sending, and finally Anne was laughing as well.

"But no, seriously," Lift said when everyone had finally calmed down. "I'll have what he's having."

Anne's eyes got very big. They got bigger as pint-sized Match placed a similarly gargantuan order. The waitress came to me. I started to ask for a stack of pancakes with eggs, then got distracted by a burger on the next page.

"Order both. Order everything that looks good," Lift told me. A glance at Anne let the waitress in on the joke as well. "It's okay. Healthy, even."

"Not sure I'd use that word here," Anne said.

Lift went on, even as she floated every piece of silverware up off the table with her brain and used them to build a perfect recreation of the Eiffel Tower. "It's the intersection of your regular teenage metabolism and the super's enhanced one. Our bodies just burn calories like FWOOSH. Just go with it. And don't worry about the tab, it's covered under team expenses."

"Never thought about how much you guys would have to eat to do what you do. That's super cool," Anne said. "And now I will never use that word again, because you guys probably get really sick of super-this and super-that."

"Not super-really," Match said. The entire table groaned, except the too-kind Anne, and Match was forbidden from speaking for a full ten minutes. Anne got a timer from the kitchen and everything.

As we waited on our food, Ruby asked me, "You're pretty new to all this, huh?"

I looked down at my baggy tracksuit and compared it to their sleekly tailored costumes. "How could you tell?"

"It's always wild at the beginning. Not that it gets much less wild ever. But you feel like you're figuring things out okay?"

"Yeah, I guess so."

"Well, you did great tonight," Match said. "You should totally join the team."

"Match!" Lift exclaimed. Her silverware tower shook but did not fall.

"I'm with the kid on this one," said Ruby. "The more the merrier. And Bounceback really had her stuff together out there."

Of course it seemed that way; I had an extra decade of life experience and the benefit of knowing exactly what was going to happen.

"Plus she's cute," Ruby added. Lift flicked a finger, and a sugar packet floated up off the table and exploded itself into her hair. "Hey! What was that for?!"

I smiled awkwardly, not sure how to respond. Most teen hero teams exist as much to provide training and peer support as they do to fight bad guys. As a result, they tend to be inclusive, happy to sign up any young person with powers or gadgets and a codename, at least on a nominal basis. Who they took into battle was another matter. I'd already fought alongside them, but it still didn't feel real to me. Nothing in my life at the moment did, for obvious reasons.

"One step at a time, guys," Lift told her teammates, then turned to me as her tower disassembled itself. "Leviathan runs an open Wreck Room for supers every Tuesday Night. You should come by. It's usually full of loners, powered stewards, and a few retired vets, but we're always there too. Some of us, anyway."

"Tuesday's my free night. I have stuff to build," said Ruby Goldberg.

"Also *UltraViola's* on," Match added. He wasn't referring to the saucy orchestral drama about the tempestuous lives of strings players, but rather the sci-fi thriller about a cross-dressing secret agent with her own starship.

"Also that. But I get a lot done on the commercials."

"She does, actually," Lift said. "You should see her Wednesday show-and-tells."

I'd spent most of the next seven years studying in excruciating detail the ways in which people would get hurt, tortured and murdered. I'd done this so the victims would be remembered, and because I was able to make a living from it, hopefully in that order. On my quixotic days, I thought perhaps the work could even help save lives in the future. Now here I was in the past, trying to save some of the same lives I'd memorialized. I'd saved at least one already. For however long I was going to be stuck here, I'd be a fool to turn down good resources when they presented themselves.

"I think I can do Tuesday," I said.

"Great!" Lift said. "But before that? We are so doing something about this."

She was pointing at my tracksuit.

My parents were asleep when I got home, but I had already arranged to get a ride to school with Mom the next morning. I woke up with just enough time to grab a Pop-Tart before heading out to take the SAT, trying not to think about how much lower my scores would be this time around. I hoped that I hadn't ruined my younger self's chances of going to college, but I was too preoccupied with my upcoming appointment with the TroubleShooters to focus.

Dad picked me up after the test with a hearty, "How'd it go?"

I'd always been a good test-taker, so I gave the confident response he expected. "No problem!"

"Great," he said. "Now that's out of the way, your mother and I need to talk to you."

Nothing good ever comes of that phrase. I scoured my memories for some big event or life change that my parents might want to talk about. Nobody had lost a job or died or anything the first time I was 16, so I couldn't imagine what could be so serious that my dad would announce an upcoming conversation. "Sure," I said. "I'm all ears."

"We'll sit down when we get home, but in the meantime, I'd like you to think about the answer to this question," Dad said, keeping his eyes on the road. "When exactly did you learn to drive a stick?"

Chapter 5: Redesign

Like heroes, villains choose their costumes carefully, often adopting recognizable logos, thematic color schemes, and one or more highly visible accessories or weapons. Research on this topic shows statistically significant correlations between the utility of a villain's clothing and his or her success, as defined by property stolen and/or destroyed (Aja & Hollingsworth, 2015). Other research has explored connections between the source of the villain's powers and the color scheme chosen for his or her costumes (Wu, 2011) and the use of logos and social media to develop a "brand" as a way of seeking popular support (Eliopoulous, 2010; Amanat et al., 2018). Fortunately, as discussed by Fraction (2006) and again by DeConnick (2018), the overall success rate for villains remains in the range of just one successful heist out of every five attempted, with more than 73 percent of all heists resolved without fatalities.

- Dying for a Laugh

Mom must have heard the garage door open because she was waiting for us in the living room. She had a serious look on her face that I remembered from the time she grounded my brother Hank for breaking his third cell phone in a month. It was one of many groundings he incurred throughout his high school years.

Dad sat down on the couch next to Mom and I perched on the recliner. Dad spoke as though he were continuing his thought from before.

"We need to know who you are spending time with, kiddo, especially if you're driving around with other teenagers. We've always liked your friends, and you're a good judge of character. But I know Sarah can't drive a manual transmission, and most of your friends don't have cars."

Mom added, "You sure didn't learn from the one lesson I gave you, where you stalled out three times and then said the truck was too hard to drive. We're okay with you borrowing the truck if you can drive it safely, but you need to show us that you are safe, first."

"You're right, I'm sorry," I hurried to say, hoping to preempt the rest of the conversation. Getting disciplined by your parents is bad enough as a teenager; as a twentysomething it's agonizing. "A marching band friend was giving lessons during breaks and she has a really easy car to drive. I didn't think you guys would mind since it means I don't always have to take the Corolla. I shouldn't have let a kid teach me, it was reckless." I hoped I wasn't in for a grounding myself.

"Okay," Dad said, and Mom nodded.

"Okay?"

"Sure," Mom said. "It probably wasn't the safest way to learn, and if anyone had gotten hurt you'd all be in a lot of trouble, but it's not that big a deal."

I slumped back into the recliner, letting out a breath. "Cool, thanks," I said. "Really, I'm sorry, I'll be more careful in the future."

"We know you will," said Dad, as I started to get up from my chair. "And now let's talk about the late nights." I sat down again.

"We never actually gave you a curfew, and that's on us," Mom said, looking at Dad. "We might have been lulled into a false sense of security after your brother left for college, since you and your friends are generally pretty responsible. But we've noticed a trend lately of our 16-year-old kid staying out later than is wise for a 16-year-old."

I slumped back again and barely stopped myself from groaning. Among the many perks of being 26 was the freedom to not have to keep an eye on the clock. My parents must have taken my frustration for petulance, because Dad frowned, and Mom's serious face reappeared.

"Look, Caro—" Mom began, but I sat up straight again and cut her off.

"No, yeah, you're right, I'm sorry, I'm really sorry," I said, still hoping to retain some semblance of independence. "I've been taking advantage of you guys being so cool. And, uh, I think my grades are dropping a little bit too," I threw in, hoping to prevent another one of these conversations a few weeks down the road. "I'm gonna work on that."

Dad looked worried at that, but Mom seemed satisfied. "Curfew is 9 o'clock on school nights and 10 on the weekends unless you're at Sarah's," she said. I cringed.

"Eleven on the weekends?" I offered.

"We'll see how those grades look at the end of the quarter," Dad said.

After more apologies and promises to spend more time on homework, I was released on my own recognizance and allowed to borrow the car. I even told the truth—I was meeting friends at the Southpark Mall in Strongsville.

On a stretch of beige temporary wall next to a mostly empty arcade, a sign proclaimed, "Soon to be the home of an *I.M. Foreman's!*" Next to the sign was a door. I slipped through casually, as if I were an employee preparing for the new shop's opening.

Two teenagers wearing jeans, sweatshirts, and domino masks waited inside, standing and chatting next to an elevator with a touchscreen security keypad beside it. One girl was Latina and very short, and the other was black and wore a Star of David necklace, so I assumed it was Lift and Ruby Goldberg. Thanks to the subliminal coding on their masks, I didn't recognize their faces, even though I'd met them only a few days ago.

They politely ignored my slight hesitation and greeted me by codename, Lift handing me her spare mask again and typing in the elevator code while I put it on. The doors whooshed open and in we went, and down, at great speed. Before I could even ask the girls how their morning had been, the doors went whoosh again, and I was staring at a very different mall.

Southpark Below was only open on weekends, but it brought in patrons from four states. I'd heard of such places, but never known if they were anything more than a rumor. It was arranged just like the mall above, but the shops along these walls weren't offering the latest gauzy fashions, smartphones, or protein shakes. They were selling battle armor, utility belts, and fear-gas antidote pills. A few dozen shoppers wandered the median, on a mission or window-shopping, a few in full hero-dress, but most just in street clothes and masks like our own.

"Are all these people heroes?" I asked.

"Some are stewards," Lift answered. "The bigger teams have stewards look after the equipment, and really busy solo heroes hire personal shoppers. Equipping a hero is an art in itself." She pulled a folded list from her pocket. "First things first! You need masks."

She led the way to a freestanding kiosk nearby, apparently the super equivalent of the Sunglass Hut. A hundred different domino masks were on display under the glass, arranged in columns by color and in rows by capability. Along the top were the basic spares, like the one I'd borrowed.

Lift pointed at one in cobalt blue. "She'll need two of those." The sales guy nodded, pulling two thin boxes from under the counter, while Ruby explained the various bells and whistles built into the regular models below.

"All of these have retractable glass lenses, which are 99.99% guaranteed shatter-proof."

"These ones, the lenses can be set to glow white as well," added Lift. "For the real *fear-me-evildoers-for-I-have-no-pupils* effect. I love that!"

"But down here they've got all that plus night-vision, which for me, that's just a minimum."

"Okay. So what am I looking at price-wise, just for the basic ones?" I asked.

The clerk said a number. I tried to play it cool, but my jaw may have dropped.

"Don't you worry about that," Lift told me. To the sales guy she said, "She'll take one of those," and pointed to the night-vision and glow-eyes model third from the bottom. "The Shooters have a discretionary budget. You helped us out last night. Maybe you will some more in the future. This is us making an investment in you."

I wasn't planning on being around in this time long enough to make good on any kind of investment. I started to protest, but my mouth wouldn't open. Literally; I think Lift was holding it closed with her powers. After a moment I gave in and nodded gratefully. When I got home to the future, this secret mall tour alone would be worth a 10,000-word magazine feature at the very least, even without photos. I had to keep going with this.

We turned into a shoe store next and briefly debated the relative merits of bulletproof running shoes and armor weave boots before settling on the latter. Lift tried to talk me into a pair with three-inch spike heels like her own.

"With these, and your natural height, you could really intimidate!" she said. "Loom, y'know?"

I'm 5'6", and have never given much thought to looming. I've always felt unbalanced in heels, even mildly in pumps, and couldn't imagine running and jumping in them. I said as much.

"Naw! You get used to it!" Lift insisted.

"Dude, you steady yourself telekinetically," Ruby said. Lift protested, but Ruby assured me, "It's subconscious, she doesn't even know she does it."

I stuck with flat boots. I found a nice pair in royal blue that laced midway up my calf, but were still stretchy enough to run and jump comfortably in. Then we were on to Gunn's, the costume shop, for the main event.

The store was one room, the size of a football field, and most of that space was taken up with rows of mannequins dressed in every variation of superhero costume imaginable. It was like stepping into a life-sized box of toy soldiers.

I found a basic look I liked within the first ten minutes, a blue-with-purple-accents jacket and pants combination, sleek enough to be mistaken for a one-piece bodysuit at first glance. It was light-weight, bullet-resistant, and flame-and-freeze-ray-retardant. I'd taken a picture of Sarah's Bounceback logo patch with my phone; at Ruby's prompting I shared it with the saleswoman. A machine in the back would have the patch copied and applied to my new jacket in just a couple of minutes.

Lift insisted I'd need a heavier winter version of the jacket in addition to the primary costume, and a thin but still semi-armored cap-sleeve shirt and pair of yoga pants which could be worn unnoticed under my everyday clothes in case of a quick-change emergency. These all received my logo as well.

We bought two of everything, in case the first got torn up in a fight, which was not unlikely, statistically speaking. Lift refused to even let me look at the receipt.

"What if I need to return something?"

"You won't."

On the way out, Lift caught me staring at a hero exiting Gadgetorium next door, an African-American cyborg with short-buzzed hair, and dark freckles at the corners of kind eyes. Even in civvies, anyone would recognize Fulminator.

"I think we all ended up gawking at somebody the first time we came here," Lift said gently. "But we try to just let 'em shop."

I wasn't staring because he was famous. I was just surprised to see him with so many of his original limbs. The Fulminator I was used to was shiny steel alloy and blinking lights from his neck straight down to his toes. This Fulminator had just one metal leg, below the right knee, and an entirely metal right arm that currently happened to be detached and carried in the crook of his left elbow.

"What the hell happened to you?!" Ruby exclaimed, striding right up to him.

"Werewolves with rocket launchers," Fulminator said, as if he had this conversation every day. And he might well have. "Turns out a one-handed rocket catch, not a good idea."

"So I'm guessing they know each other?" I said.

"Seems like," Lift said, pouting a little. "Apparently I missed a team-up."

Ruby leaned in, admiring the detached appendage. "Ripped that sucker right out of the socket, huh?"

"Not this sucker," answered Fulminator. "This is the back-up. Fight was in the woods. I found the rocket afterward, unexploded, defused it. Never did find the arm. C'est la vie, right?"

"You know it."

"Now I just need to find a better solar converter for this one. They were out."

"Gimme a call if you don't find anything here," Ruby said. "I'll hook you up."

"Thanks. I'll keep that in mind!" Fulminator said. With a gentle whirr of gears, he moved on.

We did not go into Gadgetorium ourselves. They offered an extensive range of wristcomms and earpieces, which were on the list for me, but Ruby made better ones herself. Also, she was temporarily banned, by her own request.

From The Pouch Place we picked up a Kevlar messenger bag with a secret compartment for my new costume. It was unrippable, uncuttable, thumbprint-locked, and looked like every other messenger bag in the world. Then we started towards the food court, only to pass a Coover & Tobin's along the way, the first name I'd recognized down here. The super-specialty book chain served non-heroes as well, and assuming I got home close to when I'd left, I had several events coming up in their stores.

There is a strong magnetic pull every reader knows, which makes it impossible to pass a bookstore without going in. Books weren't on Lift's list, but she adapted instantly, leading me straight to the graphic memoirs section and handing me a title by a young man with similar powers to mine.

"A friend of mine dated a jumper," she said. "This is supposed to be a good one."

I flipped through, definitely seeing a few moves I hadn't thought of yet, and tucked it under my arm to purchase. While Lift and Ruby flipped through the magazines, I found a couple of books on time travel as well, just in case.

Over lunch, Lift asked me when I planned on upgrading my hero license to semi-pro status. I said I hadn't really thought about it. She told me a bit about the testing, and offered to serve as my sponsor and help me prepare.

"If last night's any indication, you're pretty much ready already," she assured me. "You're competent with your powers, and keep your wits about you."

"And it's not like a driver's exam," Ruby said. "It's not about showing the testers that you know what to do. It's about showing you're ready and able to learn in a responsible way." As a semi-professional hero, I'd receive access to additional tools. For instance, a lot of the more specialized doohickeys for sale in Gadgetorium could only be purchased by someone semi-pro or above. I'd also be scheduled for regular training time with experienced heroes. And I'd get a regular paycheck.

"It wouldn't be anything huge," Lift said. "It's pretty much a stipend to cover costumes and whatnot. But you'll usually have a little left over you can save, for college or whatever."

It was tempting. The extra resources might be useful in accomplishing the changes I'd been sent here to make. But the additional attention could just as easily get in the way, especially as I tried to pass off my future knowledge as vague psychic powers.

I said I'd think about it.

I didn't see Sarah at all that Saturday. She was in Columbus with her parents, visiting the Center of Science and Industry and watching rats play basketball. In this case they were just lab rats trained with Cheerios, not genetically enhanced or cybernetically augmented or anything. I suppose I could have called, or texted her, but I didn't.

On Sunday morning, Sarah marched into my room unannounced, shut the door behind her, and waved her phone in my face. "Caroline, how could you not tell me about this?!"

I looked up from my computer at a PlainDealer.Com headline that read: **TEEN HEROES FOIL FAUX-VIKING INVASION.**

"Since when do you read the news?" I asked.

"I read the metro section now. I figured maybe I'd see some cases the police are working on that you don't remember and could help out with. I did NOT figure on finding out you went to meet the TroubleShooters on Friday without bothering to tell me it was happening! Your own steward and supposedly best friend! And you totally knew it was gonna happen, because they mention you using your psychic gift!"

"I didn't want you to worry," I said.

"What if something had happened to you, and I didn't know where you were? What if this had been it, and you'd gone zapping back to the future?"

"I had my phone with the note on it again."

"And if I'd had mine turned off, or been in a movie or something? What then, genius?" She was seriously upset about this.

"You're right—" I started to say.

"What did you think I was going to do, jump in my mom's car and follow you downtown into a fight?" Which is exactly what I'd been afraid she'd do. "I'm 16, not stupid. But if I'm your steward, then I need to know where you're at and what's happening, or I can't do my job and look out for you."

I stared her down for a long minute. However I looked, I was 26 years old. I didn't need looking after. But I did need someone to talk to. I needed my best friend, and I really didn't want to deal with the emo teenage version. Which for the moment meant handling the Sarah I had in a way that gave her as little excuse to freak out as possible.

"You're right," I said again. "You are my steward, for however long I'm gonna be doing this, and I do trust you. I'm sorry I didn't on Friday night."

"Darn straight."

"Can I see the article?"

Sarah handed over the phone. There was a low-res photo of the TroubleShooters and me in action, and the reporter referred to me directly by codename. There were quotes from Lift, who credited "new local hero Bounceback" with a "big assist" in Aidon Kingsley's capture. I'd dodged a bullet there, actually. For all my initial resistance to the whole codename idea, if the Shooters hadn't been available to identify me, who knows what moniker I might have ended up with? The first media name for a new super tends to stick. The Blue Flugelhorn could call himself 'Sonic Doom' all he liked, but no one else ever would. And heaven help the hero spotted by *People* or *Men's Monthly* before their local newspaper.

"It seems like you and the TroubleShooters got pretty chummy there," Sarah said.

"I don't know about chummy. But they're good kids. Very friendly. They took me shopping yesterday."

"They what?!"

I yanked my new bag out from under the bed, popped the secret compartment and pulled out the new Bounceback costume. I explained about the trip, and Lift's reasoning for the gifts. Sarah boggled. When she was done boggling at the suit, she turned and boggled at me.

"So just like that, you're joining the TroubleShooters?"

"What?" I said. "No, of course not. I'm, um, networking."

"What's the difference?"

"I'm not signing up for anything. I'm just letting them get to know me, so they'll trust me enough to help fix the things I'm here to fix."

"I thought we had a plan!" Sarah said. "You hero, me steward, we figure this out together?"

I rolled my eyes. So much for no freak-outs. "Sarah, what are you even talking about? Nothing has changed."

"Noth—! Ha—! Wha—!" She was gasping now, seriously hysterical or seriously hyperbolic, whichever was more annoying. I wondered if I should start keeping a squirt gun handy to snap her out of it. "You don't even bother to call me when you go swanning off to meet your new hero friends—"

"I already apologized for that." I may not entirely have meant it, but I'd apologized.

"You ignore me, your best friend, who worked so hard and spent a lot of money I'd been saving up for Imagine Dragons tickets to make you your own superhero costume, which you wear exactly once—once!—before going out without me and letting your new amigos buy you all this?"

She was jealous!

I mean obviously, but it took me that long. Probably because I was only now realizing myself how much fun I'd actually had in the last couple days. I wasn't just doing a job so I could get home. I'd genuinely liked spending time with the Shooters.

"Sar—"

"No, it's fine, I get it. They're good friends to have."

"No one's replacing you."

"I didn't say they were."

"No one ever could. No one ever will."

"Sure, you say that now—"

"So would you like to meet them for yourself?"

Her eyes lit up. "For real?"

I'd forgotten all about that particularly adolescent mutant ability to switch rapidly from one emotion to the next.

Just across Wade Park from the Cleveland Museum of Art sat Everett Mansion, a Victorian gothic manor that had once stood on Euclid Avenue, Cleveland's famed Millionaire's Row, before being moved to its present location in the late 1930s. In 1997 the Everett Family Trust donated the house to W.H.A.M. They soon turned it over to Leviathan to serve as their official headquarters.

The mansion shared a parking lot with the museum, and on Tuesday night Sarah and I left my mom's car there and crossed the grounds. In the shadow of a hedge, away from the lot security cameras, I pressed my expensive new mask to my face while Sarah put on one of my simple spares. The rest of my costume remained in my bag, as I assumed there would be somewhere to change inside.

At the top of the broad granite steps, the mansion's main door stood unlocked, and we passed into an immense front hall filled with row upon row of half-circular desks. I'd visited this room several times in the future, and every time I stepped inside I felt a curious but pleasant calm settle over me, as if the quiet efficiency of those who worked here was somehow communicable. Any member of the public could walk in those doors at any hour of the day, seeking aid or asylum, and Leviathan's steward-receptionists would see they got the help they needed, even as they fielded requests for back-up or emergency Google research. The hall was equal parts hero-support call center and public lobby.

One of the stewards waved to us from her desk at the center of the room. A full dozen holographic projectors ringed its surface, enabling the steward to carry on 3-D conference calls with as many heroes or world leaders simultaneously. She was a tall, full-figured black woman, with an impressive tower of crinkly hair and a smile Edison would've tried to steal from Tesla.

Lenore Williams was already a legend among stewards, a woman swift and savvy enough to gather the data and route the calls that would keep the world from ending. Later this year she would get caught up in a Leviathan adventure in an alien dimension, single-handedly organize an armed revolt against the local barbarian dictator, and end up staying there to serve as a benevolent Warrior Queen.

"Miss Bounceback, and Steward!" she said, beaming at us, and without even glancing at our amateur licenses. "Y'all are here for the Open Wreck Room. Miss Lift and the others are already waiting for you down below."

She directed us through a door and down a hallway to an elevator. Inside, the elevator offered no floor buttons. I guessed it operated typically via voice command, but before I had time to even consider which floor we might be aiming for, the doors closed and the elevator hummed into its descent. When the doors opened again a few seconds later, we faced a long shiny silver hall, and Lift was there waiting for us, along with Manaaki, Match, and Ruby Goldberg.

"I thought Tuesday nights were for *UltraViola* and building stuff," I said to Ruby.

"It's your first Wreck Room. Kind of a big deal," she said. "Also tonight's a rerun."

I introduced Sarah to everyone, then Lift showed me to a locker room to change.

Even Sarah had to admit I looked awesome in my new gear.

Leviathan's Wreck Room was really a Wreck Suite, a hollow square of specialized chambers—firing range, water tank, Zero-G box, etc.—surrounding a wide central chamber, which for the moment was closed. The first hour of the night's practice was devoted to free exercise, with attendees spread out amongst those smaller rooms, testing or refining their gifts. I recognized a couple of other heroes in passing, like the Baroness, and the speedster Jesse Zero. I also spotted Tundra, Leviathan's Inuit-Canadian icemaster, rolling between the stations in her wheelchair, offering suggestions and encouragement. Tundra never stopped anywhere I was working, probably because my entourage kept me surrounded. Not only Sarah but all four TroubleShooters followed me from room to room, showing me how things worked.

I ran on a trapdoor treadmill, which would beep at random intervals right before it dropped out from underneath you. The first time I failed to jump clear fast enough, and plummeted ten feet onto a safety mat hidden under the floor.

"Keeps you on your toes, doesn't it?" Lift said, grinning.

I used a Jumping Scale to calculate the strength, speed, and height of my vertical leaps, which established some basic variables for this nifty homework problem assigned by Ruby:

If Bounceback leaves the ground traveling 12 feet per second, and a hostage is pushed out a ninth-story window 108 feet above the ground, how fast will each be going when they intersect? How fast should Bounceback be going if she wishes to catch the hostage without breaking any bones?

In the smoke-filled firing range, I threw bits of debris at security cameras and mysterious red buttons, as the walls shook and sirens blared, simulating an attack on a secret base. I achieved a respectable score, better than Manaaki's and tied with Match, but felt thoroughly outclassed by Lift, who from thirty feet away could bullseye an escape key on a keyboard, shutting down a self-destruct sequence, with her own spike-heeled left boot. She wasn't even using her telekinesis at the time.

"Shoe-throwing is a regular part of my workout routine," she explained, pulling her boot back on. "You never know when you're gonna get caught out in a fight by someone with a power-nullifier."

I punched a practice dummy in the head repeatedly, until I could consistently get the force indicator on the wall to jump up past 'KO!' without hitting the red Danger Zone, then did the same again with several other dummies calibrated for extra-normal skull thicknesses.

At the end of the hour a buzzer sounded, and we exited the Headpunch Room to find that the central chamber had opened. The space inside was a massive cube, tall and airy as a cathedral but with walls and a floor and a ceiling that looked, felt, and smelled like knobby gray plastic. Tundra waited inside, popping wheelies in her chair while we filed in. Sarah took the stairs to the left, climbing into a small glass observation booth high on the wall, while the Shooters, the other heroes, and I lined up facing our Leviathan instructor.

The doors hissed open again behind us. A growl rumbled and reverberated right up my spine, and I jumped as a 400-pound grizzly bear pounded past me, heading straight for Tundra.

I'd gotten pretty good height on the vertical leap, so by the time my feet hit solid ground again, Lift was giggling like a fiend. Then everyone else was laughing as well, including the bear, who was now standing on her hind legs, facing us from Tundra's side.

"Brat," Tundra said, sticking her tongue out at the grizzly. The bear stuck her own tongue out right back.

By this point, I was laughing at me too.

"I'm sorry," a voice said from behind me. "She smells newbie and she just can't help herself. That's the lowest form of humor, you know that?"

The last was directed at the bear. The speaker was a stocky white guy with shoulder length brown hair, wearing a brown leather jacket and cowboy boots over his dark Kevlar bodysuit, James Baer, of Baer and the Bear. The bear was of course the Bear, also known as Petunia.

Mr. Baer had never bothered with a secret identity, something that would've been rather difficult to maintain given his near-inseparability from Petunia, so his story was well known. He was the son of Gail Baer, famed animal trainer for the Wagner Family Traveling Circus, and he and Petunia, a highly intelligent bear, had bonded from a young age. One or both of them developed a nose for trouble, and throughout their teens they wound up solving a number of mysteries along the circus' route, all over North America. Eventually they left the circus to go into heroics full-time, and were inducted into Leviathan in 2009.

"Sorry we're late, ran into a thing with The Mime." Having crossed to Tundra's other side, James leaned down for a quick kiss. Their masks-on public wedding had been celebrated two years to the day after James joined the team. Petunia was Best Bear.

"All right!" Tundra said the moment James had straightened. "Now that we're all here, everybody ready for the main event?"

She snapped her fingers, and a waist-high square pillar arose from the floor beside her chair. At its top, just beneath Tundra's hand, a round blue touch-screen blinked expectantly.

Lift quietly explained, "The entire room is covered in nano-mechanical tile. You program simulations into that terminal there, and the room recreates anything you want in 3-D. Buildings, spaceships, monsters, bad guys, whatever."

"You can even use it for kissing practice," Ruby said. "But Match wouldn't recommend it."

"That was an experiment!" hissed Match.

"His face looked like a waffle."

"Guys, not now," James Baer said.

Tundra dialed up simulation elements on the console as she laid out the drill for the night. "We're going to be running a standard Save the Citizens game." A dozen blocky people-shapes formed near the observation booth. The clattering noise they made sounded like a giant pile of LEGOs building themselves, which wasn't far from the truth. "The object for all of you is to keep everyone down there from being reeled in and eaten by this M.T.M." A Mammoth Tentacle Monster rose up on the opposite side of the room from the civilians, looking like a pixilated octopus. "Even I need a break from Cleveland winter, so we'll make this a summer game. Programmed location is Cedar Point Beach." The trappings of the beach shuffled up all around us: slatted chairs, picnic coolers, towels and parasols, while the waters of an ersatz Lake Erie formed up around the monster.

Tundra hit a final button on the control console, which faded back into the floor as the block-people ambled to their chairs and towels or down towards the water-line. "James, Petunia, and I will be playing the roles of Monster Summoners," she said, as the three of them backed up towards the M.T.M. James shook his shoulder-length hair out of his face and settled into a fighting stance, while the bear dropped to all fours. Tundra gathered condensation from the air, forced it beneath her and froze it there, shooting her chair twenty feet straight up on a column of ice, then looked down on us from the top. "Your job is to get past us, stop the creature, and save the rubes. Good luck!" Her toothy grin was even more gorgeous in person than on TV. And at the moment, just a little terrifying.

One of the block people strayed too close to the water and was snatched up by a tentacle. The victim's pixelated face showed a rough semblance of panic, like a 3-D emoticon, as the M.T.M. dangled it over a gaping, jagged mouth. The tableau froze and Tundra called, "Heroes, on your marks."

Lift immediately took command of our side, dividing us into two squads. Match, Jessie Zero, the Herald, a super-strong construction worker named Tiffany, and Lift herself would engage the Leviathan heroes directly, while the second team attacked the monster and pulled as many civilians clear as possible. Team two included myself, Ruby, Manaaki, the Baroness, the Barnstormer, and a steward called Bob who could fire medium-intensity laser bolts from his left eye. We all dropped into runner's crouches, as if we'd just come racing down the beach.

"Engage!" Tundra shouted at the room, and everything simulated erupted into motion. The tentacles resumed their writhing, the block-people ran for cover, and a classic Wilhelm Scream pierced the air. Ruby had already bragged about being allowed to program the Wreck Room sound effects.

Barnstormer flew, the rest of us ran, and my team began grabbing the nearest civilians by their plastic arms and urging them behind us up the beach. Tentacles reached for us and we punched or kicked or swatted them back. I jogged three steps closer to the monster, only to leap back at the last instant as ice exploded on the ground in front of my feet. Tundra was rapid-firing snowballs at everyone, regardless of squad.

"Oh, yeah," Match said. "Those count as ice-javelins, they're an instant out, so don't get hit!"

I nodded, running a little closer to Manaaki and his force-field.

Across the field, Tiffany picked Lift up on one hand and threw her straight at Tundra. Lift's palms were out flat in front of her as she soared, no doubt to deflect a direct ice blast. Instead Tundra ducked, tipping off her high column onto a frozen chute that had not been there the instant before. Gears in Tundra's wheelchair buzzed and whined, black metal closing over her legs and the wheels, as the chair converted itself into a bobsled, shooting away down the track.

Not missing a beat, Lift twisted in mid-air, reaching out with her telekinesis to snag the back of Tundra's chairsled. Lift's hands balled into fists, as if gripping an invisible handle. Her legs straightened out, and suddenly she was zipping down the chute behind Tundra like a water-skier pulled by a motorboat.

As I watched this, the M.T.M. rumbled, "Om nom nommmm!" and ate one of the "citizens" right in front of me.

"Focus, dummy, FOCUS!" I chanted at myself, leaping over a tentacle just in time to push down a fake sunbather about to be grabbed by another.

The Baroness called out, splitting us again. She, Manaaki, and I moved into the front line of our squad, dodging snowballs and dragging more civilians free. Ruby had one of her laser blasters, and she and Bob opened fire on the body of the creature. The monster roared in simulated pain when a shot hit one of its tentacles.

"Concentrate fire on the arms!" yelled Bob, increasing the intensity of his eyeblasts by winking harder.

A roar of an entirely different timbre startled me, and I turned to see Petunia charging across the gray plastic sands. I tensed to jump, felt a big hand catch my shoulder, and spun. I only just stopped myself from elbowing Manaaki across the face as a snowball burst all over his force field, three inches from my right cheek.

Having failed in her attempt to distract me, Petunia turned away just in time to be pounced on by a wildly laughing Jessie Zero. "TICKLE ATTAAAAAACK!"

"YES!" I heard Ruby shout, immediately followed by, "Oh crap!" She had managed to shoot off one of the M.T.M.'s tentacles, but instantly two more arms sprouted in its place. "Do not shoot the arms! Stop shooting!"

Bob heard and ceased fire, but already three more tentacles, weakened by their efforts, were falling away from the monster's body. A whole mess of new arms burst out. The new tentacles were just as powerful as the originals, and moving faster, now that they didn't have any pesky laser-blasts to slow them down. A hot-dog vendor and a sand-castle builder were snatched up and dropped into the creature's maw before I could reach for their hands. I pushed a dog-walker at Manaaki, crouched to go for the dog as well, and the next thing I knew a tentacle had snapped tight around my ankle and yanked me off my feet.

"PAUSE!" yelled Ruby.

The room beeped and froze, the monster and the civilians suddenly snap-shot still. The players took another few moments to cease fighting and straighten, everyone looking around in concern. I hung in the air over the gray beach, the blocky tentacle locked around my leg, the blood rushing to my head and fingers.

"Everyone all right?" Tundra called out from above. A bumper of snow halted her sled at the top of her latest ice-hill. "Ruby, what's the problem?"

"We're okay!" Ruby called back. "I just needed a sec to figure out—"

The Baroness pulled the kind of face that makes criminals stock up on underpants. Even from upside down, it was terrifying.

"Seriously? You kids may train here every day, but some of us only get these two hours a week. You want to shut up and let us get on with it?"

"Heroes are penalized three citizens!" Tundra said. Three simulated civilians abruptly collapsed in a shower of bricks. "Resume!"

I was whipped through the air and dropped right into the creature's gaping mouth. The next thing I knew I was climbing to my feet inside its hollow nano-mech body, slightly shaken and lightly bruised.

A minute or so later, Match got eaten as well. We sat against the plastic wall of the monster's "stomach" and watched as much of the rest of the fight as we could, staring up through the gnashing block teeth at the top.

"So how are you liking your first Wreck Room?" asked Match.

"It's different."

It was the Baroness who finally figured out the trick. She and Bob attacked the tentacles again, but all on one side of the monster's body, until the weight of all those flapping new arms caused the thing to overbalance. Trumpeting its alarm, it fell right over onto the beach. Match, The Barnstormer, Tiffany, Lift, and I all climbed free of its now lifeless jaws, and the game was over. The beach clattered away into its constituent blocks, which then rebuilt themselves into a circle of surprisingly comfortable chairs for the post-game. Sarah came down to sit in as well.

"Final score: 8 civilian casualties, 5 hero casualties, 24 civilians saved," Tundra announced.

"Ugh!" Lift said. She grumbled at Ruby Goldberg about calling the pause; the girl who would reinvent quantum engineering during a meteor storm on live TV whined back about hating on-the-spot strategy and doing her best thinking alone in her room with her tunes.

"I have to say, I'm a bit disappointed in you Shooters," said James Baer. "Especially Ruby and Match."

"Me? What did I do?" asked Match.

Tundra said, "We've been letting you two skip out on these Tuesday nights to watch your TV show on the assumption that you're getting in enough training time the rest of the week. Tonight's showing suggests otherwise."

"We'll all be here again next week, and as many more weeks as it takes," promised Lift.

"There's a new episode next week," said Match. "Can't we just—"

"We'll be here," Lift repeated.

Then Tundra and James Baer gave each of us some specific pointers, and the session was over.

"I've got some notes as well," Sarah informed me as we headed for the door. "Do you want them now, or in the car?"

I smirked. "Notes, huh?"

"Yes. Next time, suck less. No, seriously—" She held up a yellow legal pad filled with scribble. "I've got a lot here. Mostly from watching what the others did that you didn't."

"All right. Let me see that." I glanced down the list, intending just to humor her. Then I scanned. Then I was actually reading. Nearly everything Sarah had written down was succinct and actually useful to future performance. It wasn't even just about me. She'd caught on to some intriguing blind spots in the Shooters' tactics as well.

"What's this?" Ruby said, coming up behind us.

Sarah, red faced, snatched the pad back from me and clutched it to her chest. "Nothing."

Ruby gave her a suave grin. "I saw my name on there. Were you studying me?"

"A little," Sarah said, trying for nonchalant. "I was studying everyone, really."

"But I was the most impressive, right?"

Sarah pursed her lips, pretending to give it some thought. "Hmm. No, that was definitely Manaaki. I kinda expected the guy with the force field to be less observant of what was going on around him, but he's more aware than anyone."

"Uh, yeah. He's like that," Ruby said. "So what did you notice about me?"

"Mostly that you only seemed to want to fire on opponents when they were facing you," Sarah said.

"Oh my god, you totally do!" Lift said. I hadn't even noticed the other TroubleShooters crowding in around us.

"I guess. Maybe?" Ruby said, thinking about it. "Isn't that just good manners?"

"No, it's not," Lift said. "There's no manners in the field with lives on the line, so doing it in practice is just establishing bad habits."

"Also, this is you. You want everyone to know who it was that took 'em out, especially if you can do it with a gun you built yourself," added Match.

"Excuse me, when did this become Everyone Pick on Ruby Day? Besides—" Ruby snatched the notepad out of Sarah's grip, flipping pages until she found Match's entry. "You 'displayed a distinct learning curve with the new gun' you copied off me. 'Perhaps the field isn't the best place to adjust to the weight and kick of a new weapon'."

"This wasn't the field," Match said. "It was practice."

"Yeah, but when have you EVER turned down a new weapon? The point stands!"

"Yeah, okay. But that's the fun of it! I'll just have to learn faster."

"This is good stuff!" Lift enthused. "What's she got about me?"

Sarah snatched her pad back before Ruby could check. "You're good. Like really good," she told Lift. "But when you got tagged, I think you were busy trying to keep track of something over by Manaaki?"

"Okay, yeah," Lift said quickly. "But that's why we train, right? 'Cause in this life that's all it takes, a second's distraction, and WHAMMO."

"So don't get distracted," Ruby said.

"And me?" asked Manaaki.

Sarah double-checked her notes. "Manaaki, you did pretty good. But I noticed, your force field doesn't just go up around people you touch, it extends around people *they* touch too. So maybe instead of running around quite so much, you might have anchored yourself back a ways and had the team, like, pass people to you? Made some kind of daisy chain thing, to get people clear faster? Or maybe the monster would've just pulled them off, I dunno."

Lift looked at me. "Can you bring her every week?"

I looked at Sarah before I answered, but she was grinning ear to ear. "Sure, I guess."

Match and Ruby Goldberg fist-bumped.

"We'll get our *UltraViola* nights back in no time," Match said.

Lift groaned, and facepalmed. "That is so not the point, you guys!"

"Nobody from Leviathan has ever told you this stuff?" Sarah asked.

"I guess, sometimes?" replied Ruby. "But it's not nearly as annoying when you do it."

We said goodnight to the Shooters outside the locker rooms, but Ruby Goldberg ran up just before Sarah and I reached the Mansion's main door. She handed me a packet containing two TroubleShooters wristcomms and four nigh-invisible wireless earbuds. The wristcomms were indistinguishable from your ordinary digital watch—for now, anyway, in the years before smartwatches became prevalent enough to make for reliable camouflage—but the owner's fingerprint unlocked W.H.A.M's secret communications app.

"They're for both of you," Ruby said, nodding to Sarah as well. "Let me know if you have any problems or want back-ups or whatever."

"You're totally on the team," Sarah told me when we were alone in the car.

"I'm not here that long, remember?" I said, starting the engine. "But what about you? You could be wearing red and blue tomorrow, if you wanted."

Sarah giggled. "Please. Who ever heard of a steward in a costume?"

"No, I'm serious. Not about the costume, but the job. You're actually pretty awesome at this."

"You really think I could do this for real?"

"I absolutely do," I replied, pulling out of the museum lot and onto the road. "And before you ask, no, that was not your job in the future. But maybe it could be." An amazing possibility had just popped into my head.

Sarah frowned. "I thought you didn't want me to go running off and changing my timeline or whatever?"

"Then I realized I was sent here to make things better. Tonight you proved you can make things better too. Maybe the future needs your ace stewarding skills. Maybe you were chosen too."

"I don't know about that." I glanced over; doubt and excitement flickered across Sarah's face as we passed from streetlights to shadows and back again. "You're the time traveler. I think I'm just along for the ride. But hey, either way I'm in. For as long as you need me."

We high-fived, which turned into one of those tug-of-war hand-clasps. We were both on a high. Whatever I'd been sent back to this time to accomplish, it had to be easier with back-up. Having connections with Cleveland's experienced heroes, not to mention having Lenore freakin' Williams know me on sight, meant I was one big step closer to getting my real life back.

Chapter 6: Reinvent

No single inspiration for villainy is cited more frequently than the villain's experiences in high school.

- Dying for a Laugh

After six weeks of high school cafeteria lunches, the tedium was extreme. I couldn't talk about my real life in the future or what I was getting up to in the evenings, or anything else that was actually on my mind. I'd feign interest in whatever TV show, song, or sporting event the others were rattling on about—I interviewed people for a living, so I was good at faking it—while my eyes surreptitiously wandered the lunchroom, my ears stealing snatches of other conversations like a second station breaking the static on a radio.

That's how I worked out Milo's future secret identity.

Zoran "Milo" Milosevic was a pale, rail-thin boy from my math class. His tightly curled brown hair stuck up from his head at irrational angles, and his dark eyes were sometimes impish but usually just sleepy, especially during school hours. I'd never known him well, but he'd always seemed like a good guy. Today, as Sarah, Nate, Tamika, Liz, and I played Hearts after we ate, Milo sat with some friends at the next table over, talking about taking over the world.

This in itself was nothing new or alarming. Just about everyone I know has had this discussion in a high school cafeteria, probably multiple times. The divvying up is the fun part. "You want Russia? Sure! Can I get Australia and New Zealand?"

But today, Milo and his buddies were talking strategy. Still not unusual; Sarah's usually involved hatching dinosaur armies, or writing a mind-control book and getting Oprah to pick it for her Book Club.

"Any successful bid for world domination will rely on both secrecy and mega-impressive weaponry," Milo told his friends. "To that end, I'm going to recruit my stooges from a source I'm pretty sure no supervillain has ever tapped before: online forums for conspiracy freaks."

"Okaaaaay…" replied one of his tablemates.

"No, seriously, I've got this all worked out. You get all these guys in the same room, and step one: you work out the location of the *Raiders* vault."

That's when the hairs along the back of my arms stood up. I leaned over to Sarah, nodding at Milo. "Hey, what do you know about that guy?"

"Just 'cause you're old doesn't mean you get to cheat!" Sarah hissed back, slapping her cards to her chest so I couldn't peek. "Who?"

I was too busy listening again to respond. Having reminded a particularly absent-minded companion that the vault shown at the end of the movie *Raiders of the Lost Ark* was where the government had hidden away all the mysterious artifacts of ancient power and alien technology confiscated over the years, Milo was now explaining how the entire film had been cooked up at the request of the President of the United States. "Lucas and Spielberg made the whole thing just for that last scene. Reporters had already been snooping around, found some evidence to suggest the existence of just such a vault. So the government, to cover their own butts and to avoid having to expose all those wonders to actual democracy, asked the filmmakers to invent an adventure so exciting and popular that practically no one would ever believe that warehouse existed any place outside their imaginations."

"Okay, sure," laughed one of Milo's companions. "But if we're going after magical artifacts and alien junk, why not just hit one of the public superhero HQs?"

"Too well guarded," Milo said. "Duh. Who would you rather take on: a team of experienced supers, or a few bored, tired soldiers stationed in the middle of nowhere getting paid government wages? No, we hit the soldiers. We hit hard and fast with an army of giant robots built to look like Abraham Lincoln, Eleanor Roosevelt, JFK, Martin Luther King Jr., etc. That'll freak 'em out and slow down their reaction times."

"Do you have any *clubs*?" Sarah repeated in my ear. I jumped, shushed her, and threw down a six of hearts, because I didn't.

"So we use the robots to bust into the vault, and then it's like a shopping spree. We go running through the vault with our shopping carts or whatever and we cherry-pick all the best stuff we see, and we give ourselves a time-limit. Whatever we can grab in five minutes or less, and then we get out. Any more than that and we'll have superheroes everywhere. But five minutes in a place like that, it's enough. I swear, this could totally work!"

It could. My senior year of college, it very nearly did. And I couldn't believe I'd missed it up until now, when it was staring me in the face this whole time.

Sarah, reading my sudden lack of expression, whispered, "What's wrong?"

I whispered back, "There's a supervillain at the next table."

"Where?" Sarah craned her neck around, her eyes huge. "Are they invisible? Are they possessing someone? I bet it's Mrs. Schneider!"

"Not like that! A future supervillain."

"You mean like a student? Who?"

Zoran Milosevic. Zo-rann the Conqueror. I'd gone to school with this guy for seven and a half grades, he'd gone on to almost take over the world, and I'd never made the connection. In school he was always Milo. As the Conqueror he'd worn armor, with a full Vader-knockoff helmet concealing his face. But even so.

"I'll tell you later," I promised. "When I've figured out what I should do about him."

"Is he gonna kill a lot of people?" Sarah asked.

"I don't know. I know he did."

Again she read my face. "This isn't another Grammar Cop, is it?"

"No," I said.

"Oy!" Nate called from across the table. "Enough with the plotting over there! If you think you're gonna spank me with the Queen of Spades—"

"Shut up, Nate!" we both snapped.

"So we've got all our nice new toys," Milo was going on. "We just need some time to study them, to figure out how everything works before the heroes come busting down our doors. And that's where the conspiracy nuts become invaluable again. We take a bunch of those guys who think the moon landing was faked and we get them to figure out the most convincing way to film simulated "attacks" in places completely on the other side of the world from where we are. We put them in charge of all our official broadcasts. 'Cower, puny Earthlings, for I am your ruler now!' That sort of thing. That'll keep the heroes guessing until it's too late..."

"How many?" Sarah asked me.

I whispered, "Close to five thousand."

Zo-rann hit an until-that-day secret military installation in Nevada with an army of robots exactly like the ones described today. Commandeering an arsenal of advanced magic and tech, he went to ground in an archipelago near the Cayman Islands. His decoy transmissions kept the world's heroes chasing wild geese for months. And then, one day in late April, just as the news media was getting bored of the whole thing, he launched simultaneous all-out attacks against a dozen nations in Asia, the Middle East, and Eastern Europe.

The world's heroes did their job. Most of Zo-Rann's missiles were intercepted, his particle-beam disruptors deflected, and all of them traced back to their source. The Conqueror himself was reported killed, blown up by the malfunctioning guns of his own flying saucer.

But not before one of Zo-rann's stolen death rays managed to decimate the population of Saxenbourg.

"It's like that ethics question from class, 'what if you could smother Mr. Monstrosity as a baby?'" Sarah said. "Only not as bad, 'cause he's a teenager, not a baby. And we're always kind of annoying, right?"

"I'm not going to kill him, Sarah."

"Okay."

But I had to do something.

This was the mission everything else was leading up to, I was sure of it. When Zo-Rann the Conquerer died, he was fighting Ruby Goldberg. Whatever plan she had for me, Zoran Milosevic was the key.

For the next week, I made it my business to get to know all I could about 17-year-old Zoran Milosevic. At the outset, this did not actually involve *getting to know* Milo. At school I didn't talk to him any more than I had previously, which was rarely and in passing. As a crime biographer my job had been to excavate a subject's deeper feelings about what they had done. Here, I was attempting to find a reason for actions that hadn't been taken yet, which was a different sort of investigation altogether.

I found Milo after last period one afternoon and followed him to a Model U.N. meeting. I sneaked into the empty classroom next door and sat by the wall, listening to him defend a proposed Israel-Palestine compromise. Doomed optimism, or already a clever ruse? Unable to see his face, I had a hard time gauging his sincerity.

After the meeting I followed Milo home, parked a couple of streets over, then cut through the intervening backyards into his, hoping I wouldn't be spotted by a nosy neighbor. Milo had either younger siblings or highly sentimental parents, because I found shelter inside a miniature plastic castle sitting on the back lawn, and through the turret window I had a decent view of the rear windows of the Milosevics' comfortable two-story house.

I put on my domino mask and pressed a tiny button on one side. To an observer, the ordinarily clear plastic lenses would suddenly have turned a dimly glowing blue, hiding my eyes entirely. For me, the world suddenly snapped into sharp digital focus. Sliding a finger along the mask's edge allowed me to zoom in on the Milosevics' kitchen, where I spotted Milo grabbing a snack from the fridge.

Scanning the other visible rooms, I picked out the likeliest candidate for Milo's bedroom; there was a table or workbench with a computer on it, and several shiny bits of technology with lights blinking or wiring exposed or both. I was too low to the ground to make out anything more specific, and a few moments later Milo came into the room and immediately shut the blinds.

I adjusted into a better sitting position. Thankfully the evening was a warm one for February, somewhere in the mid-50s. Due to Cleveland's vacillating weather patterns it would probably be snowing again the following week, but I settled in fairly comfortably. I unslung my mini-backpack and settled in for my first psychological stakeout.

I would've liked to be reading, but the zoom-lenses made that rather problematic, so I made do with listening to my iPod. I'd finished the latest Janelle Monae and was halfway through one of Sarah's kitchen sink playlists when a man in a suit appeared in the hall, presumably Milo's dad or stepdad coming home from work. A middle school-aged brother and an elementary-aged sister were in tow, and released to play in the living room until dinner.

This was what I'd been waiting for, the chance to observe Milo interacting with the people who shaped him.

I watched the dad vanish upstairs then reappear in the hall in a t-shirt and sweatpants before going into the kitchen to cook dinner. I watched Milo's mom or stepmom come home as well, change, and join the dad in the kitchen. She made no move to help with the meal preparation, picking up a newspaper and folding it instead, maybe doing the crossword, but she kept the dad company, and they smiled as they talked. I had no skill at reading lips, but they seemed happy. They still seemed happy when Milo joined them to set the table, and when the siblings or step- or half-siblings were called and they all sat down to eat.

I watched the family until eleven o'clock that night. I never saw a hand raised in anger or a bottle hidden under the sink, or any of the thousand other details that had embroidered my dysfunctional histories of supervillains. The only dramatic tension I witnessed was a squabble with little brother at bedtime.

I persevered, following Milo after school for several more days. He went to work, stocking shelves and bagging groceries at the Giant Eagle supermarket. He went to the library, and picked up books for an English paper on Shakespeare; he was reading *Twelfth Night*, not *MacBeth*. On nights he wasn't working he returned home, and I returned to my toy castle and watched Milo watch sitcoms with his parents, or play Playstation with his little sister.

I paid close attention to the video games, looking for signs of low frustration tolerance. If Milo was the type to curse at the screen or ragequit when things weren't going his way, it could be a suggestion that his anger simply needed the appropriate catalyst to become explosive. But Milo mostly played wacky cartoon racing games and seemed equally entertained when he came in last as when he got the trophy. The one night they played the marginally more violent *Hero's Duty*, they turned it off after twenty minutes, and I was fairly certain that was because little sister had gotten bored after shooting Milo's character 34 consecutive times.

On Saturday night, after dark, I followed Milo across town to another friend's house. Both of Milo's tablemates from that fateful lunch period arrived shortly after, and the four teenagers gathered in the dimly lit front room with a plethora of snack foods, a box of dice, and three entire armies of pewter miniatures, which they spent the next four hours shoving around a large map.

I'd love to have heard their conversation, to find out if any more details of Zo-rann's future conquest had leaked through into the game. Perhaps I might have been able to identify one of the friends as one of Zo-rann's ruthless lieutenants. Sadly, at the time I didn't possess any audio enhancers, or even a bug I could've tossed under Milo's shoe. The TroubleShooters had such things, but I didn't want to involve them just yet. I had no desire to cast suspicions on Milo that he hadn't yet earned. That went double for Ruby, what with them being future nemeses and all.

Still, I had to try something different. Clearly my stakeout idea had run its course, with nothing to show for it. What I really needed was a way into Milo's house and a chance to snoop around his room, to see what he was building up there.

"So do the fake study-date thing," Sarah suggested.

"The what now?" I said. We were sitting on her bed, watching *Iron Chef: Powers Edition* while I debriefed on my latest evening playing suburban spy. Mom and Pop Milosevic had actually argued today. Then they made up and made out in the kitchen. It was kind of sweet. Or squicky, if you asked my shuddering 16-year-old best friend.

"The fake study-date," Sarah repeated. "You wait 'til you know Milo's not home, knock on his door, and tell his mom or dad or step-whoever you're supposed to be meeting Milo to study. The parent invites you in, 'cause they're all nice and stuff, and with a little luck they leave you alone at some point, and you can go snoop. And if they catch you mid-snoop, you just say you were looking for the bathroom."

Raising an eyebrow at my delinquent friend, I said, "When and why did you make use of this elaborate technique? And how come you never told me about it?"

"Oh, I've never actually done it. I don't know anybody who's done it," Sarah replied. "It's a classic because every teen TV show ever thinks it's exactly the sort of thing we do. But you could totally make it work, right?"

Unfortunately the only alternative I could think of that didn't involve calling in the TroubleShooters would be to wait until no one was home, break the Milosevic's back door lock with my super-strength, and leave an envelope full of money on their kitchen table to pay for the damage. That didn't feel right either.

A couple of days later, I found myself sitting in my dad's truck in the rain with my mask on, one street over from Milo's place. From this vantage, with lenses zoomed, I could just make out Milo's car in his driveway. At lunch, I'd overheard Milo making plans to meet some friends after dinner, and sure enough, after about twenty minutes of watching and waiting I saw him come out of the house, get in the car, and take off down the street.

I peeled off the mask, slipped it in my pocket, and ducked out of the truck, holding my hood down over my head. I hurried between the houses, but didn't really mind the cold drizzle spitting down from the sky, even as it soaked the back of my sweatshirt. I arrived on the Milosevic's porch and rang the bell, pressing wet bangs back from my eyes. Milo's mother shooed me inside before I'd finished explaining why I was there.

She was momentarily confused, informing me that Milo had just gone out to meet friends, but my reply had been carefully rehearsed. I said that a whole group of us were studying together tonight and that Milo was picking Josh up. The rest of us would meet here just long enough to decide where we'd all go next. I promised, on Milo's behalf, that we wouldn't stay in her hair long. She waved it off and went to get me a cup of hot chocolate from the kitchen.

"I'm so sorry to have surprised you like this," I told Milo's mother as we sat in the family room to wait. "I hate to be a bother."

"Oh, sweetie, you're not," she assured me.

I sipped my chocolate, which was excellent. "Does Milo spring things on you like this often?"

"Not really. Z's always been my easy one."

"Oh?" I said. "And here I thought he couldn't possibly be as laid back at home as he is at school."

Milo's mom narrowed her eyes at me. "I know what you're doing. You're trying to get me to spill some embarrassing Little Z stories."

I laughed, carefully. "You've got me."

"Sadly," she said, laughing too, "I don't really have any. Good ones, anyway. I sometimes feel like I've failed as a mother."

This gentle and largely fruitless interrogation continued for another twenty minutes. I learned a little about the Milosevics' jobs, hers as an ad executive, her husband's as an accountant for a greeting card company. I babbled vaguely about my own college plans. Milo's mom vented a bit about Enver, Milo's little brother, and his differences of opinion with his reading teacher, and then I talked her out of calling Milo to see what was taking him so long, before she finally went into her office to get some work done, leaving me alone with my cocoa and the television remote.

I switched on the TV, flipped to Cartoon Network, and dialed up the volume to just a hair shy of annoying. After two more minutes, when Mrs. Milosevic did not reappear to ask me to turn it down, I took a nonchalant walk upstairs.

Mr. Milosevic had taken Enver and Anna to the movies, so I felt no fear of discovery as I wandered down the upstairs hall to Milo's room and tried the door. The handle turned. I slipped inside.

To find Milo sitting with his computer in his lap, waiting for me.

"Hi Caroline," he said. "Mind telling me what a super wants with me and/or my family?"

"A what? I was just—"

"Please don't lie to me. Just, don't," Milo said with intensity. His fingers hovered, twitching, over one of the F keys at the top of his keyboard. From where I stood I couldn't make out his screen, couldn't see what he'd linked to that itchy trigger. Something simple, like a call to 911? Or an email ready to broadcast my secret identity to his friends, or the whole school, or the police? Or was it something more sinister, a booby trap worthy of his future self? A robot guard dog waiting inert in the shadows, vicious at a keystroke? An electrified doorframe?

As my brain scrambled for some strategy, Milo said, "You're Bounceback. I've worked out that much." He knew, and he wasn't going to let me talk around that. "People say you're one of the good guys. So I'm hoping you've got a great explanation for why you've been following me for days, watching my house, lying to my mom, and now sneaking around in my room."

And I thought my reconnaissance had been going so well.

"Your inventions," I finally said, pointing at the bits and pieces of mostly dismantled technology scattered around the room. "I'm vaguely psychic, actually, and—"

"Vaguely psychic?"

"—I had, uh, an impulse, that your inventions would be involved in a terrible tragedy."

"What kind of tragedy?"

"I don't know. It was just—"

"An impulse, you said that. Do you know when?"

I shook my head.

"But you think I'm responsible, somehow, for whatever this is."

"I don't know," I lied again. Or was it a lie? What did I know about this Zoran Milosevic? His future might already be different to the one I remembered. Even if it wasn't, when did a person become responsible for things they hadn't yet done?

"But you followed me. You spied on me."

"I thought you might be in trouble. That maybe you'd, like, attracted the attention of someone who would try and steal something from you, or steal you and make you do something for them. I'm sorry." I meant that last part.

"Huh," Milo said, relaxing infinitesimally. "But they're not even finished. Most of them are just toys. I'm tinkering with things other people have come up with. Hardly revolutionary. I mean, a few of them might be. I might actually be on to something with that one. Hey, you want to sit down?"

Just like that, he wasn't angry or suspicious any more. I was a hero, albeit a minor one, and a classmate. Apparently this was how much benefit-of-the-doubt that bought me.

I sat. It was a teenager's room, so the only seats available were the already occupied computer chair, and the neatly made twin bed with its Darth Vader comforter. I perched awkwardly on the edge.

"You believe me?" I asked.

"Sure. I guess. It makes as much sense as anything else."

"Can I ask how you worked out I was Bounceback?"

"That? I only caught that tonight. I knew you'd been following me, I picked up on that a couple of days ago, but tonight, with the rain—" He tapped a few keys, then flipped his computer around so I could see. If there had been an incriminating email or a booby trap control panel onscreen, it vanished before I could see. Instead I saw a short, silent video of myself, sitting in Dad's truck, peeling my mask off my face.

I frowned. "Where was the camera?" In a tree, a street over from Milo's house, in the wilds of suburbia? Even if he'd only planted the camera after he became aware he was being followed, it wasn't as if I'd parked anywhere near that spot before. The placement suggested a degree of paranoia and planning that was a classic sign of the megalomaniacal.

"Right there," Milo said, pointing to a modest digital camera sitting on a tripod on the shelf under his bedroom window. My oversimplified pop psycho-analysis shattered instantly.

I stepped to the camera and peered through the viewfinder. "I don't see my truck now."

"That's because it's stopped raining," Milo said.

He tapped another key, and the single video on his monitor fractured into a kaleidoscope, a hundred tiny moving pictures of me in the truck, of the side-street, of Milo's backyard, and every place in between. He swiped his finger around the corner of the screen, drawing a border around the images of the truck, and double-tapped. Now the whole screen was a hundred videos of me unmasking, each captured from a minutely different angle.

"I redesigned the camera to read the light reflected back from atmospheric condensation, like every raindrop is a tiny mirror," Milo explained. "I can see for miles. I haven't figured out yet how to make it work in less than one hundred percent humidity, though."

"When it's not actually raining, you mean."

"Exactly! And I haven't tried it with snow, yet, either. I'm forecasting a lot of static."

I raised an eyebrow.

"Sorry," he said. "I put most of my comedy stats into Star Trek trivia instead."

"See, that was funny. And this is amazing."

Potentially disturbing, too. Did the government have this kind of surveillance capability yet? Did Leviathan? Then again, was it any worse than Google Earth? With or without autocratic intentions, surveillance was a growth industry.

"Okay, I've gotta ask," Milo said. "Do you always drive around town with your mask on? Is that a super thing?"

I looked at him for a long moment before I answered, and not just because I was about to spill a minor trade secret. I'd finally figured this out.

"Not really. My lenses have a zoom feature. They can't do anything like this, though. If I let you take a look, do you think you could change that?"

"You made him your *what*?!"

I'd stopped at Sarah's on my way home. She'd just gotten back from her clarinet lesson.

"My steward," I repeated.

"But you've already got a steward. You've got a fantastic steward," Sarah said. "I'm talking about me, here."

"I noticed," I said. "Well, now I've got two. And he's a totally different sort of steward anyway. He's going to build me stuff, and then pretty soon I'll introduce him to the Shooters. Then he'll turn into their ally, and not their enemy."

Sarah kept on frowning. "You're sure this is a good idea?"

"Absolutely. This is the mission. We're building the team of the future here, with Lift, and Milo, and you."

Surely, if anything could stop the evil genius from taking root in Zoran Milosevic, it would be introducing him into the worldwide hero community at 17. Let him be friends with his future foes from the start. Worst case scenario, if Milo did go off, at least this way his future opponents would know him that much better. Of course it meant that he'd know *their* weaknesses that much better too. But there were more of them, and they'd already beaten him once, and they'd never let him go evil anyway.

"I'm gonna trust you, instead of quitting in a huff," Sarah replied after a moment. "But only because I love you and stuff."

Milo didn't waste any time getting started. He found me in the cafeteria at the start of the lunch period the next day, with a proud smile and a USB flash drive.

"What's this?" I asked.

"If it's music, it's for me," said Sarah. She'd just arrived at the table, with her tray piled high with chicken fingers.

"It is. It's polka," I told her.

"Don't care." She snatched the drive from Milo's hand.

I smiled at him. "It's cool. She's my other steward."

Sarah's eyes shifted left to right, scanning the lunch room for anyone who might have overheard that telling word. Seeing no likely suspects, she resumed breathing.

"So what's really on the drive?" she asked Milo.

"Huh? Oh, it's a program I wrote last night. It scans through local news websites and Twitter and stuff, looking for crimes in progress within a 50-mile radius."

Sarah harrumphed. "Could be useful. Thank you."

"Yes," I said, a little loudly. "Thanks, Milo. Hey, we've got an extra seat today, if you'd like to eat with us?"

"Naw, I should be getting back to the guys. Thanks, though."

I watched him shuffle away, before turning back to Sarah and reaching for the flash drive. She snatched it out of my reach.

"Uh-uh. You don't know what's on this thing."

"He just said.—"

"I'm not taking any chances," she said. "Which is to say that I am. I am taking all the chances, so you don't have to. Got it?"

"Not really. What in the world are you talking about?"

"That new tech-head of yours is a future evil supergenius—"

"*Possibly* evil."

"The program on here could make your computer explode. Or brainwash you. Or combine every appliance in your house into a giant machine-monster that wants to eat Cleveland."

"I highly doubt it."

"All the more reason to let your steward test it first, then, isn't it?"

I sighed, realizing she wasn't going to budge on this one. Still I tried. "I am the one with the leaping powers, you know. If something did go wrong, I'd have a better chance of jumping out the window before it blew up."

"Then I'll be out the window to start with. I'll sit in the tree outside, and operate the keyboard with a really long stick."

She wasn't kidding. But the computer didn't blow up and Sarah's appliances didn't savage the city, and Milo's program helped me stop three burglaries and an arson attempt that first night alone. After that, Sarah consented for Milo to join our study/strategy sessions at my parents' house or hers or even his, though she continued to watch him with a wary eye. She softened a little further after a few rounds of Mario Kart and her first taste of Milo's mom's homemade pizza.

Sarah and I went to Everett Mansion every Tuesday night now for Wreck Room sessions, and two weeks after Milo signed on, we brought him along too. Walking in, I had to hold Sarah's hand, because I was so nervous about introducing Milo to Ruby Goldberg, his hopefully never arch-foe. The pair of them immediately launched into an extremely nerdy debate about tech applications. Milo criticized Ruby's tendency to overbuild, insisting "micro is the macro of the future!" while Ruby argued there was "more to life than trying to figure out how to wear your Lamborghini and pick up chicks." The rest of the Shooters just rolled their eyes, and teased me about needing so many stewards. Yet by the end of the night Ruby and Milo had invented a secret handshake and a new kind of pocket toaster just for

Pop Tarts, and each of them independently told me it was the best talk they'd had with anyone in ages. I really expected to blip back to the future on the spot, mission accomplished.

But it wasn't, apparently, because I didn't.

Chapter 7: Recollect

Like a hero, each villain has both an origin story and a source of power. For some, the two are related. Dr. Heinous, DDS, became evil after a disreputable dentist filled young Bryant Hein's cavity with essence of demon instead of the usual composite resin. For others, their source of power is rather more neutral, and their origin is what makes them villainous. PlasmaBurn was born with the ability to spontaneously generate fire, but she says that the decision to turn villain was a conscious one. "Heroes work too hard and make too little," she said during our interview. "I saw a way to get what I wanted and have fun doing it." PlasmaBurn, aka Alison Pryce, is serving 20 years to life.

- Dying for a Laugh

"You were right. You were absolutely right. He is a good guy," Sarah finally told me a few days later. We were in her living room. Milo had just gone home after a three-hour planning session for Bounceback's next intervention, which was coming up the following Wednesday.

"I'd hate to say I told you so," I lied.

But she had a point to make. "So why don't you just tell him about the villain thing? You wouldn't have to tell him about the time travel. Just say something like, 'Hey, I had a vision. It goes badly and lots of people die and you're one of them, so don't go stupid on us in the future, mmkay?' Maybe that's all he needs."

"I don't know about that," I said. Milo wasn't entirely comfortable with my visions as it was. The whole 'vague' part of 'vaguely psychic' drove his methodical brain right up the wall. He'd started researching bio-feedback techniques that other precognitive heroes claimed sharpened one's visions. "Even if he did listen, what if that just becomes the reason he goes wrong? What if it becomes a self-fulfilling prophecy, like the parent who tells their kid they're a Bad Kid so often he believes it? I've seen that."

"Well, the alternative is what we've been doing for the past two weeks, which is lying to him a lot."

"Not lying. Just omitting. And guiding."

"But guiding him into what?" Sarah said; her voice hit an exasperated peak at the end. "He's not a supervillain! He's not even a jerk! If his part of your mission is really about getting him to use his powers for good instead of evil, just give him the message already and move on!"

"Sarah?" I said. She was standing behind her chair, leaning on the back, and she wouldn't look at me.

"I think you don't really want to go, is all I'm saying. Like, why would you? I mean, you keep talking about going back to your time, but I can't figure out why. I don't even know what you want to get back to."

What did I have in the future?

A college degree. An apartment. A fish tank currently inhabited by a bloodthirsty betta fish that ate everything else I tried to put in there. A stuffed monkey that I'd gotten on my 8th birthday. A complete set of vintage *Défenseur d'argent à la rescousse* (Silver Defender to the Rescue) comic books from my editor. I'd never learned to read French, but the comics had a place of pride on my shelf.

I had a purpose. I had a career. I had an office in my apartment full of bloody crime scene photographs, tacked to the walls, strewn across my desk. I had hours of tapes and stacks of transcriptions of interviews. I had letters and printed-out emails from the families and friends of victims, grateful just to have someone to talk to for a few hours. I even had thank-you notes on prison stationary from a few of my actual subjects.

Sarah was fiddling with the knitted blanket on the back of the chair, waiting for me to say something. "I know maybe it doesn't seem like a lot to you," I said softly. "But I love my life. I know it doesn't sound anything like what we used to talk about—"

"No, I know, you're a real author and everything, that's awesome, I get it," Sarah said, trying very hard to sound like she believed it.

"This, here, now—it isn't my life, not really. I'm just borrowing it for a while."

"From yourself! I'm pretty sure you won't mind!"

"I miss what I had. I miss stupid little things. I miss sitting for hours in the bookstore in the middle of the day when it's quiet. I miss not having to put up with condescending teachers. I get that high schoolers are barely human to most adults, but it's still really annoying to deal with every day."

"And this is supposed to be news?" Sarah's smile suggested a joke; her tone was closer to frustration.

"There's just so much of myself I have to hold back, here. So many things I like about myself that are about being a 26-year-old journalist in 2023."

"And now you're a 16-year-old superhero in 2014! How is that not better?!" Sarah said. "I mean—think about dating! You haven't even asked anybody out yet. With what you know, you could probably get anybody's attention you wanted!"

I shuddered. "Dating high schoolers? That's incredibly skeevy."

"It's not that big a difference. We're pretty much adults anyway."

"I know it feels like that now, but trust me, high school versus not high school is a *huge* difference."

Sarah gave an exaggerated pout, but I saw real tears in her eyes. "So you're not here to live, you're just slumming it with us kids?"

"You're not a kid! I mean, you are, but you've never been like that. Sarah…" I stood up, moving in for a hug, but she waved me back.

"I know. I know this is hard for you too, but I don't always understand you anymore. I miss getting you."

"I miss being got."

"I'm trying! I'm actually trying really hard."

This time, she let me hug her. I felt her tears soak into my shirt. "I know. I'm so, so grateful you get as much of me as you do. And it helps, it does. I couldn't do any of this without you."

"So do it! Just get on with it. Don't worry about me. If all this is about Milo, let's just figure out how to fix him and get on with it. Okay?"

"Okay."

Another squeeze, and then we sat back down on the couch, side by side and close together, sitting on our hands. After a minute Sarah could breathe normally again.

"So what do you think it's gonna take to get you back there?" she said.

"I'm not sure yet," I said. "We just need to keep our eyes open. Something else will come up. In the meantime, while I'm here, I'll try and do a better job of actually *being* here."

"I'd like that," Sarah said. "Especially if that includes doing more homework. I've been doing most of yours *and* all of mine and that's a lot, even with the money and all."

"Yeah, I'll get on that."

"It'd be nice if you could spend more time with the gang, too. Outside of school, I mean. Tamika's started to get pretty annoyed at you bailing on us all the time, and I'm running out of good excuses. Last Saturday I told them you'd been the victim of shapeshifter identity theft, and you and your folks had to spend three hours with the bank's telepath before they'd give you your college savings back."

"Where did a shapeshifter get my DNA?"

"Hair clippings at the salon."

"Oh. Good one. But yeah, I'll make time for them too. Promise."

I meant it when I said it, but I failed to live up to it. I was just too busy. The nights I wasn't fighting crime or training with the Shooters, I was locking myself in my room and forcing myself to do homework. Sarah kept asking why we couldn't just all go out to the library or whatever and slog through our assignments socially, but Nate, Tamika, and Liz were all compulsive talkers. That was great when we all had the same test to cram for, but it meant math homework took at least four times longer than it should.

When I did try and plan a night with the gang, something always came up anyway. Like the Friday everyone met at Sarah's to play board games. Nate brought a pizza and we all settled in around *The Game of Life*. I'd just landed on a marriage and was setting a pink pin into the passenger seat of my tiny purple mini-van when the comm-badge in my pocket buzzed. A horde of fictional Martian tripods had just stepped through a reality portal into the Rocky River Metropark, Leviathan was busy in New Delhi, and the TroubleShooters were calling for backup. While Sarah made my excuses, I slipped out.

By the time all the walking machines had been toppled, their cephalopod occupants tied up in clear garbage bags full of water like so many carnival goldfish and rolled on a cart back through the energy gate, it was nearly 11 p.m. I ducked away from the Shooters and called Sarah.

"Everybody's gone home already," Sarah said. "I kept 'em as long as I could."

It was no one's fault, but I still felt vaguely disgruntled. Only vaguely. I asked what excuse she'd used when I'd had to run.

"I told 'em Erica from band camp's dog was hit by a car. I have a flair for the dramatic."

"That you do. Did the dog make it?"

"I dunno. Up to you."

Forty-five minutes later I arrived home, in civvies once more with my costume safely tucked in my bag, to a light on in the living room and my mother waiting up, a book in her lap.

"Aw, crap," I said before I could censor myself.

"Yep," Mom yawned. "That's a grounding, kiddo. And don't even try to pretend that you were at Sarah's; Tamika posted a picture to Instagram and complained about you leaving early."

Darn Tamika and her addiction to social media. "How long?"

"'Gosh, Mom, I'm sorry I broke curfew and didn't call, I have a really good explanation that I will now share with you,'" she said.

"Gosh, Mom, I'm sorry I broke curfew," I repeated guiltily. It took me about that long to remember I *did* have an explanation. "Remember my friend Erica from band camp? Her dog Spaniel Boone got out, and first she wanted help finding him, and then she found him but he'd been hit by a car, and her parents weren't home to take him to the vet, and she was a mess, because she's had that dog since she was like 5."

"Oh no!" Mom had concerned face. "Did the dog make it?"

"Yeah," I said. "He's gonna be okay."

"Well I'm glad you could be there for your friend," Mom said. "But you still should have called."

"I know, I know, I'm sorry." I was sort of embarrassed on Mom's behalf that she fell for such a thin cover story.

"It's your first offense, and you were trying to do something good, so I'll make it a four-day grounding," Mom said.

I nodded; I'd be free again by the next crime on my list, which was the following weekend. "That's totally fair." Bad move; Mom narrowed her eyes like she was reconsidering.

"Yeah, you're getting off easy this time," she said, but didn't change the punishment.

"I'm really sorry, Mom," I said, striving to look suitably chastised. I was more humiliated at being disciplined than upset about the grounding itself. It meant missing a Tuesday night Wreck Room session, but schoolwork was an acceptable excuse for skipping once in a while. At least I'd have time to actually do my own homework.

Sarah hoped that the grounding would inspire me to spend more time with our "normal" friends (her word, not mine) and less with the TroubleShooters, but I found myself drawn to the super team. Sometimes they took me out after fights, which was great, since any night I ate out on the team's tab was a night I wasn't putting a sizable dent in my parents' grocery budget. We always went to that same Denny's, which was apparently the team's almost-official meeting place. Their actual meeting room at Everett Mansion was only used for special mission briefings or meet-ups with senior heroes. The Denny's staff and regular patrons were all used to seeing the Shooters, but they respected the team's privacy and kept this information to themselves. There were no photographs taken or requests for autographs, and the young heroes were not shy about discussing team business in the restaurant, or even their own unmasked personal lives.

"So how did you all get your powers?" I asked one night. It was only my third time out with the team, but we'd just saved a dozen bargain shoppers from Death Coupon and my adrenaline was high. That still doesn't justify the question; asking a superhero the origin of their crime fighting identity or how they came by their unique abilities is generally considered the height of rudeness. Some supers design their new personas deliberately to distance themselves from past mistakes or as coping mechanisms for some profoundly traumatic experiences. The origin story can also be intimately entangled with vulnerable details of the super's home life or biology. Supers have any number of very good reasons not to share their backgrounds with the world, as exciting and full of pathos as such tales invariably are. The rule of thumb, therefore, is to say nothing. If a super wants you to know, she'll tell you.

But the other rule of thumb is that superpowered teenagers, like supervillains, like all teenagers everywhere, love to talk about themselves. No one at the table blinked at my question.

"I was a late bloomer. My powers didn't kick in until halfway through my freshman year," said Marci. That was Lift—Marcela Garcia Gomez. By this point the Shooters all had me calling them by their civilian names, which was another reason I didn't feel as bad as I should have grilling them for their backstories. Marci was a junior this year, like me. Ruby and Manaaki were both seniors, but when the previous team leader had graduated out, neither of them had wanted the job. Manaaki wasn't much of a strategist, and Ruby felt the responsibilities would get in the way of vital tinkering time.

"I'd been doing gymnastics and cheerleading for years, and since I'm so tiny I got to do all the cool stuff, like getting thrown into the air," Marci went on. "That's how Benny and I met; he's my tricks partner. The first day we worked out together, he held me up with one hand. It was amazing! So I liked cheering all right, but what I really loved to an unhealthy degree were the outfits. Running around in the leotards, with the glitter and everything? Loved it. When my power kicked in I was like, thank god! Now I have an excuse forever!"

The actual discovery of Marci's powers was relatively boring. Like many well-known telekinetics, she had a dream one night and woke up to find all the furniture in her bedroom floating off the ground.

"At first me and my family were all like, '*Oh crap, the house is haunted!*' It went on for days, my power manifesting itself in little unconscious ways, and I had no idea. But we'd hear thumps in closed closets, and we'd open them and the cat wasn't trapped in there, or the radio would turn itself on. My papa finally called in a steward who could see ghosts. Once she confirmed it wasn't that, we figured out what was really going on. So I got the tests and my first license and everything. And then *I* was lifting *him* on *my* hand," Marci said, beaming at Manaaki.

When the family let Marci's grandmother in on the secret, she gave them a new one in return. "It turned out my great-grandfather, who died when I was like a year old, was the hero known as Cuza back when the family still lived in Colombia. He retired in the early 1960s, when they emigrated to the U.S. The hero licensing process was pretty new in those days, and they hadn't started giving out work visas to non-citizens yet."

Ruby Goldberg, who was Nicole Jemison in real life, launched into her own story the second Lift had finished. "When I was little I was orphaned in a Silicon Valley earthquake. I was trapped with no human contact for seven years in the ruins of an old warehouse, and raised by a family of desktop computers and Super Nintendo game consoles."

I will admit, for the briefest instant, she had me wondering.

"Nicole," Marci said, "That is an insult to your lovely and long-suffering mother."

"What? The SNES is a classic machine!"

Eric Glover, aka Match, was a freshman, and the first person in his family to gain a special ability. "When I was in middle school, my great-uncle Sid, who basically raised my mom, was living in an old folks' home. So I went there like every Sunday to hang out with him. And Uncle Sid had this friend there, Joe, who was demented."

"He had dementia," Manaaki corrected.

"Yeah, that. Anyway, he'd tell us these wild stories about fighting as a young man in the First World War—obviously he wasn't that old, though the nurse said Joe had been in Vietnam—and going on expeditions into the jungles of Africa, and protecting secret treasures from the Crusaders in the Middle Ages, and every wild thing you can imagine. So most people thought he was crazy, or pitied him, or both. But I was just a kid. All I thought was 'Hey, cool stories!' So what if he told them all like he was there?"

Eric's favorite stories were the ones Joe told about being a secret superhero, the Re-Creator, with a power passed down through the ages and originating with "the space aliens that built the Hoover Dam."

"Don't you mean the pyramids?" I asked.

"Naw, dude, that's racist," Eric said. "The Egyptians had mad skills."

One Sunday, Eric showed up at the home to see Uncle Sid, and Joe had died. "And then a few weeks later, I was playing Pokemon with my buddy Steve, and I was really wishing I had some more energy cards, and my hand starts tingling. And suddenly one card had become two, just like that. And then an hour later, that second card was gone. And I remembered all Joe's 'Re-Creator' stories, and I realized that at least those stories must have been for real. And somehow, Joe passed his power on to me when he died, just like it had been passed down to him."

"All the way from the space aliens," Marci added. I couldn't tell if she was gently teasing or being genuinely encouraging.

"Sure. Maybe. I wish I knew," Eric said. He'd tried to track down more stories like Joe's, or about him, without success.

"With your power being what it is, were you ever tempted to copy money?" I asked.

"Oh, come on!" Eric said. "I already get that from every adult I meet. You gonna give me the whole economics lecture, too?"

I didn't know what to say that wasn't, *No! I just spent my life in the future interviewing criminals.* "Uh..."

But Marci jumped to my defense. "Lighten up, Match. Bounceback wasn't judging you as a person. It's a fair question for anyone. Except maybe Saint Scion."

Eric sighed." I can't say I never thought about the fact that I was capable of it, but I never really thought I could do it, y'know? So instead I used it to cheat at Pokemon. For like a year. I mean, I goofed around with it, but I really wasn't thinking what I wanted to do with it."

Then one night the previous summer, Eric was working the register at his parents' corner store when a guy robbed the place at gunpoint. Or tried to; Eric filled the robber's bag with copied money.

"So you did play the counterfeit game," I said.

"Well, yes. Technically. But that doesn't count!"

Eric also managed to spot the license plate on the guy's car as he drove away. By the time the police pulled him over, the man was clutching a great big bag of nothing.

"I told the cops that I just, like, faked the guy out. Sleight of hand. That I'd been practicing some stage-magic tricks. But it felt pretty awesome. That's when I started thinking about signing up for the hero thing," Eric said.

Nicole said, "I was bitten as a child by a vampire clone of Albert Einstein. The vampirism was cured, but not the genius."

I rolled my eyes.

"I guess I'll go next," Manaaki said in his deep Kiwi accent.

Benny Tupu was born in New Zealand and lost his parents in a car accident when he was a baby, leaving his grandmother to raise him. When he was 12 his *kuia* passed away. Benny's next of kin, a cousin in Cleveland, asked Benny if he wanted to stay with the close-knit Maori *iwi* in Hawke's Bay where he'd grown up, but Benny chose to move to the U.S.

"My shield saved me in the accident, but since then I hadn't really used it," he explained. "New Zealand doesn't have much need for *tuahangata*, superheroes. Outsiders see nothing but sheep and gorgeous scenery, so villains don't bother us."

Benny's cousin and her wife supported his desire to train as a hero, particularly after Benny's force field saved his new foster sister from a fall that could have broken the toddler's neck after she worked out how to climb out of her crib. This was also the moment Benny discovered he could extend the shield; he'd come into the room just as Tenia was tipping over the edge and didn't quite catch her, but when his hand wrapped around her ankle, so did his shield, and she hit the floor safely, with a giggle rather than a scream.

Benny got his amateur hero license and started looking for a team immediately after that. He signed on with the TroubleShooters the year before Marci joined his cheerleading squad, and he recruited her in turn. Now he was starting on nursing classes at Cleveland State, since his school allowed seniors to leave campus early in the afternoons to take college courses.

"It's a good skill-set for a hero to have," he said.

While Marci showed me pictures of Benny's little cousin Tenia, now almost 10 and hoping to be a pro skateboarder, Benny had plowed through his usual post-battle Denny's order and was sneaking some of Marci's neglected fries. "Benny says that a lot of times talking just gets in the way of actually communicating," she told me, slapping his hand away as he grinned, unrepentant, "but I think he just stays quiet so nobody will notice him and he can get away with stuff." She ate a fry and made a face, pushing the plate toward Benny. "Bleh, they're cold. You can have them."

"I got a papercut from a radioactive issue of *Popular Mechanics*," Nicole said, ducking to avoid the cold fries we all threw at her.

Nicole was really just a smart kid who liked to build stuff and beat up bad guys, but she insisted that eventually her biographer would need details, and she planned to have something cool at the ready. I smiled at this, remembering how in the future Ruby Goldberg would decline numerous requests for interviews and personal features, preferring to release press statements and op-eds. I wondered if she'd decided that her origin was too uninspiring to publish. For the moment, Nicole assumed she was going to college in the fall and was waiting to hear back on her applications. She wasn't the type to get nervous about that, but I knew it didn't really matter in any case, as she'd end up taking a year off to start her own company.

When the Shooters asked about me, I made a few vague comments implying my gifts were a lucky turn in the genetic lottery and turned the conversation right back on them. Nicole hadn't said a word about my time travel since she'd winked at me that first night, so I assumed she'd rather I not discuss the details in front of the others. No one seemed to mind my mysteriousness, though. Or my nosiness.

When spring break came along, I spent almost the whole week with the team, training and patrolling, much to Sarah's annoyance. She was always invited as well, and came along a couple of times, but spent the rest of the days either humoring her mother's 'bonding outings' or hanging out with the school friends I continued to neglect.

"I'll make it up to them," I said when Sarah complained. "Promise. When I get home, and I talk the adult TroubleShooters into letting me write a book about them—with all their precarious personal information changed or redacted, obviously—I'll throw the biggest, coolest party ever."

"You realize you'll have a decade of compound friendship interest to make up as well, right?" Sarah said.

"I'll buy you a pony," I said.

"I will hold you to that."

Chapter 8: Reassess

Ramona Schultz, aka Mona Lethal: Friendship sneaks up on a villain. Not because us 'bad guys' are inherently incapable of trust or loyalty or whatever. Most of us have families, best buds. People we'd die for, same as any hero.

Caroline Henderson: Are you saying that villain teams are just like heroic teams?

RS: Not usually. If you're a realist, then the person you want behind you in a fight is someone who you wouldn't care if they don't come home.

CH: So villains are less emotional about their teammates than heroes.

RS: I ain't sayin' I didn't love the Rogue's Gallery. Some more than others, for sure. Vincent Van was as much of a windbag as he was a crummy wheelman, and Mother Whistler kept promising to bake real chocolate chip cookies and then every freakin' time showed up late with oatmeal raisin or some vegan crap. But most of my crew, sure, I love 'em like cousins. Second cousins, at least. It just takes a while.

CH: Why is that?

RS: Well, the first time you meet up for a job, you're thinking, 'This loser ain't gonna last the night.' Sometimes you're even hoping it's true. 'Cause better her than me, right?

"Villains Unmasked: Mona Lethal"
Newsnight, October 7, 2022

By the beginning of April, Marci and Nicole were dropping regular hints that a full-time spot on the TroubleShooters would pretty much be mine for the asking, as soon as I passed my test for semi-pro and they kicked out Eric. I was fairly certain that last bit was a joke, but I didn't actually want to join the team full time. I figured that adding myself to the official roster was getting a little too close to the history books. Plus membership would involve a mandated number of weekly training hours with the TroubleShooters' mentors from the senior teams, and I'd need an excuse signed by a pro hero, Grade 1 steward, or public official every time I missed a meeting. The semi-pro benefits were starting to sound pretty enticing, though. I decided to run the idea past Sarah.

"That is a really super-terrible idea," Sarah said the instant the words 'I'm thinking of going semi-pro' left my mouth. Tamika had a field trip that day and Liz was home with the flu, or didn't feel like coming to school, or whatever, so we were more or less alone in a corner of the auditorium, listening to Nate and the jazz band practice before first period. "You're not really keeping up with your homework now, and it's only gonna get more bananas with all the end-of-the-year projects and A.P. tests and everything. I can't keep up with your work and mine, especially with my parents all breathing down my neck to get a job. Not unless I stopped going out to eat and to movies with the gang, and obviously that's not possible."

"Well there you go," I said. "Semi-pro stewards get paid too. Problem solved."

"And how many semi-pro stewards are still in high school?"

"Don't worry about it. Marci already told me she'd have one of Leviathan's stewards sit in with you at the next Open Wreck Room. She's positive they'll sponsor you too."

Sarah's mouth dropped open.

"For serious? But—no, it still won't work, doofus. My parents want me to have a job they can actually see me working."

"We could make up a job. Buy you a McDonald's uniform off the internet or something."

"Yeah, no. They'd figure it out. I'm just gonna have to get a job, and suffer."

"Awww."

"I don't need your sympathy," Sarah lied. "But you watched me endure all this once before, right? So you can just tell me who's gonna hire me anyway. That way at least I won't have to waste time on pointless applications and interviews."

"And what if you have to mess up those before you can do well on the ones for the job you're supposed to get?"

"You're old and I hate you."

"I've got a better idea anyway." I did remember the job Sarah had gotten around this time before. It was retail and she hated it. "Come work at Shooter HQ."

"You think Leviathan would hire me?"

"No, but Denny's is looking for a waitress. Ow!" Sarah had punched me in the arm, and it actually hurt. Nicole must have shown her how to focus the impact in her knuckles.

"That isn't an awful idea," Sarah admitted after a minute. "At least then I'd get to hang out with you a little more often." But she still wasn't sold on the semi-pro thing. "You haven't even told your parents you're a hero yet. Won't one of them have to sign a form or something?"

"No, it's not like a learner's permit for a driver's license. As long as there's a semi-pro or professional hero in good standing to sponsor, parental consent isn't required for heroes over 15."

"And W.H.A.M.'s not worried about getting their butts sued off?"

"They're more worried about some kid getting dead because he had issues with his home life and didn't get proper training. You can't really stop powered kids from testing out what they can do. More young heroes died in the six months adolescent heroics were outlawed in 1951 than in the entire 11 years beforehand, since Greyhound and the rise of the teen sidekick."

"Well, aren't you the fountain of knowledge," Sarah said. She also reminded me how badly I'd been doing at making more time for our other friends. "I know you're trying, but now you want to give up even more of your time—*our* time? Why not at least wait until school's out for the summer?"

"You know why. Because this *isn't* my time."

"For all you know, whenever you get back to the future, you'll go right back to the moment you left anyway."

"For all I know, I'll be sent further forward the longer I wait. Maybe even longer than I'm spending here. There are probably rules to this sort of thing."

"But you don't know that! You don't even actually know you can get back at all! Would it be so bad to just enjoy yourself for a while?"

A couple of other students looked up at Sarah's raised voice. I glared at Sarah, who didn't even pretend to look apologetic. "I'm going to get back," I told her firmly after the kids went back to their own conversations. "I'm figuring this out. I've already saved Lift. I'm turning Milo from a supervillain into the Shooters' new best friend."

"Is that what this is about? You don't just think they'll let me be semi-pro, you think you can get Milo to do it too? Meaning our future maybe-villain will get even more supervision from W.H.A.M."

"I'm hoping, yes."

Sarah's tone was even more grudging this time. "That's not a hideous idea either. But do you really think that's the missing element that'll get you sent home?"

"I think something big is coming, something it's going to take all of us together to stop, and I'll take all the training and resources I can get in the meantime."

Sarah sighed. "Fine. Whatever. You're still doing your own damn homework."

"That's fair."

Milo took a lot less convincing, which surprised me. One didn't have to be a possible budding supervillain to dislike the thought of inviting W.H.A.M. to audit your life and inventions. But Sarah and I talked to him together after school, and the moment the plan was announced, his face lit up.

"Have you seen the software real stewards get access to? Let's do it!"

"Ex-squeeze me!" Sarah was pouting; I was trying not to laugh. I can hear her pout from across a room with my back turned. "You speak for yourself. *I've* been a *real* steward from the start."

The following Saturday, Marci and I drove down to the outskirts of Columbus, parked out of sight, then suited up and ran the rooftops to the regional W.H.A.M. office. As stewards with only public identities, Sarah and Milo would be checked out and registered quietly in their homes at a prearranged time by a W.H.A.M. field agent disguised as a water meter reader. For me, and for Lift as my sponsor, the process would take somewhat longer.

After half an hour of scribbling signatures on forms—mostly non-disclosure agreements and liability waivers for the testing phase—we sat down with an administrative steward to catalog my powers and experience. The 40-something blonde woman tapped her finger impatiently on her desk.

"Super-charged musculature," she barked the instant we entered her tiny glass-walled cubicle. "What exactly does that entail in this instance? Are all of your muscles enhanced or can you just lift heavy objects? Don't try to claim whole-body powers if you don't have them, kid. Benching 50 pounds might wow the gals down at the gym but it won't get you a semi-pro license, so you'd better not be wasting my time."

Lift was briefly taken aback by the steward's accusatory glare. I was just irritated. "All of my muscles are enhanced beyond normal human levels," I said. "Probably joints, ligaments, and bones too."

"Probably?" she said.

"Well my shoulders don't dislocate when I dead-lift a Holstein, so, probably," I snapped.

Lift asked, "When did you have to pick up a cow?"

The steward wasn't impressed. "You'll have the chance to show off during the testing phase. Any secondary abilities to declare?"

I hesitated, still annoyed by the attitude pouring off the steward. I wasn't sure if she would request proof of my psychic abilities, which of course I couldn't provide. I knew something that might happen in

New Orleans next week, but nothing about what was going on in Columbus that day. I looked to Lift for guidance.

"It's okay," she said. "Your profile should be as complete as possible."

Before the steward could ask, I said, "Low level clairvoyance," and Lift clarified, "Level 2, observed by myself and other licensed heroes."

"Sure, why not?" the steward said, entering something into her computer. "Anything below Category 4 doesn't require a demonstration, so go ahead and claim to be psychic. Maybe someday you can have your own radio call-in show and tell people that their dead grandmothers are proud of them." She finished typing and handed me a slip of paper with a number on it. "They'll call you back when they're ready for you."

While Lift sat out in the waiting room with a stack of magazines, a quartet of analysts ran me, sometimes literally, through a battery of tests. They took samples of various fluids, and CT scans of my brain. They tested my reflexes with a mallet borrowed from a Norse deity, had me read an eye-chart while hanging upside down from the toes of my boots, and administered a hearing test under water.

After that the real fun began. I ran laps in a labyrinth, and halfway through the first lap I discovered that random patches of the floors had been greased. I lifted exotically shaped and labeled weights; I stayed down on the "Motorcycle w/ Sidecar" end of the room, but I would've loved to watch Saint Scion or Uluru Walks bench-pressing the "Stegosaurus." I ran hurdles against three Olympic gold medalists, and bested Ms. O'Connor's entire sixth grade class in dodgeball, barely. Those kids were unreal. Then I was taken back out into downtown Columbus for a brief practical. I leapt a hot dog stand in a single bound, then a high park wall, and finally a city bus, though I clipped my heel on the roof on the way down with that one.

At last, lungs burning, exhausted, I raced through what I swear was a combination of every *American Ninja Warrior* obstacle course ever in two minutes and twenty-nine seconds.

I was then allowed a hot shower and a twenty-minute power nap before Lift helped me reassemble myself for the holo-photos. One set was taken with my mask off; these would vanish down a secure data-line into W.H.A.M.'s black box servers, only to be accessed by top security officials in case of emergency. The other set, full body-and-costume holo-shots, were publicly archived, and the best would be printed onto my new semi-pro ID card.

We were shuffled back to the blonde steward's desk for some final questions. I assumed she could see my test results on her screen because her tone had shifted from hostile to merely dismissive. "Deep memory brain scan?"

"I'm sorry?" I said.

"Seriously?" the steward said.

Lift looked guilty. "Sorry, I was supposed to tell you about this. They put your memories on file, and you come back like twice a year for a scan, so they can update, and they use the info to help train future heroes or something. It's cool, it's painless. You sit there with the thing over your head and just watch TV or whatever for half an hour."

I glanced at the steward, then back to Lift. "Will they think it's weird if I don't?" I murmured. The steward sighed loudly to let me know that she could hear me perfectly well.

"Oh no," Lift answered at normal volume. "It's like the hero equivalent of donating blood. Lots of people opt out. I mean, it sounds like a pretty huge invasion of privacy, right? I'd probably think so too, if it was anyone else asking."

As an organization, I trusted W.H.A.M. I was here today, after all. They were founded by good people, the original stewards to the Everyperson's Guild, back when it was still the Everyman's Guild. Those good people had hired and trained good successors, who had by all reports maintained those same high standards with their own recruits. Nothing I'd seen in the next few years had ever suggested otherwise.

"All memory scans remain in a closed file, and are only accessed by better-than-top security operatives in the event of a hero's death," the steward said impatiently, her fingers momentarily still on her keyboard.

"*Better*-than-top security? What does that even mean?"

"No one knows," Lift said. "Except whoever does know. Y'know."

I believed them. Mostly. But when it came right down to it, my situation was unique. So far as I knew, anyway. And if there was even the ghost of the possibility that someone might peek and notice that I knew things that hadn't happened yet, that was not a chance I wanted to take. I wasn't interested in unraveling the timelines by committee.

"Not at this time, thank you," I said.

The steward typed a few words and stabbed a button. The machine on the desk between us whirred once and spat out my brand new license. "Congratulations," she said as she handed it to me. "You are now licensed by the World Heroes Advisory Mission to put yourself and those around you in danger, as teenagers are inclined to do. Please try to keep the collateral damage to a minimum."

"Hey, I'm—" *not a teenager!* "—very responsible," I finished awkwardly.

"Of course you are. Enjoy running around in your spandex and mask. It'll be like Halloween every day," said the steward.

"'Scuse me, ma'am," Lift said, "but I think if you look at our stats you'll find that my TroubleShooters have been consistently effective in the field." Her measured tone was somewhat undermined by the stapler and the coffee mug full of pens that started to float off the desk.

The steward noticed immediately. "Oh yes, I have ever so much confidence in your self-control now."

Lift started to splutter a reply, but I grabbed her arm, pulling her toward the exit. "Thanks very much, we'll be going now," I said.

The clatter of office supplies scattering across a desk followed us out.

She turned to me when we reached the roof. "Did I just embarrass myself? Wait, no! If anyone should be embarrassed, it's that jerk! We get that crap all the time from non-heroes, I never thought we'd get it from stewards too."

I wasn't sure what kind of response would be most appropriate from a fellow teenager, and I couldn't decide how mad I was on my own behalf. The steward wasn't entirely wrong. Teenagers as an age group do tend to be more reckless than older or younger demographics, but only because the reward centers of the teenage brain require a more intense thrill to register pleasure. It's basic neurochemistry, but I didn't think Lift would appreciate hearing that. Instead I changed the subject.

"So that's it? I'm a semi-pro hero now?"

"You should get your first paycheck in about three weeks," Lift said, returning to team leader mode. "Once Sarah and Milo get checked out, they'll calculate salaries for all three of you, based on the hours you spend training and in the field, and the expenses of your particular power-set and activities."

"I don't suppose there's any back-pay?" I asked. I'd been getting along this far on my allowance, and some judiciously budgeted Christmas money.

"Nope," Lift said. "Amateur heroism is basically considered like an internship. Unless you happen to save the world, of course."

"Of course."

For the next several days, I pulled out that license and stared at it pretty much any time nobody would notice. It wasn't a narcissism thing, though the photo of me was an awesome little hologram and the likeness did not suck. It was more like the summer after seventh grade when Mom and Dad were taking Hank and me to Europe for vacation and I got my first passport. I did the same thing then. This wasn't just a license to super, which I'd been doing for months now anyway. This was my ticket home.

And goodness knows I needed something to cling to, given how regularly I was getting my butt kicked these days.

"It's NOT RIGHT!" I shouted as I stomped into Sarah's room one afternoon. Sarah and Milo were both seated at the computer, poring over some steward tech catalogs they'd received with their own licenses. They closed them in a hurry, staring instead at my hair frizzing wildly out of my ponytail and my bloody knuckles. "People are not *statistics*, you can't just *categorize* them. You can't just assign numbers to them, and the ones who don't make the cut, too bad, no future for you!"

"Holy crap, Caro!" snapped Sarah, bounding up from her chair to grab an alcohol wipe and a tube of Neosporin. She'd stashed first-aid kits in her bedroom, my room, Milo's room, each of our school lockers, and the glove compartment of each of our parents' cars. "Who was it this time?" she asked, pulling my hand into hers and scrubbing vigorously at my knuckles. It tickled.

"Determinist?" guessed Milo. "I heard he was back in town. Or, wait a minute, how many of the Focus Group are out of jail right now?" Despite the shop talk, he made no effort to close Sarah's bedroom door. We never did when Milo was here, because he was still a teenage boy, and there are rules. There were also a few motion detectors Milo had built hidden on Sarah's stairs, synched to a phone app. If one of her parents came within earshot, we'd know in plenty of time.

"Not them, not any of them. I'm talking about Mr. Parker," I said.

"You don't mean he's a—" Sarah said.

"And you had to give him a righteous for-the-good-of-innocent-lives beatdown?" Milo said, grinning at me in pure awe. "Is it evil of me to hope someone got that on film?"

"What? Ow!" I said. Sarah had just squeezed the antibiotic cream across the back of my hands, and my cuts stung. "Oh. No. This was from stopping at a building site on my way home to punch some already broken concrete. I thought it would make me feel better."

"Dumbass," Sarah said.

"True, but she's our dumbass," Milo said.

"At the end of school you said you had to go take care of a thing, I thought you meant a supervillain thing," Sarah said.

"It's why I'm here," Milo said. "We were all set, if you needed anything."

I slumped in a chair, and suddenly Sarah was thrusting an entire tray of cheese and crackers under my nose. I hadn't even seen her put away the first aid kit. "No, I'm okay," I said, even as I built a tiny tower of crackers and Havarti and shoved it into my face. "I'm just doomed. Mr. Parker made me stay after class, said he was 'concerned.' And by 'concerned' he meant that he'd already given me 2 Ds and a C on my last three physics labs, which means if I don't completely ace the last test and the final I'm gonna get a D for the course."

"Ah," Sarah said.

"Whoops," said Milo.

"Yeah. Whoops!" I said. "It's not fair. I already GOT my B in this freaking class, and I worked my butt off the first time!"

"The first time?" Milo said.

"She means last quarter," Sarah said quickly.

"Yeah. That," I said. "I just—I know this stuff. So what if I can't always put it all together on paper from memory on test day? Where else in life does a single assessment indicate a person's true knowledge or potential?"

"Hey, you're preaching to the choir here," Milo replied.

Sarah and I both turned to glare at him.

"What?" Milo said. "Okay, so I happen to test extremely well—"

"You took your SAT freshman year and were 3 points away from a perfect score. Without studying, you told me," Sarah said.

"Well, sure. Yeah. But that doesn't mean I can't feel for the rest of you trapped in a flawed system?" Milo said.

Sarah rolled her eyes. I ate another stack of crackers, then pulled my new license out to stare at it again.

"I don't know how much longer I can do this," I said. "Crap, I really don't."

"Just another six weeks, that's all," Milo said. "Then it'll be summer, and—"

"You're almost there. Focus on this," Sarah said, tapping the ID card in my hands with one finger.

"Hasn't that kind of been my problem?" I said.

"Probably," Sarah said. "But do it anyway, and let us help you focus on everything else."

"Hmm?" Milo said. "Oh, yeah! We'll totally tutor you."

"More than I was already doing," Sarah said. "You just need to put in more time."

"That's the part I hate," I said. "It's so boring!"

"It's school," Milo said. "You're not used to that by now? Not even a little?"

Sarah and I beefed up our review schedule for English, Spanish, and history. Milo started working me over on math and science. I definitely started feeling more confident about my homework, but I also woke up at least three nights a week sweating from the same nightmare, where I got back to the future only to find my past had been rewritten because my grades sucked so bad that I didn't get into Kent State. I never worked on the school paper or had profs with connections in publishing, never wrote my book, which meant supervillains never shot me and I never went back in time, so my past was NOT rewritten, and the whole space-time continuum had a conniption and imploded.

Three weeks after my licensing test, I woke up from one of those nightmares and immediately reached for my phone. I checked my bank account first thing, like I did every morning—surprise overdraft fees are nobody's friend—and found that sometime in the night W.H.A.M. had transferred in my very first semi-professional paycheck. And it was a really, really good thing they did. Because 11 hours later, the money was my only consolation as I stared at the bashed-in wreck of my mother's car.

I mean, Sarah was there too—

"Oh, you are SO dead."

—but she wasn't helping.

A massive gaping hole had been punched through the car's roof. Or stomped through, technically. The same had been done to the hood. Bits of engine had become visible in several places, once the fire had been put out. Did I mention we were standing well back, and the TroubleShooters had helpfully circled the vehicle with an emergency barricade before they left? The driver's side door bore a distinct three-toed avian footprint where it had been kicked in by a big bird. Not *the* Big Bird; even my life wasn't *that* weird. No, I'd only been called in tonight to help quell a genetically-engineered quasi-intelligent ostrich rampage. And the first and only casualty, before I could even find a secluded place to park, had been my mother's Corolla. After the fight was done, the Shooters had offered to wait for the tow truck with me, but Sarah was already on her way so I told them to go on. I sneaked into the bathroom of the nearest evacuated Starbucks and changed back into civilian clothes.

Now here I was, just a poor innocent bystander and her mother's innocent totaled car. I put my face in my hands and whimpered.

Sarah leaned over and hugged me. "Hey, it's okay. I'm your steward, I got this! You just need an airtight explanation how this happened to the car while we were all at dinner."

"No," I mumbled through my fingers.

"It's cool. This is what steward-slash-best friends are for, right?"

"No," I said again, actually lifting my face this time. "This is stupid! My parents are caring, understanding people. I don't know why I bothered keeping the whole secret identity thing from them in the first place."

"Because you never really had a teenage rebellion phase, and thought it might be kind of fun?"

"I don't think that's it. Well, probably not. But keeping this from them isn't fun, it's exhausting. They're my Mom and Dad, I should just tell them."

"Everything?"

"Everything super. The time travel stuff is a little much, but the rest, absolutely."

"You really think that can work?" Sarah asked. "That you can just *be reasonable* with parents?"

"Who knows? But anything is worth trying once, right?"

"There is SO much you haven't told me about your love life."

Chapter 9: Re-educate

Less glamorous than public hero support is the administrative and legislative work performed by the agency. The so-called Heroes' Lobby was instrumental in identifying villainy as a legal class distinct from misdemeanors and felonies, as well as adding the Right to Remain in Costume to the Miranda roll. Suspects are now legally allowed to withhold their identity during the first stage of any investigation into crimes they are purported to have committed while in uniform. This way, framed heroes are able to work with the system without putting their civilian lives and loved ones at risk.

"A Brief History of W.H.A.M.: 66 Years of Heroic Support"
Rolling Stone, Caroline Henderson, May 22, 2020

"Well," my dad said. "Thank goodness it's not drugs."

"Yes. We're so glad you're just sneaking out to fight violent sociopaths with super powers," Mom said dryly.

"I'm not thinking about that. You don't want me to be thinking about that," Dad said.

I'd found Mom and Dad sitting at the kitchen table when I got home, rather close together. I'm reasonably sure they'd been making out when I walked in, which was fine, because I'm an adult and it seems to make them happy. Also because it meant they were distracted and slightly embarrassed, which eased the tension.

"We knew something was going on in your life," Mom said. "The grades dropping and the staying out late, that just wasn't like you."

"But you weren't being as big a pain in the ass about it as your brother was at your age," Dad said. "We were worried, because we're your parents, but mostly we figured it was normal teenage stuff."

Mom said, "We didn't like having to ground you or enforce a curfew any more than you did—"

"Really, Mom?" I said, snarkier than I'd intended.

Thankfully Mom ignored that. "But we still thought you'd come to us if you actually needed help."

"I absolutely would," I said. "Luckily that's not why I told you all this today. But I may have totaled the car."

"WHAT??" my parents said in stereo.

"The TroubleShooters called me in today. Some genetically engineered birds got loose downtown—"

"Birds?" said Dad.

"My CAR?!" said Mom.

"Ostriches. But it wasn't as big a deal as it sounds. I'm perfectly fine, as you can see. And I'm insured as a hero, part of the semi-pro license upgrade I'm really glad I just got. It will definitely cover the car."

"But I *love* my car," Mom said.

"Maybe they can salvage it? I'll check in with the mechanic tomorrow."

"It's a great car," Mom said.

"But you're not hurt?" Dad asked.

"I'm completely fine. Not a scratch. Well, a couple scratches. But that was later. I didn't crash the car; a bird landed on it."

"Can I get you a Band-aid or anything?" Mom offered.

"No, I'm good. Thanks, Mom. My skin and muscles are pretty tough, and I heal pretty fast now. Plus, Manaaki—you know Manaaki?" I spread my hands wide, drawing the arc of Manaaki's shoulders in the air; my parents nodded. "He's in nursing classes, he always checks everybody out after fights."

This provided a convenient segue into the kind of support I had available to me 24/7 via the TroubleShooters and W.H.A.M.: the assessments, the training sessions with more experienced heroes, the special medical and therapeutic coverage. I pulled out some pamphlets I'd been carrying around ever since my visit to the licensing office— *So Your Teenager Is a Superhero: A Parents' Guide.* Mom started flipping through immediately, skimming. Dad put his on the chair next to him and half sat on it.

"And Sarah and Milo have been helping me too," I added. "They're my stewards."

My father blinked. "Ohhhh. Milo's your *steward.*"

"Yeah?" I said, not following where he was going with this.

"I just thought, when he kept hanging around... well, I didn't know if he was a boyfriend and you didn't want to mention it for some reason, or if he wanted to be, or what was going on there."

"Richard!" said my mother, staring at him. "Our daughter can have friends who are young men. Don't be so Victorian."

"What?" Dad said. "I just wondered, that's all!"

"But you sound relieved," Mom pressed. "I know you."

"Whoever makes Caroline happy is, y'know, tops in my book. However, if that person happened to be someone I could watch a game with, that'd be a nice bonus for me, is all I'm saying."

Mom rolled her eyes. I grunted and talked about what Milo and Sarah did as stewards, and what I'd done so far myself. Mom and Dad continued to ask questions, but they never really challenged the decisions I'd made in putting my abilities to work, despite the risk. All they asked was that going forward, I'd always let them know where and when I was going, and/or have Sarah keep them posted. They were treating me, at 16, something like an adult. Which was no less astonishing for the fact that I actually was one.

Finally I pushed it a little. "That's it?"

"Can I see you in your costume?" Mom asked.

I grinned, went upstairs and changed but left the mask off until I came back to show them.

"Whoa," Dad said when I put it on. "I know it's you, but it's like you're in bad 3-D. The angles are all wrong."

"It's giving me a bit of a headache, actually," Mom said, scrunching her nose. I peeled the mask off.

"All right, I need to see these super-jumping powers of yours," Dad said.

"Not in the house!" snapped Mom.

Telling my parents the truth did more than get me mostly off the hook for Mom's car. It also meant I avoided another grounding the following week when I came home with an F on a math test that I'd fallen asleep studying for because I'd been out all night fighting Plato with the TroubleShooters. It was actually Sarah who got upset about that grade.

"Milo!" Sarah snapped. The three of us were at my house after school. "What part of 'Caroline's math is *your job*' did you not understand?"

"It's not his fault," I said. "He explains it all in dummy-speak beautifully. He gives me practice problems, which I've been doing every night. Mostly. I just get distracted. I *want* to hear how to calculate the square root of the polynomial, but my brain's too busy trying to recall the five subtle ways to spot StainAlive disguised as an ordinary puddle."

Sarah looked at Milo and sighed. "I guess even you can't be asked to work miracles."

Milo affected a theatrical Scottish accent. "I'm givin' her all she's got, Captain!"

Sarah busted out into giggles.

"Hey! I'm right here!" I said.

The both of them just giggled harder, which made no sense. How did Sarah even get that reference?

"Okay, what the hell?" I said to her. "I could never get you to watch *Star Trek*!"

"Yeah, well, I was stewarding over at Milo's one time and he had it on," Sarah said. "And Chris Pine's eyes are ridiculously pretty. Anyway, we were talking about your grades."

"Grade," I said. "It was just the one class. The others are getting better."

"Slowly," Sarah retorted. "And the one that still sucks, it sucks really bad, and you just admitted it's your own fault."

"I admitted there's a lot on my mind," I corrected. "A lot of important things."

Sarah arched an eyebrow. "Yeah. Remember when we were talking about going semi-pro, and you said you would not officially join the TroubleShooters, because you didn't want to have to go to all the meetings?"

"I'm not going to *all* of them," I retorted. "Just the awesome, useful ones with guest instructors." How could I pass up an opportunity to learn wrestling holds from James Baer and Petunia? Or to practice bladed combat with the extra-terrestrial hero Chandi, who in her warrior aspect could extend eighteen arms and duel us all simultaneously?

"Whatever," Sarah said. "Just don't expect a refund from us when you fail pre-calc and they make you go to summer school."

After I bombed two more pre-calc tests, insuring my semester grade would fall somewhere in the D range at best, Sarah's warning turned out to be prophetic. The parents wanted me to take classes over summer break. I'd never earned less than a B- for a semester in any class in my life. I quietly fumed for most of an afternoon, fought some ninjas with the TroubleShooters, and got knocked unconscious for three whole minutes—which turned out to be just long enough for a reprise of the universal implosion dream. As soon as the police showed up to cart the ninjas away, I called my Dad and said, "FINE, I will go to frickin' summer school."

With Sarah and Milo's well-paid assistance, I finished the final papers of my junior year, built a few dioramas and made some presentations. I managed to hold on to an A in English at least, and squeaked out Bs and a C+ in everything else except math. I ended up getting called in to fight Defenestrator the night before that exam, came home bruised, and chose sleep over doing any studying on the principle that I'd already signed up for the do-over. I managed to underperform Lance Stern on that one, who filled in all the test bubbles to spell rude words on a bet. We went on to become good friends during our remedial studies.

Summer school sucked hard. The only upside was that since my parents were now wise to the hero thing, they didn't ask me to work a summer job on top of it. As I was only taking the one class, this gave me more time overall for crimefighting and training. Also for micro-analyzing everything I did with the Shooters, and occasionally embarrassing myself in the process. Like the time Marci and Benny were sharing a milkshake and I weirded everyone out by asking how long they'd been dating. The Shooters, including Marci and Benny themselves, all insisted vociferously that the two were just friends. "Practically siblings!"

"But think about it," I said to Sarah the next day. The sun was falling down, and we were sharing a bench in front of the Laketon Dairy Queen, where we'd gone after Sarah got off work. "Maybe this is another part of future-Ruby's plan. Maybe by sending me back to save Lift, she knew I'd give their star-crossed romance the chance it never had. Or maybe it was more than that. Maybe she found out through some kind of parallel universe thing or magic prophecy or whatever that they were SUPPOSED to be together. Maybe their kids are destined to save the universe."

"That's it," Sarah said. "I'm cutting you off."

"What?" I said.

"Every little thing that happens, you're all, *'This is it! This is the mission, really for real now, I know it!'* First it was saving Lift, then it was about fixing Milo and hooking him up with the Shooters, now it's, what? Playing matchmaker to two best friends who already finish each other's sentences?"

"Well, it sounds stupid when you put it like *that*, sure. But clearly the whole situation is complex. It's *Ruby Goldberg* complex, but it's all gotta add up to something in the end. I think if I just—"

"You think. You've been here for six months already, and most of what you've done is think!" Shoving the bottom of her sugar cone into her mouth, Sarah reached out with the napkin in her other hand and wiped a big streak of chocolate and vanilla swirl from my thumb. My soft-serve had melted and dripped while I filled her in on this latest twist in my mission.

"Cute," I said.

"Ah'm serra-us!" Sarah said, mouth full of cone. (I'm serious!) She swallowed. "Your whole life's gonna fly right by you and you won't even notice, but I'm already sick of hearing about it. I'm officially declaring the Time Traveler's Swear Jar is open for business."

"The what?"

"Your mom never had to use that one? Like for every f-bomb you're dumb enough to drop in her earshot, you have to put five dollars in the jar."

"Ohhhh, that," I said.

"If I have to put up with you always going on about 'the mission,' I might at least make some money," Sarah said.

"Or I can just stop," I said.

Six months," Sarah repeated "Whatever Ruby needs you to do, obviously she's taking her time about it. But you're a superhero, and you're smart. Just trust you'll know it when you see it, okay?"

"You're right. I'm sorry," I said after a moment, and not just because Sarah could get really tedious to argue with. "Whatever Ruby has me doing, it's clearly a vast and unknowable plan. The least I can do is shut up about it."

"And try to enjoy the summer?"

"Sure. That too."

I licked another splotch of ice cream that had dribbled across the back of my hand. It wasn't bad, even like that.

Of course I didn't stop obsessing over my mission. I only stopped talking about it. When I was at home, if I wasn't buried in summer school homework, I was poring over my lists of upcoming crimes, ranking and color-coding them on the likelihood that they might represent a key turning point of the timeline. Robberies and heists with no injuries and no clear links to later, bigger crimes were shaded purple and blue, and while they still needed attention, I typically just called the cops or sent in a tip to the W.H.A.M. online crime stoppers forum. Other crimes were colored yellow and orange, signifying that they involved either an especially nasty villain or moderate property destruction. I tried to get the Shooters or other heroes in on these cases without being too obvious about it. I couldn't risk using my "psychic gifts" too often, in case one of our supervising heroes tried to test them. Any case in which my intervention might save a human life, either immediately or several metaphorical dominoes down the line, was shaded a portentous red. I handled these personally.

One Thursday night, as the rest of my school friends were at Tamika's watching a *Lord of the Rings* movie marathon, I arrived at the Rock & Roll Hall of Fame & Museum in what I thought was plenty of time, only to find a massive hole had already been smashed through the glass pyramid that fronted the building.

Whoops.

The majority of my foreknowledge was gleaned from interviews conducted months or years after the fact; whether due to intentional omission or the innocent quirks of human memory, it wasn't always accurate.

Sprinting through the jagged hole, I heard my boots crunching over broken shards, and a conspicuous lack of alarms. I didn't see any red lights, either, just a few dim glimmers of night lighting. I mentioned this to Sarah, who was holed up with her wristcomm in Tamika's bathroom again. If we weren't careful, one of these days our friends were going to drag Sarah to a doctor to get her checked for a bladder infection.

"I'm messaging the cops right now," she said. *"Telling them someone's robbing the museum and has shut down the alarms, and that you're on site, with our license numbers and everything."*

I made my way up four whole floors before finding a single smashed display case. A life-size diorama inside recreated Lethe's immortal music video for "In the Ending Was the Song," with mannequins of the band performing on a precarious platform balanced on the point of the Great Pyramid as the gods descended in their space chariots. But lead singer Jared Tennant raised empty hands.

"Dammit," I said. "He's got what he came for."

"Well, crapcakes," Sarah said. *"Maybe—"*

"Nope, I've got him!" I said. My ears had caught the distinctive clatter of rollerblades over a smooth tile floor. I hurled myself down the corridor, half skidded and half fell around the next turn, and saw Train Wreck skating away down the hall, tucking Lethe's tablet into a padded box hanging from a strap across his torso.

Armored in plastic from head to wheels, with wide bulky shoulder-guards and spikes trailing from his forearms, Train Wreck looked like a refugee from Andrew Lloyd Webber's forgotten classic *Starlight Express*. His peak years of operation had been 1987-1991, but every so often he would be tempted, usually with large wads of cash, into a revival crime like this one. He wasn't subtle, obviously, but he was fast and fairly smart. He'd originally gotten away with tonight.

I poured on the speed, closing on him as he gripped the edge of a glass case to swing himself around a hard turn, but lagging behind again in the next straightaway as he accelerated, tiny puffs of black steam shooting back from his skates.

"Don't suppose," I huffed to Sarah as I ran, "you've got any clue how to shut down Train Wreck's armor?"

"Not really my area," Sarah replied. *"Don't worry, I'm patching Milo in."*

At almost the exact same time, my wristcomm buzzed. I slapped at it to answer the second line. "Milo?"

"Who?" said my brother Hank's voice.

"What the hell?!" I said.

"What?" Sarah said.

"Who's Milo?" Hank said.

"Hank!" I yelled. "Why are you calling me? How are you calling me?" The only people with my comm code were Sarah, Milo, the TroubleShooters, and the stewards at Leviathan HQ.

"Uhh, you haven't changed your number since the last time I called," Hank replied, as if I were the one being ridiculous. *"So, Caroline, when were you going to tell your only brother that you're a superhero?"*

Pink Floyd's Wall loomed above me, the giant blue alien Schoolmaster peering over ominously. Train Wreck shot through the gap underneath, straight for the long narrow escalator descending into the museum's depths. He leapt as he hit the top, twisting his body sideways, the wheels of his skates grinding down the handrail, then soared off the bottom and shot off down another dark hallway.

I jumped from the top of the escalator to the bottom in one exhilarating leap, and kept after him.

"Hank, this is really not a good time. For whatever you think this is." He'd only been home from college for two weeks, and he'd spent most of that time at work or out with his friends. How could he have found out about Bounceback? Did Mom and Dad tell him without asking me?

"This is exactly what I think it is," Hank said. *"I found the costume in your closet."*

"What? When?" I was wearing my costume, obviously.

"Just now. Hence the call."

Oh right, I had a spare. But this brought up a more important question. "What were you doing in my closet?"

Up ahead, Train Wreck took a hard right through an archway.

"I was doing laundry, thought I'd do yours too. I was trying to be nice! And here I find out my baby sister has been keeping secrets from me."

"Don't call me—"

Evidently that archway was a dead end. Train Wreck shot back out, nearly running me down. At the last second I leapt straight up and over him. Dammit! If I hadn't been distracted, I might have tackled him.

"I'm a grown woman with my own life, which is none of your business!" I snapped.

"You're a high schooler," Hank said.

"Shut up!" I didn't have the lung capacity to debate my brother and chase down a villain, so I was reduced to basic retorts.

"Look, I forgive you for not telling me," Hank said. *"Having a secret identity is a big deal, I get it. But I've seen Bounceback videos on the internet. You've got powers! Why didn't I get powers?"*

"I don't know," I said. That's what this call was about? Good grief!

"Should I get tested or something?"

"Um, you could, I guess? But it's pretty expensive. And at your age it would probably mostly tell you if your kids were likely to develop a special ability."

"Well, that could be useful to know."

Train Wreck had already scraped his way down another staircase. I bounded down after.

"Look, I'm kinda busy here."

"Wait, are you fighting crime? Like, right now?"

By this point Train Wreck had gained enough of a lead that I had to stop at the next hallway and listen to figure out which way he'd gone. "Yeah, I gotta go. Later, Hank."

"Huh. I've never thought of you as awesome before. This is weird."

He finally clicked off and I took off down a hallway, pretty sure I knew which way the wheeled wonder was headed.

"I'm so sorry!" Sarah said. She'd been keeping silent since she realized Hank was on the line; no need for him to know her part in all this. *"I have no idea how that happened!"*

"It's okay," I said. "No big."

"Here's Milo for real."

"Hey, boss," Milo said. *"Sarah tells me you need a good way to stop Train Wreck?"*

"Yes, please. Because most of the arrests I know about it, he got picked up by flyers," I said. "Literally. That's not much help."

"Gotcha. His speed is in his armor, he's not a genetic or anything. What you've gotta do is find the power source, and I can help you shut it down. Then he's just a dude in shoulder-pads on rollerskates."

"All right. What's the power source look like?"

"Should be a blocky plastic case, about the size of a paperback book."

"And it'll be safe to touch? It's not going to explode or give me cancer?"

"No no, it's not radioactive or anything. But, um, this type of energy has a negative effect on sperm motility, so it's probably not attached to his waist."

"Got it," I said, vaulting a railing and dropping into the museum lobby, right onto Train Wreck's back. I locked my arms around his bulky shoulders. My toes skidded on the floor behind his skates, but he didn't stumble, or even slow down. I heard him shout, "Hey!" as I pulled my legs up.

Then he put his head down and his forearms up, linking the spikes on his arms into a miniature cow catcher. "Okay, then. Ride at your own risk!"

Together we smashed right through a door that would have cost Train Wreck five seconds to simply open. That explained the shattered glass at the entrance.

"Car—Bounceback?!" shouted Sarah, hearing the crash.

"I'm fine!" I snapped back, shaking glass shards from my hair. Train Wreck's legs were pumping, building speed as we shot across the parking lot, but before I could think too hard about the dangers of a 100-mile-per-hour piggyback ride, I noticed a chunky decoration on the molded plastic armor covering Train Wreck's back. The heat emanating from it suggested this was Milo's power source.

"Okay," Milo said, *"on the side of the casing there should be three buttons. Gimme a sec to figure out the right sequence, and I can turn it off without shorting out the mechanism."*

"Because that would hurt him?" I said, clinging on tight as Train Wreck tried his damnedest to shake me off.

"No, it's pretty safe, but if you bring it home intact, I can reverse engineer it, figure out how to make my own. And then the next time you're fighting a tool with similar tech, you'll have a gizmo that shuts it down by remote."

"Sounds great, what's the sequence?"

"Working on it."

124

Sarah wasn't so patient. *"Dude, just take him out!"*

Digging my fingers underneath the power pack, I found a braid of wires trailing into the backplate and yanked. Train Wreck's engine cut out abruptly—just as we hit a pothole. The thief went down hard. I bounced clear, rolling across the pavement, hoping my costume would save me from the worst of the road rash.

"Aww! Why'd you do that?" Milo whined in my ear. *"I mean, you're okay, right?"*

Having tumbled at last to a stop, I patted at my battered and bruised self. "I'm okay. And it was faster."

"All right, I forgive you."

My opponent lay on his back about fifty yards away. By the time I reached him he was sitting up, shaking his head and poking at the controls on his gauntlet.

"Damn, you killed it." He sounded more bemused than anything else. I looked down at the wires still clutched in my glove.

"Yep," I said, then, "Thanks," to Sarah, who had informed me that the cops were only minutes away.

Train Wreck didn't seem inclined to run, for which I was grateful. He set the bag containing the stolen tablet on the ground near me, and said, "I'm Ron." I pretended this was news to me, as his identity wasn't public yet.

"I'll stick to Bounceback," I said. "No offense. I'm sure you're really a decent guy."

"Oh, sure." He did not remove his helmet, and I didn't ask him to.

"So," I said. "The Rock Hall, huh? And all you take is one cheap prop?"

"I know!" Ron agreed, laughing. "Place full of sequined suits and Les Paul guitars that would go for thousands on eBay, and all I grab is that. But I've learned the hard way, letting yourself get distracted, trying to shop for the wife on the side, it only ever leads to trouble, you know?"

"I guess, sure." I'd opened Train Wreck's bag and was looking at the tablet. It appeared to be nothing more than Styrofoam.

Ron shrugged. "Ridiculous, isn't it? But so was the commission! Collectors, eh?"

Pretty soon, the police arrived to take Ron away, run my hero's license, and take my statement. Clean-up crews were called in to fix up the museum, and I walked back to where I'd left my scooter. I had a scooter now. That was Mom's idea, after what I'd done to her car. I could already feel the night's bruises healing, my superior muscles popping back into proper shape like dents snapping back out of rubber.

125

"Not a bad night's work, hey boss?" Milo said.

The minimum sentence for Tech-Armored Theft was three years. Ron wouldn't even be up for parole for a year. He wouldn't be available to take another job nine months from now for the Crimson Capo, or be killed in an argument over The Phantom of the Opera.

"Not at all."

I rode back to Tamika's, arriving in time to catch Sean Bean's greatest death scene at the end of *The Fellowship of the Ring*. But not before Milo called back, saying that he'd forgotten to tell me that he reprogrammed my wristcomm to accept automatic call forwarding from my cell because he thought it would be useful.

Reformed future supervillains. What can you do?

Chapter 10: Remix

Many villains turn to music in their off hours. There are the obvious music-themed villains like Soprano, Deathstep, the Flaming Flautist, DeciBullet, and heavy metal group/bank robbers Blood-Dark Night, but even more traditional villains like Grammar Cop and Heavy Hand have been known to throw the occasional karaoke night.

Other villains are more public about their musicianship and keep their villainy private. Malatha Roberts is the given name of the supervillain known as the Bite, but her fans knew her better as the singer Vampatha. She was in great demand on the goth club circuit and had just signed a record deal rumored to be worth six figures when she was arrested for her part in the theft of nearly a thousand pints of donated blood at Red Cross locations across the country.

"The Secret Lives of Supervillains"
The Burr, Kent State University
Caroline Henderson, Fall 2017
Reprinted in *The Plain Dealer*, March 15, 2018

Just because I was a secret adult and a totally awesome superhero doesn't mean I stopped being a bit of a dork. I played clarinet in the marching band, and it was pretty much the only part of my high school do-over I didn't completely loathe. (Apart from my friends, obviously.) The feeling of playing your lungs out along with 149 of your favorite nerds is like nothing else in the world.

Still, even I wasn't dorky enough to adore sweating heavily in a polyester uniform on a Saturday evening in July. We were lined up behind the bleachers, waiting to take the field at the Parma Summer Invitational, when my wristcomm buzzed.

Surreptitiously popping the earpiece into place, I heard an alert from the call center at Everett Mansion: *"—gency in progress. All available heroes report in. Cataclysm Rating 7. Repeat: Emergency in progress..."* I blinked; 7 was a plague, minor alien invasion, or newborn god-thing, none of which I remembered happening in Cleveland in 2014. Either the alert wasn't local, or the timeline had just pulled its first major diversion outside of my own interventions.

I gave Sarah the nod. She announced I wasn't feeling well. Mr. G, the band director, managed to fit irritation and sympathy into a single facial expression, and I dashed for the nearest restroom to call the TroubleShooters.

"What've we got, and where?"

"Zombie infestation, downtown and starting to spread," said Ruby Goldberg. She actually sounded excited.

"Zombies are creepy," I reminded her.

"Kick 'em in the head," Ruby cheerfully advised. *"Where are you?"*

"I'm doing a thing," I said vaguely. "I'm kind of stranded, but I can probably call Milo for a ride."

"Naw, hang tight until we have more of a plan. We're on our way to meet the EDC now." The EDC was W.H.A.M.'s Extranormal Disease Containment division. Zombie plagues and alien bio-weapons were their sort of thing.

"Just the Shooters?"

"Most of Leviathan are still on their way back from the Andromeda galaxy. The call's been routed to them anyway, but the laws of physics only bend so far. Well, most of the time."

"So what kind of zombies are we dealing with here?"

"Kind?" That was Match's voice; presumably Ruby had me on speaker in the ShooterVan.

"There are eight distinct classes of zombie, and 14 subclasses," Ruby explained. *"Dude, don't you know anything?"*

"Hi Bounceback! It's rock zombies," Lift said.

"Mineral or musical?" I asked.

"The latter," Ruby said. *"EDC's identified the plague's epicenter at a Led Zeppelin tribute band concert at the Rock Hall. Apparently the alignment of the stars tonight and the particular chord progressions in 'The Immigrant Song' intersected to activate an ancient tablet which had been disguised as a prop in a museum display."*

And that explained why I had no memory of zombies.

"Uh, guys? I think this one might possibly be kinda my fault," I said.

I recounted the straightforward version of the story, the bit where I just had a psychic impulse and stopped a robbery. I left out the part about having lived through a version of history where Train Wreck had gotten away with his heist, and as a result the ancient artifact I'd mistaken for a cheap prop had been safely elsewhere when the stars and the music aligned.

"Don't dwell on it, cuchura, *"* Lift said. *"If I had a dime for every time a simple intervention inadvertently allowed for the awakening of an ancient evil..."*

"You'd have twenty cents?"

"Well, none that I know of. But it seemed like the thing to say. I still mean it!"

"Anyway," Ruby said. *"The tablet disturbed a seriously old, entirely literal Rock God that had been slumbering in a salt deposit somewhere beneath Lake Erie. It immediately began feeding on the concert-goers and transforming them into your typical shambling brain-dead army."*

"But you called this a plague," I said. "So it's spreading?"

"The Zeppelin tribute band keeps playing the same song—"

"The band's stuck on 'repeat,'" Match shouted over her, *"and the zombies are set to 'shuffle!' Get it?"*

I laughed, everyone else groaned, and Ruby continued. *"Each time, the music gets louder. As its audible radius pushes outward, so do the zombie sightings. EDC thinks the infected are actually being used to pass on the noise."*

"So we're dealing with a communicable concert?"

"Pretty much. EDC's working on a way to jam the band, but so far every counter-frequency they've tried has only made it louder."

"How the heck is a supposedly ancient musical deity fueled by electronically produced music?" I asked.

"We've been wondering that too," Lift said. *"Was it always like that? Or did it change over time? The EDC says they've pretty much narrowed it down to three possible explanations: time-traveler induced paradox, alien invaders from another dimension, or just a statistical inevitability of the infinite diversity of life forms."*

"Assuming we don't stumble on better information in the course of getting this fixed, the EDC will vote on the least ridiculous option in the morning. That'll be the backstory they'll include in the press release," Ruby said. I wondered how many Least Ridiculous Options I'd reported as fact in my book.

"We do know this much for sure," Lift said. *"This god doesn't just love to rock. It's actually repelled by older styles of instrumentation. Something about the pure tones and harmonic resonance."*

"Pure tones?" I echoed.

"Yeah, but they said we need live musicians," Lift replied. *"They tried to pipe in some Bach from someone's phone but it didn't work. And the concert has so many carriers at this point, we'd need an army*

to beat it back. We'd basically have to round up the Cleveland Orchestra on the back of an 18-wheeler."

I had a brilliant, terribly dangerous idea.

Wandering back out of the restroom, I turned the audio gain on my wristcomm as wide as it would go. The Laketon Marching Dragons had taken the field without me and were blasting the evening with Starship's "We Built This City."

"This sound pure enough for you?" I asked the Shooters.

"Where did you say you were?" Ruby said.

"Bounceback, we're coming to get you," said Lift, quicker on the uptake. *"We're coming to get everyone."*

As soon as I was off the line with the Shooters, I hurried to find Mr. G. on the sidelines, claiming I had a stomach thing going on, apologizing profusely, and telling him my Mom was in the audience and would be taking me home. Then I went straight back to the restroom, taking off my band uniform to reveal my lightweight Bounceback costume underneath. As I stuffed my band gear back into my duffel, I called Sarah. She and the rest of the Dragons were starting the final number of our concert show, which made it the perfect time to bring her up to speed. With all that color and noise, no one would notice a single clarinet muttering into a hidden comm device.

"I know I'm not supposed to say this anymore," I told her. "But I really think tonight is what all this time travel malarkey's been about. I'm the one who accidentally woke an ancient evil! Only it wasn't an accident, because future Ruby Goldberg planned it this way. It was bound to wake up sooner or later, but this way, I'm in just the right place, with everyone we need to stop it!"

"If that's the case," Sarah replied, *"then where's Milo right now?"*

"Call him as soon as you get off the field. Tell him to get his butt to the EDC office downtown and help out there, then call and let them know he's coming."

"Will do," Sarah promised. *"So what will you be doing?"*

Suited and masked, I bounced over the low fence surrounding the track just as my bandmates were leaving the field. While the crowd gawked at the sudden superhero in their midst, I swiped a megaphone from another band's director, then launched myself high into the air, flipped, and landed in the center of the Astroturf.

"Good evening, everyone!" I addressed the assembled marchers. "I'm Bounceback, and I'm here on behalf of the TroubleShooters. Who wants to help us save the city tonight?"

The band directors took quite a bit of convincing, and the parents even more, but by the time the ShooterVan pulled up, all five bands were already loading their buses. The Shooters split up to ride along with the bands—I stuck with the Dragons—and ten minutes later we were racing downtown, with a police escort leading the way. As we passed into the city proper, each band's drivers were directed to follow a different patrol car, peeling away from the convoy one by one, until only ours remained. Two of the bands looped around to approach the Rock Hall along the eastbound Shoreway, two more would come in westbound, while the Dragons and I came up East 9th.

We followed a pair of motorcycle cops into an empty parking lot just off of Orange Avenue. The roadies hurried to help the drum and sousaphone lines unpack their instruments from the trailer while I met with Mr. G., our field commander Laura, and the section leaders. None of them seemed to recognize me, but I pitched my voice a little lower than normal just to be safe.

"All you have to do," I told them, "is march straight up that road there, playing your parade medley as loud and proud as you can. If you get to the end, start over immediately. No resting at cadence."

Laura sighed resignedly, holding out her baton. "I suppose you'll be wanting this."

"No, you keep it," I said, and her face lit up. "I'll be right beside you, punching zombies if they get too close, but you'll still be leading. Just do what you do."

At the same moment, Lift, Manaaki, Match and Ruby were each with one of the other bands, in other parking lots, getting ready to march with their field commanders and drum majors.

"Uhh, guys?" Ruby said over the comm. *"Why am I watching the color guard warm up with the sparkly flags?"*

"Because you like girls?" said Lift. *"Just don't be a creepster about it."*

"I like lots of people," Ruby said. *"I meant, why are they here?"*

"They go with the band," I said. Obviously.

"Alrighty then," Ruby said. *"Two minutes to step-off. Everybody ready?"*

The first quarter mile passed like any other parade. Well, any other parade held at 10 p.m. through empty streets, with police officers marching beside us, lighting our way with industrial-size Mag-Lite flashlights. But the band played the school fight song, took an 8-count to catch their breaths, and rolled right into Ravel's "Bolero." The trumpets sang out for attention, while Nate and the other trombones ripped the air. The sousaphones were, as ever, delightfully flatulent. Half the clarinets were off-key, though Sarah I'm sure was dead on. I desperately wished I could be back there playing with them.

Then we spotted a massive crowd filling the road up ahead, and heard the Rock God's concert droning beneath our own song. In a perfectly synchronized piece of mass choreography that was stunning the first time the world saw it in "Thriller" but was really just derivative here, the entire zombie mob swung around to face our approach.

I gasped. Most of this block had been evacuated less than an hour ago. The group of enthralled Clevelanders staring us down had been among the last to be zombified, but even from a distance I could see their physical deterioration. Their skin was sallow and ashy, their elbows and knees arthritically bent, their cheeks sunken. The Rock God's music poured out of their open mouths, but they weren't singing. They were lip syncing, their mouths always a second behind the words.

The song battered at our brains like a Steve Perry power ballad. The EDC had assured us that the brass, winds, and drums of the bands would protect us from the Rock God's disease, but I could feel the song softening us up, making us want desperately to board that Crazy Train.

A mellophone player, three trumpets and a couple of cymbal-carriers panicked and broke ranks, ducking between the police and trying to run back the way we'd come. I chased them down and yelled them back into line.

"Bolero" ended and the theme from *Robin Hood: Prince of Thieves* began right on its heels. The zombies closed ranks again behind us, and then there was nowhere for any of us to run. But the "pure tones" theory seemed to prove itself. As long as the band was playing, the zombies stayed a good thirty feet back. The center of the mob parted before us, little by little, repelled by the music. Laura and Mr. G. strode forward with heads high, Laura's baton flashing in the darkness. The music picked up some extra vibrato, but for the next mile and a half, the band held its collective nerve.

As we neared the Rock Hall, a new sound rose on our right, just audible under our own blare: not the mind-bludgeoning rock of the god, but Rossini's "William Tell Overture," better known as the "Lone

Ranger" theme. Tonight the masked man it announced was Manaaki, leading the Normandy Invaders through another gap in the mob. No sooner had they emerged than Ruby appeared on the left with the Lakewood Rangers, to the tune of Kool & the Gang's "Jungle Boogie." Then further ahead, marching their bands in from the west and east respectively came Match and the Hudson Explorers, busting out Fleetwood Mac's "Tusk," and Lift with the Medina Battling Bees and "The Battle Hymn of the Republic."

The five bands converged, each cutting their own path through the zombie mosh pit at the center of the Dark Rocker's concert, each playing a different song. They did not harmonize, round, mash-up, or otherwise blend. The sounds collided, crashed into and over and under one another like cars piling up on a highway. The bands fell into one single cacophonous line and kept marching, right into the white vinyl concert pavilion that had been erected alongside the museum.

Inspired by the competition, the bands played louder than one would expect after a field show and a two-mile parade. The Laketon trumpets actually doubled their previous volume. I wasn't sure where they found the capacity, as they'd been blaring pretty painfully to begin with, but Milo later showed me some equations involving ego and hot air production that made perfect sense of it all.

As we approached, some of the zombies ripped right through the walls of the tent, staggering away to make room for the marchers or escape the noise or both. But they didn't go far. I could see their stooping shadows on the vinyl, ringing the pavilion and closing us in.

Before us on the stage was the Zeppelin tribute band, glassy-eyed and washed out, like a grayscale photo of themselves. They played sluggishly, each guitar-thrum and drumbeat making my entire body throb. Above them hovered the Rock God, manifesting at that moment in the form of Ziggy Stardust. The glitter on his face sparkled, hunger burned in his eyes, and glowing lines of impure light extended from his fingertips to each member of the band. The musicians were leashed by their own life energies, even as the god threatened to drain them dry.

"All the nightmares came today!" the Rock God sang out in greeting. "And it looks as though they're here to stay." Its every word stabbed needles into my brain.

Beside me, Laura the field commander blew her whistle, her baton punching the air. The Dragons kicked off a glorious arrangement of Europe's "The Final Countdown," drowning out the sound from the giant outdoor speakers on either side of the stage. My headache lifted slightly and I took a deep breath, trying to shake off the Rock God's influence.

As soon as it realized that we were fighting back, the god's seductive grin turned into an angry scowl. Its garish makeup faded and its bright hair darkened until Joan Jett floated before us. Hands in fingerless gloves pulled a guitar out of thin air as it called for us to put another dime in the jukebox, baby.

I bounced toward the Medina Bees, the better to hear their stirring rendition of "Rawhide," clashing horribly with the Dragons and their '80s pop. From the other side, the Normandy Invaders had started another round of their fight song. I found myself a place where I could see each of the Shooters; we stayed at the ready in case the baddie tried to get physical, but for the moment this battle was up to the bands.

Joan Jett hardened into Jim Morrison, welcoming us to the End, then melted into Siouxie of the Banshees and tried to set our wheels on fire. With each change the god sucked more energy from its thralls, and the more energy it drank the louder its concert grew, and the harder to ignore. Some of the musicians behind me began to drop out.

I heard Sarah stop blowing long enough to yell down the line, "Freshmen, I will CUT YOU!"

The god became Freddie Mercury, crooning "I want to break free..."

It very nearly did. But beneath its hovering feet, the tribute band was fading fast. The singer hung drunkenly from his microphone stand, while the guitarist and bass player were on their knees on the stage, cradling their instruments like babies, their bloody fingers squeaking and sliding on the frets. The drummer actually had his head down on the snare, eyes closed, one hand still tapping away at a cymbal in perfect time. They couldn't last much longer.

The Rock God kept feeding, certain that it could break us before the band on stage died. For a fleeting instant I feared we'd played right into its hand, bringing it seven hundred new musicians, a fresh source of music just as its originals were burning themselves out.

Then my wristcomm buzzed three times in a pre-arranged signal from Lift. I bellowed, "NOW!" and Laura threw her baton. 50 drummers beat out a four-count, more or less in sync.

The combined power of the Dragons, Invaders, Rangers, Explorers, and Battling Bees blasted the Rock God with the one tune everyone knew: "The Star-Spangled Banner."

By the third measure, the god started to shake. By the seventh, the tribute band threw down their instruments, snapped the light-leashes with their bare hands, and rolled themselves off the stage. Against the rockets' red glare, the Rock God put on one last face. Tina Turner snarled, "I might have been queen!" and exploded in a shower of gleaming thirty-second notes.

The bands finished the anthem anyway.

With the Rock God destroyed, the life force drained from the Citizens Formerly Known as Zombies was returned to them, and an EDC sorcerer was able to safely contain the tablet that had caused this whole mess. The EDC med-techs gave the high schoolers a quick once-over before allowing them back on the buses, checking under hats and fingernails for tablet dust, listening for unconscious humming, looking for any tiny sign that some last shred of the Rock God might be lying in wait for a sequel. Milo worked with them, wearing a mask so he wouldn't be recognized by any of our schoolmates, wielding some kind of high tech beeping scanner wand and grumbling about the messes made by ancient magic-users.

"I guess it's too much work to actually *dispose* of all their stupid-dangerous rocks and books and weapons. No, they always just go hiding them or disguising them instead. And inevitably crap like this happens, and it's up to us to fix..."

Sarah ran over to me, leaning in close to my ear. "So, are you still from the future?"

"Still here, all memories intact," I murmured back.

"Oh. Sorry."

"Me too. I mean, what the hell? We vanquish an entire GOD, and that's not important enough for me to get sent home, or at least get some frickin' answers? What was the point?"

"I wish I knew, Bounceback. I really do," Sarah said.

She moved to join the line to be scanned—some of the other clarinets were yelling at her to stop fangirling at the superhero—but turned back one more time. "But if, if you're wrong and this is it and you never go back, would that be so bad, really?"

I looked away. At the musicians and color guard in their clumps, already telling each other stories about the same adventure they'd all just experienced, hands and instruments gesturing emphatically. At the gaggle of seniors from various bands jamming together, busting out "It's Not Unusual" while Ruby Goldberg danced like a nerd. At Match copying sousaphones and euphoniums for an awed audience, and a grinning Lift balancing a giggling Manaaki over her head on the tips of her fingers, tossing him lightly from hand to hand.

I thought about spending more time with the Shooters, a lot more. I thought about college again, with some exciting new major and probably a lot more phys-ed. About dating in college, maybe, eventually. About a whole new life.

I didn't let myself think about it for long. But for that one moment, I didn't entirely hate the idea.

Chapter 11: Relocate

For as long as super powered heroes have publicly served in the United States, they have demanded special privileges to "follow their gut" at the expense of strict due process. Some heroes demonstrate unique abilities that offer some logical justification to this insistence: clairvoyance, x-ray vision, special sensitivities to danger or opportunity, enhanced luck, or communication with ghosts, gods, or other extradimensional entities. Others simply argue that continued exposure to the extranormal grants them more reliable instincts than your average human. Such arguments prove difficult to empirically verify, yet more often than not, super-heroic deductive methods do achieve a higher success and lower mortality rate than traditional police work without super involvement.

Congressional legislation has therefore pronounced "heroic intuition" legally equivalent to a limited search warrant; if a hero follows her instincts into the scene of a crime, any wrongdoing witnessed firsthand can be prosecuted as if she'd had a warrant from a judge, provided a court appointed telepath can verify that the hero suspected this particular crime to be taking place before entry. She cannot legally report on any other unlawful activities she might witness in the process, excepting those involving immediate danger to innocent parties.

- Dying for a Laugh

My seventeenth birthday arrived, again, two weeks after the zombie outbreak, and a week after I finished summer school with a B+. My summer birthday made me one of the youngest in my class, so previous birthdays had always been about finally catching up with my peers, which seemed kind of ironic now. This time, obviously, 17 was just a do-over. I should have been turning 27, but it felt more like my 26-year-old life was on pause. With luck, I'd soon get to pick it up where I left off. If I didn't, if my teenage self had been living it in my absence, then I hoped she'd taken decent care of my apartment. But with everything else that was going on, July 15, 2014, felt like just another day, albeit a day with two parties.

The first was a lunch at Chili's with Mom, Dad, Sarah, Nate, Liz, and Tamika, and proceeded more or less exactly like I remembered. There were a few small gifts, including an Amazon gift card from Sarah which she warned me had $0 on it, a cover in front of our friends for her actual present, to be opened later.

My second party was held at Denny's late that night, with Sarah, Milo, and the Shooters. Marci and Nicole had made a cake in the shape of the TroubleShooter van, complete with a big red button on a separate plastic steering wheel that played *The 1812 Overture*, and the world's tiniest fireworks shooting from the tailpipe when the cannons sounded. Once we'd all demolished that, Sarah took Marci back into the staff area, and when they came back, Marci was levitating a large wrapped box, as tall and as wide as a really nice desk.

"So here's my real present," Sarah said.

"Half a present," Milo said.

I blinked. "That's only half?"

"He means it's only half mine," Sarah said. "It was all my idea, but he built the thing. We've been working on it for months."

"Okay then," I said, tearing away the wrapping. I yanked loose the tape at the top and ripped up the flaps to find the box was the size of a desk because it contained, in fact, a desk. It was simply but elegantly carved from a dark, shiny wood, and heavy.

I hefted it easily from the box and set it on the floor for a better look. "Wow. Guys, this is gorgeous. Milo, you actually made this?"

"You're not giving up tech for carpentry, are you?" Nicole asked. "I know my competition is fierce, but—"

"Of course not!" Milo said. "Caroline, check the middle drawer."

I slid back the drawer in question, and pulled out what appeared to be a store brand universal remote control. "Okay?"

"Now double tap the fast forward button," Sarah said, her voice excitedly buzzing.

I did. With a whirr of gears and an 8-bit chorus of bleeps and bloops, the entire desk transformed. The top surface flipped up ninety degrees, exposing a backside set with hefty black metal brackets. The drawers along the sides slid open by themselves, their bottoms folding out to show off battery packs and trailing wires with nothing for them to plug into. It was all very impressive, I was sure.

"O...kay?"

"Obviously it's not finished," Milo said. "Top-notch crime computers, satellite relays, laser eyes and digital noses, that stuff's super expensive, even with a W.H.A.M. discount. So I'm designing some of my own from scratch. I should have it all installed by, I dunno, January maybe?"

"Let me take a look, we'll have it done by Halloween," offered Nicole.

"But we wanted you to see how it's gonna work tonight," Sarah said. "Milo's first idea was to talk to your dad about retrofitting your basement, so you'd hit a button and your dad's bar and all the furniture would rotate or slide away and turn into a whole crime lab—"

"I was gonna call it, 'rec room to tech room.' They had all the components for something like that in one of the steward's catalogs Sarah and I started getting after we got licensed," Milo said.

"But I pointed out that we're all going to college in like a year, so it didn't make sense to give you something that wasn't portable."

Sarah practically glowed with pride, to the point I half expected Nicole to whip out a gadget and scan for cosmic radiation. I stared at my new present and avoided Sarah's eyes. This was huge. It was months of work already, and more to come. Why would Sarah put so much effort into something like this when I probably wouldn't even be around long enough to use it? Not this me, the superhero me.

As if that was a question. As if Sarah hadn't been all but begging me to stay for months. As if it was up to me.

"So!" prodded Sarah. "Crime lab in a desk. You like?"

"I love it, you guys!" I said, grinning big enough to hurt. "I mean, right now it's more like empty space in a desk. But that's cool too."

I double tapped the remote again, making the whole thing *bleep-bloop-whirr* itself back into an ordinary desk.

"If it's too loud, don't worry about it," Milo said. "The mechanics are nearly silent, actually. I programmed the sounds to play along just for fun."

"We were going for classic," Sarah said.

"It's perfect," I said hugging them both simultaneously. My writing desk at home wasn't nearly this cool. But maybe when I got back it would be?

After the Rock God battle, I'd stripped the color-coding from my future crimes chart, focusing less on my notes about upcoming supervillain attacks and more on training with the TroubleShooters. It had become clear that my foreknowledge was only part of the trans-temporal puzzle. If something as simple as derailing the theft of a cheap museum prop could lead to a zombie concert nearly overrunning the city, then it was useless to speculate on the ultimate effects of the slightest intervention. Whatever future-Ruby needed me to do, I could only keep my eyes open, and trust that I'd find myself in the right place at the right time.

Like Sarah had been telling me to do for months.

Sarah saw my dedication to training as settling in to my second life, and I didn't have the heart to tell her otherwise. I also didn't want to risk her following through on her threat of making me pay $5 every time I talked about the mission; she'd finally convinced her parents to buy her a car and let her pay them back. It was a junky silver 2002 Honda Civic, but she loved it like a child.

On August 18, just over a week before I was due to restart my senior year of high school, I called the TroubleShooters and told them I'd had a vision. Sugar Mama had dripped her way out of prison again, and was looking to hit a bank or six on her way into hiding. I could just as easily have left the message anonymously on W.H.A.M.'s tip line. In my original timeline, Sugar Mama had tied the world record for Most Successful Bank Heists in a Single Day (Solo), but without any serious injuries to bank personnel or innocent bystanders. She'd pulled a couple more jobs in the coming months, also casualty-free, before her incredibly fitting capture by Sweet Tooth. I still had a book and a half of my summer reading to finish up, and Sarah was at Denny's until nine, so I could have been curled up in a corner booth with a milkshake and *Things Fall Apart*, but I felt like hanging out with my hero friends and getting punchy instead.

So there we were, in a dead-end alley at six o'clock on a summer evening, trying to beat the crap out of a pile of sugar. We'd blocked off the road with the ShooterVan and a couple of Ruby's port-a-barriers, but were still having difficulties containing our confectionery fugitive.

Lift tried to scoop Mama up telekinetically, but there was the tiniest gap in her concentration, and Sugar Mama slithered out like sand through an hourglass.

Manaaki had marginally more luck extending his own force-field around our foe, only to be swarmed and pinned down by a small army of doughgirls. These were a new trick Sugar Mama had developed during her time in the Cuyahoga County ExtraMax prison; now she could split parts of her mass off into an army of miniature sugar-selves, each bearing a disturbing resemblance to the Pillsbury mascot. Their fists might've been tiny, but since they were inside Manaaki's protection, their blows actually landed on his face, his arms, his legs, and worse. He let go.

Ruby theorized that even a sugar-shifter had to keep a central processing neural cluster somewhere, and just kept stun-blasting sugar clumps at random with one of her ginormous pulse rifles.

Personally, I favored the direct approach, watching for Sugar Mama to manifest a face and hitting it really hard. She thinned her face to powder, absorbing the blow, then hit back with a sledgehammer fist compacted to the density of rock candy, and with all the same rough edges. It hurt.

Match grabbed a squirming doughgirl in both hands and tried to copy it, hoping that maybe he could control the clone and turn it back on the original, but the duplicate didn't have the original's spark of life. It melted into a pasty mush all over his hands and sleeves.

"Gyuck!" he said, flapping his arms wildly. Dough droplets flew everywhere, including my hair.

Eventually Sarah, on her wristcomm from the back room of Denny's during her dinner break, asked, "Why don't you just bake them?"

I couldn't think of a good reason why not, so I repeated her idea for the benefit of the team.

The others took a moment out of the fight to turn and give me A Look, but Ruby's only lasted a second before her eyebrows shot up. "Yes. Yes! I can do that!"

She dashed for the ShooterVan, cracking open a panel on the side of her pulse rifle and yanking out wiring as she ran.

"How long?" Lift asked, using the comm so she didn't have to yell.

"Five minutes. Less," replied Ruby.

She left the comm channel open, intentionally I'm sure, so the rest of us could hear her working while we kept Sugar Mama busy. I picked out the snip of wire-clippers, the crackle and hiss of something getting soldered into place, and the occasional violent crash-bang. All the while, Ruby was muttering to herself, "Minimize force, maximize heat..."

Sensing something was up, Mama fought harder, swinging multiple rock candy fists. Her blows rained down faster, and her doughgirls multiplied.

Finally, as even Lift was beginning to droop, Ruby leapt from the van, her rebuilt rifle now not only plugged into the giant power pack strapped to her back, but also trailing a thick cable leading back to the ShooterVan's microwave.

Yes, the van had its own microwave. Mostly for after-fight popcorn.

Ruby actually yelled, "Cookie time!" as she shot the first doughgirl. Her pulse gun was now an Easy Bake Oven Ray. It caramelized the little creature instantly. Sugar Mama cried out in pain, as the tiny cookie fell to the pavement and crumbled.

Ruby kept firing, making short work of the doughy fighters. Sugar Mama started scooping up the cookies and crumbs with her grainy hands, but she couldn't reabsorb them fast enough. The larger portions of her body baked more slowly, but I could see her pummeling arms starting to turn brittle.

It was Match who broke her, not with a fist, but a well-timed, "Anyone think to bring a gallon of milk?"

Sugar Mama surrendered.

It took nearly an hour to see Sugar Mama processed at the police station, and another after that for Ruby to help the station engineers modify a set of restraints to keep the villain solid and in her cell until her trial date. By the time Ruby finished it was almost ten, we were all too exhausted and gross even for Denny's, and Sarah's shift was over anyway. I called to let her know I was heading straight home, got her voicemail, and assumed she'd gone out with coworkers.

Sarah's mom called my house in a panic at 6:15 the next morning. Sarah wasn't in her room, and her car wasn't in the drive.

"Last night, when she didn't come home after work, I assumed you'd gone out, that she just forgot to call. I was angry, but I went to bed, planning to yell at her in the morning. But now—"

I told Sarah's mom not to worry. The second I hung up I called Sarah's phone, in case she was just angry with her mother for some reason she hadn't yet bothered to tell me about. She didn't answer. I called all of our friends next, including the ones Sarah's mom said she was going to try, on the same principle. No more luck there. I tried pinging Sarah's wristcomm for a location but couldn't get a signal. We live in an imperfect world with imperfect technology, I told myself. I called Denny's, where one of Sarah's managers said she'd left just after 9:00 p.m. as scheduled, and she hadn't said anything about going anywhere other than home. I thanked her, and called Milo.

Milo hadn't heard from Sarah either.

"I don't suppose you secretly tag all your friends with radio tracking devices?" I asked, only half kidding.

"*Sorry boss,*" Milo replied. "*But I maybe could—*"

"Hold that thought." I had a call waiting. I barely had time to hope it was Sarah before I glanced at the screen and saw the call was from Denny's.

"I just checked the parking lot," Sarah's manager said. *"Sarah's car is still here."*

"Someone's taken Sarah," I almost choked on the words as I switched back to Milo's line.

"What? Was that—?"

I explained about the car. "You had a thought a minute ago. What was it?"

"Huh? Oh, her phone, most of them can be tracked like GPS. I thought I could, but the police will be doing that anyway, right?"

"Do it. Race them." On some level I probably had sensible doubts about encouraging him like that, but at that moment they were entirely drowned out by the voice chanting at the back of my head: *This didn't happen, my Sarah was never—*

I didn't have time to listen to any of that.

I hung up on Milo and conference-called the Shooters. They were all in bed, wouldn't otherwise have crawled out before ten at the earliest, but every one of them was running for their costume before they hung up the comm.

Then I called the Cleveland Police, a direct line to a special department via a number I'd received when I went semi-pro.

"I need to report the suspected kidnapping of my steward," I said, my voice surprisingly level. I gave my license number and Sarah's. The officer said the call was already going out, and took my wrist-comm number to stay in touch.

I called Sarah's mom back, told her about the car, told her I'd already informed the police. She actually thanked me.

At last I was able to drop the phone to my bed. It took everything I had not to hurl the thing into the wall. Finally I could pull on my costume, pick the stupid phone back up and shove it into my pocket. I burst from my room, nearly bowling over my mother in the process.

"Honey? What's wrong?"

I explained.

She yelled, "RICK! HANK!"

"Whaaaat?" groaned my father, but ten seconds later he stumbled from the bedroom in his shorts. He snapped from bleary to sharp-awake the instant he saw our faces. Hank emerged from his own room in rumpled clothes he'd no doubt slept in, silent and blinking.

Mom filled them in, then started on the orders. "Get dressed, eat something if you need to, but we need to be with Eugene and Dale right now."

Leaving Mom to take care of things at home, I took off on my scooter, its small but determined engine ripping a hole in the quiet of the morning. I had my helmet on, like always, and the bike's holograms were engaged, not just to obscure the scooter's own design and plates, but to make my costume less recognizable as well. The neighbors would only see that weird Henderson girl making a nuisance of herself.

As I rode, I half expected to get a call back from Ruby Goldberg at any second. Preferably from the future Ruby. Because clearly this was it, for real. This had to be it. Whatever supervillain I'd been sent back in time to defeat was on the move, they had my best friend, and I still had no freaking clue who or what I was up against. Thank you *so much*, Ruby, for that total lack of information!

Denny's was already a circus by the time I arrived, most of the parking lot taken up by two police cruisers, one unmarked cop car with a light on top, the ShooterVan, and Sarah's grungy Civic, looking lonely behind its yellow tape cordon. Three of the four TroubleShooters stood near that tape, shoulders hunched. Match's arms were folded across his chest and his head was down. Lift and Manaaki stood a foot apart, unusual for them, but bridged the gap with tightly clasped hands.

I parked my bike, dropped my helmet and joined them. Lift leaned up to give mè a hug, which I accepted stiffly. "What've we got?"

"The police are talking to everyone who was here last night when Sarah left," Lift said. "Trying to see if anybody saw or heard anything."   ·

"Is that where Ruby is? Helping them?"

"Not with that," Lift said. "She's with the guy going through the security cam footage."

"Okay. All right. So out here we're looking for clues?"

"Sure. What do they look like, then?" Match said. Lift and Manaaki both glared at him, but he was right. I realized I had no idea either. When I wrote my books about supercrime, the clues my subjects left behind were almost universally big, loud, and desperate for attention. Sometimes complex to interpret, like riddles, performance art, or poetry worthy of internet greeting cards, but impossible to miss. The subtle details of everyday police work were still a mystery in themselves to me.

"Okay," I said again. "The car. Her car. Have the cops checked it for, I don't know, signs of a struggle? Forced entry, something?"

"They looked. They found her wristcomm on the ground nearby. It had been stomped on," Lift said. That would explain why I couldn't get a location ping. "Other than that, they just said it was unlocked."

I ducked under the tape and went to have a look myself, and found a long scratch I'd never seen before on the driver's side door, just beside the keyhole. "This is new," I said loudly. The others came to join me. "This is a sign of a struggle."

I strained to ignore the scene as it played in my head: my best friend, not the brassy twenty-something I knew best, but a scared-to-death teenager, clawing at the car door with her keys as she fought to get away. From what? Who?

I didn't know. I couldn't know. I wasn't actually psychic, and imagining got me nowhere. It just hurt.

I got down on my hands and knees, triggering the tiny LED on the side of my mask as I peered underneath the car. The Shooters got down as well, looking under Sarah's Civic and the other cars nearby.

Seconds later, Match shouted, "Keys! I've got keys!"

"DON'T TOUCH THEM!" Lift, Manaaki and I yelled simultaneously.

"All right, all right!" Match said, raising his hands in surrender. We crowded around him, following his pointing finger to the set of keys that had fallen under the SUV next to where Sarah had parked.

"Yeah, those are hers," I said. "I can see the *Wreck-It Ralph* keychain."

"I got 'em," Lift said, reaching out her hand but stopping several inches short of where the keys actually lay. Slowly, jingling, the keys floated up off the parking lot asphalt and retracted through empty space towards Lift's open hand. She didn't allow them to touch, but instead kept pulling her hand back, always keeping the keys about a foot in front of her fingers, even as she stood and started walking towards the van.

"This isn't as easy as I make it look," she said. "Even just holding them with my brain, I can still smudge the prints if I'm not very, very careful."

She was that careful, and lowered the keys into the laser scanner in the van's crime lab without a hitch.

A mere 30 seconds later, the scanner pinged. The only clear prints anywhere on the keys or keychain belonged to Sarah's mom and Sarah herself. The van computer printed out an evidence form confirming these results, which Lift signed as primary and the rest of us signed as witnesses, with our codenames. This would be presented to the police for their files on the case, and I was then within my rights to reclaim the keys on my steward's behalf.

The rubber figurine on the keychain was scuffed, a black smear like a stain across the front of Vanellope von Schweetz's teal sweater. Somehow that offended me as much as anything had that day. I pulled off my glove, licked my thumb and tried to rub the mark away. I was still trying when Ruby stuck her head into the van.

"We're getting nothing on the security tapes, which don't even cover the frelling parking lot."

"How are the interviews going?" Lift asked, nodding in the direction of the restaurant.

"I wasn't really close enough to hear much, but not so good from the looks of it. I don't think anybody heard anything."

"Crap," Match said.

My wristcomm chirped.

Ten seconds later I was bounding from the van and running for my bike. Milo had finally managed a trace on Sarah's phone. I blasted down I-90, the ShooterVan speeding along behind me, its horn blasting *The 1812 Overture* to clear the way.

We found Sarah's phone in a ditch to one side of the highway, just outside of Cleveland city limits. There were no useful prints on the casing and no recent calls to or from numbers I couldn't recognize. When Lift picked the phone up out of the dirt, my name was still visible on the screen. When her abductor threw the phone from the car, Sarah had been trying to call me.

That was as close as we came that day to a clue. We drove to Everett Mansion after that, Lift arguing that a workout was the best use of our time until the police called us with a lead. We beat each other tired, but that call never came. Finally I rode home, put civilian clothes on over my costume, and had Hank drive me back to Denny's with a note from Sarah's parents, so I could retrieve Sarah's car in their stead. Mom and Dad had spent the entire day with the Gordons, two police detectives, and a negotiator, but the kidnapper never called.

The first 24 hours are said to be crucial in any kidnapping investigation. After that, it is presumed that the victim has been taken across state lines. Realistically, in a world with magic and teleportation, supervillains don't need 24 hours to get that far. Still, at 9 p.m. Saturday I was at Milo's, the two of us watching the clock on his computer. I'd asked him to hack into the network of the police station working Sarah's case, on the off chance they'd uncovered any information that they hadn't passed on to the TroubleShooters immediately. Milo committed this felony with neither hesitation nor pride. He covered his tracks well, which was good, as we received no new data for our trouble. 9 o'clock passed. So did 10 o'clock, then midnight, then 2 a.m.

I don't remember when Milo convinced me to go home and try to get some rest. I didn't fall asleep until sometime after dawn, with my phone clutched in my hand and my costume still on under my clothes.

"Hey, Caro. Hey." I woke to Dad crouched down by my bed, whispering to get my attention. "No news," he said, before I could even ask. I checked the computer anyway; no updates there either, from Milo or the cops or the Shooters. The clock on the corner of my screen read 1:12 p.m.

"It's still Sunday?" I croaked from a dry throat.

Dad was already handing me a glass of water. "Yeah. Mom's at the Gordons'. There are some people downstairs to see you. Tamika and Liz."

Nate's family was in South Carolina this week. I wondered if anyone had texted him yet. What a way to ruin a vacation.

"Tell 'em I'll be down in a minute?"

"Sure thing," Dad said.

It was more than a minute. I took a long shower, longer than I intended, bracing myself against the tile wall with my head down and letting the spray pummel my back, before putting on fresh clothes over a fresh costume. I started to sweat almost immediately, but I was still expecting my wristcomm to buzz at any moment. I trudged downstairs, heard Tamika and Liz murmuring with Dad in the kitchen, and tried to look grateful they'd come as I entered. They vaulted up from their chairs. Tamika hung back, forcing her face into a brittle smile. Liz hugged me violently and held on.

"This sucks," she said. "This sucks! This sucks so hard."

I held on back, but it didn't feel right. These girls were practically strangers to me. I'd tried, mostly for Sarah's sake, but the longer I'd been stuck back in this time, the less they'd felt like part of my life. I knew it was my own fault; I hadn't tried very hard. I'd practically ignored them for the last eight months, but here they were anyway. I felt like a phony.

"All right, all right, enough of that," Tamika finally grumbled, and I couldn't tell if she was trying to be as funny as was allowed just then, or was genuinely annoyed.

Liz nudged me into a seat at the kitchen table, where a fast food feast was spread out for the three of us. "Your dad said you missed lunch, so we stopped at Burger King on the way over. I got shakes and everything."

"That was nice," I said. "But you guys didn't have to wait for me. I'm not really hungry."

Liz glared. "Hey! None of that now. We've all gotta keep our strength up, for the hugs we're gonna give Sarah when she gets home."

"If I have to, I will tie you to that chair and play choo-choo at the station like my mom did with me when I was two," Tamika added. "You can have a meal, or you can have a mess, it's your choice."

I surrendered. Dad reheated the by then ice cold burgers and fries in the microwave, which made the fries soggy and awful, but it wasn't like my brain was really processing much of the input from my taste buds at that point anyway. We made a couple of quiet, halting attempts at conversation, fumbling numbly over all the reasonable clichés. *How could this happen? I feel so helpless. The police are doing all they can.* We snapped them down on the table between us like pieces of a jigsaw puzzle, as if by putting enough of them together we might somehow get a picture that made sense. Dad sat with us, not eating or speaking, doing a terrible job of hiding the fact that he was watching me. After maybe ten minutes I gave him a look, and he nodded and went upstairs.

The moment Dad's footsteps had faded on the steps, it was like a switch had been thrown. The pain and sadness in Tamika's face were burned out by pure rage. Her eyes locked on mine. "So where the hell have you been?"

"What?"

"Yesterday, you call us, you tell us our best friend in the entire world has been kidnapped, and that's it? You never call us back? You don't come over? Liz and I were up all night—"

"Crying mostly," said Liz.

"—and where were you?"

Anger flushed through me. My instinctive reaction when someone gets mad at me is to reflect it right back. But I didn't want to fight. Not then. Not Tamika, anyway. So I bit my tongue.

Tamika nodded. "Fine. Sit there lookin' stupid. I know you've been getting too cool for us this year, and whatever, people change, and I don't need anyone who doesn't need me. I put up with you for Sarah's sake. But right now she's—she's in trouble, and she isn't just yours!"

With an effort like swallowing bile, I forced the rage back down into my stomach. I couldn't tell Tamika that I'd been investigating the crime. I couldn't blame Tamika because I couldn't tell her that, or because between being sad, or scared, or mad, she chose mad. A lot of people do. What's disturbing is the number who choose to be mad with ray guns and vampire glass swords. I wanted to say something, to find words that could stop her feeling like this. And I didn't doubt that Liz shared some or all of these feelings. From the corner of my eye I could see her watching us, the pained look on her face. But I couldn't think of a good enough lie, and my silence stuck.

"I'm not putting up with this," Tamika decided, pulling her keys from her pocket. "Screw you, Caroline. Liz, let's go."

Liz stood, but hesitated as Tamika turned for the door. I gave her a nod. She squeezed my hand as she went. "We're here for each other, right?"

That it was a question killed me; but how could I promise to be there when I no longer had any clue what tomorrow would bring?

Dad came back down to check on me a few minutes later. I told him I was fine, and he sat down on the couch and turned on the TV, to let somebody else fill up the silence. I couldn't think of anything productive to do, so I sat too.

Half closing my eyes, I watched bad old sitcoms from under my lashes. I kept twitching, that sudden jerking spasm you sometimes do when you're just on the edge of sleep, only I was wide awake.

Eventually I twitched with a reason; my phone was buzzing in my pocket. Text message.

Milo: hey boss
Me: anything new?
Milo: no sorry
Milo: but I'm awake. mom wanted me to stay here for dinner but I talked her out of it
Milo: i'll grab some waffles or something. i'm coming over
Me: no I'll come to you

Milo's dad offered me meatloaf. I'd had Milosevic meatloaf before, and it was the rare kind, actually good, but I declined. Milo's mom just put a hand on my shoulder, not for too long, but long enough. Enver, Milo's 11-year-old brother, told me he couldn't imagine how Milo and I were feeling, that he tried and his stomach hurt and he was sorry. Nine-year-old Anna said she could kind of imagine it, that her friend Cece's dog got lost and her parents got her a new one but she still got sad whenever she thought about the old one, so they tried not to, but Anna still looked for the old dog sometimes, calling his name when she was at the park, but don't tell Cece because Anna didn't want her to think about it if it just made her sad.

That was the point I excused myself from the dinner table and went into the living room to sit and flip through a magazine. Each word that crossed my eyes hit the back of my brain and passed right out again, like a ghost through the wall, but the static helped me not to think anything else. Soon enough Milo finished his dinner, and we went up to his room to spy on the police, watching them update Sarah's file with dead ends.

Nearly an hour passed before Milo asked me, "You never had any vaguely-psychic inkling this was going to happen?"

"Of course not. It shouldn't have."

"So what about now? How's your gut telling you this works out?"

"I don't know. I have no idea."

"No feeling?"

"Nothing useful."

"Okay," Milo said. "Okay. That's a start."

"A start to what?"

"It's a parameter. For our bad guy, we're looking for someone who's psychically masked. That's gotta narrow it down some.—"

"No!" I snapped. I forced myself to breathe, fake calm. "No, I just… It's not that precise. I miss things sometimes. The Rock God, remember?"

"But that was magic, magic always makes things screwy. Maybe we're dealing with magic again here."

"Stop. Just stop."

Milo was at his desk. I was perched on the second chair, the one Sarah had bought him, looking over his shoulder at the 22-inch flat screen monitor.

"I don't understand," he said.

"Stop. No. They're simple words," I said. "We can't assume anything, when we don't actually know anything."

"If we knew something we wouldn't be assuming, that's the definition of assume—and don't get cute and say the a-s-s of u and me thing, now's not the time. But we have to make some educated guesses here. We have to piece it together. The police are being useless!"

"They're narrowing it down with facts. They'll get there." Even at 17 I don't think I would've believed me.

"So you just want to sit here? You're a hero. I'm a steward. I know it's different this time, but this—this is what we do. We can do this. You don't think the fact that the most effective psychic in Cleveland completely failed to see this coming is a clue?"

I could've told him. I came so close to spilling the whole thing out right then: the time travel, my having lived all of this except for the really important parts before, all of it. But the questions that were sure to follow felt just as heavy as the secrets and half-truths already hanging around my neck.

"I just don't think precognition is an exact enough science to justify cutting down our list of suspects," I said.

"Fine. We'll come back to that. So what else do we know? Who else might've known Sarah was connected to Bounceback?"

Milo grilled me for the next I don't know how long. Had we told any of our other friends about my second identity? Might Sarah have told them and not told me about it? Did we ever talk business at school where someone might have been listening? Could one of my parents have dropped some hint and not realized it?

"Your mother hangs out with reporters all day," Milo pointed out. "They're professionally nosy. Also your dad's a lawyer. They're evil, right? Not your dad, no offense, just statistically at a higher percentage than the general population."

I couldn't see any of these things having anything to do with Sarah's disappearance, even if she and I had occasionally talked shop at school. We never said anything outright, and people talk about all sorts of weird crap in high school anyway, all the time. It's what high school is for. And how many supervillains could be hiding out at Laketon High? I'd already found one, which more than accounted for the national average. Another fact I obviously couldn't share with Milo.

In the end, we both found our attention focused on the same place: Denny's.

"But if I wasn't there with the Shooters, if it was just me, then I wasn't in costume, I was *just me*," I said. "And with the Shooters, we always kept our masks on, always used codenames. We were friendly with *all* the staff, and the regulars. I don't think we ever made it obvious that Sarah and I knew each other in real life too."

"But you might have. And did you ever talk about any cases you were working on? Anything someone might have wanted to know that they'd know Sarah might know?"

"No. It's W.H.A.M. policy never to discuss an active case outside of the actual investigation. We hardly ever talked about cases anyway, except a few old fights."

"Okay. All right, so what about..."

Mindsaber, Leviathan's telepath, spent the next several days sitting down with the Denny's staff that had worked Saturday night and any of the customers willing to come in and speak with her. For witness scans like these, she was legally bound to examine memories only of the night in question, with any other information gleaned from their minds guaranteed to be confidential. The hope was that someone might have subconsciously picked up on something suspicious, some key element that they had forgotten or ignored. More than two dozen people volunteered, but the scans turned up nothing.

Meanwhile, Milo was working on a DNA tracker, something he'd been planning to build into my new crime lab desk. Once it was properly up and running, it could lead us to Sarah from across the city. We spent a lot of time tinkering with it, in his room or mine. Well, at first Milo tinkered with it, and I waited for the phone or my wristcomm to buzz, and occasionally handed him things. If we were at my house, sometimes Mom or Dad would sit with us. Hank even sat in once or twice, until he asked too many annoying questions and I yelled at him to just go away. I kind of think he did that on purpose.

Tamika called me on Tuesday to apologize. I guess she couldn't stand the thought of having one friend missing and being angry at another. At least she still thought of me as a friend. After that, Tamika and Liz stopped by not infrequently, always with food, and even if Milo was there and I wouldn't let them stay, they wouldn't leave until I'd promised to eat. They never just called, or asked me to come over to their houses; I think Tamika was afraid I wouldn't go. Sometimes they cried. I never could, and sometimes I could see Tamika's mouth twisting, see how hard she had to work not to be openly bothered by that. I apologized a lot.

Milo's work was slow going, involving a lot of complicated soldering, wiring, and occasional programming. He swore and burned his hands a lot. Eventually I insisted he should just talk me through the most fire-hazardous bits. Even with my superhuman epidermis, the sparks across my knuckles hurt like hell, but this was infinitely less painful than the waiting. And waiting was all there was, hour after hour. Because to not be waiting, to turn away from it, to read a book I might enjoy or watch a TV show I was actually interested in, to allow my life to go on, somehow felt like the deepest possible betrayal of Sarah.

At just after 1 a.m. on the Thursday after the kidnapping, Milo and I finally brought the DNA tracker online. It was a tall black plastic box, its front aglow with lights and buttons and dials, all surrounding a central disc like a sonar screen in an old submarine movie with a digital arm spinning around four pie-piece quadrants at ten times the speed of a second hand.

"And you were going to fit this into a desk drawer... how?" I teased, and regretted it immediately. Making jokes, even weak ones, just made my stomach hurt.

"Yeah," Milo said. "I was planning to ask Ruby Goldberg to help me with that. But it'll need to be a lot more precise at long-range first."

In the meantime, we borrowed my dad's truck to meet up with the Shooters in the Denny's parking lot and hook the tracker up in their van. Milo had one of my spare masks on, which was good, as Denny's staff and even regular patrons kept stopping by to ask about Sarah. Milo and Ruby Goldberg got the device installed with virtually no fuss and everyone piled into the van. The instant Milo powered up the tracker, a host of blue dots lit up right in the center.

Milo let out a triumphant whoop. Ruby did as well, or the start of one, though she quickly quashed it and put her serious face back on.

"That's it? That's where she is?" asked Match.

"No," Milo said. "That's Denny's. She works here, so of course her DNA is all over the place. But we can filter those signals out." He plugged a roll-up computer keyboard into a jack on the tracker's side and started typing.

"So how's this work?" asked Lift. "Doesn't DNA testing require a physical sample or something?"

"Ordinarily," Milo agreed. He went into a six minute technical explanation of how he'd managed to digitize the process and make it possible to detect specific DNA from a distance. None of which I can recall, because I was never really listening. I was too busy watching the blue dots at the center of the screen fade, and new dots appear at its outer edges.

"—and now I've convinced the machine to ignore the closest readings and anything older than those," Milo finally said. "So maybe, hopefully—"

"You just tell Benny which way to drive," Lift said, as we all buckled in.

I took the spot closest to Milo and the machine, my eyes rarely leaving the screen as my steward called out "left," "right," or "keep going straight."

"How are you picking which dot to take us towards?" I asked.

"Honestly? I wasn't expecting to get so many readings," Milo admitted. "Not after I narrowed it down to the, uhh, freshest signals. I'm thinking maybe this means she's been moved a few times?"

"Either that, or Sarah's been cloned," Ruby suggested. Everyone except Manaaki glared at her.

Milo said he was guiding us to the strongest reading, on the assumption that it would be the most current. He kept calling out directions every time we approached an intersection, even as more dots appeared on the map. Just how many places had Sarah been held in six days?

Then we turned down a familiar downtown street, and I realized where the signal was coming from.

"That's Sarah's dad's office building. It's not working, is it?"

"No, that kinda makes sense, right?" Match said. "Maybe this wasn't about her being a steward at all. Maybe her dad saw a co-worker getting up to something—"

"And they took his daughter and hid her where they both work?" said Ruby.

"If he saw the *boss* getting up to something, if the building has a lair in the basement or a sanctum up on the penthouse level, she could be here," Lift said, as if such things happened all the time.

I'd never gotten the feeling that Sarah's dad knew more than he was letting on, that he might be suffering blackmail or threats, before or after Sarah's disappearance. But I was still hopeful that maybe it was almost over and we were about to make a thrilling rescue, and that Sarah would be sore and hungry from being handcuffed to something for a few days but she'd be fine, and later she would make fun of me for taking so long to figure it out.

As Manaaki pulled the van down an alley and activated its holo-camouflage, Milo triggered a 3-D projection capability that I hadn't even realized the tracker's screen possessed. The blue dots floated into space, mapped against X, Y, and now Z axes, so Milo could direct us to the right floor of the building.

Match and Ruby stayed in the van with Milo. It was generally a good idea to leave a backup team on standby against the possibility that we had stumbled on a big operation, and this way Ruby could hack into and shut down the office's security systems section by section as we went in. Match, meanwhile, would be calling both the security company and the nearest police station, letting them know why the building's alarm systems looked like they were glitching, and providing the TroubleShooters' clearance code for confirmation.

Manaaki and I followed Lift from the van to one of the building's service entrances. We crouched in the shadows, even Manaaki's face creased with tension as our leader leaned in to the door, feeling out the lock with her telekinesis, then pouring her mental energies inside, molding an invisible key from pure force, and twisting. The lock clicked, and Lift pulled the door open from the inside.

Once in, we had Milo in our earpieces guiding us towards the source of the tracking signal and away from the few security guards or late-working staff picked up on the van's sensors. We hurried down dim, tiled corridors, the walls lined with cheesy motivational posters and random surrealist prints. A couple of times we had to duck into an empty office or copy room to avoid being caught between two or more of the life signs moving on our floor.

Nothing we saw looked nefarious or out of the ordinary. The one time we were spotted by a security guard, Lift instantly immobilized him. He struggled against her telekinetic hold, fighting to reach his radio.

"We're the good guys! Chill!" I hissed. He nodded, but Lift kept her grip on his jaw to prevent him from yelling for backup. Murmuring an apology, Manaaki gently wrapped his arm around the man's neck and squeezed his carotid arteries until he lost consciousness.

When we finally reached the target floor, we found no additional security waiting for us. Ruby's sensors picked up no life signs on that level at all, in fact.

"She could be shrouded somehow?" Lift said.

Milo's blue dot hadn't moved, was still "as bright as ever," he promised me. He led us to a particular hallway, a particular closed door. I saw the nameplate beside it, and my stomach sank.

Eugene Gordon, Director of Marketing. Milo's DNA tracker had led us to her father's office.

We engaged the lenses on our masks anyway, scanning the door for traps before trying the handle. It wasn't locked. Manaaki opened the door, slowly, and stepped in first. No one jumped him, or cried out for help. He flipped on the light. The office was empty. In the desk drawer we found a reusable water bottle, a comb, a travel toothbrush and a set of spare contacts.

Milo's tracker was sensitive enough to pick up the faint traces of DNA left on these ordinary objects, yet it couldn't tell Sarah's DNA from that of an immediate blood relative.

We spent the rest of that night chasing blue dots. Hardly any of them tested positive for life signs, and those that did gave up no evidence of Sarah's whereabouts. We checked the restrooms of a couple of gas stations and a 24 hour grocery. We skipped Sarah's own house, but spied on her mother's pastor as he practiced a sermon in his pajamas in the church at 3 a.m. We broke into a neat little ranch-house at the end of a Laketon cul-de-sac, and gave Sarah's elderly aunt a terrible scare. Manaaki made her a cup of tea before we returned to the van.

With each passing hour we grew more and more frustrated. I started snapping at Milo and Ruby to make their damn toys work, and Lift snapped me for snapping at them, "which is hardly going to help the situation!" Match snapped at everyone for snapping at everyone when obviously we were all stressed. Milo and Ruby, surprisingly, didn't snap at anyone, even to defend themselves. They just kept plugging more and more random pieces of machinery from Ruby's mobile lab into the tracker, babbling at each other in low voices, as they worked. Nothing worked. Manaaki sang softly to himself as he drove, knuckles white on the wheel.

When dawn broke through the van's windshield, there were still more than a dozen blue dots we hadn't even had a chance to check out. Rather than keep driving all day, we decided to go home, rest, and give Milo and Ruby time to refine the tracker. They tried, and we went out again the next night, and again on Saturday. Each time, the machine either gave us too many readings or none at all.

On Sunday, the day before I was due to start my senior year of high school for the second time, we were no closer to finding Sarah. I woke up intending to spend the day riding around town in costume, looking for a serendipitous clue or criminals to hurt, but Mom prodded Hank and me into helping Dad cook a big dinner instead, and the four of us descended on the Gordons' house that afternoon with arms full of Tupperware. It was a very quiet meal. Afterwards Dad stayed there, Hank went to a friend's, and Mom and I went home. We sat together at the kitchen table, so Mom could write her column while I did the last of my summer reading.

That was the plan, anyway. I opened the book, but didn't turn a page the entire first hour.

"They're going to find her. It'll be okay," Mom finally said.

"Do you really feel that? Or do you just feel like you have to say it?" I asked. "Thanks, either way."

She looked pained, and I leaned over and folded her into my arms.

"Why do I feel like you're the one comforting me?" Mom asked. "Stop that."

But neither one of us let go for a while.

I went back to school alone. As a senior with a future in the liberal arts, and having passed summer school, I wasn't required to take math any longer, so none of my classes required too much concentration, which was good, as I had none at all to spare. I sleepwalked through my days and lay awake every night, keeping my fears packed tightly down into a restless wooden box that constantly rocked in my gut, papered over with stickers that said, *I am a superhero. The villain will make a mistake. My friends and I will save her.* Nothing else was worth thinking.

I did my homework as soon as I got home in the afternoons, then put on my mask and went out, to do extra training with the Shooters or to preempt remembered crimes. I quipped a lot less than I had before, and once when stopping an electronics store robbery I broke the gunman's arm over my knee before I even noticed the weapon was plastic, a toy.

I thought I was holding up quite well.

Chapter 12: Redirect

The newly formed Stewards' Alliance, as it was called in those days, faced its first major test when an enterprising villain sent a stooge undercover to work as a records clerk. It is not known how the stooge passed the security measures, which were impressive by mid-twentieth century standards, but he was able to smuggle some information out of the secure archive. The information included enough details about a hero's secret identity that the hero was targeted out of uniform. While the names of those involved as well as the details of the incident remain privileged, secrecy and protection of heroes became a top goal of the Alliance. The event itself is something of an urban legend among heroes, with most versions of the story concluding that the plan failed because the undercover stooge confessed and switched sides soon after beginning his work at what would become the organization now known as W.H.A.M.

- "A Brief History of W.H.A.M."

I received two wristcomm calls on Thursday, September 14.

Lift called me around two o'clock, just before the end of my school day, to let me know that Manaaki had been attacked at Cleveland State that morning. She was quick to say that Benny was okay and the villain was in custody. Some new jerk calling himself Coldest Winter had zapped the college pool with an ice beam, trapping Benny and half a dozen other students in the water while they were swimming laps. Benny's force field kicked in automatically as soon as the ray hit the water, but his face was submerged at the time, so water rather than air got trapped inside the field with him. He was immobilized in a sheet of ice crusting the top of the pool and likely to asphyxiate before frostbite had a chance to set in.

Benny was stuck for approximately fifteen seconds before he managed to draw his force field in tighter around his body, pull himself up on top of the ice, and tackle the wildly ice-blasting villain. The other swimmers were broken free and thawed out with no lasting damage.

The second call, at 7:30 that evening, was from the police, asking me to come down to the station and formally identify my steward's body.

I didn't ask any questions on the call. I needed to hope that asking me to identify meant they didn't know for sure. I didn't tell anyone where I was going. I just slipped out of the house and rode my scooter downtown.

At the station, I was ushered straight through to the super-unit's bullpen, where Detective Kimberly Rockwell was waiting for me. We'd spoken a few times before, twice in person, so our greeting was nothing more than a quick handshake.

We descended to the basement of the station. In the future, I'd interviewed several medical examiners to discuss their autopsies of villains and victims alike, so I'd seen my share of these places. Now that familiarity merely added to the surreality as I walked down the steps into a dingy hallway under acid yellow fluorescent lamps. There was the low buzzing drone of powerful electronic gadgetry, which I felt through my boot soles more than heard, and the biting cool stench of industrial-strength chemical disinfectants.

We entered the morgue, a wide, high-ceilinged room made claustrophobic by three rows of dull steel tables. The acrid smell was twice as strong here, the buzzing twice as loud. The rapid increase in extra-normal abilities among the American people since the 1960s had driven a shift in autopsy technologies, as traditional methods of cutting and analyzing didn't necessarily work on a being with organic steel skin, or a victim whose entire body had been abruptly calcified by Cro-Magnum's petro-ray. Recent laser and microchip advances allowed for a new wave of non-invasive deep tissue scanners, but it would be a few years yet before many police precincts would be able to afford to upgrade. For now, stations like this one were stuck with the massive droning mainframe towers lined up along one wall, and the automated arms and assorted devices hanging down from the ceiling like some bizarre metal octopus.

I walked behind Detective Rockwell to the end of the room, spotting a tall, fat young medical examiner in scrubs and a white jacket waiting beside a small body covered by a pale blue sheet on a slab. I expected my knees to lock up, the back of my throat to burn, but they didn't.

Neither the detective nor the M.E. said a word. In the future, my interviewees were always quite chatty in this room, eager to fill up the cold space with words. This time there was only somber, compassionate quiet. The M.E. removed the blue fabric to reveal a dark-haired girl with a white sheet tucked around her from armpits to knees. Her hair was damp, as if she'd just had a shower. Her eyes were closed. There was a bluish tinge to her skin, and her fingers and toes were deep purple shading to black. It looked painful.

"How did you find her?" I asked, my voice louder than I had intended.

"We arrested the ice guy, Morgan Patterson, a.k.a. Coldest Winter. You heard about that?" Rockwell said. I nodded. "Interrogation suggested that the attack was targeted. He knew Manaaki's civilian identity and where he attended school. We searched his place and found Miss Gordon's body in a block of ice."

I nodded again, as if Rockwell was simply one more hard-working police officer relaying one more horrific event she'd witnessed and I was just a writer of books about horrific events. Sarah's hair was wet and very cold between my fingers. I saw bruises disappearing under the sheet but her face looked untouched. I turned to the M.E.

"So the cause of death." I ran out of breath and started again. "Hypothermia?"

"That's still being determined," he said, turning pages on the clipboard in his hand. His name tag said Dr. Hawes. I couldn't remember if I'd introduced myself earlier. "There were traces of psychoactive drugs in her system and her body shows signs of severe dehydration. The freezing may have contributed, or the ice may have been applied posthumously as a preservative."

"What else?"

"Her hands and feet were bound," Rockwell said. "There was some bruising to her face, and also to her hands, her knuckles, her knees, the toes of her right foot. These are all typical defensive injuries." Frizzy curls were escaping Rockwell's normally tidy ponytail, and there were dark circles like smudged mascara under her eyes. I hoped she could go home soon and get some rest. "She fought back. Those are the only signs of trauma."

Sarah wasn't wearing earrings. I could see the holes, two in each ear, but I hadn't seen her that day so I didn't know if she'd been wearing them when she went to work. I said, "It's no secret that the team hangs out at Denny's after fights. He kidnapped her from work, beat and drugged her. He interrogated her about the TroubleShooters, and when he had the information, he killed her."

Rockwell nodded. "Patterson claimed he wanted to make a name for himself by taking down a few young heroes. It was just bad luck that your steward was working that night."

"She gets the best tips on Friday nights," I said and then felt stupid for saying it. I'd put three little braids in her hair and my hands were going numb from the cold.

"We haven't yet informed Miss Gordon's family. As her registered hero, you have the right to inform the steward's next of kin personally. If you'd prefer, I can accompany you or go by myself."

"That won't be necessary, thank you," I said. I combed my fingers through Sarah's hair, untangling the braids, and stepped back from the table. Dr. Hawes put down his clipboard and picked up the blue sheet again. I waited until Sarah was covered before turning away. I had a bizarre urge to ask him to give her a heavier blanket. I couldn't fathom how it was that I wasn't crying yet; part of me was grateful for the fact, while another part wondered what sort of terrible person I must be.

Detective Rockwell led me to a desk in another room and handed me a big plastic bag with flimsy handles. I looked inside and found a stack of clothes with a smaller plastic bag on top. I opened the smaller bag to find Sarah's wallet, sunglasses, Denny's nametag, and two pairs of earrings. One pair was small silver hoops and the other was enameled cat faces with pink ears and green eyes. Sarah didn't carry a purse. The wallet was bulging; I opened it to see a thick stack of bills. Her killer never looked. If he had, he might have found her steward's license.

I shoved everything in the bag, ignoring the dark brown streaks of dried blood on the clothes, and signed the log book to confirm that I'd checked the bag against the inventory sheet. I followed Rockwell to the stairs and accidentally bounced up four steps instead of one. I turned back to the detective.

"Could I get a ride to the Gordons' house?"

"Of course."

Alone in the dark in a police van, at last I had nothing to occupy my mind. Nothing except imagining what her last days must have been like, the terror she must have felt. The tears finally came then, in a flood. I peeled my mask off, pressing my fingers to my face in its place. I was glad of the crying, the great shuddering sobs. *So it was just shock before*, I thought. *That's what shock's like*. Still I fought against the noise, turning into the window beside me and covering my mouth with my palm as hard as I could, as if the officer driving would somehow mind.

I failed. The gasps got louder, and each time I found myself apologizing. "I'm sorry, I'm sorry…"

"It's okay," the driver said. I remembered Rockwell telling me his name but I couldn't remember what it was. I looked for his name tag but couldn't read the letters. The tears slowed enough to be wiped away, and I focused again on the concrete details around me, on the cool metal door against my shoulder and the lights of each car we passed on the road.

Officer Cho dropped me at the end of Sarah's street. I saw his name tag clearly as he unloaded my scooter. He gave me a brief sympathetic smile before he drove off, and I walked my scooter the rest of the way. As I parked the scooter in the Gordons' drive and stepped up to the stoop, I felt strangely like a kid again, standing there in Bounceback's garish costume, like it was Halloween and Sarah was right behind me. I hadn't needed to ring the doorbell at Sarah's house since we were both in elementary school. Sarah's dad answered a moment after I rang.

"Mr. Gordon, I'm Bounceback. I'm here to talk to you about your daughter."

I saw his face tighten. He knew what it meant to have a hero appear on his doorstep.

"No. Oh, oh no…"

"I'm so very, very sorry."

"Oh, please just, please excuse—"

He shut the door. After a minute the door opened again, and Dale was standing there beside her husband. "Please come in," she said, trembling.

I stepped into the house. Sensing that I was indoors, the lenses on my mask clicked from night-vision into standby mode. I blinked a few times to clear my eyes, unable to rub them with the mask on, and then I gave up and took it off. Dale's brow unfurrowed slightly, and I remembered what Mom had said about the mask giving her a headache.

"Oh," said Eugene.

"Of course," said Dale. "I feel like I should have known."

We went into the family room, and they sat on the couch and I sat in a chair. I didn't want to stare, so I politely kept my eyes on my folded hands. "Sarah was my steward. She never told you, for my sake, but she helped me save a lot of lives. She kept me together. She worked with my other steward and with the TroubleShooters to—"

"Hon? It's okay to slow down a little." I looked up to see an odd look on Dale's face that might have been an attempt at an encouraging smile, while Eugene squeezed her hand and looked past my shoulder. "We've seen you on the news, and of course we knew all about that demon that you fought with the marching bands. Sarah told us she met the hero responsible for that one, but we didn't know she worked for you."

162

"With me," I corrected. "Sarah worked mostly with me, but we both helped the TroubleShooters too. That's why she was targeted. A villain kidnapped her because she worked at the Denny's where we all hung out." I realized that neither Detective Rockwell nor Lift had told me where Morgan Patterson's freezing powers came from. Were they innate or did he use a freeze ray? However it worked, he must have been pretty powerful to flash-freeze the top of the Cleveland State pool, which would have been about 80 degrees.

"That job, was that for some sort of case?" Sarah's father asked. "You needed her at Denny's to keep an eye on someone? Or to cover for you?"

"No, nothing like that," I said. "I just liked having her there with me."

"Well, I'm glad she was," replied Dale, her voice loud. "That's how it should be."

I told them what the M.E. told me about how Sarah had died. Halfway through, Eugene left the room, but Dale just reached out to take my hand. My fingers were still numb, so I fumbled a bit accepting her grasp. I had to stop to clear my throat a few times, but Dale was very patient. She cried, of course, and handed me a new tissue every so often, but she listened to everything I said.

I told her how Sarah and I had chased down the Grammar Cop together. I mentioned having a vision that someone would have been killed that day, though I didn't say who or how. I told her about all the days Sarah was a voice in my earpiece, cheering me on, or refusing to let me pass out after a nasty blow to the head. I recalled how we would order pie and tackle our homework together at Denny's after long nights battling evil.

Eugene came back as I talked about blasting the Rock God out of existence with the national anthem. He smiled a little and said something about Sarah's pride in having to buy all new reeds for her clarinet.

Finally I stood up. "As her hero, it was my job to keep Sarah safe. You have a right to sue me for negligence."

Dale looked shocked. "Of course we won't!"

"If you'd known, if you'd had a vision about this, you never would have let this happen. The only person responsible is the man who killed her, and he'll go to jail," Eugene said, gripping my shoulder. I don't think he knew how hard he was holding on; it hurt, even through the thin Kevlar of my suit. It might have bruised.

He seemed to be waiting for something, so I said, "Yes. There was a lot of evidence. He'll go to jail for a very long time." I couldn't tell if Eugene was comforted or not, but Dale stood up and put her arms around me.

"Thank you for coming," she whispered into my hair. "Thank you for reminding us she was more special than we knew. Now go home, sweetheart."

I did, and I told my parents what had happened. They cried a lot, sitting on the couch with their arms around each other. Eventually Mom got up to call Hank, who had gone back to school the week before. I had a headache and my eyes and throat were sore, so I got a glass of ice water from the kitchen before heading upstairs to call Milo and the Shooters.

I didn't get much sleep that night. At times I was too busy crying. Mostly I was too busy thinking. I didn't want to disturb my parents. I wanted my aching muscles to stop seizing. I wanted to be able to let go, to sleep and not be here and now. That wasn't going to happen, but I was better at least if I could keep my thoughts moving

The more I thought about it, the less sense Sarah's death made. This hadn't happened. She grew up. She moved in with Geoff. We had lunch three times a week and loaned each other trashy paperbacks and tormented her frenetic cat with laser pointers. I remembered all of these things. She wasn't kidnapped or killed at 17. This never happened.

But neither had anything else, I realized somewhere in the gray before dawn. Sarah never worked at Denny's. I was never friends with the TroubleShooters.

Lift never made it to her senior year.

At some point I went down and curled up on the living room couch in front of the TV, watching infomercials with the sound off. Around 5 a.m. I heard the newspaper hit the porch. When I picked it up, I saw Sarah's picture on the front page below the fold. The headline read *SEARCH ENDS FOR MISSING TEEN*.

I'd seen that story the first time I was 17. My mom wrote it, and the picture was different.

Morgan Patterson, a.k.a. Coldest Winter. I had known that name. I'd never spoken to him, he'd never warranted so much as a footnote in my book or any of my articles, but I'd read the original version of today's wretched front page. He'd killed a young woman called— what was her name? I ran through all Sarah's coworkers in my head, and a couple of them almost fit, but I couldn't be sure. Maybe it wasn't any of them. Maybe it was some lucky girl who never even got the job this time, thanks to Sarah and me. Last time she was killed instead, and Patterson started with Match, and Match was fine but Patterson got away, and so far as I could recall, no one had ever heard of him again.

Because he'd gone underground? Been recruited for something bigger, maybe? Something so big it forced Ruby Goldberg to send me back in time, to stop it all before it could start?

I'd known about him all along and hadn't even remembered. I'd spent nine months obsessing over all those damn future crime spreadsheets, and he'd never even made the cut. And Manaaki caught him anyway, and Sarah paid the price.

I was still staring at that front page, the edges scrunched in my iron grip, when Mom came down for breakfast on her way to work. She told me she'd already called me off from school. I thanked her, and went back to sitting on the couch. Dad checked in on his way out as well, asked if I needed anything. He even offered to call in sick himself. I was tempted, but decided I'd rather be alone for a bit. I'd call him if I changed my mind, I promised.

I un-muted the TV and three hours went by. I got up to use the bathroom. Mom called and asked if I'd eaten anything, so I got myself a bowl of cereal and a cup of juice. I went up to my room and tried to read, giving up when I realized I'd read the same paragraph about five times. I thought about picking up my phone, but there were still old emails from Sarah saved in my inbox, and I didn't want to delete them, and I didn't want to face them.

I checked my wristcomm, and found a voicemail from Milo. His computer program was still keeping tabs on the police, and he'd learned that Morgan Patterson had already been transferred out to Cuyahoga ExtraMax. For some reason he thought I might want to know.

I thought about setting up another interview. I imagined sitting across a rickety Formica-topped table from the man who killed my friend, letting him glower at me, his flushed face set off by his bright orange jumpsuit, talking and talking until I found the right combination of false flattery and moral authority to unlock his psychosis and make him tell me why he'd chosen a life of villainy, why he'd killed my best friend, in his own words.

But it wouldn't do any good. I was an interviewer, not an interrogator. I'd never uncovered any crucial facts or evidence the professionals had missed, was never called to testify against one of my subjects. My interviews had only fed the public's need for salacious details about the evil among us, and I already knew more than I'd ever wanted to about this one.

I called Milo back; he was probably in class, but I left a message telling him to delete his back door on the police database. I turned on my standard, legal police scanner, listening for any crimes-in-progress that could maybe use a superhero to stop them. I listened for twenty minutes, not hearing anything likely. I went back downstairs, and lost a few more hours to television.

All day, I kept expecting Ruby Goldberg to call and tell me what all of this had been for. Morgan Patterson was in custody. Surely he was the last villain I'd been expected to prevent, because what could be worse than this? Each of the other TroubleShooters had called sometime before noon, asking how I was holding up.

But when she finally called around 2:45, the first words out of her mouth were, "You could not have seen this coming." She didn't even bother with hello. "Coldest Winter was one twisted sack of crap. You couldn't have foreseen this."

I started to ask, "So what did he have to do with—"

"Nothing. He didn't have anything to do with anything. He was just one lone jerkface, and now we have to deal with it. But you can't blame yourself. And anything you need, we've got it, okay?"

"Okay," I said, and there was a little space of silence, and we hung up.

Of course I did blame myself. I had to. I had to take responsibility for my mistakes, like the adult I was. Just because Morgan Patterson wasn't part of my mission, just because he acted alone, that hardly stopped this being my fault. What happened to Sarah was still the fallout of my own actions. I got her that job.

I went back to watching TV.

A little later, Dad came home with a comic book for me. He'd left the office a little early so he could hit the shop in the mall and pick up the latest issue of *Model Citizen*, like he used to do when I was little and home with the flu. He looked sheepish as he handed me the crinkling brown paper bag, as if he'd just decided in that moment what a silly thing he'd done for a daughter going through what I was going through. I made him bend down over the couch so I could kiss his cheek and hug his shoulder, and told him he was wonderful. I didn't have to feel wonderful to know it was true.

I helped Dad make dinner, when Mom got home we ate, and after that I went to bed, finally exhausted enough to actually sleep.

I woke up early on Saturday, around 6:30, and got myself a bowl of cereal. Hank wandered in a few minutes later. He'd driven up from Columbus last night and gotten in after I'd already passed out. I hadn't even known he was coming.

We stared at each other for a minute. I'm pretty sure he was thinking about whether or not I'd want a hug. I didn't know, so I didn't indicate.

"Caro, I'm so sorry," Hank said, like everyone. A few seconds later he added, "That asshole—I can't even. I mean, she was just a kid, y'know?"

If I'd really been 17, I'd have argued with that. Instead I just said, "Yeah," and watched my Honey Nut Cheerios turn to mush in the bowl.

On Monday I went to school, though nothing much sank in. Other people were still crying, not just Tamika or Nate or Liz—in fact the people who cried the most often seemed to be the ones Sarah had spent time with the least—but I did not. I didn't even cry when extra chairs were crowded around our usual table at lunch, and people wanted to tell stories about Sarah. I could think about Sarah in the past without my gut wrenching too badly. I could even think about her in the future, the stories which could not be told because they'd only happened for me. It was only thinking about her in the now that hurt, or the future from now, the places she should be but wasn't.

Maybe an hour after I got home, Marci called. She'd been called in to Everett Mansion to meet with Saint Scion and Mindsaber.

"They insisted they weren't blaming me, or anyone. But they were, quote, 'concerned that the public nature of our meeting place may have contributed to Sarah's death.' End quote."

"We know it did," I said flatly. I'd aimed for gently and missed, and Marci reacted powerfully.

"I'm not denying that! Do you have any idea how much I hate myself right now?"

"I didn't mean—"

She ran right over me. "When I first joined up, my first night at Denny's after a fight, I thought it was weird. All of us in our costumes in a restaurant, where everybody knew us because the team was there all the time. But Nicole said it was no big deal, the Shooters had been hanging out there for years. If I could go back, make myself stick to my guns then, talk to somebody? I had a bad feeling then that it wasn't smart or safe, and I let them talk me out of it!"

I could hear her sobbing then, over the phone. I didn't say anything, didn't try to calm her. I honestly don't know if I thought she needed to let it out, or if I thought she was right, and I was okay with her blaming herself a little right now, like I was. I waited for the storm to pass. Once she'd finished, once there was silence on her end of the line as well, then I said all the things one should. That this wasn't anyone's fault but the guy who did it. That we shouldn't let him hurt us more by thinking otherwise.

"The TroubleShooters will get through this. No one's going to disband the team. The team will just meet at the Mansion from now on."

"Is that a vaguely psychic promise?"

"Sure."

Marci let out a choked half-laugh. "How the heck are you so calm right now? No offense. I love you. But are you having a quiet breakdown or something?"

"I probably am. But let's go with it for now?"

"For now. But we've got grief counseling scheduled, as a team and individually. That's the other thing they told me. I'm not gonna have to order you to go, am I?"

"Absolutely not." Counseling was standard procedure for heroes of all ages following the loss of a close friend or loved one. It wasn't technically mandatory, but the next thing to it, ever since what happened to Captain Lunar in '86. Which I suddenly realized was still a secret and not yet a scandal here in 2014. Still not a story anyone needed to relive. "I'll be there."

On Tuesday night I found myself putting on my navy blue dress for Sarah's funeral. The evenings were still warm but the dress was sleeveless and I felt exposed, so I wore a white sweater over it anyway. I'd outgrown my navy shoes so I put on some black flats, which also pinched my toes. Sarah would have made fun of me. I thought about Sarah's closet. She had at least two pairs of navy shoes and a sweater that matched my dress much better than what I was wearing. She also had a pair of my jeans and half a dozen shirts; I had two of her shirts and a dress that hadn't really fit either one of us but it was such a gorgeous deep purple and on sale for just $5 so she'd bought it and left it with me to see if I could alter it somehow. I kicked off the black flats and ran shoeless through the tickling grass to the Gordons' house.

Dale and Eugene were already gone but the back door was unlocked. I pounded up the stairs to Sarah's room and flipped through the hanging clothes looking for her belted navy cardigan. Then I dug through the shoes on the closet floor until I found the pair I was looking for: dark blue with short, chunky heels and a strap around the ankle. Sarah would have worn sandals with this outfit, but I thought they were too sloppy for the occasion.

I looked at the top of Sarah's dresser, hearing her voice in my head saying that no ensemble was complete without the proper accessories, but I'd already reached the limits of my fashion knowledge, so I left. On the way home, I stuck my hands in the pockets of the sweater and found a pair of earrings shaped like silver stars, a silk daisy with a gold safety pin through the stem, and a bracelet made of knotted purple thread. I wore them all.

I sat with Milo, my parents, and Hank in the United Methodist church where Sarah's mother sang in the choir every week. Sarah's parents and grandparents sat just ahead of us, while the TroubleShooters were several rows back, in plain clothes, holding hands in a chain. Sarah's parents were entitled to declare her a steward and celebrate her heroism, but they chose to keep it a secret for my sake.

I wondered what Sarah would think of the proceedings. My Sarah, the 27-year-old I'd left in a previous life, would be quite moved. The Sarah who had actually died would just be uncomfortable. She'd probably critique everyone's outfits to distract herself. When we stood up for a hymn, she'd probably turn to the wrong one on purpose and pretend to sing the wrong lyrics. Or maybe she'd just stand quietly, thinking about something else and waiting for it all to be over. She wouldn't be fidgeting with the buttons on her sweater or the paper in her hands like I was.

At one point, Dale turned and nodded to me, and I went to the front of the sanctuary. A hot breeze blew in through the open door at the back; I could have taken Sarah's sweater off. Sarah's casket was closed, but I'd seen her body at the viewing the night before. She wore a dark red dress that made her look like Snow White. I'd only seen Sarah wear the dress a couple of times; she thought the skirt was too short. The bottom half of the casket was closed, so I couldn't see if she was wearing leggings underneath.

I've never been afraid of public speaking, but I don't like using microphones, so instead of going up to the pulpit, I stood next to it. The acoustics were good and I knew how to project my voice. I started with the story of how Sarah and I had met, then got a couple of laughs with suggestions of our youthful shenanigans. I'd begun a third anecdote when my eyes and my brain stopped communicating, and suddenly my notes weren't written in English any more. I trailed off, and my eyes glazed.

I didn't know how long I'd been silent so I cleared my throat and folded the paper in my hands. "I don't know how to become whoever it is I'm supposed to be without Sarah there with me. I can only imagine living as if she was still here. And I think I always will."

After the service let out, after we'd waited in the receiving line in the little back hallway to tell Sarah's parents again how sorry we were and how loved Sarah was, it was after 8 p.m. and the sky was dimming. I stood outside the church with Milo and the Shooters, scuffing my shoes deliberately on the pavement, until I remembered they weren't actually mine.

After a minute of silence, Eric said, "So did you guys hear about Robo-Tiger's fight last night with Mona Lethal?"

I felt an irrational urge to punch him. Marci caught my hand and squeezed; one look at her face told me it wasn't just me she was calming.

Benny said, "Not here." He glanced significantly at the civilians walking by, drying their eyes as they crossed to their cars.

Three of those civilians crossed right to us. Liz, Tamika, and Nate.

"Hey," Liz said. That was to me, but all three were studying the TroubleShooters. "Are these your Irish dancing friends?" Since Sarah, Milo, and I attended the open Wreck Rooms every Tuesday, Sarah had told the gang from school that we were taking Irish dancing classes across town.

"Yes we are," said Nicole, introducing herself and the others while everyone shook hands. To my knowledge Sarah had never mentioned "dance class" to the Shooters, but heroes were taught basic theatrical improv as part of Secret Identities 101. Always say yes was rule #1.

"Why don't you show us a few moves?" Tamika asked. Everyone else stared at her. "What? Like an Irish wake. Sarah would've hated all this quiet."

There were nods and almost smiles, but no dancing. Tamika shrugged.

"Well. We're gonna get going. Nice to meet you all. Caroline, I saw your parents and brother still in there with the Gordons. You wanna ride with us?"

I looked at the Shooters. They would almost certainly be driving back to Everett Mansion after this, to break things. Tempting. But there were more of them, and they had at least some idea what had happened to Sarah. I thanked them all for coming, and went with my school friends. Milo said his goodbyes as well, but he didn't really know Liz or Nate or Tamika, and since I wasn't the one driving I didn't think I could ask him along with us. I saw him drive off alone as I got into Tamika's mom's SUV.

None of us actually wanted to go home just yet, so Tamika drove to the Dairy Queen. No one felt like ice cream either, so we sat side by side on the dirty metal bench out front, Nate's long legs hanging off one side, and told more stories about Sarah, the ones we hadn't wanted to share at lunch or at a funeral, the ones for just us. I talked the least and the quietest, and took the longest to cry, which surprised me when it happened. I hadn't thought I had any tears left in me by that point. Not for a thing that hadn't happened.

I'd seen Sarah grow up. That was real.

I held on to that.

Chapter 13: Remediate

Rob20 meant to call himself "Rob 2.0," as in Robin Hood, but he misplaced a decimal point in his first email to the press. No one besides Rob himself really bought the reference in any case, as he defined the poor as, "myself, until further notice." He's become best known for the music he blasts out of his giant robots while attacking financial institutions. His eclectic "Mayhem Mixes" have become popular internet bootlegs, sampling every genre from hip-hop to classical, with the exception of country. He's very particular about that, although he makes a special allowance for Dolly Parton, who he says "doesn't really count as country" due to her extensive acting career.

- Dying for a Laugh

On Wednesday afternoon I met the TroubleShooters in the Everett Mansion gym for our first group therapy session with Mindsaber. She was a tall, dark-skinned woman with chestnut curls falling past her shoulders, wearing a jacket and body armor of deep scarlet leather. Soft-spoken, like most telepaths, she started off by outlining how the whole counseling process would work over the coming weeks. We'd meet with her once a week as a team and twice a week individually, and I was encouraged to bring Milo in for sessions as well. We were not required to take leave from our crime-fighting duties but asked to cut our hours of activity back as fully as we felt comfortable doing.

"I know that's the last thing you want to hear," Mindsaber said. "I don't have to read your minds to know what you're all thinking right now: 'The more heads I go out and break, the less I have to live in mine.' And that sounds great, as therapeutic techniques go. It even works sometimes. But a lot of times, people end up getting hurt that we didn't intend. Which is insultingly obvious for me to say, right up until you see a puddle of blood on the floor. Believe me."

"Still insulting," said Match. He was the only one of us who hadn't come here willingly. He'd had to be ordered, then threatened, and finally telekinetically hoisted by Lift.

Ruby Goldberg asked, "You speaking any of this from experience?"

"Yes," Mindsaber replied, "but it was my blood that did the puddling, after a friend slipped. I was lucky. Only two of my internal organs are currently artificial."

She proceeded to tell us that whole story, but not sitting down. We met in the gym because most of our counseling hours would be spent in simultaneous hand-to-hand combat training. What better way for a group of super-charged adolescents to work through their pain, rage, and burgeoning awareness of mortality? Particularly as nearly every hero, villain, and adventurer seems to possess the logic-defying ability to receive or deliver the hardest punch mid-sentence without pausing for breath and pack thirty-second soliloquies into the time it takes a single blow to land. I still have no clue how that works, but it does, and that afternoon it worked overtime for all of us. So did the body armor built into our costumes.

When Mindsaber's tale was done, we told her about Sarah, and kept punching. I don't know if any of us felt any better at the end of that first session, but Mindsaber was a good listener, and sheer physical exhaustion felt as close to relief as I could imagine just then.

Mindsaber's office was a cramped but meticulously organized room in Everett Mansion's northeast tower, her desk covered with photographs of various heroes and civilians, all wearing masks. There was a mini-fridge under one of the bookshelves with a grade school science test stuck to the front with a magnet; the student had earned a B+, and written next to it, *"Simple machines today=simple weapons tomorrow?"* with a smiley face. It was a Friday afternoon and I'd come here for my first individual counseling session.

Mindsaber started by handing me a waiver, giving me three choices for the level of telepathy to be used in our private meetings here. If I chose "full telepathy," then the sessions would be conducted entirely mind-to-mind. I wouldn't have to talk at all. We'd just sit back and think at each other, Mindsaber gently probing for tangled thoughts I could not consciously express. "Surface/emotional scan only" would mean we would communicate mainly through regular speech, but Mindsaber would still be allowed to reach out empathically, reading the undercurrent of feeling beneath the words. "No mental contact" was fairly self-explanatory.

I chose the second option. I didn't want my thoughts to give away my time-traveler status or the things I knew about people's possible futures, especially Milo's. I'd been sent back alone, given this mission to solve on my own, and whatever mess I'd made of it, I intended to clean it up the same way. Still, an objective assessment of my emotions could be useful. I was an adult, I could handle grief as well as any adult could, but it would be nice to hear that from someone else.

I found myself talking about chess.

"I've never been any good at it. Never tried to be, really. Dad got me a beginner's book and a plastic set one Easter, and I taught myself the basics. Sometimes I'd get my brother Hank to play with me, until I beat him one too many times and he had a tantrum and broke the board. And I did sixth grade chess club, and I wasn't the worst. But I always felt like I should be better."

Mindsaber nodded, maintaining a reassuring not-quite-smile, her dark eyes intent and calming.

"I can't see ten moves ahead, or five even. I know I'll never be a master. But I always felt like I should at least consistently be able to see one move ahead. That much should be simple, right? I move a piece, and where it ends up, either it's in danger of being captured, or it's not. There are a finite number of pieces on the board, there are only so many angles my opponent can come at me from. I should be able to see that much. But still, every time I play, win or lose, I always end up getting blindsided somewhere along the line."

I was sitting in a comfortable but not too soft chair in one corner of the room; Mindsaber sat in the opposite corner next to her desk, but not behind it. Next to my chair was a little table with a digital clock, a box of Kleenex, and a few tchotchkes on it. At some point I'd picked up a paperweight, a hefty stone triceratops with a chipped horn and a sticker from the Natural History Museum on one of its felt-padded feet. I thought about replacing it. Instead I kept rubbing my thumb over the rough edge of the broken horn.

"That's how I feel about my psychic ability," I said.

"You blame yourself for not foreseeing your friend's death?" Mindsaber asked.

"No," I said. "Maybe. But I'm telling myself not to. I just have to do better. I know I can."

"And what would doing better look like? More crimes prevented?"

"That's part of it, I guess. But this isn't a numbers thing. I'm not looking to improve my Scorecard rating or anything."

"You feel like someone's keeping score?" Mindsaber said.

"Oh, no. SuperheroScorecard.com. It's a website—" Actually, it probably wasn't, yet. "It's a thing. But not for me. I just want to figure this out. I have this, this psychic whatever, for a reason."

I did not say, *And if I'd remembered Morgan Patterson sooner, Sarah would never have gotten hurt.*

"Do I sound really silly right now?" I asked.

"Not at all. It's natural to seek greater meaning in the wake of tragedy. It can be part of the healing process, as long as it alleviates rather than adds to the pressures you feel."

"Absolutely." I set the triceratops down on the desk. "I can be a better chess player. I can make this, um, psychic thing work for me, like it was supposed to. I just have to get focused."

On Saturday morning I woke up just after 6, but forced myself to wait until after 8 before riding over to Milo's. His parents were still asleep, but Milo was already awake, and unlocked the door by remote. That was new. When I got up to his room, which was thankfully soundproofed with ribbed foam panels—another new development—I found him sitting at his desk, pulverizing a circuit board with a hammer.

"What are you doing?"

"Starting over on the DNA tracker. I still can't get it to work." *BLAM!* "I'm ready to admit the problem might be with the hardware, not the programming. Or not just the programming."

"And the hammer?"

"It's therapeutic." *BAM!*

"Right," I said. "Did Mindsaber suggest this?"

"No, I haven't seen Mindsaber yet." *BANG!* "I'm gonna go next week."

"You better."

"I will." *WHA-BANG! BAM! BANG!*

"Would you take a break?"

He set down the hammer. "Sorry. You need something, boss?"

"Three things," I said, sitting down in the spare chair. "First, you have to tell your parents about me. Or about Bounceback, anyway. Telling Sarah's folks was one of the worst things I've ever had to do. Your mom and dad deserve to know what you're up to, and the risks."

I glared, expecting a fight.

"You're right," Milo said. "I've kinda been thinking about it, only I wasn't sure if you'd be okay with it. If I just tell them about Bounceback, they'll probably guess it's you anyway."

"Doesn't matter. Do it."

"Okay."

"And if they tell you they don't want you being a steward anymore, you listen to them."

"All right."

"You're okay with that too?"

"I'm thinking with my parents, they'll know what this means to me, so it won't be an issue. And it's not like I'm on the front lines. What happened to Sarah, I mean, she was in public. And I could get hit by a bus any time, you know?"

"I guess so." My 'psychic gift' wouldn't see that one coming either. I resolved not to think about that. "Thing #2: any future stewarding you do, you do it from the safety of here in your room, or from Everett Mansion. No more ride-alongs in the van. No more Denny's." Not like any of us would be going back there now, or ever. "Not unless you feel like getting yourself a mask and a full costume, with a cowl and everything."

"I don't think that's really my style."

"I'm serious. If you think you're gonna take your laptop to Starbucks someday, don't. If you need fresh air, open a window."

"You got it, boss. So what's the third thing?"

"I need you to build me a time machine."

Milo blinked.

"Or a ring, or a watch, or a portal, or y'know, two wacky ray guns that when you cross the streams send your target back through time."

"Boss?"

"I'm serious."

"You want to go back and save Sarah?" he asked. I nodded. "Setting aside the fact that temporal engineering is way beyond my skill level right now—"

"Won't know until you try," I said.

"—it won't work. Even if we could go back, we can't actually change our own history."

"It's not history, Milo. Just the past."

"Everything we know about time travel thus far, and by 'we' I mean 'science'—I've read pretty much everything, even Dr. Pi's papers, and understood just about everything, thank you very much— it all backs up the many-worlds interpretation of quantum mechanics."

"Meaning what?"

"Meaning you can travel into the past, sure, but any actions you take there can't actually affect your own life. You can shoot your grandfather all you like without causing a paradox, because your own actual grandfather will still exist back in the timeline you came from. All you'll have done is create a new, alternate, grandpa-free world, totally separate from and irrelevant to your personal past."

I stared at him, my brain grinding to a halt, stubbornly refusing to consider this possibility. "You're wrong," I said finally.

"I wish it were possible to argue with the math, but you can't."

176

"I'm not arguing with the math, I'm arguing with you." My voice remained perfectly level.

"Arguing with me how? What evidence do you have otherwise?"

"You say you can't change your own timeline. Fine. Unless you're going back to fix something that's *already* been changed, something that's not how it's supposed to be. Clearly, this is not how things are supposed to be."

"I'm sorry, boss. I just don't believe it works like that. In science fiction it does, sure. But I haven't seen anything to suggest it works that way in real life. There are worlds out there where Sarah lives. But we don't get to share them, whatever we do."

My head snapped back as if he'd physically slapped me. I uncurled fists I didn't think I'd made. "And how the hell are you so calm about that?"

"Because the alternative to the branching worlds theory is even worse. The past can't be rewritten, but it can't ever be erased either. We can't save Sarah, but at least we know she's out there. That's something, isn't it?"

"Not really."

Milo was wrong, obviously. The future Ruby Goldberg had sent me back just days before Lift's death, just weeks before Milo conceived his plan for world domination in the lunchroom. She'd sent me back to save them, to fix things, and I had. But then I messed it all up. The future couldn't be fixed without Sarah. There had to be a way to save her too.

But I couldn't tell Milo any of this. I couldn't tell him how close he'd come to turning into a supervillain, or risk him figuring it out on his own. He was too fragile right now.

I'd just have to find someone else to help me.

The problem with finding another time expert, as I'd more or less figured out during my first month in the past, was there really weren't any. So I returned to Plan A instead. I pored over my future-crime charts, determined to finish my mission and get home. If I got back to the future and my Sarah wasn't there waiting for me, then I'd hunt down Ruby Goldberg and make her send me back again to stop Patterson. Simple.

In the meantime, I stopped attending training sessions with the TroubleShooters outside of counseling, stopped riding along in the van on patrol nights. They were great kids, but they weren't my real friends, and it was long past time I accepted that and got on with the job. The frequency of their texts and emails gradually decreased, and then ceased altogether. I wondered if one of them might say something to Mindsaber, tell her I was being anti-social or something, but if they did, she never said a word about it to me.

The one time I did text the Shooters was toward the end of October, in a fit of total and knowing manipulation. I told Marci I was sorry I'd been so distant lately, and she said of course she understood. I asked if maybe I could meet everybody at the Mansion and bring pizza or something. Marci suggested Friday night, and I said I had a thing and suggested Sunday instead.

I arrived, balancing a stack of five large pizzas on one hand—one for each of us, and there would be no leftovers—to find Eric sitting alone in the team's meeting room, playing a video game on the ginormous main monitor screen.

"Hey," he said, glancing my way for a second but not bothering to pause the game.

"Hey," I said, setting the pizzas down on the meeting table. "Where is everybody?"

"Uhh." The black girl on Eric's screen jumped over three zombies, then clubbed a fourth in the face with what looked like a massive book of Sudoku puzzles. "Nicole's probably down in the tech lab, she usually is. Dunno about Marci and Benny."

"Thanks."

The tech lab was in Everett Mansion's basement, a massive vault-like chamber subdivided into individual workshops for Cleveland's various geniuses by thin but nigh-indestructible movable walls. I found her at her bench in the corner, wearing a purple helmet to protect her face and spot-welding four small rocket boosters onto the base of what had until very recently been a gaming chair.

"I keep messing them up!" she shouted at me over the hiss and pop of shooting sparks. She gripped the welder one-handed, and with her other glove tapped one of the rockets. "It shouldn't be that hard!"

Finally she turned the machine off, the sparks died out and I approached. "Ejection seat?" I guessed.

"That's the plan," Nicole said.

"For what, exactly?" Her first robot/spaceship wouldn't debut until late 2017. Unless, of course, she was early.

"No clue," Nicole said. "But you know what they say: *safety first.* How've you been, Caroline?"

"Oh, y'know. How's it going with RubyTech?"

Nicole blinked. "I'm supposed to be starting a company, aren't I? That's why I'm not in school this year. Dang! I knew I was forgetting something!" That cheeky grin came out, dimmer than it used to be, and she laughed. "Naw, I've just kinda gotten bogged down with other things lately. Like whatever this turns out to be. It'll happen when it happens, I guess."

Well, that can't be good, I thought. Whatever Nicole's future self had sent me back to get ready for, I had to think her company would be playing an integral role.

Except, then again, maybe it wasn't. Maybe the first time through she'd rushed into business and slacked on her tech. Maybe she needed her bot-ship ready sooner.

Maybe, maybe, ugh.

"So Eric's in the meeting room," I said. "Any idea what Marci and Benny are up to?"

"Try the Wreck Room," Nicole suggested. "I'll meet you all upstairs, after I get everything cleaned up here."

In the Wreck Room, Lift was throwing cars at Coldest Winter. Not the actual villain, not my best friend's actual killer. Just a pile of nanotiles programmed to mimic his shape and movement. Benny was sitting in the observation booth, bent over the long bench where Sarah used to sit on Tuesday nights. At first I thought he was doing homework but the faint smell of artificial cherry tipped me off before I saw the pack of markers next to him. There was a stack of art supplies in the corner of the lounge, which Lift said a few stewards used on their lunch breaks to de-stress.

"She fights this same simulation several times each day," Benny said. I looked over his shoulder and saw he was filling in a pattern of concentric circles. Next to him was a fully colored page with the words, "Lord Love a Duck," in between rows of mallards. "Sometimes she adds in other villains teaming up with him, to keep herself sharp."

"Does it help?" I asked.

Benny shrugged. "It didn't when I tried it. But she was worse the time I made her take a day off."

"And what about you?"

"I haven't slept much." He capped one marker and picked up another. It smelled like bubblegum. "But I kind of expected it. After my parents died, I couldn't sleep more than half an hour at a time. It will get better."

Down in the Wreck Room, a nanotile Humvee slammed down on the villain's head with what was absolutely a lethal amount of force. I wasn't sure how to feel about that, so I didn't bother to try.

Once we'd all finally made it upstairs to the meeting room, Marci lifted the stack of pizzas I'd brought off the table with her mind, telekinetically flipping them all open at once and spinning them about until all the toppings were in front of the correct chairs. We dug in.

I really had intended to let everyone finish eating, but looking around at all their faces as they looked back at me, the care and concern in Benny's furrowed brow, I panicked.

Before anyone could finish their second piece, I faked a psychic vision.

Robert Naples, alias Rob20, liked to rob banks while driving giant suits of robot armor, two stories tall with massive battering ram fists bristling with laser guns.

"So which is it?" Match asked. We were all piled into the ShooterVan at this point, speeding down the highway. "Armor, or a robot? Does he drive, or just ride?"

"It's both," said Ruby. "His mechas are capable of independent operation, they've got AI, but he usually switches those off when he's inside. So either term is accurate."

Naples had been active for roughly two years at this point, and was already responsible for eleven deaths and forty-seven serious injuries, with many more to come. He wasn't like Markus Strunkenwhite; their first kills may have been equally accidental, but there was no turning point for Naples, no clear-cut psychological divide between the bank-jobber and the mass-murderer. To Naples, anyone who got in his way did so at their own peril, and that was that.

Naples had been apprehended eight months previously by Saint Scion and had resided at Cuyahoga ExtraMax ever since. Though Naples possessed no superhuman abilities himself, his machines had been known to come looking for him, and he was therefore considered an extraordinary flight risk. If the TroubleShooters and I failed to intervene tonight, that risk would become a reality. Nine prison guards and three inmates would be killed in the process.

"One of Rob20's robots is heading for Cuyahoga ExtraMax as we speak," I informed the others, two fingertips held dramatically to my temple. I had never done that sort of thing before and wasn't quite sure why I was bothering now. "It'll be holo-camouflaged, invisible until it punches a hole through the prison wall."

Ruby nodded, calling up a program on the computer built into her seat. "I've been working on a way to detect holo-camouflage and shut it down. I haven't quite got it, but I'm close. Hey, is Milo online?"

It wasn't until Ruby asked that I realized I hadn't even talked to Milo in two weeks. "I'm patching him in now," I said, dialing on my wristcomm.

All appeared quiet at Cuyahoga ExtraMax as we drove up. Lift had called the warden before we'd left Everett Mansion, and he reported no sign of trouble, either inside the building or on the prison's long-range sensors. Nor had he employed any of the code phrases that meant *I'm actually in quite a lot of trouble but I can't say so out loud.* We parked under the cover of the last bit of woods along the road leading up to the west outer wall, where I "sensed" the robot would begin its assault, and engaged the ShooterVan's own holo-camouflage.

Unfortunately the van's disguise turned out to be a) entirely useless and b) significantly less effective than the giant robot's, as the first anyone knew the machine had spotted and sneaked past us was when it punched its way through the *north* outer wall with a resounding KOOOOOOOM!

"Okay, I see what we missed there," Milo said over the comm.

"Yeah dude, little past that," Ruby said. "Fight now, talk later."

"Do what you gotta do. I got this."

Manaaki floored it, the van careening around the prison and right through the gaping hole in the north wall, with a little help from Lift. Up ahead we could see the force field surrounding the main building flickering, sparks radiating from two points high on the translucent barrier. The sparks intensified, and then we could see the robot as well, thirty feet tall on two bent metal T-Rex legs, fists the size of Mini Coopers pushing against the energy wall.

"There, I got it!" Milo crowed. *"Wait, no, I didn't get it, the holo shorted itself out. CRAP! There goes the force field—"*

The field blew out. A ring of high-intensity lasers popped from their housings all around the robot's right fist and began blasting away at the prison. The building itself was built of hephaestean concrete, reinforced with adabranium, twice as strong as the outer wall. It still wouldn't last long.

Ruby yanked one of her plasma rifles from the wall of the van and tossed it to Match, who copied it and tossed back the original. These were a new model I hadn't seen before, finally free of the bulky battery backpacks. Manaaki engaged the van's auto-defenses while Lift waved the side door open with one hand. The team and I dropped from the van, spreading out as we charged the robot. Even with Manaaki on our side, we couldn't take a chance on those lasers hitting us all in one cluster.

I ran close behind Ruby. Her rifle fired up at the machine, but the plasma-bolts SPANG!ed harmlessly off the robot's chassis. Its gun-arm swung back from the distinctly cracked side of the building, and I dove on Ruby, knocking her flat to the ground as the lasers locked on Manaaki and fired.

"BENNY!" I screamed, even louder than Lift did.

"I'm fine," Manaaki said calmly, amplified in my ear. I could see him now, crouching on one knee, staying perfectly still as the lasers bounced from his shield. "No problem."

"Bounceback, you okay?" Ruby asked from under my armpit. "You're not usually this jumpy. No pun intended. But if you need to go back to the van, we understand."

"I'm fine!" I snapped. The Shooters had never treated me like anything but an equal. What a time to decide I was some delicate flower.

From either side of us, more laser fire PEW-PEW'd ineffectually at the robot. Two lines of Cuyahoga ExtraMax guards in riot gear had appeared around the sides of the building.

"Oh no no no!" Lift shouted, and then into her wristcomm, presumably to the warden, "Get them back inside—I don't CARE how old I am, get them the hell back inside!"

The robot turned on the guards. They dove for cover. Some were thrown there by the invisible telekinetic hand of Lift. A couple of others were pounced on by Manaaki, shielding them with his back and more importantly his force field as the laser bolts rained. I leapt up to help while Ruby army-crawled behind the cover of a large chunk of granite wall. There she dropped her rifle and began typing furiously at the miniature keyboard built into the inside of her gauntlet. I hadn't noticed the gauntlets before; those were new.

"Milo, babe?" Ruby said over the comm. "You better not be on a pee break or anything. We're gonna hack this tin can and make it dance, you and me."

"*Kill its psi-dampeners if you can,*" Lift added from wherever she had found cover, her voice tense. "*I've been poking at the stupid thing but there's something blocking my telekinesis and I can't get a grip.*"

The robot's gun arm WHRRRRRR'd in my direction. I caught a guard around the waist with one arm and bounced sideways, as a flurry of laser blasts tore up the grass where we'd been standing.

"*Problem,*" Milo announced. "*Your tin can has really good firewalls. Like, really good. I'm not sure we're gonna be able to break through remotely. Not fast, anyway.*"

"Okay, time to get creative," Ruby replied. Crouching low, she scurried back to the ShooterVan.

I popped up from cover as she went, bounding across the field in wild zig-zags, hoping if I couldn't get close enough to get some hits in that I could at least draw the robot's attention. It seemed to work. Seconds later, Ruby was inside the van. Between volleys of laser fire, over the open comm, I heard a hammer pounding, then the quiet hiss of her soldering iron, followed by a squishier noise I could not identify.

Not that I had much time to try. The robot's next shots busted through the main prison wall, which imploded with a pew-pew-POOOOOOOOOOOM! And that's when all hell really broke loose.

The robot jammed its arm into the hole in the wall, grabbing and yanking, hurling whatever it caught at those of us on the ground—first cell doors, and then guards and prisoners indiscriminately.

Lift let out a string of curses, both hands above her head, her mind reaching out to catch the falling. Manaaki ran to get her under the cover of his force field in case the robot turned its guns back on her. It didn't bother. It just kept pulling people out of the building one at a time and flinging them back at us.

Lift caught the first four, then she must have blinked, because an orange-jumpsuited body went sailing past her. I tensed and sprang, sailing into the air, colliding with the prisoner in mid-flight. His skull clipped my jaw hard and I bit my tongue painfully, even as my arms automatically locked around the man, an instinct born of many hours training with dummies in the Wreck Room. My feet hit the ground, my knees absorbing the impact as we tucked and rolled.

The prisoner climbed to his feet, shaking his head clear, none the worse for wear.

The robot kept grabbing and throwing. Lift and I kept catching, while Match and Manaaki stayed close, watching the prisoners in case they tried something. Mostly they threw themselves flat on the grass and stayed down.

After another minute of this, I heard the van door slide open, and Ruby Goldberg ran out wearing a newly-minted shoulder-mounted catapult.

"Match, I need sixteen more of these!" she called out, tossing something that from across the field vaguely resembled a purple baseball.

Match caught it one handed, then both his hands started glowing. He threw back one copy, then another. Ruby snatched each one from the air, dropped it in the bucket of her catapult, and fired.

Seventeen shots, seventeen hits. Each ball splattered colorfully against the body of Rob20's 'bot, like giant paintballs, until their formation spelled out a giant RG.

A few of the inmates on the ground actually stopped covering their heads long enough to applaud.

"Ruby, tell me that wasn't just an aesthetic gesture," I said.

"Wouldn't that be hilarious?" Ruby said, unhooking her catapult and dropping it to the grass. "But not this time. Look closer."

I slid my finger down the edge of my mask, and the lenses zoomed in. I spotted a dozen or so—well, seventeen, I suppose—little robots skittering all across the big robot's surface.

"What are those? Nano-saboteurs?"

"I mean, basically," Ruby said. "NanosaBOTeurs? Trademark RubyTech, 2014? Eh, I'll work on it. The paintballs were actually gel-based delivery vehicles for USB sticks on legs."

For ten seconds or so, Rob20's 'bot stopped firing, trying to turn its lasers at an angle that would allow it to pick off Ruby's skitterers without blasting holes in itself. But it wasn't really built for that and the little guys were too fast. One or two at a time, they found gaps in the larger robot's surface and disappeared inside.

"My USBs will crawl around in there until they can find a place to plug in and deliver a virus that will take down the firewall," said Ruby.

"*And then that thing is OURS,*" Milo added over the comm.

Only the robot didn't know that yet. It went back to throwing people out of the building, and by that point there were too many down in the yard for the five of us to keep watching them all.

As I sprinted into position to catch the next falling guard, one of the prisoners behind me took off running, straight for the open hole in the outer wall.

"Mine!" yelled Match, like he was calling a fly ball in the outfield. He zapped the runner with his copied plasma rifle. The inmate dropped to the grass, unconscious.

But now that the idea was out there, more prisoners tried to run. Every one of them got stunned into the dirt by Match or Ruby.

The rest of us kept catching the new people thrown by the robot. All we could do was keep moving as the machine coldly endangered life after life. I couldn't even take pride in our rate of success; it was obvious the robot could move faster, throw harder, and shoot better, only its logic circuits wouldn't allow it to do so under present mission parameters. With heroes on scene, killing would be counterproductive. As soon as someone died, W.H.A.M. protocol would demand we take the fight directly to the robot and end the threat as quickly as possible. As long as there was a chance to prevent casualties, we were too busy to attack the mecha directly. For us it was a plate-spinning act, unless or until the first dish hit the ground.

I had a convict under each arm when the hatch on the robot's front sprang open. Rob20 himself had appeared at the hole in the prison wall. He leaned out to catch the edge of the hatch and pull himself across, singing out triumphantly, "Hallelujah! Sweet freedom!"

No longer interested in diversion, the robot opened fire on the yard.

I threw the squirming prisoners clear, leaving myself exactly no time even to leap out of the way. My chest clenched, and I was certain I was about to die.

In that same moment, Ruby and Milo finally managed to shut off the robot's psi-dampeners, allowing Lift to get a mental grip on its arm.

Lift yanked. Instead of shooting me, the robot's arm swung down, the vault-busting guns cutting right through the machine's own right leg.

The robot lurched to that side. Rob20, still perched only half inside, grabbed at the hatch in a panic, his legs kicking free for a moment, before he lost his grip and fell, hitting the ground hard.

I hopped 30 feet backward, watching the robot for another tense few seconds, waiting for its next attack. It was crooked and unable to walk now, but still more or less upright, and its gun-arm looked just as operational as before. I didn't know that when Lift made the thing shoot through its own leg, much of its processing power was diverted to analyzing and attempting to compensate for the damage, and Ruby and Milo were able to hack through the last of its defenses and shut the robot down entirely.

As I was uselessly watching the robot and Lift and Manaaki were looking to the nearest prisoners and guards to make sure they were all right, it was Match who caught sight of Rob20 limping past us, making for the hole in the wall as fast as his legs would hobble. At point-blank range, Match didn't even bother with the pulse-rifle. He threw the gun on the ground, tackled the villain, and started hitting.

Rob20 raised his arms in surrender as Match rained down blow after thudding blow.

Match, the team's kid brother, easygoing Match, screamed at the top of his lungs, every word raw and ragged and pained. Every one of them punctuated by a punch.

"No! Killers don't get to get away! You DON'T GET AWAY!"

I ran. Ruby and Manaaki ran as well. I reached Match first, caught his fists and pulled him up and off the bad guy. Rob20 remained fetal on the ground, but Match kept fighting me. My tone was less than soothing as I told him, "You're done. He's done now. It's over."

"Get off me!" Match snarled, shaking.

I let him go but waited, watching as Rob20 climbed slowly back to his feet. I didn't think any permanent damage had been done.

"I give up," mumbled Rob.

Moving faster than I'd thought him capable of, Match snapped out a jab to Rob20's jaw. The villain hit the ground again, out cold. "No shit, Sherlock."

"Ruby actually laughed at that," I told Mindsaber in our session the following Friday. "And Manaaki of all people, Manaaki told him, 'I know I shouldn't say it, but that was a beautiful hit.' They're all grieving like teenagers. I mean, they are teenagers, I know that. But it worries me."

"You're teenagers," Mindsaber agreed, and I suppressed my irritation at being included there. "But there is no right or wrong way to grieve, at any age. Inappropriate humor happens, as do happiness, sadness, and anger. What matters is how you respond to the intense emotions throughout the grief process."

"Responding to anger is what I'm afraid of."

"Which is why counseling is mandatory. We're here to help you find ways to process your feelings without taking them out on the bad guys."

"I know," I said.

Lift told me that Match had been taken off duty for six weeks by his own request. So obviously Leviathan was dealing with the incident. The TroubleShooters would be fine. And since none of the dozen lives saved at the prison had won me my ticket home, clearly I still had a job to do. I put Match's slip-up out of my mind and got back to work.

Chapter 14: Reprise

Andreas Knobloch, aka das Dolch: You know, I saw your talk last month with Ms. [Mona] Lethal [aka Ramona Schultz], and I must disagree.

Caroline Henderson: With which part?

AK: I have found that being a villain carries with it a very deep loneliness. In my experience, my work has pushed me away from my friends and family. They do not need to know what I do each day, and I do not wish to tell them.

CH: You worked alone for many years. Did you ever wish you had a team?

AK: Not me. I hired the occasional *Spießgeselle*, you call them stooges, but no other villain could replace my *Sippe*, my family.

CH: I think Ms. Schultz would agree with you. She said that while she felt affection for her teammates, she preferred to leave her true loved ones out of her work.

AK: Ja, but I say that having a team of villains is not a good thing. When you work with people who see nothing wrong with what you do, you become a tier, a brute. You begin to think you are right to do it. It is not to forget that what we do is evil, for whatever reason that we do it, and we do not deserve the comfort of good people around us. Or bad people.

> "Villains Unmasked: das Dolce"
> *Newsnight*, November 12, 2022

Milo and I were speaking again, which was good. I still wasn't clear how we'd ended up not speaking all those weeks in the first place, and he didn't bring it up either, so we just sort of got on with things. We were both busy, so we didn't actually see a lot of one another. Milo and Ruby Goldberg had managed to talk their way onto the tech team examining Rob20's robot, so he spent most of his afternoons and evenings at Everett Mansion, but I'd call him if I needed something when I was out fighting crime. *"What's the boiling point of mercury?"* I'd ask, or *"What's the average airspeed velocity of a gold-laden dragon?"*

It felt weird, asking him instead of Sarah. Before, even if I had a tech question, she was the one I'd call, and she'd call Milo, and streamline his answer for me. I missed that. It was irritating having to ask Milo to slow down for the fourth time while I was trying to kick some dude in the face. Still, we got the job done.

I asked Mindsaber if there was anything I should be watching out for, to see how Milo was doing. I didn't actually talk to him much in school either, even though we had a couple of classes together. We'd say hi in the halls, but I spent most of my social time with Nate, Liz, and Tamika, and they still thought Milo was just my sometime-study-buddy.

"What makes you think you need to watch out for him?" Mindsaber asked.

"He seems distracted," I said. "He carries around gadgets and gizmos in his backpack, more than he used to, and fiddles with them in study hall, or during free reading time in English. I don't know if that means something."

"How are your teachers handling that?"

"They're not. In light of what's happened, they're being pretty patient with him."

"Do you trust Milo to let someone know if he needs something different?"

"Yes," I said automatically, and then stopped to think. "He's working with Ruby and the stewards here. He's got a solid support system. He'll get what he needs."

Midway through November, Liz invited the usual suspects to her house on a Saturday night for a "Some of Us Still Haven't Finished Our College Applications" gathering. It was too soon after Sarah for the word 'party,' but we were all thinking it anyway. There were chips, dip, soda, and a ton of cookies waiting patiently on the dining room table as we filled out our forms in the kitchen. I did not plan on being here for college, but some version of me might well be, so I labored on her behalf, applying to whatever schools I could remember applying to the first time.

As we worked, my friends started talking about the future.

"I know after everything it's kind of crass to say, *the good side of all this...* but it really got me thinking," Tamika said. "About the future. About what I want to do with it. Because life's too short, y'know?"

Liz said, "Yeah." Nate grunted emphatically. I signed my name for the umpteenth time, pressing harder.

"I'm doing it. I'm going for the music degree. Focus on performance. Mom wants me to save that for my minor, and major in accounting, but it's not like I won't have music education to fall back on, right?"

Liz and Nate agreed. Again I said nothing. The Tamika I knew took three years of music classes, bombed an audition the beginning of her senior year of college, and finally decided there was a big difference between a love of playing music and loving to perform it. Two years later, she finished a business degree, and went to work as a sales manager for a sheet music company.

Nate looked over at me; I noticed but kept my head down. "Caroline's probably gonna tell me what a mercenary jerk I am, but I'm gonna make bank. At some point I want to have a family and everything, but all that's a lot easier when you've got a good paycheck and benefits. I'm not crap with computers. I'm gonna put my head down in school, get an awesome job, pay my dues, and then I'll have fun. It'll take a lot less time if I get the boring crap over with, and then I'll have the resources for a lot more fun after."

I snorted, feeling a strange anger coming to a boil in my gut.

"What?" Nate said.

"Nothing. You're saying this now, is all."

"I mean it! It just makes sense. It's responsible."

"Sure," I said.

My timeline's Nate got offered a Google job right out of school, turned it down to fail a start-up with a frat brother, and last I knew was running tech support for a small insurance office.

"I'm going to travel, see the world," Liz said. "England, France, Italy. Japan. Maybe Egypt? I wonder how much the tour guides at the pyramids hate it when you start humming the Bangles at them."

"No, you won't."

"No, I wouldn't. That'd be rude." She thought I meant the *Walk Like an Egyptian* thing.

"You won't travel the world," I clarified. "You'll fill out the forms, you'll be signed up and buying luggage and *this close*, and then you'll decide you don't want to add another five thousand dollars onto your already ridiculous student loans."

I spoke a little too loud and a little too fast, and all three of the others were staring at me now, jaws agape. How could any of them guess that the adult Liz would back out of a dream semester in New Zealand just in time to start dating her jerk of a future ex-husband?

"Geez, Caroline, what's your problem?" asked Nate.

"Yeah, that was awfully specific-like," Tamika said.

"Sometimes I'm kinda psychic," I said, adding an eye roll at the last second for effect. "Didn't you know?"

Liz asked, "Did you know someone who chickened out like that?"

"I know *everyone* who did that," I said. I couldn't stop myself. "Everyone does it all the time. Because nothing goes like you plan it, because everything looks different when you get right up close. Because all you can actually do is keep your eyes open, and even then you still miss the most important things."

"That's what I'm saying!" Tamika said. She was actually smiling. She thought I was on her side here. "All you can do is figure out what really matters the most to you, and you gotta go for that."

"There's no going for it!" I snapped back, slamming my pen down on the table. "You think there's a path and you're on it, from school to college to a good job and the life you want. Teenagers always think they know what the future's going to be like."

"You're a teenager too," said Liz.

"You're all on this completely fictional track, and you're so *happy* there, only you don't even know that you are, all wrapped up in your emo crap—"

"Emo crap? Our best friend is dead!" Nate yelled at me.

"I know that, I didn't mean that!" I yelled right back. "Obviously! All I'm saying is that you think you know who you are and where you're going, but you'll spend the rest of your lives chasing the kind of contentment and self-assurance you're enjoying right now!"

"Enjoying?" spluttered Nate. "Screw you!"

I glared back for a good ten seconds, but I didn't actually have a response.

Finally I launched myself out of my chair, yanking my backpack off the floor but leaving my applications on the table, spinning for the door.

"Fine, just walk out!" Nate shouted after me. "And don't you bother—"

"Nate, shut the hell up!" Tamika snapped. "Caroline's gotta deal with this in her own way."

"Would anyone like a hug?" Liz asked.

"NO!" Nate and I both yelled, and then I was out the door and gone.

Looking back even two days later, for the life of me I couldn't figure out what my friends had said that had made me so angry. Still I couldn't quite bring myself to face them, so on Monday morning I used the voice-masker Milo had programmed to make me sound like my Mom on the phone for emergencies and called myself off school.

190

Then I rode over to Everett Mansion to hit things in the gym until I could see Mindsaber in her office.

"You're very frustrated about this," Mindsaber said after I'd recapped the conversation. "From what you've said, it seems like your friends are expressing how the death of someone close to them has inspired them to reprioritize their lives."

"But they have the same priorities they did before," I said. "They just think they're more profound now. They don't know anything about the future."

"And you do."

"Yeah, I do," I insisted. "Psychic, remember?" Talking to Mindsaber wasn't turning out to be as helpful as I'd hoped.

"Do your psychic visions tell you everything about the future?"

"Of course not. But I know enough to know that I don't know everything!"

Mindsaber tilted her head slightly. "It's been a long time since you raised your voice during a session. What's happening right now?"

I ignored her question but lowered my voice. "It's not that I blame them. Teenagers always think they're adult enough to make their own decisions, that they're jaded and invincible. I get that. But they don't have the perspective I have."

"A hero's perspective, you mean," Mindsaber said.

"Yeah, sure. I mean, it's almost like the closer any of us are to actual invincibility, the faster life teaches us that we're not. Like the faster we can run or jump or fly, the faster reality catches up with us."

"It sounds like you wish you could share your perspective with your friends."

I shuddered at the thought of telling more people my secrets. "Not that. But I wish they'd trust me that the future isn't all rainbows and butterflies."

Mindsaber sat back. "People trust who and when they want to. In the meantime, I wonder what they would say if you talked about what is important to you."

"Nothing useful," I said.

I was seven years older than my oldest remaining friends, and tired of acting like I wasn't. So I didn't. I apologized to Nate, and Liz and Tamika as well, but I also told them I needed some space and time to put myself back together. They seemed to understand. I ate my lunches alone in a deserted corner of the band hall, and used the extra free nights in my week for more crime fighting. I'd already scheduled for all the incidents I could remember, so I patched my wristcomm into the police scanner on my scooter and went on patrol, on the off chance that the last life I was meant to save wasn't one I'd written about after all.

November came and went, Thanksgiving a blur. Nobody had much to feel thankful for. Then it was December, and I was still stuck in a past I could no longer stomach, waiting for my real future to come back and get me. I kept telling myself, *Not much longer. It can't be much longer now.* Right up until the afternoon of the 13th, when I heard a rock go SPANG off my bedroom window.

I looked up to see the window thankfully intact, but no sign of the thrower. I was alone in the house at the time, studying for finals while my parents were out with work friends. Hank had finished his semester the day before and was due back anytime, but would probably be partying with his friends all night.

I pulled the compact laser-stunner out from under my pillow and keyed off the safety. Ruby Goldberg had built these for the whole team plus me, passing them out three days after Sarah's funeral. I crept up to the wall, sliding up next to the window just as a second rock rebounded. Cautiously I peered through the curtains.

The TroubleShooters stood arrayed in my backyard. Marci wore a sequined silver shawl over a hot pink swish-skirted evening gown and balanced perfectly as ever on glittery silver slingbacks. Benny looked dapper in a dark suit, with a hot pink vest. Eric's suit was royal blue, with a red vest and red bow tie. Nicole had on a purple tuxedo, complete with tails; she also had a shiny silver cane in her hand, and twirled it rakishly.

I pocketed the stunner, pulled up the window, and stuck my head out.

"Uh, hi?"

Marci grinned dazzlingly. "There you are! Stand back, we're coming up."

I really hadn't planned on being sociable. Still, I knew better than to think they'd go away without an audience. I sighed. "Go around to the side door, I'll be right there."

"No need," said Nicole, stepping forward. "I got this."

She tapped the tip of her silver cane against the ground. With a whirr and a series of clicks it broke itself apart, folding outwards and upwards to become a lightweight but solid ladder, extending up the side of my house and stopping just as it reached my windowsill.

"If you scratch the siding, my father will be very displeased," I said.

Nicole looked affronted. Marci grinned, and hitched herself up the ladder and through my window. A few moments later, Benny brought up the rear and my room was full of super teens in fancy dress.

I stood against the door, leaning back as I faced the others. Five people filled my room to capacity, and I didn't want to be sitting on the bed or the desk chair looking up at them all.

"So where are you guys headed, in this finery you had to drive all the way out to Laketon and climb through a window to show off?"

"Not to show off," said Benny. "To pick up."

"My school's winter formal is tonight, and I want all my best friends there with me," Marci said. "That includes you, sunshine."

"I appreciate the thought, I really do," I said, "but I'm kinda buried in test prep at the moment."

"It's Saturday. You have all of Sunday to study," Eric said. "Next objection?"

"'I'm not really in the mood' isn't going to cut it, huh?"

"Nope," said Nicole, idly rifling through the assorted clutter on my dresser.

"My winter formal, so my feelings come first, and I want you there, *mi carina*," Marci said. "Unless of course you choose to exercise your constitutional right to veto my feelings with your own feelings. But please say you'll come?" She made a flat shelf of her hands, rested her chin on it, and fluttered her eyelashes at me.

Benny did the same.

I laughed. It was a strange feeling in my throat.

Still it took me a minute to answer. I didn't get why my attendance was so important to Marci. To all of them. And then it hit me. It was just the same as Liz throwing a gathering that she wouldn't call a party. They needed someone to tell them that enough time had passed, that it was okay to have fun.

"I don't have a dress," I said.

The Shooters all looked at each other and grinned. Benny drew a small bundle from under his coat and passed it to Marci, before following Eric out my door and closing it behind him. Marci unfolded the bundle to reveal a dress of deep blue satin, with hidden silver threads that glimmered like water under moonlight. By some miracle of superheroic fabric compression, it was not in the least bit creased.

Nicole turned back from the dresser, having picked out my favorite sapphire earrings. "We've got you."

My new fairy godmothers did a remarkable job with my hair and makeup. I felt more detached from my own body than I had since I'd first woken up in the past. In the mirror I saw a stunning young woman, her honey-colored hair piled up and ringed with a braid like a crown.

I left a note for Mom and Dad in the kitchen, and the five of us walked down to the end of my street, where the ShooterVan waited, disguised as an ordinary red minivan.

We piled in and buckled up. As Benny pulled away from the curb, Marci beamed at everyone.

"I called Milo and he said he's busy tonight, so this is everyone," Marci said. "Even without him, tonight shall be *perfect*. I am accepting nothing less. Let's do this thing!"

There was some general whooping and cheering, which I can't remember if I participated in.

"So is everyone just going stag to this thing?"

Benny turned around just long enough to grin face-achingly at Marci and get a soppy smile in return, so clearly I'd missed something there. I'd actually been right about them, and I'd missed it. The star-crossed heroes hadn't needed me at all.

Eric said he "kind of had someone, but not quite an ask-her-to-another-school's-dance someone." Nicole said she had three someones, but ditto.

The last time I'd gotten to dress up like this had been in the coming spring, for my senior prom. Sarah and I had shared a limo that night, along with our friends and our dates, and the more I looked around at the TroubleShooters, the more those memories came flooding back. The ShooterVan suddenly felt very claustrophobic indeed. I tried closing my eyes, taking slow deep breaths. Somehow that only made it worse. The small of my back and the bare skin of my arms started to prickle and burn.

"Would anyone mind if I opened a window?" I asked.

"Only our wonderfully frou-frou hairdos," Marci said, reaching up to pull a few strands out of my updo to frame my face. "But it's just hair. Go for it."

"No, you're right," I said. "I'll be fine."

Eric passed me the coldest bottle of Coke from the bottom of the van's cooler. The others all took drinks as well, and then Nicole pulled a Tupperware tub the size of a shoebox from the ice. Apparently she'd been responsible for the wrist corsages and boutonnières. Not only had she delivered gorgeously, she followed up by pulling out what looked like diamond jewelry from the pockets of her tux: tennis bracelets for Marci and me, and cufflinks for Benny, Eric, and herself.

"Dude!" Eric said. "Do you have compromising pictures of a leprechaun or something?" Nicole would make the Fortune 500 before she was legally able to drink, but for the moment she was no better off financially than the rest of us overworked, underpaid student-heroes.

"I grew the diamonds in my lab," Nicole explained.

"Ah," Eric said. "So they're fake."

"Works for me," said Marci, whipping hers around her wrist.

I cinched the bracelet around my wrist, holding it close enough to my nose to stare into the diamonds. Fake or not, they sparkled prettily in the dim light. The Coke sparkled too, in my stomach, which I couldn't decide if I found pleasant or not, but I appreciated the distraction. For the same reason, I asked the Shooters about the scrapes they'd gotten into over the last few weeks without me. They obliged and regaled me with stories, and the rest of the drive passed just on the okay side of unbearable.

When we got to Marci's school, Benny stopped me as we were leaving the van, one large hand on my shoulder.

"I'm good," I assured him.

"No, you're not," he said quietly. "No one expects that."

"Maybe not," I admitted. "But I'm still enjoying myself more than I have in a while."

Giving my shoulder one last squeeze, he joined Marci at the front of the group, taking her arm.

Marci had bought an actual couples ticket for Benny and herself, and had Nicole forge tickets for the rest of the team and me. She'd hacked into the dance committee's registry and added our names, and Marci had made an anonymous donation to the committee in the amount our tickets would have cost. When we walked in, no one questioned us.

Crashing a high school dance: achievement unlocked.

Inside, Eric bowed and asked me for the great honor of the first slot on my dance card. He used those words.

"That's it," I said. "No more Turner Classic Movies for you."

But he pressed me for an answer, even a no. When I told him I hadn't decided if I felt like dancing at all, Marci was personally offended.

"Caro! Oh, you have to dance with us!"

I waffled. She made me promise. She asked again three more times on the way to the punch bowl. Then the DJ switched from Paramore to Imagine Dragons, and everyone else set their cups down on the nearest table. I clutched mine in both hands.

Sarah and I and our whole gang had danced to this same song at prom.

Marci caught my eye, and for a moment I thought she was going to order me out onto the dance floor.

"When you're ready," she said.

As the rest of the group headed into the music, I stepped out into to the hall. I had a weird urge to call Milo, but I used my regular phone since it wasn't hero business. He didn't pick up. I started to walk back into the dance, changed my mind, and called again to leave a message.

Milo answered on the second ring. *"Hey, boss. What's up?"*

"Milo! Hey. Where are you? Your voice sounds funny."

There was a bit of an echo, like he was in a tunnel.

"Huh? Oh. I'm in the car. With my family, we're going out of town."

"You okay?"

"Yeah, I'm fine," Milo said. *"You need something?"*

"No, I just—I'm out with our talented friends. They dragged me out to a school dance, of all things."

"Yeah. Wish I could be there instead of here, I really do."

"Yeah, it's fun. I think. Well, good luck with the family whatever."

"Yeah, thanks. Night, boss."

I shuffled back into the gym just as the DJ selected another blast from the wrong part of my past, and reclaimed my spot on the wall. After a minute I realized it was easier to ignore the song if I concentrated on watching the people dancing to it. I looked for the guy in the baby blue leisure suit, because there's always one, and assembled a mental list of my ten favorite dresses.

The next song had not played at my prom, so far as I recalled, but it wasn't great, so I sat that one out too, and waited to hear the one after that. It turned out to be "Human," by The Killers, off an album Sarah and I once spent most of a road trip to New Jersey singing along with at the top of our punch-drunk lungs. Sarah had an aunt and uncle who had a house on the Jersey shore; despite the unsavory associations with reality television, we'd driven out to spend a week on the beach after graduation.

Suddenly even teenage fashion faux-pas were not distraction enough. I grabbed up my skirt and lunged for the door.

I made my way past the bathrooms, ducked under a tape cordon while the nearest chaperone's back was turned, and stumbled halfway up a dark and empty stairwell before slumping against the wall. I sat with my head drooping towards my knees and my hands behind my head, waiting to bawl or to retch, surprising myself as I continued just to breathe. I'm not sure how long I sat there. Every time I thought about standing up and going back downstairs, a little voice in my head said, *Maybe not yet*, and I answered silently, *All right*.

The next thing I heard was Nicole's voice. "Hey, gorgeous. How're you?" I looked up to find her seated on the stair beside me, her jacket off and tie missing, probably in the pocket of the jacket. She was sipping from a bottle of water.

"I'm sorry," I said.

"What for?"

"For being selfish."

Nicole raised one incredulous eyebrow.

"I just, this is a lot to deal with. I thought I was dealing with it, but I think I've just been so busy with school and everything that it was like I didn't have to."

"That's the only way *to* deal with it, I think. To do everything else *but* deal with it, until the dealing with it just happens. You know?"

"I don't," I said. "I don't know. And now here I am. And here all you guys are, and you must feel like I've been avoiding you all, because I have been. Because I've been so caught up in dealing with me, or not dealing with me, or whatever, that I didn't really care that all of you were dealing with it too."

"I refuse to believe that you did not care," Nicole said.

"Caring that matters has action attached."

"So maybe we should've dance-napped you sooner. Or, I dunno, Laser Tag-napped you. Bowling-napped you. Something. You forgive us for that?"

"Stop it!" I snapped. "Really, it's childish, and I sincerely don't need that right now."

"What?"

"Stop being a jerk when I'm trying to apologize..." I trailed off, feeling an insistent buzzing from the wristcomm in my purse. As I went for it, Nicole went for hers as well. We checked our screens at the same moment, saw the emergency alert, and hurried to get our earpieces in place.

Lenore Williams was on the line with a Cataclysm Level 6. Leviathan was fighting sorcerers on the other side of the planet, and Rob20's giant robot was missing from the mansion lab and assumed to be headed back to the prison.

"Crap on a cracker," I said.

"Marci's gonna be *piiiiiiiiiissed*," said Nicole.

Then we were running down the stairs, Nicole struggling to keep up with my bounding strides.

As we reached the main hall I said, "You get the others, quick and subtle as you can, make sure they got the alert. I'm going for the van." Benny had the keys, but the van was programmed to recognize our fingerprints and retinal scans as well, mine included.

"On it." Nicole grinned at me. "And Bounceback? It's good to have you back."

"I'm not back, I'm just here. Go, go!"

Chapter 15: Regret

In dangerous supervillain encounters, an ordinary non- powered police officer does hold one advantage over any hero: the police are permitted to employ lethal force when necessary in defense of themselves or innocents. Superheroes are not. The same laws which grant heroes special privileges regarding unwarranted searches [...] require that a hero avoid inflicting permanent physical, psychological, or spiritual harm on their opponents.

- Dying for a Laugh

Less than two minutes later, I was pulling the van up to the curb. Marci yanked open the door, the Shooters scrambled inside, and Benny took over the wheel as I reclaimed my usual seat in the back next to Eric.

"So are you back on duty now?" I asked him as I strapped in.

"You mean after I beat the almighty crud out a prisoner who'd already surrendered? Not officially. I think I will be this week. Mindsaber is supposed to tell me after our next think."

"Doesn't matter, this is a level 6. Anything over a level 5 means all hands on deck," Marci said.

"Hopefully we'll finish it fast enough this time that it won't matter anyway," Eric said.

"That's the spirit!" Marci said. "If everybody brings their A-game, we can totally make it back in time for 'Love Shack.'"

"Umm, I meant that I can beat the almighty crud out of a robot with a clear conscience," Eric said.

"Assuming the bot doesn't already have a driver," Benny said.

"Like if Rob20 had a stooge or something we didn't know about?" Marci said.

"A stooge that just walked through Everett Mansion security?" Nicole said. Her eyes were locked on a monitor built into the side of the van, her fingers flying across a keyboard that had swung out from the arm-rest of her seat.

Eric mimicked her, fluttering his fingers. "Or, y'know, hacked through."

"No way," Nicole said. "Not with all the work Milo and I put in. We stripped out that bot's command codes and firewalls and put our own better ones in. We have to be dealing with the intrinsic AI here, a consciousness we missed when we were making friends with the rest of the software."

"If you're so friendly, how about you get the bot to tell us where he is?" asked Marci.

"I'm working on it, fearless leader."

I called Milo again, to see if he was somewhere he could get to a computer, but he was back to not answering. In the meantime, we drove for the prison. Benny deactivated the van's holograms, revealing our true red-and-blue glory to the night at large and law enforcement in particular as we hit the highway and poured on the speed.

I pulled my mask out of my purse and pressed it to my face; it was one of my no-frills spares, as I'd been nervous about accidentally losing the expensive model at the dance. The others put their masks on as well, none of us ever left home without them, but otherwise we were heading into battle in our winter formal finery.

"Don't you usually keep spare costumes in the van?" I asked.

"Usually, sure. But we had to use 'em in an ambush two days ago, and SOMEONE took 'em home to be washed, and forgot to bring them back," Lift said.

"Including mine. I wasn't even in that fight!" added Match.

"Dude, your suit STANK," said Ruby Goldberg. "And I said I was sorry!"

"A lot of good that does us now, *cuchura*," Lift said. "We're facing a giant robot rematch, we don't actually know where it is or how it broke out of our own frickin' base, and we have no body armor and no mecha-grade weapons."

"We do have one thing going for us," Ruby said.

"An impressive amount of practical experience for our age?" said Lift.

"We all look super hot?" said Match.

"Bounceback being back?" said Manaaki.

Ruby rolled her eyes. "Okay, yeah, all of that. But I was talking about these." Tugging on her right sleeve, she pressed the cufflink there with her thumb, and with a low thrumming noise, twin gloves of glowing red energy sparked into life surrounding her hands. She flexed her fingers, and the energy gloves moved with them. She made fists, and they were extended by the field to three times their normal size. "Ladies and gentlemen, I give you my latest stroke of genius: Fisticufflinks! Trademark RubyTech, 2014."

I snorted. Match groaned. Lift said, "Dude! Where are mine?"

"On your wrists," Ruby promised. I was closest, so she demonstrated on me. Taking my left hand, she tore the beautiful rose from my wrist corsage, tossing it away to reveal another of her lab-grown diamonds hidden on the elastic strap below. She thumbed the diamond. I felt the tennis bracelet tighten around my other wrist, not too much, and with that same thrumming noise I had a pair of hard light boxing gloves of my very own.

"Fisti-bracelets!" Ruby crowed. "I'm still working on that name."

Reluctantly, Lift peeled the flower from her corsage as well, and flicked her gloves on and off a few times. Match powered up his cufflinks and left them on, his fists loosely clenched in anticipation.

The computer pinged.

"I've got a location trace," Ruby said.

Manaaki jammed the accelerator to the floor and the ShooterVan roared down a two-lane road hemmed in by forest. We could feel the ground jolting beneath us long before we heard the robot's massive legs thudding against the ground.

"There?" Lift said.

"Dead ahead!" Ruby said.

"Oy, ixnay on the ead-day!" Match said.

"How 'bout an ixnay on the Pig Latin?" Lift said. "I'm trying to concentrate."

"I'm working on the holo-camouflage, but it's fighting back pretty hard," Ruby said.

"Which is ironic," Match said, "given all the quality time you and that robot have been spending together."

"Almost—" Ruby said.

"Valid use of the word ironic," I said. "Nice."

"GOT IT!"

A hundred yards in front of the van, the thin air shimmered to reveal Rob20's giant robot running down the road before us, its car-sized feet pounding the pavement. In the white glare of a nearly full moon, a dark line of carbon scoring was visible across the machine's right thigh, where the steel had been welded back together after Lift forced it to shoot itself at the prison.

That same leg was looming very large in our windshield, and larger, and larger still.

"We're sure this is a good idea?" Match said.

"Everybody HANG ON!" Lift yelled.

Manaaki altered course just slightly to the right, fully centering the robot's leg in our view. Lift closed her eyes and hummed, projecting a battering ram of pure telekinetic force out ahead of the ShooterVan. Not that any of us could see it.

"You know how in the comics they color TK blasts like pink or something?" Match whispered. "I'd really like that right now!"

"SHHHH!" I hissed.

We braced for impact.

At the very last second, the robot kicked its right leg high, and the ShooterVan sailed right under the machine.

Trees reared up before us. Manaaki stood on the brakes and swung the wheel hard left, overcorrecting, rocking the van on its wheels. We started to overbalance; I felt gravity punch me in the stomach, my head swimming as we tipped hard to one side, but Lift reached out with her mind and pushed us back upright. As it was, the van spun 180 degrees, giving us a great view through the front windshield as Rob20's robot lifted its arm, its lasers popping out to say hello.

"Out, everybody OUT!" shouted Lift, as if we weren't already yanking our restraints and kicking open the doors. We dove clear into the grass between the woods and the road as green lasers strafed the van's left side. Amidst the PEWPEWPEWPEWPEW I heard at least two of the tires pop and hiss. Match had landed closest to me, and I grabbed the back of his suit coat with both hands, shoving him forward under the cover of the trees.

The others made it there too. We all whipped around, fighting to catch our breath as the mecha turned in the road to face us. Our pretty clothes were grass-stained and torn. The sharp December breeze tickled my bare arms and legs, but with all the adrenaline I had going I couldn't really feel it.

I waited for the machine to raise its lasers again, but it didn't. Not yet.

"No retreat!" Lift called out.

"The van's tires will self-repair," Ruby said. "If we just—"

"Not fast enough! This piece of scrap demolished my fancy night, we're demolishing it right back! Direct frontal attack," Lift said.

"That's the whole plan?" Match asked.

"We've got Ruby's new toys. Just remember your robot drills: go for limbs, break joints. We can do this."

"Don't get squished!" I cheerfully added as we all triggered our fisti-whatevers.

My shoulders tensed as we ran back into the road, staying close to Manaaki, expecting more fire to rain down at any second. Instead the robot tried to sprint past us. I crouched and sprang onto the roof of the van, then kicked off again with both feet, enjoying the burning in the muscles of my super-charged legs as I shot up at the metal giant, intending to land on its left arm and do some up-close damage to its guns.

Faster than it had ever moved before, the robot twisted, slapping me right out of the air. I fell fifteen feet to hard pavement, hitting hands first, my energy gloves shooting red sparks as they impacted. I suddenly missed my Kevlar very much as I rolled across the road, skin scraping through the thin satin of my dress. But my wrists and hands were more or less unscathed, protected as advertised by the bracelets, and I pushed myself back to my feet.

By this point Manaaki and Match had started pummeling the machine's metal ankles with their power-gloved fists, while Ruby and Lift hung back by the cover of the ShooterVan. Ruby was typing away on her phone while Lift telekinetically hurled small rocks at the robot's body at near-bullet velocities.

I circled around behind, staying well clear of Lift's projectiles. Meanwhile the mecha opened fire on Manaaki with the full power of its bank-busters. Manaaki stood calm under the assault, one arm raised to protect his eyes from the glare, as the deadly green bolts went PANG! off his energy bubble. Lift panicked for the both of them, hands raised and waving excitedly at the machine, trying to telekinetically divert its gun arm. "Start hitting yourself! Why aren't you hitting yourself? Ruby, I thought you killed the psi-blockers the last time!"

"I did!" Ruby said. "Then Milo and I fixed them and made them way better!"

"Why would you DO that?!"

"Because it was supposed to be ours now! And you're not the only telekinetic in the world. Wouldn't you love to drive that thing into battle against the bad guys sometime?"

"Not really, no!"

"Well, I would! But I'm working on it!"

I took another running jump at the robot's leg, actually connecting this time, but my shoes weren't made for kicking, and I barely made a dent. Match seemed to have had better luck punching at the left ankle with Ruby's energy gloves. The robot diverted its fire from Manaaki for a second, long enough to make Match jump back, but as the 'bot raised its leg, the distressed joint blew out in a shower of sparks.

The mecha's leg crashed down, but no longer able to bend at the ankle, it couldn't push off the ground fast enough to run. It could walk, but it was hobbled.

Now we were getting somewhere! I punched the air, and Match and Ruby cheered.

The leg came up again, and this time its heavy foot crashed right down on top of Manaaki.

Lift screamed his name and leapt forward. Ruby tackled her as the robot's lasers turned their way, tearing up the road around them. I yelled and threw myself into the air, delivering a flying punch to the back of the robot's right knee. My power-gloved fist left a wicked mark, but the machine was unshaken.

I bounced away, falling back to the ground, tumbling back on my butt as I landed. That was partly from the impact, but partly just sheer relief as I heard Manaaki's voice gasping in my ear: "Force field holding... not crushed..."

The relief did not last.

"He can't breathe, HE CAN'T BREATHE!" Lift wailed. She was on her feet again, shoving at the air in front of her like a mime in a box, with as little actual effect on the world. "His shield's not meant to stay on continuously! If it's repelling constant force, it's not letting air in! Ruby, get those psi-blockers down NOW!"

"Just another few seconds!" Ruby begged, her thumbs flying across the screen of her phone.

I rolled to my feet again, springing forward under the 'bot's arm. It shot at me. I leapt away, expecting every moment to be outclassed by its computerized reflexes, to feel the lasers cut through my body. Somehow I stayed always two steps ahead. But I couldn't seem to get close to the leg pinning Manaaki.

Match ran towards Lift. "Maybe if you push at the ground underneath—"

"THERE!" shouted Ruby. "Psi-blockers are down!"

Lift punched two fists forward. "GOT YOU, YOU—"

Her entire body rocked backwards as if she'd been shot. Match got to her just in time, barely catching her before she could hit the road.

"She's unconscious!" he yelled. "I don't know how bad—"

I ran straight at Ruby Goldberg, furious and shouting. "The hell happened?! You just said the blockers were down!"

"I thought they were!" Ruby yelled back. "Every indication was they were, but it must've been a false reading..."

We were interrupted by the scrape of metal on pavement. I twisted around to see the robot backing away from us down the road, its electric eyes watching us as it continued towards the prison.

I roared and ran straight at it.

The 'bot raised one arm, the guns cycling around its wrist and firing. I didn't care; I had eyes only for the giant pothole left in its wake.

I ran at the hole, and the robot's lasers fell wide to either side of me, like it wasn't even trying. I reached the edge, and there was Manaaki. The road had cracked and recessed beneath him, but his force field seemed to have done its job. Near as I could tell he wasn't even bruised, let alone crushed, his suit barely rumpled. His face looked a little purple, but he was breathing just fine on his own.

I called to the others, "I've got Manaaki, he's all right! He's out, but—"

"Good, that's good!" Match answered. "But I can't get Lift to wake up."

"We need to get her and Manaaki off the road," I said, already throwing Manaaki over my shoulder in a fireman's carry. But as I turned towards the trees, the robot was turning as well, facing forward again. Suddenly I could see a sizable gap low on one side of its chassis, where Lift had been hurling stones only minutes before.

"MATCH!" I yelled. "Fire in the hole!"

"What?" Ruby peeked out from behind the ShooterVan. "Crap oh crap oh crap—"

Match followed my pointing finger to the chink in the robot's armor. With a pinch near each wrist he shut down his energy gloves, the light retracting back into his cufflinks. Raising his hands, he conjured one of Ruby's laser rifles from the air. The rifles had proven useless when we'd faced this thing the first time, but Match had tagged one before we left the van anyway, just in case. Now the bot was damaged and some part of its innards exposed. Hopefully parts that would blow up real good. Match raised the rifle to his eye, taking aim at the hole.

I bounced clear, taking Manaaki with me.

Ruby dropped her phone and leapt straight in front of Match and the gun, screaming, "DUDE, STOP—*MILO'S IN THERE!*"

The rifle fired.

Ruby's fisticufflinks activated automatically. The laser beam struck Ruby's energy-gloved palms and bounced right off.

Right back at Match.

Match screamed as he was thrown back off his feet, and he wasn't as lucky as Lift. I heard the crack as his head hit pavement. Dropping Manaaki on the grass beneath the trees, I scrambled, half running, half crawling. Ruby was already dropping to her knees, cradling Match's head in her lap.

"There's blood," she said, and then I could see it, wine-dark in the moonlight. "But head wounds bleed a lot. And it's just at the back, where he hit the road. I think my gloves absorbed most of the actual blast."

Shutting down her fisticufflinks, she yanked off her tuxedo jacket, balling it up to sop at the back of Match's head. I dropped to my knees beside them, hands flailing uselessly.

The robot did not try to attack us as we ministered to our friend. It kept walking towards the prison, one ponderous pounding step at a time. THOOOM. THOOOM. THOOOM.

Ruby called Everett Mansion with her wristcomm, reporting heroes down and our location. I couldn't hear the receptionist's response, but the gist was obvious enough as Ruby shouted back, "Don't tell me there are no speedsters available! Somewhere in the world there's a speedster who can be here RIGHT NOW! Well, there should be!"

"You said Milo is in the robot?" I'd missed something important.

Ruby nodded. "I thought, when Lift went down—who else would be cunning enough to give a robot a psi-blocker upgrade that makes it looks like it's shut down, then hit the telekinetic attacking it with massive mental feedback? Instant TK-KO."

That's what had happened to Lift, and it did sound like Milo's sort of cleverness. And I knew better than anyone the potential he possessed for this kind of mayhem. But Milo was our friend. He wasn't on that path any more.

"Milo!" I shouted into my comm. "Zoran Milosevic, are you there?"

No answer. I estimated we had maybe five minutes before the mecha was within firing distance of the prison wall.

"Plus, there's the way he was hacking back my hacks when I was trying to take over. Not like a machine at all. Like a person. A very specific person I know," Ruby said. "Trust me, I know how Milo codes."

"If Milo's driving that thing, why's he still heading for the prison?" I asked. "What could he possibly want from Rob20?"

Ruby shrugged. "Maybe something's driving him?"

"You think it could be mind control?"

"I always think it could be mind control."

What if it was? What if it always had been? Was that why I never managed to figure out how a good kid like Milo became a mass-murdering supervillain? Maybe Zo-Rann the Conqueror had never been anything more than a pawn in the same game I'd been playing since the Vice Admiral and Tomás Pain crashed the book signing.

Milo's voice rang out over our comms. *"It's not mind control."*

"Milo!" Ruby said. "What's happening?"

"It's me, this is me, doing what needs to be done, because it needs doing. I'm sorry, I'm so sorry. But if you'll just back off, please, then I won't have to hurt you anymore. No one will have to get hurt anymore."

"Milo?" I said. "Milo, I trust you, but you've got to tell me what you're trying to do."

"Yeah, dude, we just need a little more information right now," said Ruby.

No reply, and the robot was still walking.

I muted my wristcomm and caught Ruby's eye. "Someone's making him do this. I mean, obviously, right?"

"But if he's under duress, that's why we have signal phrases," Ruby said. "Which he hasn't used."

"So he can't. So it's someone who knows our signal phrases. Someone like...?"

And now, Ruby Goldberg, would be a FANTASTIC time for you to tell me who it is we've been fighting across time, I thought.

"Yeah, I've got no clue either," Ruby said.

I couldn't tell if she meant it, or if she just had some all-important reason not to say the name out loud. She wouldn't meet my eye; she was too busy tying the arms of her tuxedo jacket in place around Match's head, a makeshift bandage.

"Okay, so it's plan B," she said. "Kick his butt first; sort out the why later."

"We're teenage superheroes," I said, with a levity I sure wasn't feeling. "Isn't that plan A?"

"Yeah, pretty much. C'mon, first let's get our friends clear."

I picked up Match, careful to support his head and neck, and jogged him to the cover of the trees. Ruby hooked Lift under the armpits and dragged her there too, Lift's beautiful silver stiletto sandals scraping across the gravelly road. As if her night hadn't been ruined enough already.

"Milo, talk to me," I tried again, setting Match down in the grass alongside Manaaki. "What's this really about?"

"You know exactly what this is about!" Milo snapped.

"I really don't," I said. "Why don't you tell me?"

No reply. The road curved up ahead, and Milo and his mecha would soon be out of sight.

Ruby handed Lift off to me, and I settled her in beside the others as Ruby ran back towards the ShooterVan. I assumed she was going for more pulse rifles, or some other useful toy she hadn't thought to mention she had. I also assumed the van's tires would still be somewhere in the middle of their self-repair cycle. Assuming was easier right then, with my body torn up by the road and the robot and my gut torn up by three badly injured friends and Milo.

"Don't you want us to understand?" I heard Ruby's voice through the comm as she ran back to the van. *"This would all be a lot easier if you'd just talk to us, Milo."*

"Of course I want you to understand! But I can't, I just can't…"

"Milo, please," I said. "Just hang on, just wait—"

"No, I can't wait!" Milo shouted. *"How long were you waiting, Caroline, on the night Sarah died? How much time was wasted on containment for a multiple escapee? On frickin' paperwork?!"*

"So what're you saying?" Ruby asked in a flat voice. *"That the last time Sugar Mama broke out, we should have killed her when we had the chance?"*

"That's not what I meant."

"You're saying Sarah's death was our fault? That it's on the Shooters?"

"No, no!" Milo said. I'm pretty sure he was crying. *"I'm just saying I can fix it!"*

Behind me, the ShooterVan's engine roared to life.

I turned just in time to catch a glimpse of Ruby Goldberg's face through the windshield, wild-eyed and teeth bared, before she barreled past.

"Yippee ki-yay, mother trucker!" she yelled, accelerating directly at one of the robot's legs.

Ruby timed it perfectly. This time, there was no stepping over. The robot's foot came down on the top of the van like a dad stepping on a kid's skateboard that had been left in the driveway. The robot's whole leg went flying out from under it, and it fell hard on its steel back.

Whatever was left of the van was kicked away, skidding off the road and crashing side-on into the trees.

My throat seized up, every muscle in my body tensing, more terrified than I'd been since the morning Sarah's car was found abandoned in the Denny's parking lot. Hitching up my dress, I ran, faster and harder than I'd ever run in my life.

Before I'd crossed even half the distance, the robot was already pushing its big steel-beam arms against the road and sitting up. Its head hung at on odd angle on its neck, trailing wires—thick laser-optical cables. Unfortunately the head's purpose was primarily cosmetic, offering little to the automaton's function; its central processors were buried in the main body below the driver. There were a number of new dents and scrapes across the metal of its back as well, but on the whole Ruby Goldberg's stunt didn't seem to have done any significant damage. The 'bot pulled its legs in and began to rise.

With a guttural roar, I leapt upon the crouching machine. I executed a twisting somersault as I ascended, sailing over the robot's left shoulder. Reaching out as I passed over, I managed to catch hold of the exposed neck cables with both hands, and slammed hard into the robot's chest.

I dangled there by the cables, a mere six inches of titanium hatch plating now separating me from Milo. Choking up on the cables, looping them securely around my hands, I shouted his name.

Ruby Goldberg shouted back instead. *"Bounceback, I'm okay!"*

"Oh thank god," Milo said. His voice echoed, a murmur through the hatch followed by clarity in my earpiece.

Looking back over my shoulder, I picked out the ShooterVan lying several hundred feet up the road. The rear two-thirds of the vehicle were an unholy mess, but the cab was largely intact, thanks to emergency force bubble generators that kicked in upon impact to protect the occupants. The generators in back had failed, too quickly crushed by the robot's foot, but the front was saved. Unfortunately the doors were too warped to open.

"I'm trapped, but I'm okay!" Ruby said.

"Is anything on fire?" I asked.

"I don't think so."

I didn't see any smoke from where I was either, which was good. "We're coming," I promised. "We'll get you out."

"Who's we?"

The robot shook, finally extending to its full height again, leaving me hanging twenty-five feet above the road by two chunky cables, staring at an impassive titanium hatch.

"Milo?" No answer. "Milo, you're going to use this stupid machine to help our friend, right now, and then you're going to get out and talk to us!"

Nothing. The robot stomped, every footfall sending a shudder down the cables and through my arms.

A dent from one of Lift's earlier projectiles caught the moonlight. It was barely a dimple, really, but I kicked at it. The tips of my pretty shoes split open, sending blinding spikes of pain shooting up from my toes to my brain, but I kept kicking anyway, giving myself half a foothold. "Milo, stop!"

"*I scanned the van. It's stable. Ruby will be fine,*" Milo said. "*You should drop off now.*"

Letting go of one the cables, I punched at the edge of the hatch with all the extra force Ruby's fisti-bracelet provided.

"*Dammit, Caro, STOP!*" shouted Milo.

I punched again and again, hammering at the metal. "You—want me—to stop? Then—tell me—who's making you—do this!"

"*I told you, it's just me!*"

Oh holy crap, I thought.

Because what if it was?

His robot reached for me. I pulled up on the cables, spun and kicked the metal hand away.

Who was Ruby Goldberg fighting in the future? That had always been the real question. And then I just happened to stumble on Ruby's nemesis in my own high school lunchroom. Someone who had *died* fighting Ruby, and I never once thought—what if he didn't? Yes, W.H.A.M. confirmed recovery of the Conqueror's body in a press release, but no one ever actually saw it. That was like the Fourth Law of Supervillains: if you don't see the body, they're not actually dead.

What if Zo-Rann the Conqueror lived?

What if he was the one who sent me back in time and gave me powers, not Ruby?

And I went back and picked him out and marched him right into Everett Mansion as an honored guest. I'd handed him all the tools he needed to destroy the TroubleShooters. He'd taken them out one by one, and now I was all that was left between him and whatever stupid plan he was enacting.

Blinking behind my mask, my vision blurring with tears, I punched the hatch again. "So were you just pretending to be our friend? All this time—"

"*Of course I wasn't!*" Milo insisted.

Was he a time-traveler, an adult stuck in a teenager's body, just like me? And if everything that had happened to me wasn't Ruby Goldberg's doing after all, if it was all part of Zo-Rann the Conqueror's latest whacked-out scheme, then why me?

Had he read my book, in the future? All those villains with all their weird science weapons—I'd practically written him a catalog. Stealing other people's inventions had always been Zo-Rann's M.O. I remembered Milo getting upset that time I fought Train Wreck, when I destroyed the power pack he'd hoped to study. And now here he was, in Rob20's wicked mecha, which I'd just about delivered to him gift-wrapped.

But why attack the prison? Was he trying to steal himself an army? Did he have allies in there waiting to be freed?

My next thought made ice boil inside me. *Did Zo-Rann hire Morgan Patterson?*

My whole body shook, my foot slipping in the dent with each ponderous step the robot took. I grabbed the cables with both hands again, and it was all I could do to hang on. Was my best friend's murder an attempt to uncover the secrets I'd only shared with her? Had Milo known where she was all along?

No. No! Even tonight, even after all this, I couldn't believe that. Two minutes ago, when he talked about the night she died, he was crying, I was sure of it.

He was still crying, I realized, as he begged, *"Caroline, please, please, listen to me. Just listen! I couldn't do what you wanted. I couldn't build you a time machine, I couldn't save Sarah! So I hijacked this robot instead. I can kill her killer, and I can kill a whole lot of other killers in that prison, before they kill again. I can prevent them from killing a whole lot of other Sarahs in the future. How does that sound, boss?"*

"On paper it sounds great," I said. "But you're a freaking genius, Milo, you have to know that's not how things—"

"—not how things work? I'm an engineer. Don't tell me how things work! The jackhole who built this kick-ass robot, how many people has he killed in how many banks already? How many more would he have killed if you hadn't had your vision, if he'd escaped and you guys hadn't been there to shut him down?"

Twelve, just to start with. I knew that precisely.

"This is how it works," Milo said. *"Villains kill people. Heroes fight villains. Heroes capture villains. Villains escape and kill again. Or they just keep the heroes so busy that they're not there for the people who really need them."*

"So you do blame us," Ruby said. I'd forgotten she was still listening in, still trapped in the wreck of the van. *"Because we should've finished the job?"*

"Killing is the last thing I want for you! But someone has to."

"They really don't," Ruby said.

As short as my career was as a super-villain biographer, whatever success I enjoyed rested on my finely honed bullshit-detector. And right then, I believed that Milo believed what he was saying. He thought this was about justice, and about saving lives in the future.

So maybe he wasn't a time-traveler after all. Maybe he really was just a scared, grieving kid. So what, then? Was his future self was manipulating him somehow? Sending him messages? If so, he was clearly leaving out a lot of vital information. Like just where Milo's future was leading him.

But what could Zo-Rann actually want? To goad Milo into eliminating his rivals? Maybe clear the way for future-evil-Milo to raid the dead prisoners' secret lairs without fear of discovery or reprisal? Another bloody shopping spree, literally.

"Milo, I get how you feel. We all get it," I said. "But you have to trust me, you have to stop. He's using you!"

"*He who?*" Milo said.

"Okay, *you're* using you!"

This time he didn't even answer. The robot stomped on. And the one iron-clad certainty I had was that for whatever reason he did it, going through with this would wreck Milo. He could do it for power and money or children and puppy-dogs, and my friend would be destroyed all the same.

I wasn't having it.

I started bashing again. Milo was in there. My future supervillain, wrapped tight in a steel cocoon. But there would be no transformation today. It could've been the whole purpose I was sent back for, my one and only way home, and I still wouldn't care. I punched the hatch, the metal thundering.

Again, Milo pleaded for me to stop. "*Stewards do what heroes can't, Caro. Heroes have powers, most of you. If you started killing, even the worst bad guys, people would freak the freak out. No one's gonna get scared of stewards because no one knows who we are. Please, let me do this for you.*"

I kept punching, felt the hatch starting to give under my glowing red fist. "And what about all the guards that are about to get caught in the crossfire?"

"*They won't. I'm better than that.*"

"Villains have families too. What about the people who will grieve for them?"

"*They'll learn to deal. Just like they've dealt with loving a homicidal douchebag inmate.*"

"What about you? What do you think happens to you after you kill a bunch of prisoners in cold blood?"

"*That's up to you and the Shooters. If you turn me in, boss, I'll accept it. But if you don't, I'm walking away, and they'll find this robot*" empty, and everyone can think this was another botched escape attempt from Rob20's corrupted AI."

He had an answer for everything.

My knuckles finally hit air; I'd opened a gap at the hatch's edge. I wriggled my fingers into the gap, ready to rip the door from its hinges.

Milo answered that by electrifying the hatch.

The current carried right through my energy gloves. My fingers spasmed open, and I plummeted twenty-five feet onto the unforgiving road. I hadn't been prepared for the drop, so my normally springy knees locked, and I hit the ground hard on both heels. I fell onto my back, barely managing to tuck my neck and keep the back of my head from cracking on the pavement.

My vision swam anyway, as Milo stepped right over me. I was pretty sure both of my ankles were sprained, my spine was definitely bruised, and the rest of me just hurt a lot, as if I'd messed up a drop from the high dive.

For a moment I lay flat on the ground, staring up at the moon, listening to Milo walk away.

THOOOOOOOM.

THOOOOOOOM.

THOOOOOOOM.

Then I heard a voice, that might have been mine and might have been Sarah's, screaming in my ear. "Get up. Get up. GET UP!"

Barely even aware of what I was doing, I tore the ruined shoes from my feet and threw them away, then unclasped the fisti-bracelets from my wrists and secured them around my ankles. The energy fields winked on around my feet, conforming themselves to the shape as I'd hoped, becoming glowing translucent boots to support my ankles. I stood.

Milo's robot was maybe five hundred feet up the road. We'd come farther than I'd realized as I was hanging there arguing with him, and I could see the prison wall in the distance beyond. The guards there would spot him any second now, if they hadn't already. Stumbling, I ran after him, shouting his name and various epithets.

I made it maybe half a dozen steps before my abused legs refused to cooperate any longer, and I collapsed back to my hands and knees on the gritty pavement. I could only watch as the mecha lifted both arms, as Milo took aim at the wall.

With a ragged voice I shouted into the comm, "Milo, don't do this!"

"*If I don't do this,*" Milo said, "*if someone doesn't, then she just keeps dying. I have to fix it! It needs a permanent solution, not some duct-tape stopgap!*"

"There are no permanent solutions. Believe me, I know, better than anyone. Because I'm from the future too, and I know how this ends. I've always known!"

"*You what?*" Milo said.

"It's why I spied on you, why I recruited you, to stop you becoming a supervillain. To stop you becoming the person who does this."

"*A supervillain? What are you talking about? You know me, you know I'm not—*"

"You're a freaking genius," I told him, "and you'll only be remembered for stealing other people's toys and using them to kill!"

"*Even if that's true, just because people won't understand, that doesn't mean it's not the right thing to do.*"

"Violence escalates. It always does. You'll kill, you'll keep killing, and innocents WILL get caught in the crossfire. You'll allow some to die to save more, and in the end you won't be a steward any more. You'll be—"

"*No. No! I'm smarter than that! I would never—*"

"Milo, you just beat the living hell out of our best friends in the world. Where do you think your life goes from here?!"

Milo's robot stood, guns out, staring down the wall. I waited, my ankles throbbing, my muscles tense and ready for action.

After an eternity, Milo's voice whispered in my ears. "*You're from the future. How did I not see it before?*"

Chapter 16: React

For fans of daytime superhero dramas like Capes and Tights, there are few story tropes more poignant than the hero and arch-villain who were once the greatest of friends. The long-running series won its first Daytime Emmy for writing for its 17th season, which featured a critically acclaimed and highly rated plot arc involving the hero Lightwalker and her high school sweetheart-turned- nemesis ShadowScythe. Over the course of 6 weeks, the hero convinced her lover to turn back from the path of villainy, finally marrying him in a ceremony attended by both heroes and villains under a flag of truce.

Yet in real life, 67% of those polled by SuperheroScore-card.com said they would be in favor of heroes using lethal force against the Apostate, the supervillain once known as the hero the Absolver, compared to 54% who favor lifting restrictions against superheroes using lethal force all together.

"The Redemption Myth"
The Burr, Kent State University
Caroline Henderson, Fall 2018

I really didn't see how we had time to get into this right now.

"It was just a figure of speech. I'm psychic, you know that," I said.

"Yeah, but that never made any sense. The things you were extremely specific about, the things you didn't know at all. Most psychic visions are actual visions. The future is seen in the mind. But you pretty much never described yours in optical terms. It was like you were getting the psychic Cliffs Notes. I thought that was odd, but I figured you were just something new. But now you're telling me that you knew tonight was going to happen way back when you first recruited me?"

"Not tonight," I said. "Not exactly."

"You're from the future. That's how you know things." There was wonder in Milo's voice, and a little fear. I could hear the last not-quite-year shaking itself up in his head, the facts of me realigning. *"But we were in fourth grade together. Was that when you first came back? Did your whole family come back too, or are you like adopted? Have you always been...?"*

"Milo, I'll tell you the whole story, how it all works. But not right now." I would have been angry, I would've snapped, but I was too bone-tired. I pushed back off my hands, forcing myself up on to my aching feet. "Right now I need you to step out of the mecha and help me walk."

"*Are you—*"

"I'm fine," I assured him. It was only half a lie. "But we have to go back and help the others."

The robot's guns stayed fixed on the prison wall. "*The world will still be a better place without Coldest Winter in it. You know that.*"

"It's never that simple. No matter how much we know, or have seen, or can do, none of us is smart enough—"

"*To outwit fate?*"

"Fate's nothing but the sum of the choices we make. Make a different one."

Another long moment passed.

Finally, slowly, the mecha turned around. It knelt down, and as it did so its hatch popped and swung open, an extremely loud sound in the suddenly hushed night.

Behind a bank of levers and buttons, Milo hung inside in a motion control harness, like some twisted marionette. He flailed, struggling to pull himself free of the harness. I was too tired to help, and not sure I wanted to.

"I never meant... I didn't think you'd be the ones who took the call," he said. "I'm so sorry."

"You should be."

At last Milo managed to shake himself lose, clumsily dropping the last few feet from the robot to the ground, stumbling forward. I stumbled forward myself to catch him. He held me up as we walked back up the road. Pain shot through my ankles with every step, but Milo held on tight.

The TroubleShooters waited for us by the crushed and crumpled hulk of the van. In the time it took Ruby to improvise a laser sword from spare parts and cut herself free, Lift, Manaaki, and Match had all regained consciousness. Young heroes have thick skulls.

There was a tense moment as everyone glared at Milo.

"I formally surrender," Milo said. "Whatever you have to do—"

Lift cut him off with a jabbing finger. "This was my happy night! You can shut up now!"

I wanted to defend him, but nothing he had done was defensible.

"Guys?" said Ruby. "Back-up's gonna be here in like no minutes. We sending Milo to jail or what?"

"We could take a vote?" said Match.

"No!" Lift said.

"Why not?"

"Because he's standing right there," replied Lift. "That's just mean."

"And kicking all our butts with a giant robot isn't?"

"Our actions have consequences. Big consequences," said Ruby. "Isn't that the first rule of what we do? Not saying I don't hate it, but—"

"But jail?" said Match.

"Guys, it's okay," Milo said. "If—if that's where I need to be right now—"

Lift looked at Manaaki. Manaaki shook his head.

In the distance, we heard the first sirens approaching.

"No. You need to be with us," Lift determined. "Guys, we're lying our asses off. That robot went rogue all on its own. Everybody cool with that?"

Ruby stepped forward and punched Milo hard in the face.

"Dude!" said Match.

"What?" Ruby said innocently. "He needs to look like he was in the same fight as the rest of us."

"That is logical, and also fair," Milo replied from the ground.

"Also, he stole my robot."

Lift and I each took a hand, helping him back up.

"Thanks," Milo said. "No, really, all of you. I don't—"

"Thanks later," Lift said. "Match, give him your coat. We were at a school dance tonight, he needs to look the part."

Milo peeled off his own sweatshirt, tossing it to Match, then pulled on the charred and torn suit-coat over his t-shirt. Otherwise he wore jeans and bright red Converse All-Star sneakers. Slacker-hip was a style, so it just about worked.

Manaaki looked at me. "So when you told Milo just now that you were from the future..."

They'd heard everything on the open comm channel. All of them.

"Not now, *mi carina*," Lift told him. "Later."

The post-battle adrenaline was wearing off; we were all starting to feel the cold through our ruined party clothes. Manaaki's force field kept flickering on every time there was the slightest breeze; when there wasn't, I noticed him sucking in deep and grateful lungfuls of air. Ruby, Match, and Milo all paced back and forth at varying speeds, rubbing their arms or breathing into their hands. The stabbing pain in my ankles was getting worse by the second, so Lift helped me sit down while we waited, the sirens growing louder.

I stared at the wreck of the dear old ShooterVan, which turned out to be neither as old nor as dear as I'd previously believed. Ruby caught me looking and said, "Caro, it's okay. It happens all the time."

"What?"

"Oh yeah, the van's no big," Lift said. "We've killed at least two of 'em just since you started hanging with us."

"I think I'd have noticed a replacement ShooterVan!" I thought they were having me on.

They weren't. "We keep detailed holo-scans on file," Ruby said. "A computer repaints the new ones exactly, down to the last scratch. The ShooterVan is an icon. Continuity matters to our people!"

"Maybe I could help assemble the next one?" Milo asked. "Assuming I'm not, y'know, in prison or anything."

"You won't be," Lift assured him. "You're not my favorite person right now, but we'll deal."

The police pulled up less than a minute later, and an ambulance was close behind. There would be extensive reports to file, technically perjuring ourselves in the process, but first we all received a ride to the nearest hospital. Ruby and Milo, who were relatively unscathed, rode with the cops. I'm sure that was pretty nerve-wracking for Milo, but he'd kind of earned it.

The intake nurse at Southwest General didn't bat an eye at our no longer quite formal attire, but saw our masks and called a 38 Blue, medical code for supers who need help. This meant we were ushered into a private room and treated by specially trained stewards who could deal with everything from normal broken bones to alien goo infestation.

As the rest of the medical team got to work, one clerical nurse looked up our codenames and logged the injuries and treatments into the WHAM database. Lift explained that pro hero teams tracked their members' medical history this way, and copies of our reports would be sent to our Leviathan supervisors. Apparently we could opt out of this if we really wanted, as HIPAA applies even to secret identities, but I figured it didn't hurt to have someone making note of these things.

Ruby kept up a carefully calculated stream of distracting chatter as I was given shots of cortisone in both ankles and fitted for anti-gravity boots. From the outside they looked like plastic splints that anyone might get for sprained ankles, but they would keep the weight off my joints and let me walk normally while I healed. Bandages covered my various scrapes, of which there had been more than usual due to the sleeveless dress, and a medicated layer of artificial skin was rolled over my burned palm. Most of the others were finished before I was, but Lift was being kept over for observation. Psi-feedback can have disturbing and occasionally dangerous effects. Manaaki was staying with her. We all agreed to meet the next day, to discuss the night's events more fully, and with a significant glance at Milo, I apologized again to Lift for the ruination of her winter formal.

Lift waved it off. "Y'know what, *cuchura*? Getting you back was worth it. Both of you."

I smiled, before shuffling out to the lobby to call for a steward to drive me home.

When I finally got home, Mom was sitting up, as she and Dad usually did when I was out late. For most of my life, Dad had a pathological aversion to daytime naps that meant he was out like a light around 11 p.m., barring birth, death, or natural disaster. On previous occasions I'd found him nodding off at the kitchen table with his hand still wrapped around a coffee mug, but Mom usually sent him to bed and stayed up herself. I'd thought about telling her not to wait for me, that I'd wake her when I got home and let her and Dad know that I was okay, but I was pretty sure she couldn't sleep if I was out.

I could only imagine what Mom thought when I climbed carefully out of the car, still wearing my sadly tattered satin dress. By the time I got halfway up the driveway, she was coming down to meet me.

"Need help, sweetie?" she asked, taking in the shredded dress and stylish ankle boots.

"Tea, please. And pajamas," I said.

Inside, I found Hank passed out and snoring in a chair near the window.

"He insisted on sitting up with me," Mom explained. I ruffled his hair, my big-little brother, and went into the downstairs bathroom to change. Mom brought me a t-shirt and a pair of shorts that slipped on easily over the boots, and a few minutes later I was settled at the kitchen table with some tea.

Once we'd gotten the necessaries out of the way—how the battle had gone, how all my friends were doing—she smiled and asked, "How was the dance?"

"The music was terrible," I said, and then corrected myself immediately, "it wasn't that bad. I don't know what I was expecting."

"Sarah should have been there." I wasn't sure if she said it or I did.

"Mom. How do you do this?"

"What's that, honey?" She was looking at me intently. She'd washed off her makeup from the day and I could see dark circles under her eyes.

"When I go out at night, when I fight supervillains, how do you sit here drinking coffee, not knowing if I'm coming home?" It wasn't what I'd wanted to ask and I cringed at the bluntness of my question, but Mom barely hesitated.

"I'm a parent. That's what I do." She took a drink before elaborating. "It's my job to make sure you grow up happy and healthy and capable of doing the right thing, whatever that is for you. Sure, I'd expected to have you for a couple more years before you went off to college and took over your own life, but superpowers happen."

She reached over and gently tugged my hair, which I'd taken down and put back in a plain braid. "Of course I worry about you, but you're smart. Tonight was rough, but you got through it, and your teammates got through it, and that stupid machine never even had a chance to hurt anyone else." I'd only shared with Mom the official version of the story. I still hated lying to her, but she didn't need to deal with everything Milo was going through. "If I didn't trust you, I wouldn't have done my job as your mom.

"But that's not what you wanted to know," she finished before I could respond.

"Not what I had in mind," I said, "but I'm glad you told me."

My tea had gone cold. I stood up to reheat it in the microwave, and the bandages pulled at my skin.

Mom said, "Let me see if I can help. You're not a mother, but you feel responsible for your friends?"

"Something like that."

She came to stand with me, and hugged me carefully with one arm. "Sweetie, bad things happen. It's up to you to decide how to deal with them. Some paths are riskier than others, both for you and for the people you love. You need to do what's right for you.

"If that means wearing a costume and fighting bad guys, I'm with you all the way. If you want to graduate from high school and major in accounting and sit behind a desk for the rest of your life, you can do that instead. It's your choice. And I might add, nothing says you can't change your mind at any point."

I hugged her back hard enough to feel every one of my bruises. "When Sarah was... when she was missing, did you ever think... were you glad it wasn't me?" I struggled to get the words out.

"Yes," she said calmly. "And if it had been you, I'd be glad it wasn't her. I know her parents feel the same."

The following morning I picked up the very much not arrested or in any sort of official trouble Milo at his house, and we rode downtown to Everett Mansion, where the TroubleShooters were already gathered and waiting in their meeting room. The door hissed closed and locked itself behind us.

Everyone looked horrendously tired. Marci nursed a headache and the largest coffee mug I'd ever seen, the steam rising from the top smelling fantastically good. Benny, outwardly unscathed, sat beside her, one hand resting on the back of her chair. Eric had a swollen lump on the back of his head where he'd slammed into the ground after Nicole deflected the pulse rifle blast, while Nicole herself was bending and stretching a sore elbow.

"Oh man..." Milo said, seeing everything he'd done to them through a wicked purple shiner of his own. "You guys can change your minds and send me to prison at any time." I couldn't tell if that was supposed to be funny. I doubt Milo could either.

"Oh, we know," said Marci.

I shifted uncomfortably on my anti-grav boots; the gently humming energy field keeping the weight off my injured ankles had a tendency to put my feet to sleep. Nicole sprang up, nearly shoving me into the chair beside hers. Milo sat too, but kept his seat pulled a little back from the table, maintaining a wary distance.

A moment passed, none of us quite sure how to start.

"So," Eric said.

"So," Marci said.

"So when you told Milo you were from the future, that was true, wasn't it?" Benny said.

Nicole looked aghast at Benny. "Wait, you actually fell for that? Obviously she was saying whatever Milo needed to hear so he'd get down off the stupid. No offense," she added, nodding to Milo.

"None taken," Milo answered.

"Actually it wasn't a bluff," I said. "I really am a time traveler from the future."

"No way!"

"Shut the front door!"

"Seriously!?"

"No. No! That makes ZERO sense," Nicole insisted. "We've known you, what, almost a year now? Time travelers never stay in the past that long, not without being noticed."

I frowned at her. "Nicole, what the hell? You're the one person who always knew I was a time traveler, even before I met you guys."

"Dude, what are you talking about?" said Nicole.

"When I first came back, I sent you that message through your website."

"You did?"

"Yes!" I said. "And I saw the secret message in the reply: *the first rule of time travel...*"

"*...is do not talk about time travel,*" Ruby said. "Yeah, okay, that explains it. If you select 'time travel' from the drop down box, your message automatically deletes itself before it sends you the auto-reply. I don't mess with time travel."

"You don't mess with time travel, but you've been listening to my 'psychic visions' for months?"

"That's totally different! Psychic visions are an established crime-fighting tool, one that doesn't come with 'Risk of Deadly Paradox' in bright red letters on the label."

"But that's not how time travel actually works," Milo said. "Most quantum physicists these days agree that any attempt to alter the past via time travel merely results in a new universe branching off."

"Sure, *most* of them say that. But a significant minority still think any attempt to change established events would cause the entire space-time continuum to suffer a massive existential breakdown. Never thought that one was worth risking the test," said Nicole.

"But when I asked about what happens when someone travels back along their own timeline, you winked at me!" I reminded her, hoping to drag the conversation back on point.

"I don't doubt I did," Nicole replied. "But the wink was just a wink."

My stomach sank. I'd spent the last year, ever since I got thrown back in time, wildly jumping from one conclusion to the next.

"And when you told me there was no way I could've seen Morgan Patterson coming?" I asked.

"You were supposed to be psychic. I didn't have to be, to know what you needed to hear," Nicole said, reaching over to squeeze my shoulder. "So, are you gonna tell us how you traveled through time, or what?"

"I still don't know how it works," I said. "I barely know how it happened."

The meeting table was piled high with an assortment of sandwiches, fruits, veggies, cheeses, and pastries, even more than was usually on offer at Shooter gatherings. Healing was hungry work. I nibbled on whole bunches of broccoli as I told my friends about my future career as a supervillain biographer, my encounter with the Vice Admiral and Tomás Pain, and waking up in my own teenage body in 2013.

"So you're saying, what, that you time traveled with just your mind? Nicole's right, this doesn't make any sense," Eric said.

"It doesn't," I agreed. "But it happened."

"No, I get it," Milo said.

"You do?"

"Well, duh," said Nicole. "It's a *Quantum Leap* thing."

"A what?" Eric said.

Milo looked horrified. "You've never seen *Quantum Leap*? Classic TV show from the early '90s?"

"No?"

"We'll go back to my place after this and watch a marathon," Nicole told Eric. "We'll fix you right up."

"Uh, guys?" Marci said. "I think Caroline was talking."

I explained how I'd seen the Shooters on the news and decided that Ruby Goldberg's future self must have sent me back on purpose, to use my knowledge of future crimes to improve the past.

"Yeah, sorry about that," Nicole said. "But even knowing now that the paradox thing isn't a problem, I can't really see myself ever doing that to someone."

"No, I know. I never actually had a reason to believe that," I said. I'd committed the journalist's cardinal sin. I went looking to confirm what I thought I already knew, instead of letting the truth come to me. "Last night, I even started thinking maybe it was a future version of Milo instead."

"Yeah, I can't imagine doing that either," Milo said. "But then, I couldn't imagine doing what I did last night before I did it, so maybe I'm not the best person to ask right now."

I continued the story. For the first time, I revealed my part in the fight with Grammar Cop.

"Of course that was you," said Nicole.

"And Sarah," I said.

I alluded to Grammar Cop wreaking more havoc in my original timeline, but left out any implication of Lift's former fate. I didn't want Marci feeling like her life had been traded for Sarah's. I didn't want to think about it much myself.

"Okay, so you stopped Grammar Cop from doing whatever, you hooked up with us, helped us stop Kingsley and his Vikings, all that good stuff. You saved lives. You changed history," said Nicole. "That does seem to pretty solidly confirm the branching-worlds theory. But just because it looks like you experienced time travel, that doesn't mean we have to take it on faith."

"You think there's some way to prove all this?" I asked. "I mean, besides all the crimes I knew about in advance." Perhaps Nicole knew how to test for temporal energy residue or something.

"Tell me about my five best future inventions. If I'm working on any of them already, then we'll know your time travel's legit," Nicole said.

"Hah," I said. "Nice try."

Nicole grinned.

"I'm sorry, I know I'm being dense, and it's all just like some fictional TV show or whatever," Eric said, "But I still don't get how any of this actually happens."

"Caroline says it did," Benny said. "What more sense does it need to make?"

"What *I* don't get," Marci said, "is why you didn't trust us with the truth before now."

I'd spent most of the last year making excuses to myself about exactly that. Now I couldn't think of a single good reason.

I picked up the story again, telling Milo how I'd overheard him and his friends discussing world takeover strategies in the lunchroom, plans that I knew too well could almost have worked. I described the brief and bloody career of Zo-Rann the Conqueror, ending in his death in battle, but glossing over Nicole's involvement in that final fight.

"So you spied on me, to see what kind of guy I was, and when you didn't find anything incriminating, you hired me as your steward," Milo summarized. "Keep your enemies closer?"

"More like, if you know a baby's going to grow up to be a supervillain, you make sure the baby gets raised right," I said. "Okay, that sounded weird. Please let's never speak of that metaphor in this context again. But you get what I mean?"

Marci frowned. "Wait. Wait a sec. You're saying you knew all along that Milo was a future supervillain—"

"Potential supervillain," Nicole corrected.

"—potential supervillain, and you didn't have any idea how or why he got that way, but you brought him in to work with the team anyway? We got our butts handed to us last night. He knew how to bring every one of us down with the minimum of fuss—"

"Also the minimum lasting damage," added Benny, which I found spectacularly magnanimous coming from a guy who'd been stomped on by a giant robot.

"He knew everything about us, and we had no idea what he was capable of, because you didn't bother to tell us?"

Beaten and bloody myself as I watched my friends get taken out one by one, I think I'd only felt very slightly worse than I felt in that moment, staring down the betrayal in Marci's eyes.

"I am so, so sorry…" I started to say.

"It's what I would have done," Nicole said right over me. Everyone turned to look at her, and she spread her hands wide. "It would have been stupid and wrong, we all get that now, but at the time? Not wanting to burden anyone, especially Milo himself, with knowing the terrible things he'd hopefully never even think of doing? Totally would have made the same call."

I wasn't sure if she meant it or just thought it needed to be said, but I was grateful either way. Some of the hurt faded from Marci's eyes.

"I forgive you," she said to me. She turned to Milo. "And I don't really want to forgive you. I'd been looking forward to that dance for a really long time, and also there was violence, and my head hurts. But I'm going to forgive you too. Because I don't think you're a bad person, and not forgiving you is just going to make you worse, isn't it?"

"I don't know," Milo said. "I still don't know how it happened, how I got to be where I was last night. That's what scares the crap out of me."

"It should," Benny said, mostly gently.

"I can see the choices I made, one by one. I can see what I was thinking, and how I thought it could all turn out for the best. That scares me too, that I can still see that as a possibility. But now, in the light of day, I pull back and look at everything, and I can't imagine how I thought that killing people was likely to lead to anything but more hurting."

"That's the question to keep asking yourself," Nicole said. "Every day."

"So what if it's just something wrong with me intrinsically? Maybe there's something in the way my head works that will always make such ideas attractive to me. Maybe I'm destined to be evil."

"*No*," I insisted. "No. Milo, look at me." He turned away, tucking his face into his shoulder, but I pulled his chair around to face my own. "Last night, what did I tell you about fate?"

"That it's mathematically derived from our own decisions," he mumbled.

"Close enough," I said. "You make the choices. Nothing just happens to you. And we're never going to let this happen to you. You get that?"

It wasn't just hubris talking this time. Because I'd finally figured out where Zo-Rann the Conqueror came from.

He'd lost someone. He'd always lost someone. In the timeline I'd come from it obviously wouldn't have been Sarah, but someone. And just like last night, he'd stolen the shiniest, deadliest toys he could find. He'd been ready to blow up a whole lot of people for the dream of keeping a whole lot more from dying later. The nations Zo-Rann attacked in my time, like Saxenbourg, were the ones most often accused of harboring or allying themselves with supervillains.

It was wrong as hell, but I understood how it happened. How the Zoran Milosevic I knew became Zo-Rann the Conqueror. How my Milo became the Milo of last night.

Milo looked from me to the Shooters. Most of them smiled back at him, a little sad but encouraging. None of us would let him fall. Not again.

"You screwed up," I said. "But I screwed up too. I wasn't paying attention, right when you needed me the most."

Milo shook his head so rapidly it must have hurt. "How could anybody expect you to be worrying about me after what happened to Sarah? How did that even happen? Everything you knew, and how come we couldn't stop it?"

I didn't answer right away. The room was suddenly very still, my friends all staring at me sympathetically or trying not to look at me at all. I'd known this was bound to come up today, but that didn't make me prepared.

"The Sarah Gordon I first knew was never a steward," I explained softly. "She was never a waitress at Denny's, either. Morgan Patterson kidnapped and murdered some other poor girl who never even made it into my book. She made one headline, and I didn't remember that until it was too late. My Sarah, the first Sarah, grew up and had a life, and we saw each other almost every day."

Tears rolled down my cheeks, and down the faces of my friends as well. The apple held between Marci's tiny hands compacted to the size of a golf ball with a wet popping noise, presumably with the help of her brain. Sticky juice ran over her palms, and Benny rubbed circles on her back.

"She's still out there," Milo said. "It's a different world, but she's still there."

"I know," I said. I pulled him into a bear-hug, right into a bruise and I didn't care. "I know she is."

Eventually I pulled back, rubbing tears away from the corner of my eyes. Milo held onto my arm, and Nicole took my other hand.

"So we get you back there," Nicole said. "Someone built a machine to send you here—"

"Possibly two machines," corrected Milo.

"—possibly two machines. We can totally build one to send you back!"

"I know I said it wasn't possible before, but that was before I knew it had already been done," Milo said. "That's a totally different ballgame."

"It's a sweet thought," I said. "Thank you, both of you. But where would you even begin?"

The look Nicole and Milo exchanged was clear; they didn't know, and they didn't want to tell me they didn't.

"It's all right. You both have much better things to do with your genius. Even if you could get it to work, could you guarantee it would send me back to the life I came from, and not the future I've made from here?"

"Probably not," Milo said.

"Well, maybe. I mean, if we found a way to calibrate the..." Nicole trailed off. "Yeah, I got nothing."

"No, it's okay," I said. "If I'm going to take a chance, then I should take it on the life right in front of me. Sarah was always trying to get me to see that."

I studied each of my friends in turn, fixing their faces in my memory, anchoring myself there in that moment.

"For the longest time, I thought that Ruby's future self had orchestrated my journey so I could make time better," I said. "I thought, with everything I'd seen, that the future was something I could pick and choose. But it doesn't work like that, no matter who you are or how smart you are or how much you know."

"You can't just fix it," Milo said.

"Sarah's death wasn't supposed to happen. But it did happen. And also it didn't. But here we are, where it did."

"That's kinda what I said, way back," Milo said.

I didn't look at him, or shush him. I just squeezed his arm.

"The future's just something that happens. Something we get stuck with."

"Like the check!" Eric quipped.

Nicole looked over at him, shaking her head.

"After I—" *After I lost Sarah*, I was about to say. But she wasn't lost. I knew where she was, in both my realities. "After Sarah died, I avoided you all for so long. I thought I was focusing on fixing the future and getting back to my real life. Only last night I realized it was never about that at all. I just couldn't stand the thought of seeing any more of my friends get hurt. And because of that I almost lost Milo, and you all got hurt anyway."

"You can all punch me many, many more times," Milo said.

"Sarah is gone. I will never be okay with that, but it doesn't make it any better to pretend I'm not already living with it."

"And if a way back to your old life presented itself tomorrow?" asked Nicole. "If future-me or some alien or wizard or something turned out to be behind everything after all?"

"I don't know," I said. "Honestly. I miss Sarah. I still miss things about being a real adult. No offense. But I'd miss the hell out of you all, too."

For all the wonders I'd seen in my new life, I could no longer imagine that happening anyway. There really is no going back. Not in life. Not even in time travel.

"Maybe destiny doesn't offer a menu," I said. "But I'm done telling myself I don't have a choice. Right now, this is exactly where I want to be."

Marci's face was still glistening wet, but at least she could smile at me now without looking pained. "Does this mean you'll officially join my damn team?"

Tuesday Dec. 23, 2014

"The team got me in to see Dr. Pi yesterday at PiLabs in Boulder. She's not a medical doctor, obviously, but as the world's number one meta-physicist, she's still the best person to talk to about the kind of energies I got shot with back in—

I do the math.

"Holy crap. A year ago. I've really been here a year?"

I'm standing in a long corridor in Everett Mansion, lit from overhead and lined along both walls with empty knee-high plinths: cubes and cylinders, each with the name of a fallen hero engraved on a silver plate bolted on to the front. The platforms are motion-sensitive; movement triggers a holographic projection. In most cases, the base is suddenly topped by a spandex-clad crime fighter, posing dramatically. From here I can see Stonehenge, Beta Max, and Roller Derby.

"Anyway. Dr. Pi ran me through a whole battery of tests and scans and stuff, just to make sure. They all seemed to confirm that what happened to me, with the time travel and the powers, was pretty much a bizarre fluke, caused by the combination of Tomás Pain and the Vice Admiral's weapons and my own latent super-gene. So here I am."

Some variation of this Valhalla Hall is present in every super-team headquarters I've visited. As an adult, as a journalist, I loved these halls. They made death feel tidy, bearable and worthy. I'd take my time strolling through, study each figure. Now every day when I come here, I always go straight to the same faux-marble column, stare into the same face. There's a thought somewhere in the back of my head that if I don't keep staring, then one day I'll forget what she looked like. That scares me.

"I'm still not entirely used to this. It still doesn't feel entirely real. But I like it here. I hate it here every time I think about you not being here, but I'm getting better about not doing that so much. I think."

Sarah rolls her eyes, but then she grins. And then she does it again, and again after that. Her hologram is a five-second loop. She's wearing a green top, and the light hits her at angles in conflict with the lamps overhead because she was holo-scanned in her parents' living room, with spring sunlight coming through the windows, by the steward who issued her semi-pro ID card.

"What else? Oh! Milo finally finished my crime-lab-in-a-desk. Your transforming desk, it's amazing. So thank you for that. Milo's still my steward, but when he's not working on something for me, he's asked Lenore Williams to start interning here, with her team. It's

229

gonna be really good for him, I think. I'm worrying less that he'll have an evil relapse. He says hi, by the way. I keep telling him he can come down here himself, but I guess he's not quite ready for that yet."

In many hero HQs, fallen stewards are given a room or a hall or a building all their own, but someone at Everett Mansion had insisted that they be interspersed with the heroes. Sarah is one of several women and men in ordinary clothes, of various ages, scattered among the more garishly-garbed supers.

I look down at my own attire, brand new in red and blue, with my Bounceback logo on one side of the jacket and the TS patch on the other.

"I showed Milo and the Shooters my future crimes spreadsheet. They had some great ideas, like how to be more proactive about it, how to track down some of the bad guys I thought were just laying low before their next big crime."

My hair is in a thick braid, falling heavily over one shoulder. I tug on it.

"I should have let you see it too."

Again, the eye roll and the grin. Even knowing, even looped, I smile back.

"So Mom and Dad and I have been seeing your folks for dinner every Wednesday, ever since. Y'know. They're doing okay. Not really okay okay, but as okay as they could be, I guess. And I'm trying to hang out with Tamika and Nate and Liz a little more often. I'm not sure how long we'll last after graduation. We don't have a lot in common, really. But they care about me, and they cared about you. They still do."

I reach for the image of Sarah's shoulder. It isn't solid, but the hologram is slightly warm, and tingles against my palm. I stand like that for a minute.

Then Lift is there in the doorway, in her costume, mask on her face. "Bounceback, it's showtime. You ready?"

"Right behind you, fearless leader."

Giving Sarah one last nod, I press my own mask to my face. Then I'm running, right behind Lift in her high-heeled boots, through the halls of Everett Mansion. I drop down three flights of stairs in three mighty bounds, Lift floating down behind me. We emerge on the garage deck, where the rest of the team is already waiting in the brand new, battered old ShooterVan. They slam the door behind us as we leap inside, and we roar into the night.

Acknowledgments

Infinite thanks to *Bounceback's* own heroes and stewards:

Caitlin McDonald of Donald Maass Literary Agency - Your feedback made Bounceback a far stronger book, and your belief in this story made us stronger writers.

Mackenzie Walton - After we'd worked on this book for over a decade, you still zeroed in on details we'd missed. Ruby Goldberg especially owes you a great debt.

Cory Thomas, not just for an incredible cover, but for being the first person to draw characters from this world ten years ago. Every day, your art on our wall inspires us.

To Jaydot, for giving W.H.A.M. the flair it deserves. To Christopher Fletcher, for inspiring Milo's story with an anecdote at your wedding rehearsal dinner, and Zoran Jovanovic for lending Milo your awesome name. To Cathy Derrick, Laura Wallman, and Lizzy Bartelt, readers of our earliest drafts, for continued encouragement (despite those early drafts). To Alyc Helms and Sheila Lane, for writerly advice. And to Ross Hick and family, from whom we borrowed the perfect dog's name.

About the Authors

John and Rachael have been writing together since 2006. After almost ten years of marriage, they deemed *Bounceback* ready for public consumption. Under the name John Clifford, John wrote and directed a one-act play, "The Dream in Question," as well as several short plays for sci-fi conventions. Rachael worked in journalism and international education before becoming a child and family therapist. They live with their daughter and two cats in Indianapolis.

Find us @SuitsandCapes on Twitter and Facebook, or suitsandcapes@gmail.com.

Made in the USA
San Bernardino, CA
01 July 2019